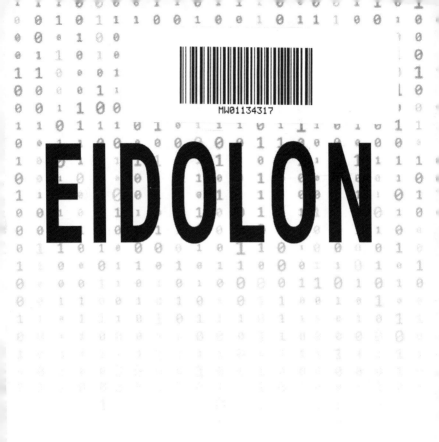

EIDOLON

RUBY DUVALL

ISBN-13: 978-1514140000

Cover design by Ebooklaunch.com

This is a work of fiction. Names, characters, places, and incidents either are the product of the author's imagination or are used fictitiously. Any resemblance to persons, living or dead, actual events, locales, or organizations is entirely coincidental.

Chapter One

Foss, Lily. "The Illusion of Acceptance"
National Technology Review. *29 May 2043*

No one really understands what happened. I'm not talking about the crimes he committed, what the agency did to him and many others, or even the way it all ended. The depth of that tragedy is largely lost on the peddlers of sensationalism and their gossip-hungry consumers. I'm talking about a relationship the media callously and ignorantly labeled as "unhealthy."

Though it means sharing a deeply personal experience, I have to set the record straight. To deny that submission and empowerment are mutually exclusive. To point out that the pretense of non-consent is merely that—pretense. To contend that proper BDSM is not only safe, sane, and consensual but also more vetted and more demanding of voiced, enthusiastic consent than some if not most vanilla sexual encounters.

Not only did he offer me the fantasies I'd craved, he also helped free me from my shame, allowing me to accept a part of myself I had denied all my life.

It wasn't until the very end that we were both faced with the real demon between us, a revelation that will haunt me until the day I die.

December 2032
Redmond, Washington

L ily had more than one reason for masturbating in a dark room. If the lights were on, the dusty Code-to-Play toy robot in the corner would be a jolting reminder of where she was, and nothing was less arousing than her parents' house. Sure, she had entertained plenty of sexual fantasies in this room, on this bed, but only out of necessity, only because she'd had nowhere else to go. After the relative freedom of a year and a half of college life, being back in this room poked at her self-loathing as if it were a bruise.

With the lights off, she couldn't see the way she had contorted her limbs. She could distance her mind from her body, could dig deep into the secret caverns of her imagination to quietly indulge herself. When her parents returned from the airport with her older brother, she could pretend her relaxed state was thanks to Christmas vacation and a successful semester rather than the temporary gratification of her carnal fantasies.

Her imagination did wonderful, terrible things in the dark. She wasn't on her bed but on the floor of a castle's torch-lit dungeon. She wasn't manipulating the touch of a clit tickler with the roll of her hips but squirming under the oral onslaught of a handsome, broad-shouldered man. The wet sounds of his lips eating her out weren't coming from a porn video—playing on a cheap tablet no one knew she owned—but coming from between her legs.

But the fantasy could only go so far. She had shoved her pajama bottoms down to her ankles and sat on the excess material to keep her legs bent and immobile, but she was too desperate for climax to thrust her hips less wantonly, and her cotton pants repeatedly escaped the weight of her pelvis. More than once, she had to stop and make adjustments.

After crossing her forearms again in the small of her back, she resolutely closed her eyes against the dark room and let her imagination envelope her, although it meant that she wouldn't notice the lights of the nearby security alarm panel blink out.

She knelt upon a pile of furs, naked, blindfolded, arms bound behind her. The furs cushioned her from the dungeon's cold stone floor. She had been caught spying on the prince, who now sought to make her his lover and slave. Her ankles were tied to the backs of her thighs to keep her legs bent and her pussy available. Escape would be nearly impossible.

A man ordered Prisoner Lily to beg for forgiveness and she recognized the prince's voice. He wished he didn't have to punish her, but she had committed a crime against the crown and justice had to be served.

After that, he flogged her. A truly cruel captor would start with a flogger sporting thin, hard tails and would use the strongest blows, but the prince didn't want to injure or abuse her—just punish her. He knelt next to her with one hand on her bound forearms and a soft leather flogger in the other. Gently but firmly, he folded her over her thighs until her forehead brushed those velvety furs.

Real Lily wished to know the snapping bites of pain and the blossoms of heat, but with no one to administer the strokes, she never would. She had only her imagination and the descriptions she found online.

The prince's hand replaced the flogger after ten well-spaced blows. He wanted to feel her hot skin, massage it tenderly, and lightly slap her ass just to savor the impact on his palm before returning to the flogger. Its strokes were harder than his hand, which rubbed and tormented her stinging skin at irregular intervals.

Prisoner Lily would come to crave his touch. The flogger created distance, but the warmth of his hand created intimacy and connection, reminding her that all his concentration was on controlling what she felt, heard, and saw—or didn't see.

It was her first punishment, so he was gentler than she knew he could be. Real Lily shuddered at thought of her prince's sadism being fully unleashed, even as he quickly pushed Prisoner Lily to the white-hot threshold of what she could withstand—just close enough to the edge to peer over. She cried out under the thundering *smack* of his hand, and he somehow knew to relent.

She was panting and sweating. Her legs ached, but not nearly as much as her backside. It was covered with welts and would be discolored with bruises that would last several days, perhaps an entire week. Real Lily liked the idea of looking into a mirror and seeing those marks.

Her captor repositioned her onto her back. Prisoner Lily couldn't conceal that her nipples had hardened, but she held her thighs shut in a vain effort to hide how he had affected her lower half. When the prince's warm fingers lit upon her knees, her legs jerked, both in the fantasy and in her dark bedroom. His hands slowly eased between her thighs, his palms far rougher than one would expect of royalty.

Prisoner Lily resisted only the space of a few breaths before allowing him to part her legs. He nipped the inside of her thigh, his teeth scraping and pinching her skin. An open-mouthed kiss followed pain with pleasure. His warm tongue lapped at the reddened flesh. Lily could only imagine it, just as her blindfolded, fantasy facsimile would have to imagine it—a strong, smooth-shaven jaw beneath the parted lips of a man with calm restraint. For him, her torture and her pleasure were of utmost importance to his own satisfaction.

More nips followed by soothing kisses oscillated between her thighs, moving closer to the apex of her legs. She craved his firm lips, his hot breath, and his seeking tongue. Prisoner Lily didn't want to need him, but Real Lily mewled. If someone really saw inside her head, knew her real desires, and forced her to experience them...

The prince's strong hands slid under her bruised backside and squeezed. Prisoner Lily cried out. He hummed with hunger and sealed his lips around her clit. Real Lily, close to orgasm, bucked against her vibe. Her fantasy lover tongued the opening to her vagina before returning to her clit and testing its sensitivity. He flexed his fingers

4

and Prisoner Lily cried out. Real Lily was certain she would come at that moment if she were as pinned between pleasure and pain as her imaginary copy.

But Prisoner Lily wouldn't be allowed to come yet. If she came before the prince gave her permission, another punishment would be in her future. He might leave her in her cell another day or, even worse, he might not fuck her until she learned to obey him.

Real Lily waited as long as she could, wishing the sucking sounds coming from her tablet were instead coming from between her legs. Any second, her prince would tell her to—

A sound downstairs made her eyes pop open. What was that? A car outside backfiring? Or was it the porn video's terrible music? Lily lay motionless, listening, hoping, but the next sound was unmistakable. A door opened and shut.

Her parents were home. Guilt swamped her. *Why would you look at that garbage? I didn't raise a weak-willed daughter.* She hastily grabbed her tablet to silence the porn video, spun the dial of her vibe down to Off, and drew her cotton pants up her legs. As soon as she had the chance, she would shower and change her underwear.

The interruption served her right. She was getting off to the fantasy of being the prisoner of a man who beat her and ate her out. No more. She wouldn't do this again. Every time she succumbed to such fantasies, the guilt-shoveling put her deeper into a hole that was becoming difficult to climb out of.

She slipped her hand into her panties and drew out the slick egg of her vibe with a whimper. Her engorged clit was a moment away from climax, but she couldn't chance rubbing it out. Not only was her mother notoriously quiet on the stairs, but she had also burst in without knocking on more than one occasion. Her mother would immediately realize her error and leave, but it was almost a guarantee that Lily would later have to endure a passive-aggressive comment thinly veiled as an "apology."

Lily once asked for a lock on her door, but her mother shut her down by saying, "Families don't keep secrets from each other." Lily resorted to putting a chair under the knob if she really needed privacy.

The wetness on her fingers pulled her lips into a frown. Despite what she wanted to believe, her body's arousal betrayed how much it liked the fantasies her mind wove. Washing the vibe would have to wait until she could slip into the bathroom, so she wiped her fingers with a hand towel, wrapped her vibe in it, and squirreled the bundle inside her suitcase.

She contemplated lying down and pretending to be asleep so that she wouldn't have to see her family until morning, but her mother had asked her to stay awake until they returned with her brother. She went to the door and had her fingers on the knob when she realized no light was coming through the gap at the bottom.

The hairs on her arms stood up. She could've sworn she'd left a light on downstairs. And why hadn't anyone called out to announce they were home? Why didn't she hear the shuffle of feet, or the sounds of conversation, or the *thump* of a suitcase rolling over the threshold between the kitchen and the garage?

Her eyes slid to the dim neon glow of the bedside clock. Her brother's flight was supposed to land at 11:30 p.m., and it was still 10:55. If his flight was delayed, why would her parents come back rather than wait at the airport? They had checked his flight status just before leaving, though, and it had left Los Angeles on time. The weather was clear in SeaTac. Could that have changed in the last hour?

She slowly tightened her fingers around the doorknob and prayed the sounds downstairs had come from a neighbor's house. Either that or her usual paranoia. *Please just don't let there be anyone in the house.*

She tried to breathe normally, but her breaths shuddered and whistled through her nostrils. The handle didn't squeak as she slowly turned it, but she had to apply more torque when it stopped moving and the latch escaped the doorframe with a soft *click*. She froze for a moment, listening intently over the thumps of her heart, which seemed to echo right between her ears.

But she heard nothing and cracked open the door. The hiss of air coming from a heating vent in the hall grew louder. Her sweaty palm, still gripping the knob, kept the latch pulled into the door so that she could quickly and quietly shut it if necessary. For a long moment, she stood frozen and impotent, one eye scanning the sliver of hall in front of her room.

She could see part of the top of the stairs and the transom window above the front door, but the solid balcony wall blocked her view of the first-floor entryway—and of anyone lurking down there. If she wanted to know for sure who was down there, she had to leave her room.

Thankfully, the door opened silently. She leaned forward inch by inch to peer down the hall. The door to her mother's office, on the opposite side of the hall at the end of the balcony, was shut. Leaning farther and still death-gripping the doorknob, she confirmed that the doors to her parents' room and her brother's room were also closed. She couldn't remember if they had been that way when she went into her room.

The door latch silently slid out as she released the handle. Her clammy palm ached. She took a step into the hall, her bare feet quiet on the carpet. A little more of the first-floor entryway came into view. The front door was shut, but she couldn't see enough of it to tell if it was locked.

Something nudged her backside. She nearly jumped out of her skin, but it was just her bedroom door relaxing into its jamb.

Another step toward the balcony. More of the front door came into view, including the broken sidelight window and the unlocked deadbolt.

The hall tilted sickeningly. She held her breath. Backed up. Slipped into her bedroom. Her throat convulsed and she hastily covered her mouth. The five seconds it took to quietly shut the door felt like thirty. She didn't stop to think why she couldn't find the alarm panel without running her hands over the wall on the hinge side of the door. She didn't stop to wonder why the buttons didn't light up when she punched in the panic code.

Only when a few seconds passed and nothing happened did she realize the panel was dead. No status light, nothing on the LCD display. She muffled her gasp a second too late. How had they killed the system from outside?

She could call. She could call the police on her phone. She just had to block the door first. It was instinct to want to grab her desk chair and jam it under the door knob, but as soon as she turned around, she remembered her parents had junked her old desk. The chair was probably in the garage.

She went to her nightstand and fumbled for her cellphone. Her hand knocked something off—her cheap tablet. It hit the carpeted floor with a loud pair of thuds.

Both hands went to her mouth this time. Her wide eyes locked on to her closed bedroom door and the dark gap at the bottom. She waited for heavy footsteps to pound up the stairs. The bathroom door would bang open first, but then they'd find her. They'd shout with rage or maybe whoop with glee, their hands grabbing at her, bruising her and dragging her, twisting her arms, yanking her hair, sealing her mouth with tape that would rip her skin when later pulled off—if she survived. Should she hide under the bed? In her closet?

The scent of her arousal still clung to her fingers. She used the back of her hand to wipe tears from her eyes at the frightening thought of being raped if the burglar found her. Or maybe they'd kill her. A gunshot to the head, strangled with rope, with hands, her neck sliced open, beaten with fists wrapped in black leather gloves until those gloves were soaked with her blood.

No one stormed upstairs. The bathroom door didn't bang open. She briefly closed her eyes and more cautiously felt around for her cellphone. It wasn't on her nightstand. She went to her purse on top of her suitcase. It wasn't in there, either.

Her search stopped when she remembered it was downstairs on the kitchen counter. She had been eager to take advantage of what little alone time she'd get that week and had raced upstairs as soon as her parents left to pick up her brother. Her secret tablet device was so cheap and bare of programs that it couldn't make calls. It couldn't even text the police. *What do I do?*

Her mother had a landline in her office. It was the only one in the house connected to a handset. That meant going back into the hall, and she *really* didn't want to. It seemed so much saner to hide under her bed and hope the burglar wasn't thorough. Even if she had to stay under there for two hours, she would know it was safe to come out when she heard her parents come home.

And if the intruder waited for them to come back? No, she needed to call the police.

She took a few bracing breaths, but it didn't help. Her hands were shaking as she eased the door open. The heater was still going. No other sounds. She prayed the burglar had grabbed the Christmas presents under the tree and was long gone. The house was quiet. The doors were all still shut. She stepped out of her room, instinctively avoiding the one squeaky spot.

With her next step, something strange happened. Her breathing and heartbeat slowed. She almost felt calm. No one could know she was upstairs. They would have either cut and run or flushed her out if they knew. She would reach the phone, and the police would be there in no time.

In fact, *I'm going to make it* was her exact thought right before he grabbed her.

Chapter Two

February 2042
Seattle, Washington

The hotel room was quiet. Declan's client was asleep and tucked under the covers. The pillow was a little wet from the client's damp hair, but the wet spot, like the lingering impressions of a ball gag on the cheeks of that sleeping face, would fade before the client woke. Declan took his eyes off the bed's reflection in the mirror above the dresser and finished buttoning his shirt. He pinched his collar to ensure it was crisp and even. He adjusted the way the shirt hung from his wide shoulders and carefully tucked the hem into the waist of his slacks. The fine material resisted wrinkling, so it didn't take many adjustments to make it look right.

Next was the belt. Supple, well-oiled black leather and a flat silver buckle inset with onyx. Another moment saw him affix matching cufflinks to his sleeves. No tie—his client had asked to keep it as a reminder, and such things were allowed. Reminders created repeat customers.

He was careful not to disturb the client as he stepped into polished black shoes and tied small knots in their laces. Over his hand-tailored jacket he wore a navy wool coat and matching scarf. Nothing needed mending or dry-cleaning. The agency was thorough and professional, as expected.

A whisper of sound told him his client was no longer asleep.

"Tonight was amazing," the client said in a rough voice.

Declan turned with a predatory smile. It would excite his client. The deep breath his client took as well as their slightly unfocused look indicated he was correct. He walked to the bed in measured, deliberate steps. His client shifted under the covers. He leaned down and gripped just under their chin. His client grew still. Those eyes looked sleepy, but he knew he commanded their attention.

"Because you were very obedient. Now you will rest. You used up a lot of energy. Close your eyes." His client complied. He released his hold, and his fingers brushed the client's neck as he straightened. Gooseflesh rose in response.

"I look forward to next month." He said the last with gravity. His tone more than the words would heighten the client's anticipation and nearly guarantee a future booking.

The payment was already in his inner coat pocket, so he left the room's key card on the dresser and quietly shut the door on his way out.

He checked his calendar as he walked to the elevator lobby. No clients scheduled tomorrow, though that could change at any moment. He marked tonight's session as complete so the agency knew he was free. The phone went back into his pocket, right next to the payment. He would have buttoned his coat, but raised voices coming from one of the rooms caught his attention. His pace slowed.

"Red, *red*! What the hell are you doing?" a woman yelled. A man's response was too low to make out clearly, and the couple's conversation was barely audible after that.

He kept walking, and it was only a few doors farther to the elevator lobby. He double-checked his appearance in the large mirror taking up the entire wall opposite the elevator bank. Everything was still in place, as expected. He turned from the mirror and reached to call the elevator, but refrained when he heard a room burst open.

"Where are you going? Don't you have to do what I say?"

Declan turned his head and saw the woman's reflection in the mirror. She wore a black pencil skirt and an unbuttoned gray silk blouse that hung open. Her black, lacy bra cupped a pair of breasts that would just barely spill out of a man's grip.

"Did I do something wrong?" the man asked as he knotted a towel wrapped around his hips.

"You have to ask?" the woman scoffed. "You have no clue what you're doing, do you? I specifically said gags were a hard limit. I can't enjoy myself if I'm trying not to throw up."

"I thought that meant you wanted me to force you to wear a gag."

Her jaw dropped. "Who the hell was I talking to online? Did you copy-paste your résumé?" she asked, trying to fasten the buttons on her blouse while holding her coat, purse, and heels.

"Come on, you're being irrational. We can try again," the man pleaded. He reached for her wrist, and she slapped his hand away. "Ow! You crazy bitch."

"You can't give me what I need." Her long, dark brown hair impeded her efforts to close her blouse, and she gave up in favor of putting on her shoes. "A real Dom never violates a hard limit. He doesn't balk when the safe word is used. He doesn't act like a short-tempered, selfish *amateur* with no—"

"Stop fucking insulting me." The man snatched the woman's wrist. She gasped and tried to wrench her arm away. "You're the freak. Didn't you come here for some kind of rape fantasy? It's why you wanted to fuck a stranger, yeah? Why's it matter how I do you? Or do you need me to call a couple friends?"

Declan had heard enough, and the opportunity warranted his involvement. He rounded the corner of the elevator lobby. The woman swung her purse at the man, but he dodged it. Declan detected a touch of fright in her eyes.

"Let go of me, *frat boy*," she ground out.

Declan was two steps away when the man noticed him.

"Mind your own business, asshole."

He clamped on to the man's wrist and squeezed the pressure point hard enough to entice the attached fist to open. The man yelped and let the woman go. Declan then turned the man around and tested how far up the man's back his wrist could go. The man yelped again and rose onto the balls of his feet. His voice went up an octave.

"What the fuck?"

"You will return to your room without her," he said, maintaining a calm tone. "If you understand, I will release you, and you will walk in far enough for me to close the door. Do you understand?" From the corner of his eye, he saw the woman hurriedly put on her coat.

"Yeah. *Yeah*, I understand!"

"So, what will you do?" He pulled a little harder on that wrist.

The man tried to rise to the tips of his toes like a ballet dancer. Declan knew he could push the man down to his heels and get a scream out of him.

"G-go back inside far enough for you to close the door," the man reiterated.

Declan released the man, who quickly retreated into the room and threw an appalled look over his shoulder. Declan quietly closed the door and, without a single glance at the woman, walked toward the elevator lobby. He could guess how his behavior and involvement would affect her. Giving her distance would allow her a moment to collect herself.

At the elevator bank, he stood where she would have space to use the mirror or call an elevator without being within arm's reach of him. His hands were in plain sight, and he knew he looked like a well-groomed businessman perhaps heading out for a quick drink before last call. The assistance he had rendered would also make her feel somewhat grateful, though that was more up to chance. Not everyone appreciated a Good Samaritan.

She didn't look at him at first. Her body was turned away while she finished dressing. She stood in her high heels with stiff knees, as though not used to wearing them. Once her top was closed, she smoothed her hair and coat with steady hands.

A quick swipe under her mouth removed a smudge of dark red lipstick. The color suited her complexion, bringing out the subtle pink in her pale skin. Not uncommon in the Pacific Northwest, especially Seattle. No one here seemed to get much sunlight.

"Thanks," she said as she turned away from the mirror. Her gaze was on his face barely a second before she looked down at the mobile device in her hand. Brown eyes.

Scared eyes.

"Are you all right?" He maintained a concerned tone but didn't approach her. "Your wrist?" Again, her glance flitted between his face and her phone. She was embarrassed and feeling vulnerable, as expected. He would need to tread lightly.

"Yeah, I'm fine." She rotated her wrist to illustrate while deftly tapping through an app he recognized with her other hand. She was requesting a Safe Cab pickup.

"I'm glad. I hope I wasn't out of line putting him in that hold." The man and woman seemed to have met merely for a sexual encounter, so they probably were not in a relationship, but he would need to confirm it.

"No, he deserved it. I don't know what I was thinking." She put her phone away, winced, and shifted her weight as though her feet hurt.

"One would assume it'd be easy to find a Dominant online," he said, watching her reaction. He carefully chose his words and how he said them to offer empathy as well as acknowledge just how much he had heard. She widened her eyes as she straightened and subtly reared back. Her eyebrows pinched. Her jaw hardened.

She was affronted. He could still work with this.

"I appreciate the help, but that is *none* of your business." She walked to the Call button and reached for it.

"In fact, it is my business." As expected, his response aggravated her but also stopped her from pressing the button. He took a business card from his coat pocket. "My last one."

Rather than take it, she cocked her head to read the white lettering. "Tailor Made. Discreet and professional entertainment."

"The web address is on the back," he offered.

"Very fancy," she said, looking at him with her chin down and eyebrows up. Her lips had a sardonic twist. Ah, she was being facetious. "But I'm not taking a card from a pimp." She smacked the Down button. "Hmph, 'last one.'"

"I'm actually the merchandise, not the seller."

She blinked at him, and the anger left her face. It wasn't the first time a potential client assumed he was the purveyor. She looked at her surroundings as though remembering where she was, and her mouth slowly fell open as she made the connection that he was here because he had just seen a client. He dropped his arm and used her stunned silence to make assurances.

"Every escort is vetted and trained. The agency ensures total discretion and ideal encounters. I happen to specialize in your...particular needs."

A blush lit her from the collar of her blouse to the roots of her hair.

"No, I-I can't," she said. The right elevator dinged and opened. No one stood inside. The mirror in the back reflected her conflicted expression as she boarded.

Ah, well. He had known his chances of success were small. Respectfulness required one last gesture.

"Of course, ma'am. I'll catch the next one."

She looped her purse over her shoulder and pressed the button for the main lobby. He stayed where he was, watching her while she waited for the doors to close. She licked her lips and kept her eyes on the array of buttons next to her.

The doors eventually responded and began to slide shut. He would wait a few seconds before calling another elevator. Perhaps his calendar had updated.

"Wait," she blurted, slapping her palm on the inside edge of the door just a few inches short of it closing. The door relented and slid open again. She took a deep breath and gave him direct eye contact—determination.

Desperation. He stepped forward and extended his hand.

"I just want to keep my options open," she said as she took his card. He allowed a tight-lipped, lopsided smile.

"Your pleasure is not an option. It's my singular goal."

He remained a small step from the door track and swept his coat back to slide his hands into the pockets of his slacks, knowing the pose emphasized his narrow waist and wide shoulders. She coyly appreciated the view he presented before her gaze dropped to the card in her hand.

Just as the door attempted to shut again, she swiped her hand across the back of her neck to pull her hair over her shoulder. In the mirror behind her, he saw—

A chill stole up his spine as the elevator door settled into its frame. His heart responded instinctually, but to what? The elevator lobby remained quiet and empty. No footsteps or doors opening. Yet his skin puckered as though doused in cold water. Sweat broke out on his forehead.

Was he feeling ill? The hallway was cooler than the room he had just left, but he wore several layers. He carefully ran his hand over his hair and found it still damp from the quick shower he had taken. No wonder he both sweated and shivered.

His head whipped up. Had the lights blinked?

No. No, of course not. Breathing out, he reached for the Down button and jabbed it harder than necessary. He would need to take a hot bath and drink plenty of water when he got home, just in case, but an illness wasn't likely. Dr. White was thorough.

The elevator was taking its time. He listened for the hum of the pulleys or the dings of a traveling cab, but all he could hear were his heavy breaths. His shirt was damp under his arms. He loosened his scarf. A sensation like falling swirled in his chest, disconcerting for how much it made him want to run as well as squeeze up into a ball.

Another shiver screamed down his spine. His skin tingled from his scalp to his toes. Something was wrong. His heart raced. He couldn't get enough air, could only swallow with concerted effort.

Don't turn around.

A bizarre thought. Nothing behind him but a mirror. He'd only see himself. Would his cheeks be flushed? He could check, but he didn't. Couldn't. In fact, he held that much more still, as if he could somehow convince his reflection to fade away.

His head swam, thirsty for oxygen. His lungs upped the pace, tried to compensate. He blinked, and the lights seemed to come on a split second too late. The urge to curl his shoulders over his chest was powerful. He steeled his spine and stood straight. Straight and still. Very still. His fingers tingled. He slowly unclenched his aching hands. His palms stung from his nails digging in.

Was the elevator coming? He glanced at the Call buttons. The flat, steel-gray plate with two white blobs, one brighter than the other, drifted in and out of focus. The prickling sensation was in his toes now. He had to calm down.

Ding. A downward-pointing plastic arrow lit up. The left elevator opened. But now it was here, he didn't want to get inside. Nonsense. Descending thirty flights of stairs in his condition?

He lurched into the elevator on unsteady legs and avoided looking at the large mirror in the lobby as he turned to the buttons. He blinked hard a few times, opened his eyes wide. The button array came into focus. It wasn't enough to hit the Lobby button. He rapid-fire punched that little light-up circle with one thumb and mashed the Close Door button with the other. The compulsion to escape was a cold knot in his stomach. The longer it took for the doors to move, the tighter it pulled.

The door rattled in its track. Slowly, loudly. As if it fought against centuries of rust. He didn't let go of the buttons until it banged shut with finality. He wanted the elevator to plunge down, to let gravity yank it back to earth. Panting, he gripped the rail next to him as the floors flew upward faster and faster.

A few more seconds. He'd be on the ground in just a few more seconds.

An insistent buzz rippled the back of his neck. That strange thought came to him again. *Don't turn around.* What could possibly happen, though? He would only see his reflection. No danger there. He knew this. The elevator slowed.

He'd look. Just to prove it to himself. One look before the doors opened. Jaw clenched, he took a deep breath and spun around.

Every hair on his body stood. He couldn't inhale to scream. Could only flatten himself against the door. He had no face. No eyes, no mouth. His head was ashen, smooth, featureless. An abstract mannequin made of human skin.

He threw his arms in front of him, dug his heels into carpeted floor. He couldn't look away. Couldn't blink. His faceless reflection stood there, frozen in place.

Something slid against his back—the elevator doors. He fell backward with a terrified howl and found himself on the polished floor of the hotel's main lobby. A few steps away, a woman gave a shrill cry. With a glance, he found her standing next to another, shorter woman who had grasped her by the arm. Both stared at him with mouths agape.

"Oh my God, are you okay?" the taller woman asked.

He sucked in a breath and looked back at the elevator. No one stood in the mirror.

Someone from the hotel staff jogged over, a desk clerk.

"Is everything all right? Do you need any help, sir?" The clerk helped him to his feet. Already he was breathing easier.

"I..." he began, but he didn't know what to say. He always knew what to say. He tried to remember what had happened, where it had started. The brunette had taken his card and said she liked to keep her options open. He had liked making her blush.

"Are you feeling ill?" the clerk asked. The elevator doors closed.

"You look so pale," the tall woman said. Her friend's gaze swept down his body in silent, licentious appraisal. His stomach clenched, and he looked away.

"The elevator...lurched and—and I'm afraid of heights," he lied.

"Lurched?" the clerk repeated with alarm. "I'm so sorry, sir. I'll have maintenance look at it. It's an old hotel. Is there anything I can do for you? A glass of water?"

"I'll be all right in a minute. I just need a taxi." He buttoned his coat.

"Of course, sir. If you'll come this way, please."

"Thanks," he mumbled as he followed the clerk away from the elevators.

"Poor thing," one of the women whispered.

His heart still raced, but his vision was clear. No more light-headedness. He hid his shaking hands in his coat pockets. The brunette was nowhere to be seen—likely long gone. He wondered if she would end up tossing his card in the trash.

No, she was hungry and wanted to keep her options open. Her options...

She had pulled her hair over her shoulder, and in the mirror he saw the petals of a flower tattoo peeking above the collar of her coat. It wasn't a rose or a lotus but a vibrant, red lily.

0 1 0 1 1 1 0 0 1 0 0 0 1 1 1 0 0 0
0 1 0 0 1 1 0 0 1 0 0 1 0 0 1 1 0 0
1 1 0 0 0 1 0 1 1 0 1 0 0 0 0 0 1 0 1
1 1 0 0 1 0 1 0 1 0 0 1 1 1 1 1
0 0 0 1 1 1 0 1 0 1 0 0 0 1 0 0 1 0
0 0 1 0 0 0 1 0 0 0 1 0 0 1 1 0 0
1 1 0 1 1 1 0 1 1 1 0 1 1 1 0 0 1 1
0 1 0 0 0 0 0 0 0 0 1 1 0 0 0 0 0
1 0 1 1 1 1 1
0 0 0 0 0 1 0 1 0 1 0 1 0
1 1 0 0 0 1 1 0 1 1 0 0 0 1 0 1
0 0 1 1 1 1 1 0 1 1 1 1 0
0 0 0 1 0 0 1 0 0 0 1 0 0 0 1 1 0
0 1 0 1 0 0 0 1 1 0 0 0 0 1

Chapter Three

"**E**leventh and East Thomas," Lily said as she slipped into a driverless taxi.

The correct cross streets appeared on a screen built into the back of the front passenger seat. She tapped the green Confirm button. Human-driven cabs hung around the hotel to pick up fares, but Safe Cab had its name for a reason, and she wasn't sociable even on her best days. At least a computer didn't have feelings to injure.

"Confirmed. Welcome aboard Safe Cab. Before we depart, please buckle your—"

"Audio off," she commanded, reaching for the seat belt. The red hexagon on the screen disappeared once her belt was buckled, and the cab smoothly entered traffic.

She really had done this to herself. User "MstrFul," or Matt Owens as she had learned far too easily when searching for the man behind the misleading alias and the low-quality, shirtless photo taken in a bathroom mirror, was a thirty-two-year-old banker and car nut. His various online profiles painted a picture of someone with many friends—most of them from his college fraternity—even more ex-girlfriends and who not only hated his job, but didn't perform it well, based on his rants about being passed up for a promotion.

Still, his Kinkster.com profile suggested a Dominant who, like her, lurked on the fringe of the BDSM community. His promises to "give her what she needs rather than what she wants" and to "leave a lingering reminder of their scene on her ass" had "whet" more than just her appetite. An exchange of messages over a couple of days quickly led to him suggesting they meet, and she had been so keen to tamp down her rising desires that she agreed.

She turned away from the silent ads on the seatback screen toward the rain-streaked window and curled around the purse on her lap.

As it turned out, MstrFul was just another sexist creep trying to reenact what mainstream porn had taught him—that all women secretly wanted to be controlled and just didn't know it. He didn't actually wish to earn the trust it took for total submission. That required believing women had their own sexual agency.

Whether he was aware of his misconceptions or not, *she* should have known better. The flags had been red and flapping wildly. They'd agreed on a safe word but only after he asked why she might use it. Red flag. While emphasizing her hard limits, she didn't know what to think when he'd smiled and wiggled his eyebrows in response. Red flag. They started with a low-stakes goal, but he'd tried to pressure her for more. Red flag. He'd fumbled with simple bonds, but she told herself he was simply nervous. Red friggin' flag.

Just seeing a ball gag among his small selection of cheap implements could have been an intense mind fuck, but then he'd moved to put it in her mouth and she knew she had sabotaged herself yet again.

How many more times would it take? Would she have to get hurt for it to sink in that she was a freak who should resign herself to a solitary life? She knew there were better places to find a Dom. Local groups with vetted, unattached members who could mentor her and make introductions. But that required real names and more commitment than she could handle right now. Maybe ever.

She didn't want to think about what could've happened if the well-dressed man hadn't intervened in the hall. She felt grateful in the moment but now hated the thought of someone rescuing her or, even worse, knowing something so personal about her.

Half a second's glance had confirmed that he was her ultimate ideal—big, stern, and in an expensive suit. His good looks were hard, almost brutal. In that half second of eye contact, he'd jerked his head halfway to his shoulder like a boxer juicing up for a fight.

Their conversation kept replaying in her mind, especially the line he'd nonchalantly thrown out about finding a Dominant online. Anger had given her the courage she needed to look him in the eye, but she'd surprised herself with a response more diplomatic than "you're an asshole."

Just remembering his large hand holding out his card made her squeeze her thighs together. She imagined that hand holding her down while his other hand made a red imprint of itself on her rear, or maybe he'd use that black leather belt around his waist.

The first real Dominant she had ever met, and he was up for sale.

For rent, technically.

The cab turned off Broadway and headed into a residential pocket of Capitol Hill, where Bungalow-style homes sat shoulder to shoulder with modest apartment buildings along tree-lined streets broken up at each intersection with a small roundabout. She dug into her purse and pulled out some cash and her compact umbrella.

Her total fare appeared on the screen as the cab pulled over, and animated icons indicated various ways to pay. She would've tapped the smart card in her phone, but she didn't want to leave a record of this particular taxi ride on her bank statement and instead fed a couple of bills into the money slot between the front seats. She had also paid for her half of the hotel room in cash.

Once she collected her change, the cab doors unlocked and a friendly message appeared on the screen. She had taken enough cabs before they allowed passengers to mute the audio to know just how it sounded.

"Thank you for using Safe Cab," she mocked.

Cold rain sprayed her bare legs as she stepped out. Her umbrella opened with a click and *foomph*. Rain pelted the stretched nylon in a dull roar. She was still a couple of blocks away from her building, but she didn't want even Safe Cab to know exactly where she lived. Paranoid, sure, but privacy was worth protecting.

She touched as little of the wet cab door as needed in order to fling it shut, and wiped her palm on her coat. Though she was careful in traversing the three-foot-wide gap of soggy grass between the curb and sidewalk, water quickly permeated her stilettos, and wasn't that just lovely? The taxi flashed its security lights before pulling away to pick up another auto-assigned fare, and she almost regretted disembarking early.

Walking in these shoes felt like walking on bare bone, but she couldn't manage a faster pace to hasten the end of her plantar misery.

The sidewalks were slick and uneven, bulging where tree roots had burrowed underneath. Any faster and she'd be nursing a skinned knee. She tried walking more naturally, but the second her ankle wobbled, she went back to her awkward gait. When she crossed the street, she was forced to make a daring leap from the curb across a wide puddle.

Yes, it rained often in Seattle, but usually it was just a pathetic drizzle. Tonight was a deluge. Rain battered her umbrella. Icy water dripped down her legs. Her thighs would be red and itchy when she got home. Another jump to the opposite curb and she was halfway there. The light of her building's lobby beckoned. The sidewalk on this side was newer and flatter, so she sped up despite her screaming soles.

Once she reached the shelter of the awning between the sidewalk and the security door, she hit the button on her umbrella to collapse its arms. Her security fob already in hand, she hurriedly tapped the sensor next to the door. An acknowledging beep let her into the lobby.

The night-shift security guard looked up and lifted his hand in a lazy salute before returning his gaze to whatever method of entertainment he had hidden behind the counter. She walked to the elevator, punched the top button, and only had to wait long enough for the door to open.

Once it closed with her inside, she shut her eyes and took a deep breath, rejoicing that she was back in her own world. It seemed harder each time to release a little control and venture into the unknown beyond her physical door. So much of her life existed online—from work to friends to hobbies—that she hardly left her place anymore. Her new refrigerator even took its own stock once a week and ordered home-delivered groceries for her. If only it could order her a sane, experienced Dom.

Every step from the elevator to her door was paired with a wince and a hiss. She gave up halfway and walked the last twenty feet barefoot. It didn't hurt much less.

Inside her apartment, she resentfully flung her shoes against the wall, dropped her coat on the floor, and slid her feet into cushioned slippers that provided immediate relief. With a sigh, she stood there a moment in near ecstasy before shuffling into her bedroom and chucking her purse onto the floor next to her cluttered desk.

In a ratty armchair in the corner, a lithe male body slumped like someone passed out on drugs, knees spread and arms lying to either side of his thighs, palms up. He wore what he'd arrived in—a close-fitting body suit made of opaque vinyl like the kind one would peel off new electronics. His blond head rested on the back of the chair. His mouth was closed, but his open, unseeing blue eyes stared at the ceiling. A wire plugged into the side of his head ran over his shoulder down to a spool of cabling on the floor that eventually wound its way to the back of her computer.

The Eidolon twitched, his head rolling on the back of the chair. She was home earlier than expected, so the gamut of tests was still running.

She stepped over a pile of clothing and went to her overstuffed closet. Her new skirt and almost-as-new silk shirt joined several other items that had been worn only once or twice. Her bra and thong both went into the already-full hamper. She slipped on regular panties, a white short-sleeve top, and fleece sweatpants with "University of Washington" down one leg. She then grabbed a glass of water from the kitchen while ignoring the dirty dishes and flopped into her leather desk chair.

At her desk was where she held her power, and it felt so good to be in control again. No painfully ignorant banker, no escort with a tempting offer, and no freezing, sopping-wet feet.

She waved her hand to wake up her monitor and typed her password one-handed since she didn't have space to set down her glass. The current window showed a news article she had been reading before heading downtown to meet MstrFul. A tech writer who wrote for the same e-mag where she published her Eidolon security reviews had some interesting comments on the latest rumors about software and robotics giant SystemOne, the same company whose latest and soon-to-be-released model of Eidolon she was currently testing.

A blinking icon on her display caught her attention. She switched windows.

You have a new video conferencing request from F-b0mb.

Frowning, she let out a discomforted sigh and rubbed the back of her neck. Her ex was calling yet again, though he wasn't exactly her ex. She wasn't really sure what to call Finley or their relationship. Was there a word for an online friend you only met once IRL and who you sort of banged? Someone you used to talk to all the time and then suddenly didn't anymore?

At first, F-b0mb was just another username in the forums when she released "Exorcise," a program she wrote to jailbreak any currently sold Eidolon and allow owners to install third-party applications. It was supposed to give Eidolon owners the freedom to try personality improvements the brand-name store didn't offer, but instead owners used it to pirate the official add-ons. SystemOne scrambled to release a patch that, a week later, rendered her program useless.

Some forum members praised her for being the first to jailbreak the Eidolon, even if only for a short time. Some praised her for putting a leak in SystemOne's profits and causing a ruckus. Some called her careless, asserting that she was as guilty as those who'd pirated the add-ons. Finley was one of the few who didn't resort to straw-man arguments or ad hominem attacks.

She never would have guessed that the F-b0mb who had nuanced criticisms of SystemOne's add-on store would someday have his head between her legs.

By the time the discussion thread finally died down, he had friended her on a couple of social sites where her main alias could be found, and soon they found other interests that intersected. Finley was also a gamer, and he gave her helpful feedback for a mod she had written for a fantasy RPG. They both sported ink. He was considering another tattoo across his shoulders. He listened to some of the same obscure DJs as she did, hated the same foods as she did—though they disagreed on licorice—and pointed her at the open-source software project to which she'd recently submitted a security fix.

She would never forget his expression the first time they video chatted. The way his face had gone blank was like a computer crashing.

He had assumed she was a he.

And that's how Lily preferred it. Like every other woman online, she'd learned early what kind of welcome anyone who wasn't a cis, white, straight male received on the Internet, and in tech especially. Being one step outside that group meant bearing aggressions both macro and micro. Any tactic would do, from the careless to the cruel to the illegal, if it shut you up and pushed you out.

Staying under the radar meant a lot of those who interacted with her defaulted to assuming she was a guy because sexism just never died, but their misconception kept them at a greater and far safer distance.

She also masked her IP address, used a PC with disk encryption and a physical lock on the machine, and compartmentalized her interests behind different aliases—a few dozen at this point, only a couple of which were out as female. She hated the idea of someone searching for a single alias and tracking her across the entire Internet, to know all of the things that made her unique without ever contacting her.

So, she couldn't help feeling a bit smug over fooling Finley into thinking she was a guy. He was one of the more thoughtful and observant people with whom she regularly interacted, so if he had been tricked, she could control how practically anyone saw her.

Because if anyone found out she was not only a woman but a sexual submissive, she could kiss all her hard-earned respect good-bye.

After the initial shock of her gender reveal wore off, she and Finley had talked as though nothing had changed, which pleased her far more than she'd admit. The more they interacted over the subsequent months, the more he wanted to know about her. He knew she lived in Washington, but what part of the state did she call home? How did she get into coding? Any family?

Lily hedged as best as she could, doling out the least risky information or obfuscating when possible. She lived in Seattle, got into coding in middle school, had a regular family. *That I never talk to.*

To his credit, Finley quickly caught on to her hesitance and took a different tack. He talked about tech news that excited him, sent a photo of the new tattoo on his calf, and shared funny stories about his family. He introduced her to his girlfriend of three years, an artist who mainly worked with acrylics.

Midge would wave at first, but after a while, Lily got the sense that Midge disliked how often Finley chatted with her. She never received any dirty looks because Midge began avoiding the camera, but it got to the point that whenever Midge was home, Finley tended to end their call early, the only exception being the times they watched RFL games together. "You two and your robots," Midge would say before secluding herself elsewhere.

Finley and Midge had broken up about six months ago. Lily did what she could to offer comfort and sympathy without knowing any specifics. He didn't offer that information and she didn't ask. She understood his need for privacy—only too well.

Then last month, he'd asked her to lunch. Rather than demur as usual, she was tempted by the prospect of a real face-to-face with Finley—and, if she were being honest, some body-to-body interaction as well, but she didn't put much stock into that happening.

She had discreetly asked a mutual friend about him, mostly to confirm that Finley wasn't secretly a psycho, even though she had already spent enough time both talking to him and stalking him across the Internet to know the answer to that question.

And yet she still hadn't been prepared to hear that Finley might be a Dominant.

Nah, Bomb is mint. His ex was sick of him tying her up during sex, but you don't need to worry about that LOL

With her stomach in knots, she had sent Finley a reply email agreeing to lunch. His response was joyous, to say the least. He suggested a restaurant that served her favorite cuisine, and she set the date and time.

It had been both bizarre and distressing to see him in person, to have more than a 2D version with which to interact. So many more details stood out than what she saw streaming from his webcam.

The glare of his display had been completely washing out the healthy glow of his sun-kissed skin. His eyes were a brighter green than she recalled, and he stood much taller than she'd expected. In sneakers, she was half a head shorter than he was. She already knew he had a body she wanted to explore because webcams couldn't hide a pair of guns like his, but that didn't mean she didn't look him up and down as casually as possible.

Tattooed around both of his forearms was a pair of black bands, one wide and one narrow. They somehow looked more permanent in person, or maybe the little hairs growing on his arms simply gave them texture. A blue-and-green roaring-lion tattoo on his right biceps was partially hidden by his shirt sleeve, but it, too, looked more colorful than she remembered. The only thing that hadn't changed in the transition to offline was his easygoing attitude, such as his frequent, disarming smiles that revealed dimpled cheeks.

But as carefree and casual as he seemed, she knew they had both taken extra time to get ready, had both carefully chosen what to wear. His short-cropped, brown hair was neatly combed. Though he usually got away with a bit of stubble, he showed up smooth-shaven. Rather than wearing a retro punk T-shirt or—the times she'd caught him just after work—a partially unbuttoned dress shirt, that day he opted for a plain black tee, new jeans, and a silver chain around his neck. She also opted for jeans and had chosen her most flattering pair. Rather than a snarky T-shirt, which easily made up a quarter of her wardrobe, she wore a red, off-the-shoulder top.

Merely taking each other in took longer than was probably socially acceptable, but they eventually sat at a table and ordered food and fidgeted with their silverware. When she wasn't staring at how his shirt molded to his shoulders, she watched his gaze roam from her hair to her hands to, of course, her chest. They both relaxed once they broke ground on their usual conversation, but the heat in his eyes when he watched her speak sometimes made her tongue trip.

Lunch turned into an afternoon at the downtown market, then dinner, then a drink, then two drinks. They strolled to sober up, and he asked if he could hold her hand. She enjoyed it so much that she asked if she could kiss him.

That stolen moment in the shadows beneath the awning of a closed shop still gave her wet dreams—his weight pushing her against the locked doors even as his hands on her hips pulled her close, the low sounds he made in the back of his throat. A taxi ride and a whole lot of anticipation later, he was showing her around his apartment.

Where it all fell apart in spectacular fashion.

Pretending that she needed to refresh her memory—because of course she hadn't read the damn thing a hundred times—she switched to her email and opened up the apology he'd sent the next day.

From: Cook, Finley <fwcook@...com>
To: codemonkkey <codemonkkey892@...com>
I'm sorry for last night. I guess I'm still sore over Midge, though that doesn't excuse the way I snapped at you or the things I said. I'd like to explain when you're available.
Wish I knew your name.
F-b0mb

In her reply, she lied and said she was really bogged down with work, so she didn't know when she'd have time to meet him, but she'd let him know. That was almost three weeks ago, and they hadn't spoken since even though he kept sending her face-chat requests. Meeting MstrFul at the hotel had been a desperate bid at a few minutes of punishment for avoiding Finley, but she wasn't going to get redemption that easily. And she had to face him sometime.

0 0 1 0 1 1 1 0 0 1 0 0 0 1 1 1 0 0 0 0
0 0 0 1 0 0 0 1 1 0 0 0 0 1 0 0 0 1 1 0 0
0 1 1 0 1 0 0 0 0 1 0 1 1 0 1 0 0 0 0 1 0
1 1 0 0 0 1 0 1 0 1 0 0 0 1 1 0 1 0 1
0 0 0 0 1 0 1 0 1 0 0 0 1 0 0 1 0
0 0 1 0 0 0 0 1 0 0 0 1 1 0 0 1 1 0
1 1 0 1 1 1 0 1 1 1 0 1 1 0 1 0 1 1
0 0 1 1 0 0 0 0 0 0 0 1 1 0 0 0 0 0
1 0 1 1

Chapter Four

0 0 1 0 0 1 0 1 1 0 1 0 1 0
1 1 1 0 0 0 0 1 1 1 1 1 0 0 0 1
0 0 1 1 0 1 1 0 1 0 1 1 1 1 0 0 1 0
0 0 1 0 0 1 0 0 0 1 0 0 1 0 0 0 1
0 0 0 0 1 0 0 1 0 0 1 0 0 0 1
0 0 1 0 1 0 0 1 0 1 0 0 0 1

C learing a space for her glass of water took some doing. She could've walked any of the three empty glasses still sitting on her desk to the kitchen, but she didn't want to see that pile of dishes again. Instead, she stacked the empties, shifted her keyboard's orientation border a couple inches left, and set the glass next to it on the right. Her custom keyboard layout blinked into its new position.

She accepted Finley's video-chat request, but kept her end audio-only.

I'm such a coward.

Finley sat at his desk with his chin braced on the heel of his hand and the bored expression of someone browsing a news feed. He lifted his head in surprise. Looked right into the camera. And he was shirtless. She leaned closer to her display.

"Oh, hey." He sounded unprepared, as if he hadn't counted on her picking up the call. She winced.

"Hey," she said. "Is this a bad time?"

"No, it's great. I was just…" His shoulder flexed as he shifted his mouse. He squinted at his screen. "Why isn't your camera on?"

She knew he was going to ask. "It just isn't."

"Your place that bad right now?" It was a familiar joke, and though part of her heart warmed, another part prickled. "I want to see you, Monkey. Turn your camera on."

"We can talk like this."

His mouth tightened, and he shifted in his chair

"You're still hiding from me." She was. No denying it. "I want to talk about what happened, but not when I can't see you. I need a face to talk to."

Even she didn't want to know what her own face looked like right then. "This is how it's gonna be tonight, okay?"

"It's not okay." He was calm, but somehow his words were more forceful than she was used to. "You share some of the blame for that night. We've got to be on equal ground here."

What? How was that disaster *at all* her fault?

"I'm the one who was kicked out," she reminded him.

Finley looked at the camera dead-on. "And also the one who lied about her name...among other things."

She put her head in her hands. She had no answer for that. Concealing her identity had been paranoid instinct. At her silence, he kept going.

"Why would you lie about something like that? I wouldn't have been happy about it, but if you'd told me to use your alias, I would have. I'd have understood."

Her eyes burned, but she blinked hard and took a deep breath. She was stronger than this. She had simply protected herself. That was all.

"We were meeting in person for the first time, and I figured we'd stick to Bomb and Monkey, but you immediately gave me your real name. And I didn't want to hurt you, which...of course, I did anyway," she finished on a sigh.

Finley stared at his keyboard with disappointment. Well, what did she owe him, really? Her identity, and who knew it, was one of the few things she could control. Giving that up arbitrarily... Then again, she had arbitrarily given up a different kind of control to MstrFul. Silence reigned for probably only fifteen seconds, but it felt like fifteen minutes. Finley didn't hang up, though.

"Can't we just talk like we used to? Please?" she pleaded. She almost said "sir," but snapped her lips shut. He lifted his gaze, and though she knew he was looking at a webcam, she felt as though he could see her, as if he almost heard that last word. His expression softened.

"Sure, Monkey." He sighed and leaned back in his chair, revealing more of his chest and abs. He still looked good enough to eat—and a second helping sounded too good. "Sure is pissing rain tonight. You weren't out earlier, were you?"

"Just for a quick errand." She definitely didn't want to tell him about the MstrFul debacle and changed the topic. "How's work been for you?"

"Hellish." He laced his fingers behind his head, putting his biceps on full display, not to mention his pectorals, his deltoids... She realized her mouth had fallen open and shut it. "You remember that SPD project I've been working on, right?"

"Of course," she said. Finley's employer had been contracted as a technology consultant to the Seattle Police and was upgrading the department's databases.

"Well, they want the new UI done by next Thursday, but my boss only told me today, *and* we're supposed to be doing the database migration this week."

"Ouch. I'm guessing they're asking for overtime?" The words came out just fine, but she was imagining tracing her lips across his chest. She'd never had the chance to at his place.

"Not yet, but it's inevitable." His stare had weight to it, and she almost worried that her webcam was on after all. He seemed to be able to see her.

"Yeah, I'm under a real tight deadline myself. Doing some benchmarking." She turned her head to check on the Eidolon. Those all-too-realistic plastic eyes still stared at the ceiling. "I usually get at least ten days to finish, but they need it done in five."

Her editor at *NTR* had sent her an email the day before the new model was scheduled to arrive. Apparently, more had changed with the new line of Eidolons than just their hardware.

A special courier is delivering the test model tomorrow morning, and I need your article by eight a.m. this Friday. I know you asked for at least a week to test everything and do the write-up, but the SystemOne rep said he couldn't give us priority access anymore, and I couldn't get him to send out the test model any earlier. The editor in chief is on my ass to get the review up before those hacks over at EW, but he did agree to pay you an extra fifteen percent if you come through for us on time.

"Why the rush?" he asked.

"I can't really say much else on account of the NDA."

Finley dropped his arms. "I told you about my project. Do you think I'll tell anyone what you're working on?"

He didn't use the word "trust," but it was there in his question. Didn't she trust him, even a little? They were talking shop like usual, though, so maybe things between them could be okay again. He was easily the person to whom she was closest, and the idea of losing that connection…

The problem was, her Eidolon reviews were one of the few things to which her real name was attached, though as "L. Foss." Even if she stuck to her NDA by waiting to tell Finley about her work until the new Eidolon released in a few weeks, she'd still risk linking her real identity to the one that wrote Exorcise.

If Finley leaked that connection, intentionally or not, SystemOne could decide to sue her. At the very least she'd lose her job with *NTR*, and "L. Foss" would be outed not only as a woman, but as the woman whose program had cost SystemOne quite a lot of money.

And it would only be a matter of time before the real dirt got out.

So she obfuscated. "It's a pretty scary NDA. Legs will be broken and all that." His dimples made their first appearance when he smiled, and his shoulders shook under a silent chuckle.

"Does that mean you have time in a few days to meet up?"

"Uh…" A string of expletives flew through her mind. She had to submit the review by Friday morning, but she had no other time-critical work lined up for the weekend, which was exactly what Finley suspected.

A notification sound from her computer announced that her current test series had completed.

"What was that?" Finley asked.

She jumped at the distraction. "Uh, work calls. I've got to get back to it if I want to get done on time. I'll catch you later, Bomb."

"Wait, when can I see you this weekend?"

Damn it. She wasn't sure if she could handle seeing him in person yet.

"Well, I never know when work will come my way, and you might be pulling extra hours, so—"

"I'll always make time for you if I can, Monkey." He sounded so sincere and generous. He *was* sincere and generous…and sexy and intelligent.

And she was such an asshole.

"Can you call back tomorrow night? I'll have a better idea then."

And a better strategy for avoiding him. He sighed and looked at his webcam with resignation. He knew.

"Sure thing. Good luck, Monkey. Bomb out."

The call ended, and she thrust her fists at her forehead. God, why was it so hard to trust anyone? Well, maybe because her trust had never been vindicated, not even by Finley.

That night at his place came rushing back. She'd never been given a "tour" when they video chatted, so it had been her first real chance to take a look around. Compared to her apartment, his had been immaculate. He didn't have a lot of furniture—in fact, his place was half-empty—but what was there looked comfortable and as though it hadn't been assembled out of a box.

The art on the exposed-brick walls weren't posters hung with sticky tack or a digital frame with rotating images but real pieces of various styles in stylish custom frames. While Finley was getting her a glass of water, she studied a vivid abstract painting of oranges, reds, and blacks hung on one of the cream-colored inner walls. Next to it was a rectangle of unfaded paint where another work had hung that was now missing. Midge must have taken a few pieces with her.

Lily tried to distract herself with the Eidolon's latest test results, but she couldn't forget the tingle of heat in her cheeks or how fast her heart had raced when Finley returned with a glass of water in his hand. They were both nervous, both excited. She sipped from her glass as an excuse for being tongue-tied. He breathed deeply, and his hot gaze was all over her. She had never felt so desired. Neither of them had moved or spoken for a solid minute. Her fingers stilled above her projected keyboard as she closed her eyes and recalled what he had said next.

"Show me your ink. It's on your back, right?"

Oh, he was so clever. She handed him her water, which he set on a side table. She then turned and crossed her arms to lift the back of her shirt over her shoulders.

"Stay just like that," he said. She gripped her upper arms. Anticipation thrummed through her, and she closed her eyes. He stepped close. "Wow, amazing work. Where'd you get it done?"

"A parlor on the Ave. I heard it closed last year, though." She wanted his hands on her again. He had held her close under that awning, but his hands hadn't strayed from her sides and back.

"Too bad," he murmured. "Must have taken a few trips to finish it all."

"Only two. I can tolerate pain." He inhaled swiftly. She wanted nothing more than to feel how hard he could whip a flogger against her ass. He had the upper body strength to make her breath catch before she cried out in ecstasy.

"May I touch you?" he asked.

Her answer was quick. "Yes."

Two red lilies, one higher than the other, stretched from her nape to the small of her back. The stylized stems intertwined. She bit her lip hard when she felt his fingers slowly trace the tattoo. His other hand, warm and possessive, lay against her waist. If he noticed her shiver, he didn't say anything.

He tugged on her bra band. "May I take this off?"

"Yes," she whispered before saying it louder. Finley did it one-handed, and her pussy clenched.

"What kind of flowers are these?" he asked.

"Lilies. They're just my favorite flower," she tacked on. After all, she had given him a fake name—Jill—which, when he'd asked, was apparently short for Jillian.

"I'm going to play with you a bit." The heat of his body came closer, and his hand slid around to her bare stomach. A few inches lower and he'd find out just how much he affected her. She wanted to say "Please, Sir," but she didn't know where things were headed yet.

"Okay," she said instead.

His hands were reverent as they slid up her torso. When they slipped beneath her unfastened bra, she had to lift her elbows to give him room. He tenderly cupped and shaped her breasts, swirled his fingertips around her nipples.

"Are you responsive here? I know sometimes a woman isn't..."

"Pretty sensitive." She let out a strained sigh, wishing she could see his hands on her.

"I'm going to take off your top," he warned.

She nodded. Once she was naked from the waist up, he pressed her wrists against the outsides of her legs. She understood not to move.

"That's right," he said. A shiver slipped down her spine. If he was affecting her this much now, how could she possibly handle real restraints? She wondered if he had a set, if he'd use them on her that night. Should she mention her hard limits?

He stroked his hands up her stomach and held her breasts again. She opened her eyes and shuddered at the sight of his tanned hands on her fair skin. Right, he had just come back from a beach vacation.

"Just feel right now. Lay your head back," he bade.

Finley was tall enough to make the position comfortable. She shut her eyes and sucked on her lower lip while he left tender kisses on her shoulder. He was gentle with her breasts but wrenched so much sensation from them, swiping his thumbs over the tips and pinching them. Was he imagining how they would look with clamps on them?

"May I take you to my bedroom?"

She wanted to reply by taking a running leap toward the bed, wherever it was, but opted to simply say yes.

His hands never left her skin. He stepped around her and skimmed his fingers down her arm to take her hand. His gaze drifted down to her pert nipples, and he exhaled hard. He then nailed her with a heated look, pressed a kiss to her knuckles, and led her up the wood-and-metal staircase to his bedroom.

She recalled thinking that *of course* his bed was made. The pristine white comforter looked cushy and inviting. More art adorned the walls. No clothes on the floor, no overflowing hamper, no inch-thick layer of dust on the side table. He'd probably be disgusted by her place.

"Anything wrong?" he had asked. He sat on the edge of the bed and tugged her closer by the loops of her jeans.

She smiled and shook her head. "Just jealous of your cleanliness. I'm surprised I don't have a rodent problem."

"I'd love to see your place," he said with a wide grin and her stomach did a somersault. He pulled her between his knees and filled his hands with her ass. His grin softened. "I want to know everything about you, Jill."

Her earlier lie made her smile falter, but his gaze dropped to her breasts before he saw it.

"Put your hands on my shoulders." He slowly drew one hand over her hip and up her side. "You're going to need something to hold on to."

He hauled her against him with an arm wrapped behind her and molded his lips around her nipple. She gripped the soft cotton of his shirt, all the air rushing from her lungs. Her eyes closed, and for a moment she concentrated on the wet heat of his mouth, the firm latch of his lips, and the puffs of warm air from his nostrils.

The sight of him was just as amazing. She watched the tip of his tongue draw circles around her areola. His lips locked on to it, and he drew back, hollowing his cheeks to keep hold of her nipple, but it popped free. After another suck and pull, he rapidly flicked his tongue across her distended nipple, and she swore it felt as though another tongue was working her clit.

Her other breast wasn't neglected. He swirled his tongue around one nipple and his thumb around the other. He sucked one and pinched the other. When he curled his tongue around one rosy peak, he teased the other with light touches.

She didn't think she could handle much more, but then he switched sides. Her spine bowed. Her fingers dug into his hard shoulders. He grunted but didn't stop, only clutched her closer. Her grip on his shoulders was all that kept her on her feet. She could barely focus her eyes when he leaned back a minute later. The long ridge of his erection was easily discernible underneath his jeans. She thought he would move right on to intercourse—no complaints from her on that count—but he was still warming up.

"Good and pink." He tapped the flushed peak of her breast, and her whole body jerked. "Now show me that wet pussy of yours."

"Y-yes," she said on a sigh. It was the closest she had come yet to saying "sir."

"Drop your jeans, but leave your panties on for now."

No "may I." No "I'm going to."

These were orders, but she knew instinctively that he'd relent if she called a time-out. She toed off her sneakers, released the button of her jeans, and slowly drew down the zipper tab. The desire and pride on his face made her heart swell.

Her jeans hit the floor, leaving her clad in only a pair of yellow cotton panties. She stepped out of her jeans, and Finley obligingly swept them aside with his foot. He then stood and twirled her about before pushing her onto the bed. A thrill ran through her, making her gasp, and she flopped back with a smile that only grew at his possessive stare. Leaning on one knee, he hooked his fingers into the waist of her panties. She lifted her hips so he could pull them off.

In her fantasies, her Dom wore a full suit rather than a T-shirt and jeans, but she loved that Finley was fully dressed—still wearing his shoes, no less—while she was completely undressed. The sight of his naked body was a privilege she had to earn, but if she was good and obeyed his instructions, he might allow a thorough examination as a reward. She *really* wanted her reward.

She was shy to part her legs, but he took his time, kissing her knees and running his hands over her hips and thighs, which gave her time to relax.

"You're so beautiful," he said as he eased his fingers between her knees and drew them apart. She watched for his reaction, wondering if he liked her pussy as it was, unshaven, or if he preferred it bare.

With a sound more like a growl than a groan, he dragged her to the edge of the bed, pulling the comforter with her. He then knelt on the floor and tossed her knees over his shoulders. He nipped and kissed her thighs, homing in on her vagina.

She worried she'd buck him off as soon as he touched her there, but he clamped her down with one arm across her hips, and with his other hand, spread her open.

Her legs jerked, and her shoulders came off the bed, forcing a strangled noise out of her. She pressed her lips shut, but it lasted only a second. He looked at her over his tattooed forearm and sucked her flesh into his mouth. Her eyes rolled up, her lashes fluttering. She pressed her head into the mattress with a long, loud groan.

She remembered clamping her thighs around his face and tugging hard on her nipples. She remembered struggling when the sensations had been too much. He'd held her down and told her how good she tasted while his slick fingers had rubbed up and down the seam of her vulva. She remembered him asking if she wanted him to fuck her with his fingers. She had shouted yes so loud that he'd laughed.

He'd pressed his longest finger into her body while tonguing at her clit. A drop of her arousal rolled down the cheek of her ass. He slowly drew his finger out, pushed it in, drew it out. She had whimpered when a climax ebbed away before she could get there. A guy hadn't given her an orgasm this way before, and she really wanted it to happen with Finley.

Another finger joined the first one, and she keened. He upped the pace and moaned against her pussy. It had been so long since she had been with anyone, and Finley was blowing her mind. She reached for him, wanting to grab his hair, but it was too short for her fingers to get any purchase. Just when she thought it couldn't get any hotter, Finley pulled his fingers from her and pinned her wrists to the bed.

It launched her right off the edge. She writhed against his lips, jerking her wrists not to free herself but to feel how strong he was and how completely restrained he had her. Her orgasm rose up, and the power behind it threatened her sanity.

Rendered mute with pleasure, she convulsed and creamed onto his tongue. Her heart beat so hard she could feel her pulse in her throat. When she could breathe again, the air shuddered out of her. She had wanted Finley all evening, to know if he could be her Dom, to find some damn acceptance for once, and she didn't know if her heart could take how happy she was in that moment.

Without really seeing it, Lily stared at the Eidolon sitting limp and docile in the ratty armchair. Her eyes stung. She wished the memory went somewhere different after that, but what followed that soul-shattering orgasm was the part she remembered most—over and over again.

Finley had released her wrists in favor of gripping her thighs and spreading kisses on her skin as he straightened up. His expression as he licked his lips was nothing but self-satisfaction and lust. She remembered being amazed that he treated oral like its own sex act, not just a run-up to penetration. Her climax had been a given, not luck.

"I really want to fuck you," he rumbled as he leaned over her to press more kisses to her stomach. Breathless and wobbly, she rose onto her elbows.

"I brought condoms if you need 'em," she said, lifting one eyebrow and nudging his sides with her knees. He smiled at the admission that she had planned ahead and stood to tug his shirt over his head.

"I've got some. Latex okay with you?"

She sat up and nodded. Finley turned to his dresser, giving her an excellent view of his broad back. His movements made the dreamcatcher tattoo on his left shoulder undulate strangely. He turned around with a condom packet, which he tossed onto the nightstand before kicking off his shoes. His abs tightened when he reached down to shed his socks. Well-defined obliques outlined his hips and disappeared below the waist of his jeans. She looked forward to watching those muscles work.

"Sorry about holding you down at the end," he said. She blinked and looked up, but he avoided her gaze. "Hope I didn't hurt you or anything." His eyebrows were drawn together, his mouth set in a flat line.

"No, it's fine. I liked it a lot. In fact, you..." It had been so hard to get the words out. "You can...do that kind of thing to me anytime. Y'know, holding me down or s-spanking me."

Her heart pounded harder in that moment than when she had climaxed. His eyes met hers, and his lips were thin, guarded. She wanted to talk about what turned her on and what turned him on, to learn what would ramp up an already erotic evening, but she had been in a vague state of denial for so long that she nearly choked on her words.

"I know you're into stuff like this, and so—"

He raised his hand. "What do you mean, 'know'?"

Wait, had she been mistaken? She crossed her arms across her body, covering her breasts.

"Well, you were telling me how to stand and where to put my hands. Then, you know, holding me down. It's just...I heard a rumor."

She regretted it as soon as she said it. Finley went stiff.

"What rumor?"

"Please forget I said that—"

"No, you're going to tell me. What rumor, Jill?"

"That...Midge left because you tied her up." Finley took a step back. "That's all I was told, and I *swear* I didn't know they were going to overshare."

"It was Dan, wasn't it?" he asked, though he said it like it was a foregone conclusion. He stabbed his finger at her. "Well, it's not fucking true."

"Oh God, was Dan just messing with me?"

"No, he... You know he has the worst sense of humor and doesn't mind his own damn business, but I am not into that sick shit and I don't want you spreading lies about my sex life."

"I-I would never—"

"So, you can forget about this," he sneered, waving at the air between them. "I'm not going to play this fucked-up game again. I'm *done* with it." He picked up her clothes and tossed them at her. "Get out of here."

She held her breath. No way. No way did he just say that.

"But Finley, I—"

"Get out of here!"

The next couple of minutes were a blur, but her body must have started dressing itself on autopilot. The only thing she remembered before returning half-clothed to the living room was a painful emptiness in her chest and a prickly ball in her throat that swallowing didn't dislodge. She barely held back her tears as she tugged on the last of her clothes and zipped her coat.

Finley waited at the edge of the room, and she shot a glance at him as she looped her purse across her chest. He stood next to that unfaded square of paint on the wall, his arms crossed. Disgust curled his lip, but his eyes shone. He kept her at the edge of his vision rather than look at her. She walked to the door.

"Jesus, what is it about me that attracts women like you?" he asked snidely.

Lily paused at the door, both hands clenching the strap of her purse. The heat of those barely contained tears spread to her cheeks

She hated that Finley, of all people, had just made her feel like a freak, especially when she had been so literally vulnerable. She hated that the one time she had lowered her guard, she'd only found reasons to put it back up. Worst of all, she hated that a part of her agreed with him. She *was* a freak. Why else would he kick her to the curb?

She whirled around, teeth bared.

"Women like me? You don't *know* me," she seethed, her voice trembling with rage. He finally deigned to look at her, but his discomfort seemed only to grow. "You see what I *let* you see. You think because you saw more that you've seen it all? This—this is the tip of a fucking iceberg," she shouted with her fists pressed to her chest. "You don't know *anything* about me. My name isn't even Jill."

She might have smirked at the shock and hurt that flashed across his face, but the burn of anger was already turning to acid in her throat.

"So don't you dare pretend you can compare me to anyone," she croaked, "especially not her."

She wrenched the door open, slammed it shut behind her, and took the stairs as fast as she could to the ground floor while furiously scrubbing hot tears from her cheeks. She ended up walking five blocks in the wrong direction before realizing she would need a taxi home.

Thankfully, Safe Cab didn't care if she wept in the backseat for the entire trip.

Chapter Five

B ack in the present, Lily slouched in her desk chair and laid her head back. *Damn it, wet cheeks again.* Both vanilla and nonvanilla guys had disappointed her before, but nothing like that. Usually, the guy either didn't know how to be a Dom—often didn't want to be one—or he was an abuser masquerading as a Dom.

And she had really liked Finley. If he had been a Dominant, it would've been more fate than coincidence, and she had gotten her hopes up that he might be the one for her.

As usual, she'd fucked it up quite handily. Not only did she bring up Midge right in the middle of sex, she also gift-wrapped it in a bit of gossip that—if their situations were reversed—definitely would've made her feel violated.

What devastated her most in the hours before Finley's apologetic email was thinking she had not only lost his respect, but that she had lost his friendship altogether. Consoling herself by thinking she might've been right to lie about her name only made her feel worse.

Crying had started a dull ache in her temples, so she concentrated on the hum of her computer and the very faint *whoosh* of late-night traffic driving on wet pavement. The patter of rain on the bathroom window was especially soothing, as if the weather were sympathizing.

I happen to specialize in your particular needs.

Lily wiped her cheeks and looked down at her bag, which was unzipped and still spotted with rainwater. She sat up in her chair, grabbed her purse, and dug out the escort's card.

Glossy cardstock and a classy typeface. The agency's name and its slogan were on the front. She flipped it over for the URL, a sixteen-character code, and the escort's name. The Stranger. *How fitting*, she thought with a swallow.

She tucked the card under her orientation border and typed in the address.

Damn. Some graphic designer out there had serious taste. On the left side of the webpage was a high-quality graphic of a woman in a black dress, only visible from her chin to her knees. Her hand rested on her hip. On the right was a man in a black suit with the jacket open, again only visible from his chin to his knees. The placement of his hand mirrored the woman's, and the skin of both models was painted gold. Text matching the font on the card simply restated the business name and slogan. The only link on the page was a button below the slogan that read *enter code*.

Wait. Lily squinted at the models and realized the graphic wasn't static. She could tell the models were breathing. A looping GIF?

Besides a site certificate, which the site did have, no other metrics spoke to its security. She opened another browser tab and spent some time searching for Tailor Made in Seattle, hoping to find a forum post somewhere talking about the agency. Perhaps she'd find comments amounting to "don't waste your money" or "it's totally a scam," but surprisingly the agency had practically no digital presence. The search result leading to their website was buried a dozen pages back.

Okay, so they were actually discreet. Good to know.

Clicking on *enter code* revealed a blank field and a Submit button. The graphic of the man and woman reacted. In perfect sync, they took their hands off their hips and gestured to the blank field. She copied the code from the card into the website and clicked the button.

The man and woman beckoned the user before fading from the screen. Lily raised her eyebrows. She was brought to the Stranger's profile, which was simply a photo of the man she'd met, his escort alias, and a few intriguing details. She pressed her hand to her chest.

Six years of experience with every level and slant of domination imaginable. The Stranger is a calculating Dominant and delights in crafting the right punishment to suit the crime. He will give you what you deserve.

The solitary link at the bottom of the page read, *Do you wish to meet this person?* The escort's black-and-white photo glared at her, daring her to click. Her finger tapped the mouse button before she could talk herself out of it, and she was taken to a page asking for her first and last name as well as an email address, username, and password.

Without hesitation, she wondered which of her aliases would work best—or perhaps a new one? If their escorts had names like "the Stranger," then they likely didn't care if her name was real or not, so she created a user account under the name Jillian Lloyd.

After confirming her email address—a simple throwaway account—she was taken to her new and therefore mostly empty profile page. A note at the top provided brief instructions. *We encourage honesty when completing your profile. When you are satisfied with your answers, click "submit." Your requested person will then schedule a time to meet.*

Lily checked the clock. It was still early. She dove into her profile. The topmost section asked for demographic information, including orientation and role. Clicking on the drop-down menu next to *role* offered a wide variety of answers, including *submissive.*

She wasn't sure what to make of the next section, which asked for her height, weight, and measurements, including her shoe size. The section after that returned to more relevant questions and asked that she list any health concerns.

After filling in a small selection of her favorite hobbies and her likes and dislikes, she answered a few questions on what kind of man would attract her most. Finley popped into her head, but she resolutely forced him aside. *A guy who is disgusted by me is definitely* not *what I find attractive.*

The last section took the longest and was the most interesting by far. It was an extensive list of sexual activities, many common to dominance and submission. She was asked to rate her curiosity about each and to admit whether she had experienced the activity.

She was squirming in her chair when she reached the bottom of her profile, where she had three buttons to choose from—Save, Cancel, or Submit. The significance of the last was not lost on her as she clicked it.

Another glance at the clock had her doing a double-take.

"Oh shit," she exclaimed. Filling out the profile had taken almost two hours. It was nearly three in the morning.

Not that she needed to hit the hay. She hadn't been able to fall asleep before dawn ever since the burglary and highly doubted she'd have any luck that night, but she did have a deadline to make.

Lily went into full-on work mode and pulled up her checklist. She had scheduled most of the automated testing for when she needed to sleep, but combing through test results, writing up her observations, and completing a visual inspection of hardware performance was going to take nearly all of her waking hours for the next few days.

She had to make up for lost time, so she rearranged a couple of items in her list and grabbed her tablet from the top of a pile of clothes. After kicking some floor clutter out of the way while tapping on the tablet, she leaned over the Eidolon to double-check that the cable was securely plugged into the android's head. *Good to go.* She backed up.

"Okay, let's get the mobility testing out of the way." She slipped on a pair of glasses to record the test and tapped a button to take the Eidolon out of sleep mode and into test mode. The android lifted his head, pulled his knees closer together, and laid his arms on the chair's armrests. He briefly scanned his surroundings to orient himself before looking straight ahead and waiting for instructions.

The current developer and manufacturer of Eidolon-brand droids was only about as old as she was and hadn't even started out in robotics. SystemOne was once a small-time custom computer systems company, but after a quarter century and several successful iterations of their own operating system as well as software suites, they had the money and market share to dip their thumbs into new pies.

"Mobility and spatial interaction testing for the SystemOne Eidolon version four, model two of eight total base designs, aka David, slated for release in summer 2042," she said while looking over the android. She double-checked that her tablet's voice-to-text was properly transcribing her words before moving on.

"The Eidolon conforms to his seat in a natural manner. Visually, he is far more realistic than version three." She leaned over the Eidolon and palpated his face. He was only room temperature. "The skin has elasticity, pores, the ability to blush, and small, randomized imperfections or discolorations. The texture of his hair and the look of the follicles is lifelike." She tapped a button on her tablet to enable voice commands and took a small step back. "David, blink once every second for twenty seconds."

David did exactly as she asked. She watched and listened closely before disabling voice commands.

"Hm, something still isn't quite right yet. I think it's the lack of facial muscles twitching underneath the eye. Blinking has definitely improved, though. The lids at least move right, and the eye motors are nearly silent. Good job, SysOne." Indeed, one of the creepiest things about the first two versions was the whirring of their eyes, which blinked too slowly and the eyelids of which were obviously hard shells rather than a fold of skin.

The original developer of the Eidolon, Human Squared, had been trying to engineer humanlike droids ever since Lily was in her teens, but their best prototypes were seriously flawed and far too expensive to continue development. They were facing bankruptcy when SystemOne swooped in with an offer. The line of droids that debuted a few years later, "Version Prime," was leaps and bounds more advanced than Human Squared's best attempt. Primes were still more expensive than what ninety percent of people could afford, but the amount of progress was cause for excitement.

Landing a review article with *National Technology Review* of Version Prime's hardware capabilities was a major achievement for Lily, especially when it was received well enough by the tech crowd to give her access to every subsequent model. Getting her hands on such cutting-edge technology had taught her more in ten-day stints than any robotics graduate program could have.

After testing the android to simulate breathing, chewing, and a variety of facial expressions, she gauged his ability to track objects and sounds in the room—meaning she was throwing around socks.

"The Eidolon shifts his eyes first, if not doing so simultaneously to adjusting his head when looking for a new object or a source of sound, as opposed to any previous version."

She commanded David to stand up. The Eidolon leaned forward and slid his feet back to shift his center of gravity. He pushed himself up with his arms as well as his legs—much more lifelike. She wanted to listen to how loud his motors were, but his vinyl body suit made a strange sound as he stood. She picked up a pair of scissors to cut them off, but paused just as she grabbed the hem of his shirt. After a moment's thought, she stepped back, toggled voice commands, and held out the scissors.

"David, cut off your clothes," she ordered. He looked at the scissors in her hand, took them, and made quick work of shedding the plastic. After returning the scissors to her hand, David reverted to his original position—arms down and eyes straight ahead.

"Very impressive," she said. "Version two would have asked me to clarify, and version three would have stated it did not have the right tool. Four looked for a tool, recognized the scissors in my hand, and completed the task. This new model is pretty amazing."

Of course, Lily confirmed that the Eidolon was as anatomically correct as all previous versions, but though the droids were capable of operating as a highly overpriced dildo, she was far more interested in the hardware's strength, resiliency, and motor control. Rather than test its ability to seduce, she wanted to test how well it resisted hacking and how much stronger it was than the average person. An android that could kill because of a bug or an exploit was far more alarming than one that could fuck.

The rest of the mobility tests went well once the distracting sound of the Eidolon's clothes was gone. The motors driving the endoskeleton were still audible but far quieter than version three. He was still strong enough to lift her fridge a few inches off the floor, so the cheaper hardware still retained the same motor strength as version three.

He walked more loosely than his predecessors, but his hips still didn't drop correctly, and he still had as much trouble keeping his footing when intentionally thrown off-balance. If pushed lightly or even moderately, he was fine, but a harder shove that would make a normal person flail or try to brace their fall made David freeze up like a posed action figure and topple onto the clothes she had piled to break his fall.

Even so, if this was just version four, she couldn't wait to test version four-point-five, which was already rumored.

A quick check of the time put her on schedule for completing the next item on her list. She ordered the Eidolon to sit and returned him to sleep mode. He went slack again, and she tossed a towel over his lap, though not to preserve his dignity.

At her desk, she took a second look at the latest test results, and her world narrowed to include only her monitor. Hours passed. Her eyes felt sticky by the time she had a few pages of useful notes, but the long winter night meant she had more darkness to endure. She got to work on an outline for her article and then on completing part of it. Her editor wanted a minimum of 12,000 words, which she told herself was a piece of cake since she had previous articles and hardware models to refer to, but producing something as polished as her other reviews in half the time was a different matter entirely.

When she realized she had read the same paragraph ten times, she turned away from her desk and felt as though she had woken from a daydream. The physical world came into focus, and her senses reengaged. The light of dawn had brightened the sky, as sodden and gray as it was, and the rain seemed to have taken a break, for now at least.

The Eidolon remained in the same position she'd left it in, unable to move unless at her behest. It couldn't touch her, talk to her, or even look at her without her permission. If she allowed it any freedoms, it would know exactly what was expected of it and would do everything within its programming's capabilities to meet those expectations.

It wouldn't judge her, insult her, or abuse her. It wouldn't reject her, hate her, or leave her. If she were David's permanent owner, he would put her commands and her needs before anyone else's. No other companion would be as safe, but he would never be able to dominate her.

Exhausted, she visited the restroom, brushed her teeth with half-open eyes, and double-checked that the next series of tests was running before flopping onto her disheveled bed.

She hoped that sleep would swallow her up, but Finley and the Stranger were both still in her mind. Their shadowy forms stalked around her, inspecting her and devising a punishment. She chewed her lips at the idea of two Doms disciplining her.

But of course, Finley wasn't a Dom, was he? And that was the problem. It was always the problem. Her fantasies—her delusions—kept getting in the way of reality, and the only thing the Stranger offered was more fantasy.

When was she going to wake up?

"Not today," she whispered.

L ily wondered when she next opened her eyes if she hadn't slept at all. Her limbs were heavy, her skull seemed one size too small for her brain, and her stomach was cramping for food. She swore her eyelids were glued shut, and the taste in her mouth made her cringe.

When she was able to peel her eyes open, she looked blearily at her cluttered nightstand. The light in the room had hardly changed, and a gust of wind threw a sheet of rain against her bathroom window. *More rain?*

"Ugh," she groaned, fumbling for her phone. The light of the display made her squint. Another long groan and a curse left her mouth. She hadn't set her alarm, so she had overslept. It was already past four in the afternoon. Sunset wasn't far off, and it'd be dark in her apartment in about an hour.

Winter was already hard to get through, but the long nights this far north meant she hardly saw the sun. She had tried sleeping with all the lights on at night, but her body knew the difference. Her mind knew the difference.

After a few taps on her phone, she listened for and heard the acknowledging beep from the coffeemaker in the kitchen. The whir of the machine punching into a new packet of grounds and the soft suction of water were drowned out when her music system turned on. It could play anywhere in the apartment, but she isolated playback to the bedroom speakers.

She normally started her day with quieter, more comforting music, but as soon as the delicate voice of her favorite singer-songwriter poured from the sound system, she frowned and switched to a louder playlist. Electronica never failed to get the heart pumping, and some classic dubstep hit the sweet spot that day.

She swung her feet to the floor and scrubbed her face. Through the open bathroom door directly in front of her, she glowered at the runnels of rainwater on the sash window beyond her sink. It would've been nice to see the sunset at least. She hauled herself upright—and promptly sat back down with a gasp and a whimper. It seemed her feet weren't yet on board with the whole walking thing.

Stupid fucking shoes, she railed inside her head as she massaged the balls of her feet. Each touch set off a jolt of pain. She reached for her slippers, which did a lot to cushion her abused soles. After using the toilet, she washed her hands and brushed her teeth while glaring at the mirror and contemplating various revenge schemes on the poser Dom who had said those instruments of torture were the shoes a "good little sub" wore. She'd like to see him clomp around in a pair of—

Oh, but then MstrFul had already gotten his comeuppance. The Stranger with his calm decisiveness had put a quick end to their argument in the hall and she'd gone home with his card.

The rest of the night came rushing back. Had the agency responded to her? Had the escort? She quickly rinsed her mouth and returned to her bedroom.

Her shriek pealed over the music blasting from her speakers as she stumbled back, her shoulder hitting the doorjamb. The Eidolon stood with his feet close together and his arms at his sides as though back in his shipping container. His eyes were open—wide open. His jaw hung loose as though the mechanism that normally kept it shut was not in operation.

He wasn't in front of the armchair, though. He stood inches from the edge of her bed and stared at the spot where she had been sleeping.

Chapter Six

"**O**h Jesus," she breathed with one hand against her chest. Apparently one of her test series had hit a snag. She wanted to check her messages, but the Eidolon had to come first.

She hobbled to her desk. The monitor woke after an aggravating two-second delay—her machine was getting too old—and she entered her password with one lightning-fast smack of her fingers against the projected keyboard. A couple of clicks and she was reviewing the event log.

The stress testing seemed to have found the new Eidolon's threshold for the number of parallel processes it could handle. Version three hadn't lasted nearly as long, although instead of standing at attention like David had, it had simply spasmed from the chair onto the floor. The new hardware was far more resilient and had automatically returned itself to initial start-up mode. No real harm done.

After recompleting the new-user setup and returning David to sleep mode in the armchair, she checked her email. Most of the new messages were pointless notifications or digests, and she homed in on two new emails in particular, one from "Tailor Made Client Relations" and one from simply "The Stranger." She read the escort's email first.

From: The Stranger <strange-r@...com>
To: j-lloyd239 <j-lloyd239@...com>
Ms. Lloyd,
I'm very pleased you used the card. Normally, I would clarify any ambiguous items from your profile via email as well as make certain that you are aware of your rights and responsibilities as a submissive client, but I am eager to play with my shiny new toy.

I say "shiny" because clearly you have craved a Dominant for a long time, one to whom you can entrust control, but that you have never been properly trained and certainly never owned. The gift of your submission will be mine to respect and cherish.

I will meet you for dinner at your earliest convenience to discuss these matters in person. Are you available tonight at seven?

Someone from client relations will have contacted you regarding your user account as well as payment information. They can answer any related questions.

Don't make me wait too long for a response. I look forward to seeing you soon.

The Stranger

She pressed her fingers to her burning cheeks and reread the email. Oh God, she really had requested to meet a male escort—and not just for sex but for domination.

The escort's alias was perfect. He didn't know it, but he was the star of her darkest fantasies, ones in which an ambiguously dangerous stranger tied her down and punished her for a variety of misdeeds, but such fantasies had yet to translate to reality. Her encounter with MstrFul had merely been the latest in a long string of failures.

What if this time could be different? Unlike her other encounters with professed Doms, the Stranger's real incentive wouldn't be his own pleasure but good old cash. He'd have to satisfy her if he wanted to get paid, and he'd never ask for more of her outside the bedroom than she was willing to give. She could keep that part of her life secret and separate from everything else.

The client relations email was basically a form letter, so she skipped to the payment information, and her eyes bulged.

"Whoa."

Base packages were listed from most to least expensive, and the ultimate fantasy package was more than she would make in her most successful year of freelance work. Even discounted thanks to her being a new client, the basic package was a sizable dent in her savings. It included a single evening with one escort who would cover a certain amount of expenses such as a meal or gifts.

Caffeine withdrawal—that's what it was—hit her hard, so she limped to the kitchen. Bobbing her head to the music as she stirred sugar into her coffee, she tried not to think about the escort's suggested meeting, but she kept looking at the time on her fridge. Seven o'clock wasn't far away.

While spreading cream cheese on a bagel, she told herself her evening plans were already set. The Seattle Sprockets were playing the Denver Fenders at six thirty, and she did have a serious deadline on her plate. *Or my bottom could become acquainted with the flat of a man's hand in a few hours.*

She could easily record the RFL game. The Sprockets would wipe the floor with the Fenders, anyway. The extra fifteen percent pay from *NTR* would take most of the sting out of the basic package fee, and she did have some fuzz testing to run on the Eidolon, which would buy her a few hours.

But this was what had gotten her into trouble with MstrFul—impulsiveness.

She could be smarter about it, though. Any red flags and she'd tell the escort to take a hike. She took a gulp of coffee and returned to her computer.

Yes, I'm free tonight. Where do I meet you?

Despite what she decided was a very rational perspective on her impending date, her body reacted as though she had gotten in line to bungee jump. Her heart fluttered with the kind of restlessness that made her want to scream. Her fingers were clumsy with excitement, and she made more typos than usual while preparing the next test series and catching up on her other email.

When even sitting down was too much, she took a shower. By the time she finished drying her hair, the sun had gone down. She then leaned over her desk in nothing but a pair of hip-huggers to check her email again. A new message from the Stranger had arrived.

We'll dine at the Italian restaurant near Eighth and Virginia. If you have it, I want to see you in something red tonight, a skirt or dress that ends above the knee. Wear your hair back but loose. The makeup you wore last night is sufficient, but toss the heels. Wear whatever comfortable shoes you have that would match.

You are inexperienced, so I'll forgive you this time for not referring to me as "Sir"—with a capital S. When you contact me in this manner, you will refer to yourself with a lowercase i. Any future infractions will be corrected with punishment.

I expect you to be on time. If being tardy is unavoidable, I expect you to send me a message. Otherwise, I will be counting the minutes—and the number of minutes will matter.

She was sitting down by the time she reached the end of the email. This guy was for real, at least when it came to etiquette. Before sending a reply, she went to her closet in search of a red dress. She had one in mind, but she hadn't worn it in a long time, so it was possibly as wrinkled as a prune.

Rarely used clothes joined the used ones already lying in heaps on the floor near her closet. She had to put spring cleaning on her to-do list. *This year, definitely.*

"Aha," she said with a smile. It had been one of many sardines in a can but nary a wrinkle, and nothing a lint roller couldn't clean up in a couple of minutes. She carefully laid it on her bed and returned to her desk.

Thank You for Your patience, Sir. i do have something in red that meets Your requirements.

As the taxi splashed its way downtown, Lily felt like someone staring over the side of a bridge and entertaining the notion that her bungee cord might snap. Worse, she was in danger of arriving late. She figured summoning a cab half an hour before she needed it would be fine for a Sunday night, but a boilerplate message from Safe Cab said otherwise.

Due to high demand and heavier than expected traffic on I-5, your Safe Cab is scheduled to arrive for pickup at approximately 6:44 p.m.

Sixteen minutes seemed like enough time, though, even with the amount of traffic coming off the interstate. That is, until her Safe Cab pulled over way too early. The speakers piped out a smooth, masculine voice with a prerecorded explanation.

"To improve safety and efficiency, your Safe Cab will now download and install a software update. This will"—She wailed plaintively.—"only take a few brief moments. You will not be charged for the duration of your wait. Thank you for your understanding."

"God, of all the days to—"

She absolutely loved technology, but it could be a real pain in the ass sometimes. She briefly considered bailing and trying to hail a human-driven cab, but heavy rainfall meant taxis were the more attractive alternative to walking, and she likely wasn't going to catch one. Walking wasn't an option at that point, though even if it were, the prospect of hoofing the last mile and a half down steep, slick hills would have stopped her.

And so she watched helplessly as the time on her phone rolled right past seven o'clock. She knew she should let her date know she'd be late, but she hadn't dreamed she would need to and therefore hadn't taken the time to sync her burner email account to her phone, or even input his phone number, for that matter.

She told herself it was fine. It wasn't her fault she was late. Traffic and an ill-timed patch had conspired against her, and the escort probably wouldn't do anything about it, anyway. He'd grit out a toothless warning, and that'd be the end of it.

While the patch finished installing, a chipper voice barked an ad at her. "Did you know you can use Safe Cab to make, change, or cancel dinner reservations as well as—"

"Audio off," she yelled. The cab went silent, but an ad appeared on the screen in front of her, which she pointedly ignored even though the idea of canceling was sounding pretty good.

Perhaps this whole thing was a mistake. She was crammed into a dress much more formfitting and revealing than she remembered it being, she had a deadline to meet anyway, and the amount of cash in her clutch was obscene. It was barely under her daily ATM withdrawal limit, which was far higher than the default.

She should change the cab's destination, go home, and redeposit the cash in the morning. That trip to Hawaii she wanted to take wasn't going to pay for itself. Why spend so much on just a few hours with someone who was only with her to get paid when she could put it toward ten days on a sandy beach sipping rum?

Then again, being with a Dominant was much higher on her wish list than ten days by herself with nothing to show for it but a sunburn. And why should she be nervous? The escort was a pro. She had no obligation to seduce him or prove anything to him, and if anything seemed off, she could back out of their date at any time. No pressure.

Contrary to its claim, the cab's software update took more than ten minutes, but it did eventually get her to her destination. After paying the fare, she dodged under the awning of the boutique hotel next door to the restaurant. Her feet still ached, but ibuprofen and shoe inserts had dulled most of the pain.

In Seattle's nicer months, Migliori d'Italia offered open-air seating, but the railed-in area of sidewalk was currently empty. Red rope lights delineated the large front windows. On either side of the pine-green entrance, neon signs displayed the name of the restaurant. Another neon sign assured customers they were open.

She approached the entrance, a rain-speckled glass door with a few credit card decals. The brass handle was smooth and cold. She took a bracing breath and went inside, but before she could appreciate the delicious smells and the comfortable warmth of the softly lit interior, a strange sight at the host's podium nearly had her rubbing her eyes in disbelief.

A current-generation Eidolon stood next to her owner, who was having a heated argument with the host. Not just any version three. The most infamous one.

"I don't understand the problem," the owner said as he stroked one hand over his receding widow's peak. "I've been a regular patron here for nearly ten years."

"Sir, you must understand our position," the host pleaded.

The most popular version-three base model was petite, white, blonde, blue-eyed, and big-breasted. If SystemOne brought a lawsuit against an Eidolon owner for breaching their owner's agreement, which usually meant the owner was renting out their droid for sex, then nine times out of ten, Jessica was the model involved. However, SystemOne wasn't nearly as concerned with the prostitution of an Eidolon as they were with redirecting "rental profits" back into their own pockets. It was still extremely easy to find porn online starring Jessica, and after nearly two dozen "pimp suits," she had become the face of anti bot sentiment, especially among religious conservatives.

Widow's Peak pointed at the bar area. "If you're so anti bot, then why are you showing tonight's RFL game, huh? Do you not let NFL players dine at your establishment?"

The gynoid wordlessly looked in the direction he was pointing. Version threes were adept at following the conversations of others, but not so good at contributing. They often didn't speak unless directly asked a question or unless interacting with only one person.

The host sighed. "Sir, we also show the Triple Crown every summer, but that doesn't mean we allow horses to dine with their owners."

"The Triple Crown," the owner parroted with a simper. He chuckled and fisted his hands. "That's just so fucking funny. You are the funniest fucking person I've ever met."

Jessica laughed as well, a feminine trill that she half covered with her dainty hand. Widow's Peak had painted her nails purple to match her dress.

"Shut up, Jessie," he hissed, cringing with embarrassment.

Without any offense taken, she quieted and put her hand down. Version threes didn't always understand context, especially sarcasm. Lily checked the time on her phone, grimaced, and tried to catch the host's attention.

"Sir, your companion doesn't eat and—"

"Is that it? Do you know how much she cost? I can buy two dinners if that's what it'll take," the owner said.

"We'd be happy to box up some food to go, sir, but you cannot bring your companion to one of our tables. We...we all know what she is. Our other patrons would be very uncomfortable."

Jessica's infamy wasn't constrained to a right-wing talking point. She was also held up by feminists as distilled misogyny. Jessica *was* objectification, a mere thing meant to replace a real woman with a traditionalist idea of femininity—physically perfect, passive, without opinion, and always available sexually. No ambitions, no objections. Lily couldn't count the number of times Jessica had been described as "submissive" by guys in the tech industry who unabashedly preferred a talking, moving sex toy to a real woman.

The host leaned to make eye contact with her. "Miss, may I help you?"

"Yes, I'm meeting...someone." Oh God, she didn't know the escort's name.

"Come on, Jessie." Widow's Peak took his Eidolon by her elbow and led her past Lily to the entrance.

The host sagged with relief. "Your name, please?"

"Jill Lloyd." She checked her phone. Fourteen minutes past the hour.

"Your party is waiting at the bar," the host said. "May I check your coat?"

I'd rather wear it the whole evening, actually.

"Sure," she said reluctantly. She shucked her knee-length wool coat and immediately missed the armor it represented, not to mention the added layer of warmth. The dress really was far shorter—on both ends—than she remembered.

She glanced at the bar area as she handed over her coat and umbrella, wondering if she'd see a pair of blue-gray eyes glowering at her, but the bar was packed with people watching the Sprockets versus Fenders game. She squared her shoulders, stowed her phone inside her clutch next to the fat white envelope holding all that cash, and walked toward the bar.

A quick "pardon me" gave her passage between two crowded tables. With her heart firmly lodged in her throat, she scanned those seated at the bar, most of them men sitting alone and nursing a drink. She spotted the black sleeve of a suit jacket behind a couple of guys in Seahawks T-shirts and immediately wanted to leave. *No jumping off bridges today, thank you.*

One of the Seattle fans reached for the beers he had ordered. That black sleeve led to a jacket lapel and the crisp collar of a sky-blue shirt against honey-colored skin. Beers in hand, the two football fans left the bar, giving her an unobstructed view of her date.

The Stranger was casually reclined on a high-backed barstool, one elbow on an armrest and one polished shoe braced on the foot rail. A half-full glass of amber beer sweated on a napkin in front of him. His striped tie matched his finely tailored suit and shirt. His black hair was combed back but not shiny with product. Not one wrinkle in his clothes or a single hair out of place. This man couldn't possibly be waiting for her.

He looked at his phone, no doubt to check the time. *It wasn't my fault*, she thought. His phone then disappeared into his breast pocket as he turned toward the entrance.

That sky-blue shirt made his irises bright and cold. She expected him to smile or wave her over, but his blank expression didn't even twitch with recognition. He stood, slipped his hand into his pants pocket, and pointed at his feet.

Come here, girl. You're in trouble.

Time to leap off that bridge and hope she didn't hit bottom.

Hard limits—gags. Soft limits—same-gender interactions and anal. Wanted bondage, impact play, a little mind fuck now and then. Wanted a touch of danger. *It's why you wanted to fuck a stranger, yeah?* Perhaps more than a touch.

Declan's mind cycled through the possibilities and constraints of tonight's scene. He knew how to keep her relaxed yet on edge, how to toe the line of trust, how to guide her through the evening and tempt her into wanting another.

Yet his stomach roiled and his heart thudded as though his internal motor was about to flash a check-engine light. Anxiety was not an unfamiliar emotion, but one he rarely felt—and one currently without cause.

I'm hoping she won't come, but I want to see her. I want her at my mercy.

Irrational. She was no different from any other client. She needed something she couldn't get anywhere else or in any other way. After the evening proceeded to its expected end, he would mark their session as complete in his calendar, like any other. The only logical explanation was that he associated her with his experience in the elevator—*Don't turn around*—which he had chalked up to exhaustion.

Ignoring the pounding in his chest and in his head, he took a swallow of his IPA and reached into his pocket for his phone. The time in the corner turned from 7:14 to 7:15. No messages from her.

Such things happened, of course. Not often, not to him, but his completion rate wasn't perfect—merely ninety-six percent. Perhaps she thought he was seated on the other side of the restaurant? He had told the host where to send her, though. He put his phone away and turned on his seat.

The bar area was at capacity. Groups of all kinds and sizes crowded around glossy mahogany tables, throwing back alcohol, pointing at the TV screens, and talking among themselves. A waiter weaved through the crowd with a tray of drinks, and a busser collected empty glasses. In the midst of all that, his newest client stood as still as a mannequin, all her attention focused on him. Even if she hadn't worn fire-engine red, he would have spotted her instantly.

She's no different.

Her dress covered only enough to be legal and barely decent. Her hair was pulled back at the temples and fell down her back in large waves except for one rebellious lock curled over her collarbone. Her black flats matched the clutch she gripped in both hands like a shield. Her pursed mouth and the way her eyebrows turned up told him she was nervous, perhaps contrite.

The first impression was essential. She had not completely obeyed him, but she was untrained, so he beckoned her to him as a disappointed parent would a child. Her lips parted. She broke eye contact and walked toward him, that little black purse held tight against her thighs. He would have to proceed carefully.

She stopped within arm's reach, and he tugged her clutch from her hands to set it on the bar. Without something to grip, she twisted her fingers together.

"Hands at your sides," he said calmly. She complied quickly. He could tell by the rise and fall of her breasts that her heart raced, could practically see the pulse in her neck.

"I'm sorry for being late, Sir," she blurted. "The cab was delayed and then it pulled over to install a patch. I know I should've sent you a message."

"Then you disobeyed me deliberately." To test the rules. To learn whether he was really strict or merely pretended to be. To find out if he cared.

"But I didn't—"

"Right now, you will listen," he said. Etiquette had to be enforced. "I made my expectations very clear, which means you'll be disciplined later."

She almost raised her head at the mention of punishment, but refrained from protesting further.

"In the future, when greeting me in public, you will do as you've just done, but with your hands at your sides and shoulders back. Eyes down, but head level. Walk with confidence. Put your lovely breasts on full display. Do you understand?"

"Yes, Sir," she said with a small nod.

"I choose when to draw you closer." He took half a step and pulled her toward him with one hand on her hip. He had to establish intimacy early.

"Close your eyes, Ms. Lloyd." He tilted her chin up and pressed a kiss beneath her ear. Her floral perfume was light and clean. She made a small, needy sound. He slid his hand to her lower back.

"I'm pleasantly surprised by what I assume was hiding in the back of your closet," he said next to her ear. "What would I see if I told you to bend over, hmm?" A puff of air on his cheek told him she found his words shocking. "You're absolutely stunning."

She shuddered, and he laid his other hand on the tiny bumps on her arm. His words affected her greatly, as expected. Though she gave the impression of someone cynical and self-possessed, she didn't seem used to displays of desire. He straightened to find a blush on her cheeks. She blinked as though coming out of a trance.

"Have a seat." He indicated the barstool he had occupied.

"We're not sitting at a regular table?" she asked in a breathless scramble while grasping at the hem of her skirt.

A knowing grin split his lips. "You wouldn't be concerned about the length of your dress, would you?" He took her hand in his and guided her toward the stool.

"I'm not sure the designer took barstools into account when they made it."

"You will sit here, Ms. Lloyd," he commanded.

Those lashes floated down again. "Yes, Sir." She kept her other hand on her hem as she boosted herself into the chair. She then tugged the skirt as far down as she could and held it in place as she lifted one foot to cross her legs.

His hands on her knees stopped her, and he leaned in close. "No. I want you constantly thinking that if you don't keep your knees together, your hem might slide up"—His fingers played at the edge of her skirt.—"and give me a sneak preview."

The mildly dejected look she gave him said more than any objection she might have made. He took the neighboring stool, which he positioned to block the line of sight of other patrons, and sat with his knees splayed.

"Your profile said you enjoy the RFL. I suggest we watch the game, talk a bit, and share some appetizers."

"That sounds great, actually." Her eyebrows jumped and the corners of her mouth turned up. She was surprised and pleased, as expected. Her rigid posture eased a notch and she breathed easier—already more relaxed.

"You'll need to explain the rule differences to me, though. I only know NFL regulations." It wasn't true, but she didn't need to know that. The point was to give her something familiar to talk about.

"It can get a little technical. There's a reason they're still only broadcast on ESPN Turbo, but most of the differences are easy enough to understand."

He waved at one of the bartenders, who headed over. "A glass of your best Merlot for the lady, and we'll start with the classic bruschetta."

"Coming right up." The bartender retrieved a bottle, free-poured a generous serving, and set the glass on a new napkin.

"You remembered my favorite wine from my profile." She reached for the delicate stem with a small smile.

"I remember a lot about you, Ms. Lloyd," Declan purred.

Scared eyes.

Desperation.

He blinked and found her setting her glass down, having taken a sip.

"You can call me Jill." She faced the bar but watched him from the corner of her eye. "It's a little weird to be so formal when…"

"When what, Jill?" he asked after too long a pause.

"We're not exactly here to discuss business." She lowered her voice and angled her neck toward him. "Is there something else I can call you? Besides the Stranger?"

He took a swallow of beer to delay his answer but already knew what to say.

"I must disagree. We are here to negotiate what amounts to a business relationship. We simply haven't yet reached an agreement and made the transaction. You will continue to use Sir, but if you're a good girl and take your punishment well, I'll tell you my first name at the end of the evening."

Jill looked at him fully. Her open mouth conveyed her shock, and her eyebrows—if he was reading the slant right—held a bit of anger. "That's not fair. You know my name."

He narrowed his eyes and lifted his glass. It would unnerve her almost as much as his response.

"Do I?" he asked before taking another sip. She looked at him like a doe after it heard a twig snap. So she had given the agency a fake name after all. No matter. Most clients did so.

The RFL game returned from commercial, and as the announcer gave a quick recap of the game so far, two opposing rows of robot players lined up on the field in an orderly fashion. Jill seemed grateful to have a reason not to look at him.

"You'll notice," she said as she pointed at the screen, "that each side has the same number of players as regular football, but regulation requires all droids to stay under a weight limit for their position..."

He listened carefully, taking in her tone and body language as well as the content of her words. Satisfying his clients took more than creating and following a script based on their online profile. The questions were meant to be personal, but everyone held something back. Jill was holding back more than most.

"It's fascinating that what a human receiver does by instinct after years of training, any robot player can do with programming. Once the program works, any of the team's running-builds can chase down passes with equal ability, assuming no hardware failures. All that's left is upgrading the software whenever they improve the hardware."

"So is the software as good as a human player?"

She smiled as she shook her head. "No, but you see huge improvements from season to season, sometimes even from game to game. The Sprockets' programming team is still working on the action-figure problem."

Declan pretended not to know what she meant. "What's that?"

"Here, watch," she said, gesturing to the screen again. "It happens on almost every other play."

He glanced at the game only long enough to see the issue, preferring to keep an eye on her mood. One of the Sprocket safeties tackled a Fender tight end, both of which froze up midstride and fell—

"Like life-sized action figures, right?" she said. "The Sprockets are closer than any other team to solving that."

"I think you may know more about the technology than the announcer," he remarked. Her smile told him she appreciated the compliment.

"Akerman used to be the lead programmer for the Chicago Gears before the team folded, so he has the cred to call the games."

"Ever been to a game in person?"

She shook her head. "I don't get out of the house much."

Their appetizer arrived, and he ordered another beer. When it came, he took a gulp and watched Jill carefully sink her teeth into her slice of bruschetta with one palm under her chin. She closed her eyes, shyly swiped her upper lip with her tongue, and hummed in pleasure.

"Mm, this is amazing," she said around her food. "I know you know this, but I *love* Italian food."

His eyes wandered to her thighs, where her hem had done some wandering of its own. Though normally he would do something to bring her attention to it—and thereby stir the pot—he casually leaned his elbow on the bar and shifted his angle. Black, no lace. He ground his molars.

She's no different.

For many of his clients, he was their dirty little secret. They were closeted gay men or older straight women, both often married to a vanilla spouse. Occasionally, married couples came to him for a cuckolding fantasy. Though any of his customers could find an outlet for their fantasies in a local group of like-minded adults, they ended up using a card from Tailor Made. They were buying discretion.

Jill appeared to be just another secretive client, but she was only in her twenties, likely unmarried, and rather inexperienced. Something else was going on.

"When did you first know you were a submissive?"

Jill froze before she could take a second bite.

Chapter Seven

One thing was for certain—Lily had never gone out with anyone like the Stranger. When she thought she might get comfortable, he threw her off-balance. His confidence and composure were absolute, and the way he studied her rather than the RFL game made her feel as if she were being dissected. In fact, he never looked at the TV unless she pointed at it.

His laser-sharp focus unnerved her, and for some twisted reason, she loved it. She tugged her hem down her thighs, somehow convinced he might detect her enthusiasm. She then set her half-eaten bruschetta on the small plate in front of her and picked up her glass of Merlot.

"No, Jill. Answer me first," he said. From the corner of her eye, she saw no hint of relish or cruelty. In fact, his face was blank. She set down her glass and glanced at the TV just as the game cut to commercial.

"I've dealt with it for a while."

"Hmm, interesting choice of words," he said mildly as he picked up a slice of the bread. "But I didn't ask how long you've known. I asked when you knew."

She heard the soft crunch as he took a bite. Thing was, she wasn't sure when she first knew. Was it the time she'd bypassed her parents' nanny software to look at the bondage porn site her school friends had denounced as perverted? Or the time she'd fucked her high school boyfriend in the backseat of his car after he impulsively spanked her hard enough for it to hurt? She didn't recall any sort of eureka moment when the word *submissive* had suddenly applied to her.

She shrugged and gave an exasperated sigh. "I...I don't—"

"Let's try this," he said as he wiped his fingers on a napkin. "What was your first obsession? Something you didn't realize until you were older."

That one was easier, but like every other increasingly warped step of her sexual awakening, it ended painfully.

"I used to follow my older brother around a lot. His best friend Mike was always at our house, and sometimes we'd wrestle." Ugh, it sounded awful when she said it like that. They were just kids, and all she'd wanted was to hang out with her cool brother and his friends.

"I always lost, but I kept begging to do it again. I liked being held down and... Anyway, Mike came over one day and I ran into the living room. He gave me this look, and my brother said I couldn't play with them anymore. I didn't understand at the time, but..."

"Mike had become aroused, and you were so young."

"Yeah," she said, deflated. On the TV, a hardware store commercial promised their products were top-of-the-line. The one before that had been selling cars and the one before that had been peddling processors. She knew because she couldn't look at her date.

"Why haven't you been owned before?" he asked.

"I...can't really handle that. I don't think I'm the type for something steady." She reached for her wine again. The Stranger didn't stop her this time.

"Ever come close?"

She remembered an undulating dreamcatcher and a pair of warm, green eyes. She intended to take a sip of wine but instead downed the rest of her Merlot in three deep swallows before setting down her glass.

"Only in my head. Reality never fails to disappoint."

"Mm, is that what you suspect will happen tonight? Disappointment?"

The commercial break was over. The Sprockets had the ball, first and ten. Two sets of droids faced off at Seattle's forty-two yard line. She glanced at the smile that didn't reach his eyes.

"No offense, but yeah."

The bartender appeared and pointed at her empty wineglass. "Care for another?" She opened her mouth to tell him "Heck yes," but her escort interrupted.

"We're good with water at this point." The Stranger then pointed at her. "Are you a fan of olives?"

"Uh, sure," she said. The bar crowd groaned. The Sprockets still had the ball, but now it was second down and nine yards to go. Her escort turned back to the bartender.

"We'll take an order of the olive ascolane."

"You got it," the bartender said before walking away with Lily's empty wineglass.

"I'd have liked a little more wine," she said.

Her date finished his beer, pushed the glass away, and used his napkin to blot the corners of his mouth.

"Perhaps in the future I'll allow you to drink more, but tonight I want you sober."

Warmth suffused her cheeks, and she wasn't quite sure of the reason. She was going to go with anger, though. She straightened her shoulders and leveled her best glare on him.

"I haven't even decided if anything will happen after dinner, let alone if I'll see you again."

The Stranger slowly turned those frosty eyes to her. His forehead was smooth, his mouth relaxed, and his body loose, but something about him made her want to shrink into her seat. He wasn't angry or frustrated—or anything at all—and yet she could barely meet his stare.

"Then let's not waste any time on that decision," he said. The pervading din forced her to lean closer to hear him. "After we're full on damn good Italian food, we're going to pay, get our coats, and hail a cab. My place isn't far, but your feet undoubtedly still hurt, and I don't intend to cause you that kind of pain."

The insinuation that he did mean to cause her a different kind of pain was unspoken but unmistakable. On TV, Akerman was excited about something. The bar crowd was getting louder.

The Stranger leaned forward and gripped her knee. His voice was no longer mild and dispassionate but warm and rough, like the sear of whiskey in one's throat.

"I have many ways of restraining you in many vulnerable positions, but not tonight. You haven't earned it. I might show you my toys if you're curious, but only after we're done."

Whereas before she was intimidated by his gaze, now she couldn't look away, not even when a couple dozen people around her erupted in cheers.

His face was so close. Their upper bodies were drawn together as though pulled by an invisible rope. She felt his hand drift up her thigh. He slid his other hand to the side of her neck, brushed his thumb across her throat, and pressed it against her pulse point.

He could simply squeeze and cut off her air. She knew she didn't have permission to touch him, but she gripped his wrist out of need and fear—need for more and a fear of liking it. She couldn't tell which emotion was stronger.

"Once I train you to undress for my pleasure and to kneel like a submissive should, you'll be punished for your tardiness. I won't remove any of my clothing except for one item." She looked at his striped silk tie, but the Stranger shook his head.

"Oh God," she whispered. She pressed her knees together and looked lower at the black belt around his waist.

"If you are obedient and please me, I will permit you to come."

Her vision was slow to focus on his face. She shouldn't have drunk her Merlot so quickly—or maybe he made her dizzy. He pulled her closer by her throat until their mouths nearly touched.

"What'll it be, little girl? Do you want to go home alone, or come home with me?"

"Welcome back, folks. One minute remaining in the third quarter here at Mile High. The Sprockets are leading by ten and have possession. First and ten now on their own forty-two yard line..."

Finley glanced at the laptop sitting next to him on the couch. He knew nothing on the screen had changed—a generic beep would have alerted him the second his video-chat request was accepted—but the time in the corner would tell him how long he had been waiting. Over an hour. He took a swig of his beer.

"The Fenders have worked hard since their last bout against the number one Sprockets to improve their linemen's dynamic strategy suite, and it has been very effective tonight in shutting down the Sprockets' running game. The Seattle team still has possession, but didn't make much progress. Second down and nine yards remaining..."

It was past seven thirty and had been dark for a couple of hours, so codemonkkey had to be awake. She was an unrepentant night owl who set her own schedule, which meant her freelance work sometimes consumed her for a few days to a few weeks at a time, but she was also a big RFL fan like he was, and they always watched the Sprockets together. At least, they used to. Tonight was the third game they hadn't watched together ever since their blowup.

"The QB is looking to pass, fires off a long one to number twenty-three!" The announcer was at least thirty-five, but when a big play was going down, Akerman sounded like a fifteen-year-old waiting for his voice to drop. "Twenty-three's running with it. The defender just doesn't have the speed to catch him."

Another TD. He knew what Monkey would say. *And that's why the Sprockets are the Yankees of the RFL.*

"Fuck." He sighed.

He laid his head back on the supple leather of his new couch. Midge had taken the old one when she left, along with the glass coffee table, the spindly dinette set, the mismatched bookcases, the dishes, half of the art, and a couple of lamps. He kept the major appliances, the bed, and of course his own stuff.

Furniture was replaced easily enough, although he still hadn't bought a new coffee table or a lamp for the living room or shelves for his sci-fi books or real tableware rather than the flimsy plastic utensils that came with takeout.

Seeing a new couch in place of the cheap fabric one had been jarring, as if he had wandered into someone else's place. The larger, heavier dining table had seemed too big even though it fit the space perfectly. The day he'd returned from work after a contractor had repainted the inner walls, he really thought he had accidentally walked into the wrong apartment. His was painted pale yellow, not dark gray.

However, the number on the door was correct.

He had abhorred the new color for more than a week. It was too dark, too different. It didn't matter that it was the apartment's original color, the one he had liked so well when he first moved in but that Midge had hated so much. It didn't matter that the change further distanced him from that unhappy time.

Then he noticed how well the classy gray went with his new furniture, which hadn't ended up too big at all despite the number of times Midge had claimed that anything bigger than what they had would make the space too cramped. The couch was long enough for him to stretch out on. The new table could seat twice as many friends. For the first time in a long time, he looked forward to going home.

A beep made his head pop up. He glanced at his laptop, but it wasn't Monkey answering his call. The sound had come from a cellphone commercial on TV.

His body relaxed, but his mind screamed. He hated this. He wished he could hit a Redo button on that day a month ago when he had lashed out at the smartest, sexiest woman he had ever met. He wished he could replace his memory of the crestfallen look on her face while she huddled naked on his bed.

It had just been all too familiar—a confident and intelligent woman who not only exuded passion but who also had a well-hidden vulnerability. Midge was a voracious consumer and producer of art and could debate an artist's mastery of any style or medium, but the characteristic self-doubt of any artist often plagued her.

In the beginning, she had also been shy yet eager to submit to the beast he barely kept leashed. Before he'd seen her for what she really was, she had manipulated him with contradictions and emotional blackmail, begging for more and blaming him afterward for "making" her like what he did to her.

The notion that Monkey was Midge 2.0 and that it was only a matter of time until she ranted and cried after sex, every time, whether it was vanilla or not... He couldn't go through that again, couldn't endure anew the accusations of force and deception, the loathing, the pleading, the threats, and the allegations that he didn't love her if he wasn't willing to dominate her the "right" way.

Midway through his relationship with Midge was when he met the author of the first program to jailbreak the Eidolon, and at first "code-monkkey" was simply the latest addition to his social circle—someone mint he enjoyed interacting with, whose interests often aligned with his own. It wasn't long before they were IMing practically every night and he suggested chatting via webcam. He valued face time far more than words in a chat window, for which Monkey called him a Luddite even though she later admitted that she appreciated a break from typing, but their first video chat had changed their friendship so much more than he'd anticipated.

He wasn't sure whom he had expected to see on his screen, but it certainly wasn't someone who made him white-knuckle the edge of his desk. For a shameful second, he thought he was being pranked, that the beautiful, dark-haired woman with fair skin tinged pink from nervousness was Monkey's girlfriend, which somehow had seemed enormously unfair—only because he hadn't thought Monkey was dating anyone, of course. The next shameful second was the realization that he had never considered that his friend might not be a man.

Even after he managed words and social niceties, he didn't fully recover from his shock for a good ten minutes. The rush of pleasure every time he made her smile or laugh took even longer to get used to. However, he was determined to treat his friend as he always did, and unreservedly agreed to keep referring to codemonkkey as "him" in online public spaces, even though his perceptions of her were irrevocably altered. Easier said than done, he had thought, but his friend was still there, still the same. Conversation came easily to them.

He was definitely attracted to her—he couldn't kid himself about that—but even when his relationship with Midge was at its worst, and they were curtly discussing who would get what when she moved out, he never considered asking Monkey out. Inviting her to lunch last month was more impulse than intention. He was certain she'd pass, as always, but then he was meeting her in person for the first time.

He couldn't keep his eyes off her during lunch, not that he was obligated to stare at his plate, but he caught himself innumerable times staring at her hair, the delicate slope of her partially exposed shoulder, or the swell of her breasts beneath her cherry-red top. He tried keeping his eyes on her face while they talked, but he kept wondering how soft her lips were and how sweet they tasted. A few hours later, he found out.

God, he had wanted to kiss her from the moment she walked into the restaurant, and almost every moment since, but he'd held off. Though he'd felt like some awkward tween boy when he asked to hold her hand, he hadn't been able to think of any other way to test the waters. Then she had asked for a kiss only a block later, and he silently dragged her to the nearest semi-private space he could find.

He still remembered every detail of that miraculous moment against the locked doors of a shop—her fingers clutching the front of his shirt through his open coat, the flare of her hips under his hands, and the overpowering compulsion to hold her down and milk from her every drop of pleasure he could.

Finley upended the beer in his hand and sucked it dry. He didn't own a coffee table to set the empty bottle on, so he took it to the kitchen and grabbed another beer. After making quick use of a bottle opener, he returned to the couch.

"Here's the snap. QB passes...intercepted by Sprockets' thirty-nine," Akerman shouted. The fourth quarter was half over. Nothing had changed on his laptop.

Going into their lunch date, he had already known Monkey was a very private person. Of all their mutual friends, only he knew her real gender. She avoided talking about her family and her past. He knew next to nothing about her love life. Her interests were hyperfocused, as though she only circled one small island of the Internet.

He knew there was more to her and had wanted it. All of it. And yet the second she came out of her shell...

How could he have fucked up so badly? She had all but admitted she was sexually submissive and he, genius that he was, had only been able to think of all the ways it could go wrong rather than all the ways it could go right.

He had to believe it wasn't too late. He had to believe he could coax her out of her shell again. She had denied her nature for too long, and the beast in him that wanted her wouldn't remain leashed. It was time to put *her* on a leash and take ownership of what should have been his a month ago.

But damn it, she had to accept his call first.

Chapter Eight

The torrent of rain had slowed to a trickle. They didn't need the umbrella when hailing their cab or when the driver pulled over only a dozen blocks later. The Stranger paid in cash and tipped very generously before drawing her from the taxi.

Considering the quality of his suit and the enormous fee he charged, Lily expected her escort to live in a posh penthouse atop a twinkling tower, but his apartment building was modest. The brick façade of the eight-story edifice was dark with age but well maintained, and the bottom floor looked recently renovated. The residents' entrance was squeezed between a nail salon and a boutique clothing store, both closed for the night.

Discreet, as promised.

With his hand in the small of her back, the Stranger guided her to the secured entrance. The shielded call box offered no resident list or even an LCD screen for scrolling through anonymous apartment numbers—you had to know what to type into the number pad. Her date reached across her to tap his fob on a flat, black sensor, and a small bulb in the corner went from red to green.

"After you," he said as he held open the security door.

With a deep breath, she preceded him inside. The retail space left no room for a lobby, so the front hall led straight back to a set of stairs. Rows of wall-mounted mailboxes on the right were labeled by apartment number. They somehow looked overly pristine, but perhaps they had just been installed. On the left were the polished metal doors of a single elevator. Her escort pressed the Up button.

While they waited, he rested his weight on one locked hip, his hand tucked into his coat pocket and his other arm hanging at his side. She wondered what he was thinking because his relaxed pose was completely at odds with the way he was staring at her—as though she was already naked and laid out before him. She just wasn't sure if he was preparing to play with her or torture her. She shivered at the cold gleam in his eyes and looked down at her feet.

"Mm, the first of many," he murmured. She could hear a smile in his voice but couldn't bring herself to verify if it had warmed his gaze at all.

Even so, the crotch of her panties was moist. Her mind kept returning to the picture he had painted of what would happen in his apartment. An undercurrent of fear beneath swirling, frothing waves of lust was a heady cocktail she wanted to drown in.

No wonder Finley hadn't wanted her. She really was cracked.

The elevator opened with a ding, and Lily was momentarily distracted from her thoughts by the beautiful woman inside. Her wavy, wheat-blonde hair tumbled past the collar of her white fur coat. Her full lips were as red as Lily's dress. Either she was on her way to a costume party, or she was the reincarnation of old-Hollywood actress Veronica Lake. In either case, she did not shy away from meeting the Stranger's eyes, and he gallantly moved aside. A light cloud of sandalwood and vanilla wafted out as she passed between them.

The Veronica lookalike didn't give her any kind of disdainful look, but Lily bristled anyway. Her gaze slid away from Lily's face with all the awareness and concern of a security camera, as though Lily weren't even worth acknowledging.

A middle-aged man with thin, brown hair who looked like he belonged in a high school biology classroom followed the woman out of the elevator. His eyes were cast down, and he slinked around the Veronica lookalike to open the front door for her. He didn't smile or even look at the blonde. It was faint, but Lily spotted a band of reddened skin around his neck.

"The point of no return," the Stranger said. Lily found her escort standing just inside in the elevator, his arm braced against the door to keep it open. The look he gave her was as intimate as Veronica's had been aloof, and unease filled her as she boarded the elevator.

A corner of his mouth twitched with amusement. He pressed the button for the fourth floor, and as the doors rolled shut, she was chagrined to realize he was messing with her. It was probably pretty obvious that she was nervous.

Well, who wouldn't be? The Stranger was handsome, confident, and incredibly intense—an already intimidating combination without adding in the fact that he was a professional escort who offered domination—and she was going to be alone with him after only a couple of emails and a little over an hour of conversation at a restaurant.

Granted, it had been very scintillating conversation.

The doors opened again, and she jumped when his arm slid behind her. As he led her out of the elevator, she couldn't bring herself to look up from her feet and didn't see anything of the hallway besides the plush carpeting. She didn't feel anything but the warmth and weight of the Stranger's arm around her back, his hand on her waist. She didn't hear his key turning the lock of his apartment door over the hammering of her heart.

"Easy, girl," he said as he pushed open the door. "You're going to be fine."

The switch by the door turned on the lamp in his living room. He tossed his keys into a shallow dish on the entry table and closed the door behind them. No plastic sheeting on the floor or odd stains on the walls or taxidermied roadkill. So far, so good.

"May I take a look around?" she asked as she set her clutch next to his keys. His expression didn't harden so much as freeze in place. She scrambled to rectify her mistake. "May I, Sir?"

"Good idea," he said with a slight nod. "I'll take your coat first."

He stepped close, his wide shoulders filling her field of vision. Now that they were away from the scent of Italian cuisine and out of the cold, breezy night, she could smell the musk of his cologne. Her coat was already unbuttoned, so he slipped his hands through the gap in her armor and peeled it away.

His head dipped to kiss one of the shoulders he had just exposed. She heard something hit the floor and realized she had dropped her umbrella. His hair was silky against her cheek, and his warm mouth lingered as her coat fell away. She couldn't help remembering the last pair of lips to touch her skin. It seemed so long ago.

I'm not going to play this fucked-up game again.

She closed her eyes and shivered.

"You'll feel warmer soon," the Stranger said against her shoulder. Feeling warm wasn't the problem, though. Her cheeks were flushed, and a fine sheen of perspiration was already forming on the back of her neck. Even her ears radiated heat.

The problem was how much she wanted this, to feel taken over. She needed it so badly that she was literally willing to pay for it. Her head swayed to the side, and she leaned into him as if inviting him to lock on to her jugular. But her escort stepped away, taking the entrancing spell of warmth and musk with him.

"Leave your shoes here and take a look around," he said over his shoulder as he hung her coat on a hook by the door.

She unclenched her fists and released the breath she had been holding. This guy was turning out to be worth every dollar she had handed over in the cab to get here. She wiggled her aching fingers and slipped off her black flats.

The front entry opened directly into a large common room furnished with a black, modern-style sectional sofa and a matching tufted-leather lounge chair over an ivory shag rug on oak, hardwood floors. The glass coffee table supported a decorative vase holding a single, deep blue iris that appeared fresh. Two pieces of landscape art on the white walls looked as though they belonged in a dentist's waiting room.

The space wasn't empty yet still seemed that way. The lonely furniture was contained within the rug's dimensions and surrounded by a moat of unused floor space where other occupants might've placed bookshelves or a TV.

To her left were two doors, one leading to the open bathroom and one to the closed bedroom. Heading to her right, she crossed a corner of the shag rug on her way to the dining room and its adjoining kitchen—more dental-office art on the wall and a fake plant in the corner. The kitchen's laminate counters were bare of the usual clutter, but someone like the Stranger probably ate out a lot.

"Is it normal for you to bring clients here?" she asked.

The Stranger stood patiently next to the lounge chair, his suit jacket unbuttoned and both hands on his hips. A lock of his black hair had fallen onto his temple. Even in the soft light of the lamp and ten feet away, his blue-gray irises were crisp and bright. She wondered how good he must look out of his clothes but remembered that he wasn't taking off anything more—except for his belt.

"Some clients prefer a hotel room or their home because they know I like them naked and kneeling when I arrive." He dropped his arms and took a step toward her. "Do you know how to kneel, Jill?"

She broke eye contact and lowered her head, as much instinct as it was nerves. "I think so, Sir."

"Other clients cannot be themselves at home and cannot put a hotel room on their credit card," he explained. His polished shoes entered her field of vision. "And not all of my tools are portable, especially the bed. Hotel beds often lack the...structures for anything more than the simplest bondage."

He had a custom bed? It was difficult to imagine something so kinky in an apartment that looked like the model unit a leasing agent showed to potential renters. In fact, the only thing within eyesight that stood out from the décor was a flat, black box wrapped with silver ribbon on the dining table.

"So you think I'm in that second group?" she asked while staring at her warped reflection in his glossy shoes. "I can't be myself at home?"

"Someone like you can't be yourself anywhere, especially not at home. You wouldn't have used my card otherwise. But you will not wear your mask here. I won't allow it."

He was close enough now for her to simply press against his chest, but he didn't touch her, and she knew not to seek contact without permission, no matter how much she wanted it.

"But it's...not easy to look underneath," she said.

"You know what's underneath. What's hard for you is letting others see. You think they'll come to the same false conclusion as you." He sounded so reasonable. He had probably gone through this with a dozen other submissives, which still didn't make it any easier for her.

"What if I can't do it?" she asked.

"I promise you can," he said. "Now no more talking unless I ask you a question, to which you will answer honestly with due respect. You're not allowed to make eye contact unless I say otherwise. Do you understand, pet?"

Heat permeated every square inch of her skin. This was it. He was in control. Her body and what he did to it were for his pleasure, which would give her pleasure, but he wouldn't do anything she couldn't handle. She was certain of that.

"Yes, Sir." She knew some of what would happen next, but not how. Anticipation thrummed through her, making her rub her prickling palms against her dress.

"Let your eyes follow my hand," he said as he pointed. "Stand there on the edge of the rug and face the flower vase."

She kept her eyes down as she quickly walked to the spot he indicated. The shag rug cushioned her aching soles. She looked at the solitary iris without seeing it as the Stranger's footsteps stopped somewhere behind her.

"Do you know the stoplight rule?" By the echo in the room, she could tell he stood several feet away.

"Yes, Sir. Green for more, yellow for help, red for stop."

Red was supposed to signal that the scene had gone too far or was about to. She had called out red many times, but always to abort a scene that couldn't even begin. She had a feeling that wouldn't happen this time.

"Bend down and touch your toes," he said. "Show me those black panties."

How did he...? God, did anyone else see? Had she flashed the diners behind him?

"Stop thinking and start doing. Now," he said in a hard voice.

With red cheeks she drew her hair over one shoulder. The glide of it across her bare skin was sensuous, but the cool air on the back of her neck did nothing to calm her. She smoothed her hands down her legs until the tips of her fingers touched her toes. Her hip-huggers tightened between the cheeks of her ass and the slit of her vagina.

The Stranger made no sound. He didn't take an audible breath, shift his weight, or clear his throat. She was tempted to sneak a look through her thighs to see if he was affected at all, but he hadn't given her permission, so she kept her eyes on the rug.

"Spread your feet and flatten your hands on the floor."

The impulse to look at him was powerful, but the need to obey was more so. Her hem and her heart rate rose even higher as she complied.

She heard a footstep. He was coming closer. Her body was already clenched from the position, her pulse already pounding in her head, but the sound of his approach had her trembling. He stroked the back of her thigh just underneath her hem, urging her skirt ever higher.

"Your skin is a blank canvas," he murmured, brushing his fingertips along the edge of her panties. A whimper escaped her lips.

"This is one of the most painful positions for punishment," he said. "Maintaining it involves your whole body and compromises the cushion on your ass. You can't twist away from the pain, mustn't fall forward or stand up."

"P-please, Sir," she groaned.

The flat of his hand struck her backside with a crack, and only his other hand against her back kept her from rolling right over her toes. The initial jolt strangled any cry of pain she might have made. The lingering sizzle of her abused nerve endings made her grimace—and made her vagina weep with need.

"I didn't say you could talk. Do not defy me again," he said tersely. "Stand up."

Her legs shook as she brought her feet together. She savored the warm tingle radiating from her left cheek. Memorized it. His hand was there to steady her when she stood straight, but then he released her and stepped away again.

"Strip," he ordered.

Her heart jumped up, lodged itself in her throat. She quickly reached back with both hands to pinch apart the hook-and-eye clasp of her dress.

"Slowly. This isn't just sex. You're giving yourself to me. Every inch of skin you reveal becomes mine."

She tried to focus on the task, but her mind latched on to the parallels, and she remembered another man watching her undress, his green eyes full of dark promises.

Wrenching herself out of the memory, she held her hair up in one hand while the other grasped her zipper. As it buzzed down her spine, she told herself she was shedding not only her clothing but her inhibitions. He wanted her submission, nothing more.

She bent forward to push her dress past her hips, keeping her back arched and her ass out. With her left hand she skimmed the spot he had struck. The skin there was warm and still tingled. Her dress quietly landed on the rug, leaving her in nothing but her hip-huggers.

"Don't stand up," he said. She heard him move and from the corner of her eye saw him crouch right behind her. "I want to see the fabric peel away from your pussy."

Her face went from warm to red-hot as she slid her thumbs into her panties. She slowly pulled the material down, felt it separate from her slippery vagina until it fell from her fingers to pool around her ankles. The Stranger didn't move, but she could feel his breath on her skin. It nearly sent her over the edge.

"Good girl," he purred.

This was insane. He had barely touched her, yet she was ready to curl her fingers into his fancy rug and give him a front-row seat to her orgasm. She ached for him to spread her open, consume her, and dangle her off the edge of sanity, but instead he walked around her to the sofa and sat. He was torturing her, and God help her she loved it.

"Come here, pet. Show me your submissive pose."

Rather than walk, she knelt onto her dress and crawled. She then sat on her heels between his feet—her back straight, her knees shoulder-width apart, and her eyes down. Her hands rested on her thighs, palms up. She had never displayed herself like this to anyone. It felt...right.

"Beautiful. Unless I say otherwise, you'll use this pose whenever I tell you to kneel," he said. "Now tell me about your gag limit."

Something she wished she could change. Being able to wear a ball gag would only enhance her fantasies.

"Having something strapped into my mouth makes me panic and think that I'll choke before it can be removed," she explained. She hoped he didn't ask why. That wasn't a story she wanted to get into now—or ever.

"What about tape or a hand over your mouth?"

"I...I don't know, Sir." She tried to keep her eyes on the wedge of carpet between her legs, but they drifted up. Though the Stranger wore black slacks and sat on a black chaise, his arousal was obvious.

"But I can definitely give head or...be forced to give head," she added. He said he wasn't taking off anything more than his belt, but he wouldn't need to take off his pants for her to pleasure him. It was just one little zipper. She wanted to see his cock, to hold it and taste it, to feel it flex in her mouth as he shot streams of cum into the back of her throat.

"Did I say you were allowed to look at my cock?" he asked.

She quickly lowered her eyes. "No, Sir."

He paused and took a deep breath. She wished she could see his expression. "I've read enough profiles to know being forced and threatened is something you often fantasize about." He leaned forward and cupped her right breast. His hand was warm. He squeezed her nipple between his splayed fingers. "Are you ashamed of that?"

Forming an answer while he was touching her was difficult. She wanted to arch her spine and push her breast into his palm, but that would earn another reprimand. "Yes, Sir," she said. "It's just that...I don't get excited unless..."

"Unless you're being controlled," he finished for her. She nodded. "If I were to ignore your safe word and force you to do things I know you don't want, not even deep down, would that be the same?"

"No, Sir. Dominance is not about abuse."

"Are you worried you won't always know the difference?" His hand rested beneath her breast. He lightly brushed her nipple with his thumb, sending out tiny shocks.

"N-not...not really."

He leaned closer, trailing his fingers down her abdomen. His mouth brushed her temple. His musk enveloped her. He brought his other hand forward to play with her left breast.

"Then why are you ashamed?"

"I..." She moaned when his fingertips reached the damp, springy curls between her thighs. She couldn't help inching her knees farther apart.

"Why are you ashamed?" he repeated.

"Who *chooses* pain and bondage?" she choked out. "Who *wants* to crawl and beg?"

Chapter Nine

God, she was such a hypocrite. She was naked and kneeling in a display pose for a fully clothed Dominant while he fondled her. Her pussy was plump and wet, and she was lamenting her fetish even as she enjoyed it.

"Look at me, Jill." He released her breast and wrapped his fingers around her neck just under her chin. She blinked to put his face in focus. They both exhaled hard when he slipped his fingers between the slick folds of her pussy.

"What you want is a deep trust, one you can test to prove its existence." His two longest fingers made a languid come-hither motion between her thighs, sliding past her vaginal opening and grazing her engorged clit. She grimaced and moaned, dying to squirm against his palm.

"It takes a lot of courage to do that and a lot of self-love. Denying your needs is denying yourself. You want to entrust yourself to another's will, someone who knows the things you're too shy to ask for and tells you to do them. Someone who disciplines you when you deserve it, when you undermine yourself. Someone who fucks you when you need it."

At his words, an ache formed in her throat. He caught her clit between his fingers, rubbed slowly up and down. Her hands on her legs formed tight fists.

"You might be tempted to think that the submissive gives up all the power, but that's not true. You must accept that what we do during a scene is what we both want. You know what to say if you want things to stop. Do you understand, pet?"

"Yes, Sir," she said. He brought his hand to his mouth and sucked his fingers clean. When he released her chin, she knew to lower her gaze.

"You were fifteen minutes late to the restaurant tonight, and you didn't send a message to tell me you were delayed."

"I'm sorry, Sir. I won't do it again."

"When you make me worry, you have to face the consequences. Bring two towels from the cupboard under the bathroom sink."

She stood on unsteady legs. As she walked to the bathroom, her gaze strayed to the closed bedroom door, and she wondered what else was in there besides a custom bed. He said they wouldn't play with any of his toys, and perhaps that was for the best. After all, she wanted to walk out of there.

The bathroom was like the rest of the apartment, gorgeous and arranged. Besides the lingering scent of the Stranger's cologne, it was nothing but clean white tile, stainless-steel fixtures, and pale wood accessories. She retrieved two white terrycloth towels from underneath the sink. She figured she'd be returning to the chaise, but the Stranger was standing behind the lounge chair.

"Lay one over the back of the chair and the other one on the sofa," he ordered.

As she arranged the towels, she quickly understood how she was going to receive her punishment. It was no cold dungeon floor, and the Stranger was no sadistic prince, but her mouth went dry all the same.

"Bend over the chair. Heels off the floor. Hands on the seat." His voice was dispassionate, controlled. Hot shivers raked down her body.

The solidly built lounge chair bore her weight without trouble as she draped herself over its sloped back. The height of the chair automatically lifted her onto the balls of her feet. She laid her hands flat against the seat. She wasn't blindfolded, but with her head upside down and facing the seatback, her range of vision was limited. She wouldn't be able to see him standing behind her or know when something was coming.

"You'll receive a strike for each minute you were late," he said as he slowly circled the lounge chair. Fifteen hits? That didn't seem too bad, and yet the jangle of his belt buckle made her tense up. "You will count each strike aloud, and your hands will not leave the seat."

He disappeared behind her. The carpet muffled his footsteps, but she heard the belt whip from his slacks in one yank, then the creak of folding leather. She squeezed her eyes shut.

Something touched the back of her thighs, making her jerk. The belt buckle clinked as the Stranger drew the leather strap up her legs. His fingers dipped between the lips of her vagina and stroked up her cleft as he grazed her backside with the belt. She pressed her face into the towel and sucked her lower lip between her teeth.

"I see the imprint my hand made." He used the belt to touch her there. His other hand moved up her spine and over her tattoo. "I'll make your cheeks as bright red as these lilies," he whispered, so close that his slacks brushed her leg.

For a second, she was surprised he recognized the flowers on her back. Then in one swift move, he left her completely and swung the belt. The impact was loud. Pain seared through her. She cried out and instinctually tried to twist away.

"O-one," she stammered, "Sir."

"Good girl," he grunted. "A fat strip of your skin just lit up."

Her *entire body* just lit up. Heat suffused her everywhere, not just her backside. Her head was swimming. That first strike had hurt a lot more than she thought it would, and she had loved it far more than she should.

The nearly silent whoosh warned her a split second before another blow landed a couple inches higher than the first. She held in another cry, but fisted her hands against the seat.

"Two, Sir," she said through her teeth.

"Your pussy's plumping between your thighs." The edge in his voice made her curl closer to the lounge chair. He landed another strike where her rear met her thighs, then another one in the same place. She yelped, pulling her right hand off the seat to shield her backside. She couldn't help it. Without touching any other part of her, he grabbed a fistful of her hair and pulled her head up.

"Never do that. If I had gone for another strike, I could have hit your hand or wrist. Keep your hands on the seat or we'll start again from one. Give me the count."

With her head hinged back, her words were guttural. "Four, Sir."

He released her hair, and she prepared for the next blow, listening intently for the rustle of clothing as he swung his arm. Perspiration was seconds from breaking onto her skin. Her face felt hot and puffy. Hit number five left a sting so fierce it almost felt cold. The drop of moisture that trailed down her leg wasn't melted ice, though.

After the sixth strike, her legs were shaking. At strike seven, her body betrayed her again as both her hands shot back to cover herself. She tried to take it back, but it was too late. The Stranger wrested her forearms behind her, crossing them in the small of her back.

"I'm sorry, Sir! I'm sorry," she whimpered. He held her arms in place with one hand.

"Starting again at one." His words were clipped.

"No," she gasped. "Please, Sir."

"If anything comes out of your mouth besides the count, I add another strike." The belt came down on one cheek and then the other. Once her body unclenched, she was able to speak.

"T-two, Sir." She heard a low groan, and the Stranger pressed his erection against her side. His hand that held the belt pulled her tighter into the well of his hips.

She wanted him to fuck her. He'd implied they wouldn't do that tonight, but if she begged for it after her punishment, he might change his mind. He might drop his pants and take her right there.

He took half a step back. Three hard hits landed on the top, center, and base of her ass, the belt squarely impacting both cheeks. She cried out and struggled against his hold, but he kept her in position for each perfectly aimed blow. She recited the count with a grimace.

"You won't be able to sit without remembering this lesson." He lashed her again. Air burst from her lips. "Every time you see the marks I've left, you'll think of me." Strike number eight, or was it nine? The fresh flare of pain faded into the din of sensation. "You'll know I own you. I do whatever I want with you."

She heard another trio of slaps, then another, but her mind couldn't do the math anymore. Her vision blurred. A squeeze on her arms reminded her of the count. How many was it? Fifty?

"I-I dunno," she slurred. He released her arms, but she couldn't move them anyway. He leaned over her and gently brushed her hair away from her face. His thumb wiped a tear off her forehead.

"Look at me, pet," he said. His cheeks were flushed, but his eyes were clear. Even more of his perfectly arranged hair had fallen onto his face. "We're not done yet. What color is the stoplight?"

Could she take any more of this? Every inch of her backside stung, her hips ached terribly where they lay atop the chair, and her knees were quaking. She hadn't received her entire punishment, though.

"Fourteen, Sir," she mumbled. "Green." She lost sight of him as he stood straight.

"It'll all be over soon," he said. Her stomach clenched. She'd heard those words before, years and years ago. "Just one more." *All over soon.* She flinched when his hand gripped her wrists again. The jingle of the belt buckle made a chill race up her spine. *Shh, shh. It'll all be over soon.*

She heard the last strike coming, heard his grunt of effort. She couldn't help tensing up, which made the impact even worse. Pain sliced through her, halting her breath. Only his hand on her wrists kept her from shooting off the lounge chair.

"Fifteen...Sir," she gasped out.

The Stranger panted as he bound her wrists with the belt. His cock dug into her thigh. Once the belt was secure, he eased her onto her feet and wrapped her in his arms to support her. His scent surrounded her. Dark spots burst in front of her eyes as the blood rushed from her head. He walked her a few steps to the sofa, and she dazedly worried she was leaving sweat on his fancy suit.

Her feet left the rug when he picked her up with one arm under her knees. He then walked a few steps and gingerly lowered her onto the towel covering the chaise. Her rear nearly hung off the end of the sofa, but he held her in place. The ceiling wavered above her as he parted her knees.

"Beg me to stop," he said. "Beg me not to look at your soft mouth and force my tongue inside."

"Don't, please." She writhed ineffectually. Her legs felt like jelly. "Don't do this."

His eyes were merciless yet exhilarated. A ribbon of fear knotted somewhere in her stomach, but her vagina throbbed. He bent over her, using his body to keep her legs open. His silk tie whispered up her torso. She turned her face away when he would have kissed her, but he gripped her jaw and pulled her back. His crisp gaze ensnared hers for a heartbeat before dropping to her mouth.

"No," she said even as her mind yelled *yes*.

"Your lips are mine." He sealed their mouths together.

She expected a bruising kiss that would leave her lips as puffy and tingly as her backside, but the Stranger left a much more lasting impression. He seduced her with his restraint, used just the right pressure. His thumb on her chin pulled her mouth open. He coaxed her to meet his kiss and parry his tongue. He stroked his hand down her neck and over her collarbone. He molded his fingers to her breast. Before she could stop herself, she arched into his touch.

"Stop," she gasped, tearing her mouth away. His cruel smile made her stomach flip, but she couldn't tell if it was from desire or fear.

"Your breasts are mine," he said roughly. He shifted down and filled his hands with her flesh. "I want to see a pair of clamps on these beautiful nipples."

"Please," she groaned haggardly. Though she shook her head in feigned resistance, her plea was for him to use the clamps, not to spare her.

He bent his head over her breasts. Every flick of his fingers, every drag of his mouth, every scrape of his teeth pushed her that much closer to the edge.

"Sir, I...I can't take any more."

"We'll stop when I've wrung everything I can from you." His gaze dragged down her body, stopped between her thighs. He inhaled through his teeth and exhaled on a rough sigh.

"Don't look at me there," she moaned.

"I could fuck you right now." He hooked his hands under her knees and pushed them toward her shoulders. "What's to stop me?"

Her heart kicked. This was what she had wanted, what she had fantasized about. He knew exactly what to say, how to muddle the emotions of the scene.

"You want that, don't you?" he asked. "You want me to fold you in half and fuck you through my pants. The truth."

"Y...yes, Sir," she whispered. A strange delight lifted his face, wild and almost unhinged. She blinked and his expression became sober resolve. He bowed over her, and his voice dropped low.

"Beg me not to."

Had she imagined that unsettling visage?

"Let me go. Please don't make me."

The Stranger knelt on the rug, stealing all her attention. His hands on her thighs kept her knees back and her legs open. Oh God, was he really...?

"I'll do whatever I want with my property. Right now I want to play with your sweet pussy. Watch me do it, pet."

She lifted her head, and he licked his bottom lip while his icy stare bored into her. His tie was tossed over the bunched shoulders of his jacket as though he were about to dig into a meal. She tested her bonds, relished the lack of control. Maybe he *was* her sadistic prince. He lowered his head.

"No, don't," she cried even as she canted her hips toward his mouth.

She didn't want to think of Finley, but when the Stranger laved his tongue up her cleft and sucked her clit between his lips, she remembered a white comforter crumpled beneath her, a strong arm pinning her hips, and the heat in Finley's eyes as he staked the same claim on her. She wanted the Stranger to overwrite that claim, to make those memories fade away.

Her head fell back, and the room spun. His *mouth*...

His lips were bold and deliberate. He unabashedly groaned. His tongue swirled, teased, and plunged. He opened her legs even wider, pulling her pussy tight. She couldn't believe she had worried about the final climb to climax. She was flinging fast, propelled like a rocket.

"Please tell me I can come, Sir," she panted. "I can't s-stop..."

"Come for me, baby," he growled against her skin, "and keep coming."

Pleasure was a great wave that rolled her beneath it, enveloping her body in effervescence. She tried to grab his head, the edges of the sofa, *anything* to orient her, but her arms couldn't pull free of the belt. The best she could do was to fist her hands in the towel beneath her.

And he wasn't done with her yet. His tongue buffed her clit, making her flinch and twitch. She could hardly catch her breath between each shuddering gasp and exhausted moan. Another orgasm was about to break over her.

"God, *yes*!"

Something inside her snapped loose, probably her sanity. The new wave kept her under longer. When she came up for air, his mouth was still on her, wanting more. Sweat rolled down her temple. She writhed against his lips, couldn't feel anything else. Her body was no longer hers. It was his toy. He had lit a fire inside her, and if he wanted it, she would burn away to nothing.

A harsh sigh resounded in the room. She was dragged under another crest, felt its weight tumbling over her, drowning her.

Her eyes fluttered open when she felt her knees near her shoulders. The Stranger crouched over her, his black hair in disarray. He looked as though he would eat her alive.

"You can...use me, Sir," she gulped.

"Yes, I can." His voice was deep and rough. "I can fuck and fill any hole I want." She breathed out hard. "But that's not what you need right now, and you've already pleased me so much. We'll stop here tonight."

Tears welled immediately. She wasn't sure why—probably for many different reasons, but she didn't want to look too closely at them right now. She could pick apart her emotions when she was back home and in control.

"Shh, it's all right. I'll take care of you." He eased her farther up the chaise, turned her onto her side, and released her wrists from the belt. After a quick examination of the reddened skin, he covered a throw pillow with the towel from the lounge chair and slid it under her head.

"Want a blanket?" he asked, but she was still too warm and shook her head.

He went to his kitchen and returned with water and a couple of cookies. He sat down on the rug, pulled her head onto his shoulder, and held the water while she ate. He then made sure she washed the sugary snack down with the entire glass.

She didn't want to think—couldn't. Her skull was stuffed with cotton instead of brain matter. She wanted to lie down on a bed with his arms around her and take a nice long nap, but where they were was pretty good, too. His hand rested on her upper arm, warm and soothing as he brushed her shoulder with his thumb. He pressed his cheek to her forehead, and she could smell his cologne. When he grunted and shifted next to her, she tried to lift her head, but he laid his hand on her cheek.

"Don't move yet."

"I can... You're not...comfy." Her words came out garbled and husky. She wanted to sleep. Her head weighed so much. "Can I help...your sh-shoulder?"

"No talking for a little while. Just stay right here. It's where I want you, okay?"

"M'kay."

Sated, that's how she felt. A starving person who had been stuffed with all her favorite foods, someone with an itch she had finally scratched. All she could ask for now was that the hunger—the itch—never found her again.

But she knew it would. She'd only want more, and the Stranger was the only one who had ever so completely satisfied her. *Oh, Lily, what have you gotten herself into?*

"Hey, let's try standing up. I want to show you something."

She opened her eyes and wondered how much time had passed. Her head was a little clearer, but her body was achy and wobbly. He helped her to her feet and kept her steady as they slowly made their way to the bathroom. When the light came on, she was shocked at the woman in the mirror. Her hair was a bird's nest. Her eyeliner was smeared. Her skin was red in too many places to count.

"Here's the best part," the Stranger said. He turned her to look at her reflection over her shoulder.

"Holy shit." Her backside was bright pink and crisscrossed with fat, rosy strips. She lightly traced a welt from what she guessed had been the last strike, savoring the sting of even the barest touch. She probably wouldn't bruise, though, which was amazing, considering how badly her ass ached.

"Do you ever think about wearing a collar?"

He pulled her against him and slid his fingers around the base of her neck. She loved how his jacket felt against her bare breasts—and he was still erect.

"I do like the idea, but for right now it's...too permanent."

"Or perhaps too visible, hmm?" He traced her tattoo from flower to stem. "But you like that I've branded you." She closed her eyes and laid her head against his shoulder. He gripped her arm to keep her in place as he skimmed his fingers across her abused backside. "You like knowing that I've left something on your skin."

She hissed but didn't try to pull away. Though his touch hurt, it was also comforting and acknowledging. He had done this to her because they both wanted it, and he still cared for her—for as long and as much as an escort could, at least.

Don't.

"You're frowning," he murmured. "Why is that?"

She smoothed the scowl from her face. "No, I... I need a minute alone."

"You know how to make that request properly."

Despite a twinge in her gut telling her not to, she pulled back and looked at him directly.

"Look, you did a great job, but the scene's over, and I'm not into the 24/7 thing. I just need to use the restroom. Then I'll get dressed and be out of your hair." His eyes narrowed, but she kept her spine straight.

"I am to take aftercare seriously, Jill. It's an important part of a scene. You may have a moment of privacy, but you may not dress yet."

He released her arm and shut the door as he left. She sagged with relief and turned to the toilet. After awkwardly relieving herself, she washed her hands, combed her fingers through her hair, and used a washcloth to cleanse her face and the back of her neck.

When she emerged with her determination in tow, she found the Stranger next to the dining room table. He held a small jar, and her dress was carefully draped over the back of the lounge chair. His belt still sat on the towel covering the chaise.

Why couldn't she get dressed yet? She felt fine and didn't need to be debriefed—she knew how to care for herself in the hours and days to come—but curiosity kept her from disobeying him. Just curiosity, of course.

"Is your bedroom as vanilla as the rest of this place?" she asked, walking toward him.

He shook his head. "The apartment came furnished. You'll see my toys soon enough."

Ah, that explained the modern-design décor as well as the model-home feel, and she had almost forgotten about the tour of his bedroom he had promised. She wouldn't want to miss that.

"What's that in your hand?" she asked.

"You're about to find out. Bend over the table."

It had to be some kind of healing balm—and he intended to apply it himself. The hardwood floor was less kind to her soles than the shag rug, but the cool surface of the table felt good and was more comfortable than bending over the lounge chair. The Stranger stood behind her, and she heard him twist off the jar's lid.

A soothing pine scent wafted to her. He set the jar on the table and, to her surprise, pinned her down with his hand on the back of her neck. Something cool touched her sore backside, and though he was gentle, his fingers might as well have been wrapped with steel wool. She arched up instinctively, but he kept her where he wanted her, massaging the balm into an ever-widening circle until it was time to move to the other cheek.

"I enjoyed marking your beautiful skin," he said gruffly. She grimaced as he spread a second glob of balm. Already the side to which he had applied lotion stung a little less, though the deeper pain remained. "The strips will fade in a day or two, but I can lay down welts that linger more than a week."

"Why are you telling me this?" *Why are you tempting me?*

"Because you need to feel owned, to see my authority on your skin and feel it in your flesh whenever I'm not around." He splayed his fingers over her right cheek and squeezed. She inhaled sharply through her teeth.

"But I...can't afford you," she said with her forehead pressed to the table. "You're my Hawaiian vacation."

"Mm, come with me." He helped her up and guided her toward his bedroom. After all the anticipation, she wasn't so sure anymore that she should see his collection of toys. She wouldn't be back to enjoy them anytime soon—if ever.

The door to his bedroom might as well have been a door to someone else's house—specifically, the house of a dedicated Master or Mistress. His bedroom alone was easily as large as her kitchen and living room combined. The hardwood floor continued, but a dark-colored, low-pile area rug stretched nearly wall to wall. The black walls reflected little of the soft overhead light. So many things tugged at her attention that she wasn't sure where to look first.

The four-poster bed was most obvious. Its size and steel-frame construction would easily accommodate three people, perhaps four. A large, angled mirror above the padded headboard offered an alternative view of the ebony-and-ivory bedding.

Several rows of pegs and hooks ran along the far wall. She couldn't guess at the function of most of the leather and metal fetish items on the bottom rows, but the top rows held dozens of short- and long-range implements, including a wicked-looking bundle of birch branches bound at one end in a leather handle.

Floggers of various colors and severity were arranged by length. Paddles came in wood, leather, or rubber. A pair of crops hung next to a supple bullwhip and a few rattan canes. The shelf closest to the ceiling held a row of mannequin heads displaying standard hoods and blindfolds alongside a pair of masks that wouldn't be out of place at a Venetian-style masquerade.

Opposite the bed, something that looked like another upholstered headboard was anchored to the right-hand wall, its long side oriented vertically. A pair of leather cuffs hanging from one of many small rings evenly spread along the varnished wooden frame gave away the board's function.

The first thing she approached was the cushioned bench a few steps in front of her. Though it was as high as a bondage table and long enough for a tall woman like her, it was only a few inches wider than her hips. Similar rings as those on the restraining board were spaced halfway down its padded sides.

She touched the cool purple vinyl, and her vision blurred as she imagined all the ways in which she could be bound, all the fantasies she could experience.

On her back, a sacrificial virgin on an altar, wrists bound above her and waiting for the virile sorcerer to crawl between her legs. Or perhaps bent over the narrow side as if it were a desk, tied down with her arms spread for a drawn-out spanking from her disappointed boss.

Both severe and cajoling, the Stranger's voice was right behind and above her.

"I'd love to see you on this. The only question would be how." His wide chest spanned across her bare back. He drew his palm down her arm.

"I..." She paused to clear her throat. "I know what you're trying to do." She continued forward to the many implements hanging on the far wall. Her escort remained silent. "It's working, of course."

She combed her fingers through the falls of a silver-handled flogger. She had once eyed something similar at a store not far from her apartment. The young clerk had told her it was half off and gave her the kind of sweet and sincere smile meant to put her at ease, but she had left the store embarrassed and empty-handed.

The flogger in front of her was clearly much more expensive. Lily wanted nothing more than to feel its many strands bite into her skin, over and over, until she had paid for all the times she had run away.

She turned to face the Stranger, her shoulders back and her chin firm.

"When may I see you again, Sir?"

Chapter Ten

F inley watched his biceps contract as he curled a fifty-pound
dumbbell to his shoulder. It was a bit late to be lifting, but he
wasn't going to get much sleep in his state of mind. He had been
waiting over three hours for that generic beep from his laptop, which
now sat on his bedroom desk, but Monkey still hadn't responded. He
knew he should give up and head to bed—he had a long week ahead
of him and hadn't exaggerated his looming workload—but the more
he thought about her and her arm's-length policy, the more agitated
he became.

So out came the free weights. He started with a rotating shoulder
press and then moved to his triceps. When he felt only more restless,
he did some calf raises, weighted side bends, diamond push-ups, and
biceps curls.

He released the final rep and took a deep breath, resisting the urge to
sit back in his chair because he was covered in sweat. Instead he stood,
grabbed a second dumbbell from the compact rack against the wall,
and faced the bed. With his palms in, he lifted the weights laterally,
then directly in front of him to shoulder height.

Monkey had been on that bed, naked and ripe. When he slid her
panties down her legs, the urge to seize one of the spools of rope in the
kit beneath his bed had clawed at his insides. He had wanted her arms
behind her head, her perfect breasts encased in a rope harness, and her
ankles tied to the backs of her thighs. He wanted her vulnerable so he
could seduce her at his pace, torment her with promises, and make her
beg for a simple touch. He wanted to take care of her, to make her feel
desired and safe with him.

He wanted her to need him as much as he needed her. As always, he was the one who called first, who waited and longed. He was the one who reached out and shared his life only to come back with less than he had given, far less than he had craved.

And the one time she had been willing to open up—just a little—he had flipped out and bounced her from his place. No wonder she had lied about her name and wouldn't accept his call.

He regretted not covering her soft form with his body, pinning her legs back, and fucking her so deeply she'd still feel his cock in her the next day. He'd have made her breakfast and taken her again in the shower.

Finley dropped his arms with a grunt, though not because of exertion. His erection tented the front of his workout pants. Perhaps lifting wasn't what he needed in order to let off steam.

A nother satisfied client, as expected. Declan watched from his seated position on the sofa as Jill bent and stepped into her dress. She drew it up her legs, her movements slow and careful as the cotton slid up and over her angry bottom. Her back stiffened and she paused.

It still hurt. Good.

The night had gone as planned. Never mind the moment his cock had strained the zipper of his slacks merely from seeing her bent over, or the moment a surge of lust had him grasping her close, or the moment he'd nearly fucked her while she was slung over the lounge chair—on her back and legs spread—coming out of the bathroom...

Never mind the ripple on the back of his neck every time he looked at her or how it made his teeth clench. Never mind the erection still wanting her or *how* it wanted her.

Screaming. Crying.

Jill zipped her dress and straightened the thin straps stretched over her shoulders as she turned around. Her panties had gone into her clutch.

"What do you want me to wear on Friday, Sir?" Her eyes were cast down, and so she didn't see his erection pushing against his fly. She expected another command.

Yes, the script. He had to follow his script. Smiling indulgently, he made a low sound that would excite her.

"Open that box on the table."

She glanced up at him in surprise. The corners of her mouth twitched, but her teeth pinched her lower lip, suppressing a smile of anticipation. She walked to the table, where she slid her fingers along the box top before she grasped the ribbon, tugged it apart, and lifted the lid.

She was faced away from him, so her soft gasp was his only clue to her reaction. She set the lid to the side and hesitantly touched her gift, a dress of autumn-yellow satin with black beaded lace embroidered on the plunge and along the hem of the formfitting skirt. She carefully lifted the dress to find matching lingerie and shoes underneath.

"It's beautiful." She turned, still holding the dress. Rather than feel pleased at the sincere awe on her face, he was restless. He maintained his smile, but his hands drew into fists.

"It'll be even more beautiful when you wear it for our next date."

He dreaded Friday night.

Jill cleared her throat, put her back to him again, and returned the dress to its box.

"I assume the fee covered it," she said. He didn't understand her mood. Her tone was light but too high.

"Of course." He stood and walked toward her, wanting to wrap his fingers around her slender neck. He could still taste her mouth and her skin. "I'll always ensure you have your money's worth."

He stopped behind her, pausing to relax his convulsing fingers and set his hands on her shoulders. His hard cock jumped when it brushed her ass.

"What do you say when you receive a gift, pet?" The words came out wrong, spoken through his teeth instead of seductively whispered.

"Th-thank you, Sir." Her stiff shoulders seemed small and thin under his palms. He had to get himself under control.

Finish the script. Hurry.

With a deep breath, he took a step back.

"I'll send for a cab and see you off," he said.

Her shoulders relaxed. She turned around with flushed cheeks. "I'd like that."

They donned their coats. Jill retied the ribbon around the dress box and slid her shoes on at the door. He carried her gift down to the front entrance where they waited only a couple of minutes for the Safe Cab. A young, lean man holding a lit cigarette shared the sidewalk awning with them.

When Declan spotted the unmistakable white-and-green cab coming up the street, he impatiently clutched the box in his arms even as he took a deep breath of the cold night air, hoping it would calm him. The taxi pulled up, and he popped the door handle.

"Send me a message when you get home."

"Yes, Sir," she whispered after a pause and a glance at the smoker, who had lit up a second cigarette. Ah, she didn't want the other man to hear them. He gave her a crooked smile and leaned into the backseat to set the box on the far side of the cab. When he stood straight again, her cheeks were redder.

"Tonight was amazing," she said.

Not amazing. Alarming.

"Because you were very obedient." His answer was automatic, but he spoke loudly enough for the smoker to hear. His balls tightened when her eyes fearfully flicked to the young man.

He jerked her into his arms and let her feel his erection. Her hands were full, so she pushed against his chest with her forearms. He knew she was embarrassed and trying to minimize their contact. He dropped one hand to her ass and squeezed. She shut her eyes and sucked in a hiss. Her body pressed against him.

"And because you were so obedient, I'll tell you my name." Her eyes opened, looked at him. "It's Declan."

Another name wanted to come out—almost did. It was right on the tip of his tongue, but no, he had given the right name. The agency allowed such liberties.

"Nice to meet you, Declan." She still spoke softly to evade their eavesdropper.

"But just so we're clear, you'll continue to use Sir whenever possible." He took his hand off her ass but didn't let her go.

"I understand, Sir."

"One more thing..." He speared his fingers into her hair, bent her back, and laid one last kiss on her. This final touch would stick with her, would make her touch her lips on her way home and anticipate their next date.

She'll be the only one looking forward to it.

Jill struggled for a few seconds, probably worried about their voyeur, but then she relaxed and met each thrust of his tongue. His cock would've jutted straight out from his hips if his pants hadn't been in the way.

Of all his clients, why did *she* affect him? He had role-played forced encounters innumerable times, and yet when *she* begged for mercy and fought against his superior strength, the urges that stirred from a dark and terrible place inside him threatened his finely honed script.

When she moaned, he pulled back. Her eyelids were low, her lips rosy.

"Do not pleasure yourself until I say you can. I want you horny on Friday."

Her surprise quickly gave way to disappointment, but she nodded. "Yes, Sir."

"Tell me what you're going to do."

She licked her lips and blinked to regain her focus. "I'll message you when I get home, and I won't pleasure myself until you say I can."

"Good girl," he hummed. "Until Friday, then."

His hands shook as he assisted her into the taxi. She didn't seem to notice. After shutting the door, he stuffed his hands into his pockets. He didn't want to let her leave, but he had to. He didn't want to find out what he was capable of—or how far she was willing to be pushed.

The cab pulled away and turned at the first intersection. After a glance at the smoker, who inexplicably gave him a thumbs-up, he retreated into the building.

He called the elevator out of habit, but when the doors slid open, he didn't want to get in. His skin prickled. *Don't turn around.* No, it had nothing to do with that. The incident at the hotel had been a fluke. He turned and walked down the hall toward the stairs. The cold night air had dried the fine sheen of sweat on his forehead. That was all. He'd take the stairs to warm up.

His eyes were on his phone as he punched through the fire door and ascended the first flight of stairs. He kept one hand on the handrail while he tagged the night's session as complete with the other.

But I'm not done with her at all.

The stairway was quiet, solid. He passed the second floor while tapping out notes.

Gift given. Client pleased. No masturbation allowed until next session. Client most interested in bondage table.

As he ascended another flight, a familiar falling sensation grew in his chest. He tried to ignore it even as it expanded. It was simply shortness of breath. Not urgency. Not the need to run, hide. A good night's sleep and he'd feel better.

He put his phone away and continued upward. The railing was cool and dry under his palm. His footfalls fell quietly on the carpeted stairs. He tried to concentrate on these sensations, on reality, but he stared hard at the floor number at the top of the next flight. He climbed a little faster. Just to warm up. Halfway there. He turned and started up another flight.

A metallic pop echoed from somewhere below. He jolted, gripping the handrail tight. His legs tensed to run, but he forced himself to pause a few steps shy of the third-floor landing. The sound of a door opening was no reason to run.

Simply curious, he peered over the handrail. An angled shadow on the bottommost floor swung away. The door that had cast it solidly clunked back into its frame. Someone had entered the stairwell from the parking garage, a neighbor coming home, and yet he couldn't continue on his way.

Slow footsteps slid along the concrete floor of the basement landing. A bulky shadow lengthened as its owner passed under the red light thrown by an exit sign. A man? But his shadow was strangely shaped.

From the corner of his eye, Declan confirmed the placement of the exit sign on his floor. The man's unnatural shadow couldn't be blamed on the angle of the light. Why did it look as though his head had split open? As though something like entrails spilled from the gap in his skull?

Nonsense. The uneven shape of his head had to be a hat, the entrails simply hair, perhaps locs or braids.

A drop of sweat escaped his hairline and slid down his temple. His head involuntarily jerked toward his shoulder. That falling sensation ballooned, making him sick to his stomach.

Run.

He heard rapid footsteps, but they were not his. The shadow was gone. Its owner was tearing up the stairs. He couldn't move. His intestines cramped, pulling his upper half toward the floor.

Run. Move your feet!

It wasn't real, couldn't be. The faceless man in the elevator hadn't been real. It couldn't be in the stairwell with him. It was an anxiety attack, a fever dream.

RUN!

One hand yanked on the rail. The other reached out, grasped at thin air as if hoping it were solid. He scrambled up to the third-floor landing, lurched toward the next flight, grabbed at the rail. His hand clamped the cold metal, kept him upright, propelled him when his legs seemed barely able to move.

Someone was panting harshly. Was he doing it, or was it that thing coming up the stairs? Gritting his teeth in terrified frustration, he fought desperately against the instinct to simply freeze. His legs couldn't seem to hold him any more than a puppet's could. More than once, his shins smacked the risers. His knees almost gave out halfway up the flight. He wasted precious time looking back, both afraid of whatever was catching up to him and hoping he still had a lead.

Only by pulling himself hand over hand up the railing did he reach the top of the last flight. The half-digested Italian food in his stomach threatened to greet the stairs and the front of his pants.

He careened toward the fourth-floor exit. His sweat-slick palm fumbled for the handle and slipped when he tried to turn it. Those giddy, murderous footsteps grew louder and louder.

With a roar, he wrenched the handle and flung the door open. Only by instinct did he yank it shut behind him. Momentum carried him forward a couple of steps, but his legs still refused to stay under him. He hit the left wall, leaned heavily on it to remain standing. As he stumbled toward his apartment halfway down the hall, he glanced over his shoulder. The door to the stairs was still closed.

His key. Damn it, he'd have as much luck using his fingers as a boxer wearing gloves. He plunged his hand into his pocket and grasped clumsily. His two smallest fingers wrapped around the leather tab that served as his keychain.

Don't drop it. He maintained a fist as he shuffled the last ten feet to his door.

A thump behind him made him wheel around, eyes wide, mouth slack. Something was just beyond that door. He took a step back. A soft rustling was followed by another thump, as though a mindless body was struggling to understand the obstacle in its path. Another step back.

A very loud bang nearly sent him to the floor. The door shuddered in its frame.

"No," he groaned.

His lips were dry, but his face was covered in sweat. The door shuddered again. He felt his way backward along the wall, couldn't look away from the stairwell door. The next bang brought with it an ominous splintering sound.

He felt the wall recede. He had reached his apartment door and had to look down at his nearly uncontrollable hands to locate the apartment key. He laboriously peeled open his thumb and index finger to get at the larger of two keys hanging from the keychain clamped in his other digits.

The leather tab slipped out of his grasp. He snatched at the falling keys but instead hit them farther away.

"Fuck," he spat. He chased the keys a few steps from his door, leaned on the wall, and stooped to grab them. The squeak of a metal handle jerked his head up.

This time, his legs worked. He shot up. Ran to his door. Shoved his key into the lock. Turned. The stairwell door groaned open as he ducked into his apartment.

Teeth bared, he slammed his door shut, threw the lock, and backed up. His chest heaved. His heart boomed. Body shook. He didn't turn on a lamp, just stared at the line of light at the base of his door.

A moment passed with no change. His heart's breakneck pace slowed to a brisk jog. The tightness in his gut eased.

Safe. He was safe. Whatever had just happened, it was over now.

He wasn't sure how long he stood there, but only when the sweat had dried on his face was he willing and able to move.

With a swallow, he leaned to flip the light switch near the door. He saw his keys on the floor nearby, thrown aside once their use had been met. His apartment remained quiet. So did the hallway beyond his front door. He took a deep breath.

An anxiety attack after all. He was lucky his client hadn't witnessed it.

He shucked his coat and suit jacket, wrenched his tie loose, and toed off his shoes. He needed a shower. After hanging up his clothes to be dry-cleaned in the morning, he shambled into his bathroom.

The row of bulbs above the mirror flooded the bathroom with light and illuminated the remnants of his breakdown still evident on his face. Flushed cheeks, hair stuck to his forehead.

He turned the water on full blast and as cold as possible. Throwing icy splashes onto his face, he ignored the raised hairs on the back of his neck. He filled his hands and drank. Twice, he went back for more.

Once his thirst was sated, he reached above his head to turn off the water and groped for the towel hanging above the toilet. He brought it to his dripping face. The cotton smelled fresh and clean. He stood straight, rubbing the towel across his face, along his hairline, and under his chin. He tossed the towel to the counter and opened his eyes.

The faceless man stood in the mirror's reflection. Where a hat might have covered his head, his skull was missing. Beneath a puddle of blood were the unmistakable bumps and whorls of brain matter.

Declan's scream rent the air. Backpedaling, he pulled the bathroom door with him and slammed it shut.

Clearly, he was sick. He needed help. Where was his phone?

A massive migraine made itself known halfway to his bedroom. He fell against the bed and grabbed his phone from the side table. Its display wouldn't come into focus. He shook his head, blinked a few times, and squinted at his contact list. He gripped his phone tight, his hands still clumsy from adrenaline.

"Dr. White here," a composed voice said.

"I-it's Declan. Something's wrong. I think I'm sick." He couldn't stop shaking, couldn't make his mouth work right. He was sweating again.

"Where are you?" White had snapped into no-nonsense mode.

"A-at my apartment." A surge of light-headedness had him grabbing a fistful of bedding to keep him upright. He was going to vomit.

"I'm not far. Stay right there."

"G-got it." The call disconnected with a beep, and he tossed his phone onto the nightstand, not knowing whether to lie down or put his head between his knees.

His stomach made the decision for him. He pounded onto all fours over a small trash can he kept by the bed. Its main reason for being there wasn't to catch vomit, but that was its job tonight. Everything he'd eaten at dinner came rushing up.

A minute later, he sat back on his heels and wiped the sweat from his forehead. His headache was worse, but the nausea had subsided.

He wasn't wearing any clothes, and Dr. White would be there any minute, but he didn't think he could make it to his dresser. His erection was long gone, at least. He then remembered his front door was locked. He'd have to go let the doctor in.

A knock sounded. He groaned and twisted away from the trash can. When his stomach didn't clench up in preparation to reverse engines, he used the nearby bed to keep his balance and surged to his feet.

Another knock, more insistent.

"Declan?" the doctor called.

"Yeah, just...just give me a second. I'm having some trouble."

The front door unlocked. She had a key?

His apartment door opened when he emerged from his bedroom, both hands clamping the doorframe. White wore her usual, a black trench coat over a white button-up and dark gray dress slacks. Her blonde hair was almost long enough to conceal the ID badge clipped to her shirt—*TM Medical, E. White.* She never let her hair get any longer. The next time he saw her, it would be several inches shorter, and her gray roots would be dyed again.

Her wrinkled forehead and downturned mouth said she was concerned, but it also could have been frustration.

"Why are you naked?" she asked with a sigh as she shut and locked his door. Yes, it was frustration. He spotted her hands-free suitcase behind her, which followed her as she approached him.

"Why do you have a key to my apartment?" he asked.

She stopped, and an emotion he couldn't catch flickered across her face. Slack muscles and a blink. She tilted her head, pursed her lips. Confusion?

"Let's take a look at you," she said slowly.

She came toward him, and his migraine spiked. He nearly sank to the floor, but she appeared under his arm. He leaned heavily on her as they walked back to his bed. Once he was seated, White turned to the suitcase behind her and pulled out several implements, which she laid carefully on the nightstand. She then spotted the trash can and what it contained.

"When did that happen?" she asked, turning to him with a penlight.

"Just now," he said. "I have a really bad headache and—" Words left him. The doctor flashed the penlight in his eye, and more pain flared in the back of his skull.

"Did any of your recent clients show any flu or cold symptoms?"

"No." He would have made a note in his calendar if they had.

"Do you have any other symptoms? Sore throat? Runny nose?" She passed a handheld device over his forehead, looked at the readout, and then palpated the glands in his neck.

"Anxiety," he said.

Her hands stilled, and that slack, blinking expression reappeared. Startled. That's it, she was startled.

"What do you mean?" she asked as she stood straight.

He struggled to put it into words. "A feeling in my chest, like I want to scream. I-I want..." *I want things beyond the script.* "I see things that aren't there," he whispered as he looked up at the doctor.

"Like what?"

"A man with—his...his head is cracked open and—"

Tears gathered in his eyes. Strange. He couldn't remember the last time he had cried.

White laid her hands on his arms and held his gaze. She spoke slowly and clearly. "Did any of your recent clients do anything different than usual? Did you black out for any period of time?"

He shook his head.

"Was this just tonight?"

"It happened last night, too. Everything was fine, and then I..."

And then he'd met Jill. White grabbed a pair of glasses and a tablet from the nightstand behind her. She slipped the glasses on, swiped at the tablet's display for a moment, and then turned back to him.

"What's wrong with me?" he asked.

"Nothing I can't fix," she said confidently. "You're going to sleep for a little bit, and when you wake up, you'll be a brand-new man." She smiled reassuringly at him and tapped her tablet.

Chapter Eleven

Foss, Lily. "The Illusion of Acceptance"
National Technology Review. *29 May 2043*

Only one person ever asked me how I felt about what I found on the agency's website rather than simply cutting right to whether or not I found a list of clients—and if such a list existed, were any famous Seattleites on it? Certain nuances, such as my firm belief in privacy, which I still hold despite everything, never crossed their minds or dissuaded them from wasting their breath, but when such people earn their living by invading privacy, could I really expect them not to try?

Rene Clement from the alternative newspaper *The Wanderer* asked me if I had any suspicions the night I found Declan's full name of what I would ultimately learn about Tailor Made. The question surprised me, because rather than ruminate on what had gone through my mind that night, hindsight demanded I ask myself what might have happened if I hadn't taken Declan's card—or if I hadn't met him in the first place.

Would all of this have happened anyway, to someone else? Or would the agency still be quietly ruining lives?

No, I told Clement, I had no real grasp of the truth. It wasn't even a speck on the horizon. Clement followed his question with another. When did I start to understand just what the agency really was?

Unfortunately, not soon enough.

Chapter Twelve

With her head resting on the seat and a soft smile on her face, Lily watched as the passing buildings went from tall, always-lit shopping centers and overpriced restaurants to one- or two-story businesses leaning on the steep main drag of what was otherwise a largely residential neighborhood. Most buildings were dark except for a corner drugstore and a generous scattering of coffee shops. The rain was picking up again.

"Did you know you can use Safe Cab to...?"

"Audio off," she said distractedly.

It was funny that just a few hours ago, she was headed in the other direction and honestly convinced her date with the Stranger—Declan—was going to end in the usual should've-known-better. Being pessimistic meant life hardly ever proved her wrong. Better to be right and occasionally surprised than to be almost constantly let down.

But this was one of those occasional surprises, a night she would remember for the rest of her life. She touched her lips, still tingling from that last kiss he had given her, and couldn't wait for another night of surprises on Friday.

That was still days away, and she had lots of work ahead of her even though her body wanted to hit the sack for ten or twelve hours. Her time with Declan, if that really was his name, had gone on longer than she expected, so she'd have to play catch up for the second night in a row. Because her Safe Cab had been summoned on Declan's phone app, not hers, she deigned to send it directly to her apartment rather than her usual drop-off.

Once the cab released her, she gathered her things and dashed around the taxi to the protective awning over her building's front door. With her arms full of a light-but-unwieldy dress box, she waved her clutch at the sensor next to the door, which thankfully read the fob inside her purse and admitted her.

In the elevator, she braced the dress box between her hip and the wall while she dug her keys out of her clutch. Her heart fluttered when she saw her balled-up panties. She set her purse and umbrella on the box and balanced it on one arm as she walked from the elevator to her apartment. A turn of the key and her door swung open.

Everything in her arms loudly hit the floor, but her scream was far louder. Without thinking, she threw her keys at the man standing just beyond the rectangle of light thrown by the sconces in the hall.

The man was naked, and his face was a contorted, tightly stretched mask of horror. His arms were thrown up in front him, his fingers curled into claws. His eyes were shiny, unblinking marbles. If his jaw opened any wider, it would unhinge from his skull like a snake about to swallow her whole. Something had gone wrong with David.

"What's going on out here?" she heard to her left.

With her hands over her heart, she pivoted toward her neighbor who lived two units down—or at least, the frowning, middle-aged man in a disturbingly off-white bathrobe standing in the doorway two units away. She had never met him before.

"I thought..." *I thought the android in my apartment was a naked serial killer.* "I thought I saw a spider," she lied, "but it's nothing."

"Well, some of us have work in the morning." Her neighbor twisted his mouth sardonically before disappearing back into his apartment and slamming the door shut. She would've muttered something about him also disrespecting quiet hours, but her chagrin died before she cared to.

With a swallow, she turned back to her door and, with one eye on David, collected her things off the floor. He didn't move. Probably another crash like before.

"All lights, max," she called. Every light fixture in her apartment wired to her voice-command system turned on, though they'd need a minute to reach full brightness. She kicked the door shut behind her, sidled past David to the kitchen counter a few steps inside, and pushed the haphazard pile of recyclables aside to set down her things.

Her keys were still on the faux hardwood floor of the entryway, having hit David's chest without a single twitch from him. She wished she could use a voice command to lock her door rather than go near the Eidolon again, but her building's leasing agency wouldn't let her mess with how her lock worked. Something about maintenance needing occasional access. *Pfft.*

She took a deep breath and walked around the droid, leaving as much space between them as possible. She locked the door, toed her keys toward her, and scooped them up. David didn't budge.

After taking off her coat and dropping it over the back of her sofa, which was more of a repository for empty shipping boxes than a place to sit, she followed the Eidolon's cords into her bedroom and leaned over her desk. Once her display woke up, she ignored a couple of flashing icons and went straight to the testing suite.

"Huh," she said. *That's strange.* The fuzz testing had completed an hour ago and found nothing wrong. Without thinking, she flopped into her chair. When she could breathe a few seconds later, she whimpered and released the weight that her arms had instinctively lifted off her abused bottom.

Though her backside hurt a *lot*, she didn't want to take a painkiller. After all, her Dom wanted her to remember the lesson he'd taught her. She would, however, sit down more gently next time—and on a cushy pillow.

Rebooting David seemed to do the trick, and she didn't have to recomplete his initial setup. Within minutes, he was back in his ratty armchair and passed out.

Had she received a defective model? She typed up her observations of his two crashes and spent a few minutes more closely combing through the event log from the past few hours but found nothing that would explain his hardware failures.

Tell me what you're going to do.

Right, she was supposed to message Declan. She switched windows to Jill's throwaway account, filled in her Dom's email address, and stared at the blank message box. So many things wanted to pour out of her, but none of them sounded right. The words that came to mind were close but didn't quite capture how she felt—how he *made* her feel.

She went back to Tailor Made's website, logged in, and was sent to an overview of her profile. Her account was marked as "current" and included a calendar appointment to meet Declan on Friday at eleven p.m.

Declan's name was a link that took her back to his escort page. The black-and-white photo did not do his soul-piercing eyes any justice. She licked her lips when she looked at his mouth, which in the photo had a slight tilt to it as though he were about to give the photographer a sadistic smile.

That mouth had been on her lips, her breasts, and between her—

She snapped out of it, knowing she had to get that email sent off sooner rather than later, but the website address caught her attention. Part of the URL designated the optimal site design to display, having learned which web browser she was using. Another part tracked that she had reached Declan's profile from a calendar appointment link. One part read "host=26" and another read "id=621."

On a whim, she changed 26 to 25 and hit Enter.

She arrived at the profile of another escort, a stunning woman with rich black skin and sapphire undertones. "The Spoiled Brat" gave the camera a pretty little pout and dared "daddy" to punish her for demanding "too many toys."

So, the host parameter determined escorts.

Escort twenty-four was a young Asian man named "The Newbie." He looked coyly at the camera, one hand on the back of his neck. Escort twenty-three was a willowy white woman named "The Pretzel."

"I think we can guess her specialty," Lily said from the side of her mouth.

The id parameter was probably for determining users like her. Did that "621" mean that 620 other people had already become clients of Tailor Made? She returned to Declan's profile, a little sick to her stomach and not all that willing to wonder why.

Right, the email, but she wanted to try one last thing and changed 621 to 0.

The browser remained on Declan's profile, but more information appeared on the page—a *lot* more. The topmost section was titled *Demographics* and listed his name, birthdate, race, sex, and a host of other items. He was a white male—*already knew that*—would turn thirty-four next month, and his full name was Declan Martin.

"His name really is Declan," she whispered. Her cheeks warmed.

Holy and shit. She had a root view of the Tailor Made website. Only administrators were supposed to see the information on this page.

If she wanted, she could probably wend her way to other TM clients and get their names, the information off their profiles, and which escorts they had requested as well as how often and when. She was never more grateful for her paranoia. She would be safe behind her fake name if anyone ever found the same vulnerability as she had, assuming they hadn't already.

She scrolled down the page, her eyes narrowing when she noticed strange data attached to the bottom of Declan's profile.

A street address was listed next to a tag named *base*. The address repeated on the next line, tagged *current*. She was pretty sure the address was where Declan lived.

The info below that was even weirder.

Assigned handler: E. White
Health status: Good
Most recent check-up: 01/16/2042
SPE Build: 4.02

"SPE Build?" she mused.

The street address was a link, probably to an online map, which she clicked to verify that it was indeed Declan's building. Instead, she was taken to a page with three tabs at the top—Site A, B, and C. The link had automatically selected Site B for her. At the top was a photo of Declan's building, its address, and a long list of names numbered sequentially from 201 to 812.

No, wait. She scrolled down. After 212, the numbers skipped to 301. They were apartment numbers. She skipped down to 407 and found Declan's name next to it.

"What *even*..." she said. Did Tailor Made own the entire building? And had they filled it with escorts? What in God's name was she looking at? Company housing?

Clicking on Declan's name took her back to the root view of his escort profile. Though it took some time, she went back and clicked on other names in search of one person in particular.

"No way," she breathed. The name Susanna Bazelon took her to a profile for an escort called "The Veronica." It was, without a doubt, the same frosty-eyed woman she had seen coming out of the elevator with a wormy guy on her heels. Her diva-like behavior and impersonator appearance had been on purpose.

Okay, she wasn't feeling so hot anymore. What kind of company was Declan working for? TM's kind of business was definitely still illegal in the state of Washington, so...

A mob operation? How would she even find out something like that? The website certainly wasn't going to have a link to something called *how our mob-run escort service works and who's at the top*. She did know someone who could do a little digging for her, though.

First things first. She went back to the list of names living at Site B and saved it somewhere she could access it again but where no one else would find it. She then fired off an email to Declan.

Sir, i am home safe and sound. Thank You for a wonderful night.

Short and sweet and not full of revealing platitudes that some even half-competent hacker could get their hands on. She switched to her video-chat program.

"Oh shit," she said with a grimace.

Finley had already sent her a video-chat request—hours ago—and she had *asked* him to call her tonight, obviously with the understanding that she would pick up this time. The request was still active, so he was awake and still waiting even though it was getting real late on a Sunday night. Finley wasn't like her, burning the midnight oil. He was a Monday-to-Friday, nine-to-five kind of guy. This would be awkward.

She hit Okay, though she left her webcam off because she didn't want to explain her outfit. She only had to wait a second or two for the video stream to start.

Before the metaphorical iron curtain had dropped between them, Finley would use the webcam on his laptop for their once-nightly chats. He'd cart her around wherever he needed to go, such as the kitchen for cooking, the couch for an RFL game, or his bedroom desk just to talk. Whenever a call connected and the video feed began playing, she usually didn't immediately know what she was looking at.

In this case, however, she knew *exactly* what she was looking at. Finley, in his desk chair, completely naked and masturbating. The only other detail her mind could register was the white towel draped over his shoulder.

Her eyes bulged, and she slapped her hand over her mouth. Finley tensed and stopped his hand midstroke. His glance shot to his computer. She was certain he'd slap his laptop closed, but he relaxed and kept going.

Hadn't he heard the call-connected sound? Didn't he realize she was watching his fist go up and down his cock, root to head and back again? She realized she should say something. It had already been at least ten seconds, though. Was that too long before interrupting with a "hey I can see your religion"?

That's when her brain blocked access to propriety, and her eyes started feasting.

Finley was sitting on the edge of his chair, the same model as hers, because of *course* it was—he'd gotten it after she couldn't stop bragging about hers. His immense shoulders spanned farther than the seatback on which they rested. His knees were spread.

She could see everything from the size and breadth of his sac to the length and thickness of his cock to the sheen of sweat on his abs and chest. Those abs would twitch every few seconds, and he'd grunt softly as he grazed his palm over the top of his erection like chalking a pool cue. He would lift his head off the back of the seat, his neck long and his mouth open. Then he'd lay his head back again and his eyebrows would turn up because it just felt so damn good.

She squirmed like a child wanting her toy. Every movement made her ass light up with an aftershock of pain. She imagined Finley in the chair beneath her and moving her up and down his shaft, having already spanked the living hell out of her. He'd tell her the chair was indeed very comfortable and tauntingly ask if she preferred sitting on it or on his cock.

Even though she drank in every detail about him she could, from the snake tattoo on the front of his right thigh to the spot beneath his sac where he liked to press his finger, she stared at his cock the most, naturally. It wasn't an impossible length, but it was very thick.

She slid to the edge of her chair and smoothed her hands up her thighs as she spread them. She imagined him braced over her, his hips between her knees and lowering toward her. Her pussy clamped around the empty space where his cock belonged.

Finley groaned, an incredibly deep and needful plea that wrenched a whimper from her. His body bowed upward and his hips punched into the tight grip of his fist. But it wasn't time yet, and though he didn't relax, he did settle onto the chair.

She slipped her fingers under the hem of her skirt and, with no panties to get in the way, stroked the sensitive crease of skin between her thighs and her mons. She wanted so badly to join Finley in that swirl of self-pleasure, but her Dom had told her not to touch herself.

How would he ever know? Oh, but that wasn't the point, and she knew it.

With a pained frown, she forced her hands onto the arms of her chair. Finley's fist was going fast now. His chest heaved with big, deep breaths. Even if she didn't touch herself, she might come just from clenching her lower body and watching him ejaculate.

She really wanted to see that, to watch jets of hot semen jump up to his chest and spray across his abs. She wanted to hear him moan her name as he came.

But he didn't know her name. Surely it wouldn't hurt to tell him her first name? The L in "L. Foss" could stand for Leonard or Larry or Logan.

No, that was both a terrible reason and a terrible time to tell someone your name.

Finley groaned again, louder. His back arched. He slowed his hand, pulling back hard as if a couple more thrusts would do him in. Pleasure didn't make him sneer or pinch his face toward the point of his nose but instead was carried in his clenched jaw and furrowed brow. He groped for the towel.

"N-no," she blurted. She wanted to watch it shoot out of him.

Finley kept the towel in hand but didn't use it. A rough sigh forced his mouth open. A long, thick stream of semen flew onto his heaving chest. God, it caught the light and everything. A second and third stream failed to go as far as the first, both landing farther down his sculpted front. The fourth jet was determined and made it a little higher, almost to his collarbone.

Technology was amazing. It transmitted his orgasm so clearly that she heard every sound he made as though they were in the same room. The gravel in his throat when he breathed. The smack of his shoulders hitting the back of his chair. The catch in his throat when yet another spurt of cum shot straight up and landed somewhere near his navel.

His body went limp. His thick cock rested on the flat plane of his lower abdomen. He seemed utterly spent, yet when he rolled his head and raised his eyes—looked right at her—she felt like prey. She knew if she said the word, he would be dressed and out the door in less than five minutes to finish what they'd started almost three weeks ago.

But she didn't just need a good hard fuck. She needed a hand around her throat, a rope holding her arms back, and a bruised backside criss-crossed with welts. She already had what she needed, though admittedly not in the most ideal of people.

"Monkey?" The word was both a plea and a challenge. She closed the video chat, red-faced and as conflicted as ever.

Heart racing, she pressed one hand to her forehead and whispered "Oh my God" a few times. She had just watched her friend—no, her ex? Ugh, whatever complicated noun he was, she had just watched him stroke his cock until he came.

And it had been unbelievably hot. She was certain steam was rising off her cheeks. Her heartbeat still pulsed in the swollen flesh of her vagina. She hadn't been penetrated in a long time, hadn't had something to clamp on to while she shuddered with pleasure. How long had it been since Finley had been with someone like that?

She saw double at the thought of all that cum splashing inside her. She had an IUD, so no worries there. No, damn it, she had to pull her mind out of the gutter, no matter how fun and dirty it was in there. She had no doubt he'd call back any minute. What was she going to say? *Looks like all those push-ups were worth it?* Yeah, right.

Sure enough, a happy yoo-hoo a couple minutes later announced that she had a new face-chat request from F-b0mb. She took a big breath, let it out slowly, and hit Okay.

Finley reappeared on her screen. He had obviously cleaned himself up and had probably put his pants back on, though she couldn't see lower than the first two beers in his six-pack. The look on his face nailed her right in the chest. His firm mouth and the twin shallow creases above his nose said it all. *I'm not done with you yet.*

"I'm sorry, Bomb."

"Sorry for what?" His voice was so much deeper than usual, and the emphasis of his question said he knew exactly what she had done wrong. He just wanted her to say it. Arousal warmed her insides like a swallow of hot cocoa. Damn it, he'd make such a good Dom.

"For making you wait all night and...for watching you."

"Why would you be sorry for watching me? Didn't you like the show?"

A needy mewl burst out before she could stop it. "Y-yes."

"I waited all night. Where were you?"

Her mouth popped open. She couldn't tell him that. No way was she going to admit to him she was beaten and eaten by a paid escort.

"I was working," she lied. She hugged herself and wondered how she'd ever receive enough punishment to make up for that.

"Damn it, Monkey," he said, sighing with disappointment.

"I'm sorry," she said again. He took a deep breath, his eyes closed. When he opened them again, they stared straight at his webcam. His lips hinted at a smile.

"Guess I'll have to punish you for it later."

Her heart skipped a beat. *Wait, what?*

"Look, I really should get some sleep...if I can," he added under his breath. "Do you know if you're free Friday night? I'm sure Deepak will call me in on Saturday, but I'd rather see you sooner than Saturday night."

How many times was a cuss word going to fly through her mind that night? She already had plans to see Declan on Friday. Then she remembered why she had wanted to talk to Finley in the first place.

"Can I get your help with something, actually?" she asked.

Finley crossed his arms. Man, his biceps were enormous. "Is it the project you're working on?"

"No, I came across something strange," she hedged.

"Can you be more specific?"

"I'd be able to if you could...possibly...look up a name in the SPD criminal database for me?" She said the last in a rush and pleadingly pressed her palms together even though he couldn't see her.

"What?" He was understandably stunned.

"I know it's *a lot* to ask."

"Jesus. Yeah, you could say that. Who the hell would I be looking up?"

She froze, completely stumped as to what she could say to that. Thankfully, she didn't have to say anything.

"I mean, I really shouldn't," he said, "but...since we're doing the database migration this week, I guess I could."

She let out a silent sigh of relief.

"I don't want any kind of email record of this, though," he said. "If you want my help, Monkey, you have to come to my place and hear me out. No more delays or changing the subject. Are you free Friday night?"

Checkmate. Finley had her.

She supposed she could see him in the early evening and duck out in time to meet Declan, assuming they didn't learn anything criminal about her escort.

"What's it gonna be, Monkey?"

"Okay, deal," she said. "When should I be at your place?"

"Six thirty?" he suggested.

"Perfect," she replied. "Sorry again to keep you up so late."

"Sorry isn't getting you out of anything," he said smugly. "You might score a point or two if you wear that red top, though."

It was her turn to be stunned. "What?"

"The one you wore last time? I want you to wear it again."

Who the hell was he kidding? Himself, obviously.

"I don't have it anymore," she fibbed.

"Yes, you do. You already have a couple strikes against you, Monkey. Don't make it any worse. Wear the red top," he ordered. A thrill went through her.

"Good night, Bomb," she said, not acknowledging his instruction. Finley gave her a smile that had her clutching the seat of her chair.

"Good luck on your deadline, Monkey. See you Friday."

The call disconnected.

Chapter Thirteen

F ive nights passed in a blur of test results, technical specs, and turning half-realized conclusions into coherent sentences. Lily felt like a sack of potatoes when rereading her article for the hundredth time half an hour before her eight-a.m. deadline. She was technically awake and cognizant of what she was reading thanks to frequents trips to her coffeemaker, but no amount of caffeine would keep her from passing out at 8:01.

The Eidolon had proven itself superior to all predecessors in practically every way, but she had waffled endlessly on whether or not to mention the android's two crashes earlier in the week. Nothing like them had happened since, and she hadn't discovered any possible cause. In the end, she mentioned them only in passing.

With a minute to spare, she sent the almost 14,000-word essay to her editor. Then she unplugged the Eidolon, set an alarm, and crumpled onto the tangle of bedding that had seen far too little use in the last few days. It felt as though her head had no sooner hit the pillow than an insistent chirping pulled her out of her coma.

She sucked in a big breath, flung herself from her stomach onto her back. The space next to her bed was empty. No one stood there, staring at her in horror.

Her bedroom was minutes from darkness, though. The light of a cloudy sunset struggled to illuminate her blank white walls, cluttered desk, and the ratty armchair in the far corner where the Eidolon still sprawled, its eyes closed in peaceful repose.

"Bedroom lights, level two," she croaked. Her desk lamp and the overhead light banished the invading darkness. She grabbed her phone and sat up, rubbing the sleep from her eyes.

Five p.m. She ignored the solitary butterfly in her stomach and got coffee started, which was hot and ready by the time she turned on the shower. She gulped down half a cup, stepped into her tub, and took care of some much-needed self-grooming. Though her coffee was considerably cooler when she toweled off, she drank it anyway and went back for more.

After blow-drying her hair and applying lotion and deodorant, she stood for the longest time in front of her closet, holding her red top. Wearing it sent signals she wasn't sure she was ready to send, but not wearing it sent a message she wouldn't be able to take back.

Her phone chirped again, telling her she had run out of time. Decision made, she got dressed, pulled her hair back into a ponytail, and went downstairs to the curb, where her Safe Cab showed up a moment later.

Traffic was heavy on the 5, so the taxi avoided the clogged on-ramps and headed north on city streets. It only ended up being two minutes faster, but that was computers for you. Opening the cab door cued a prerecorded message thanking her for riding with Safe Cab, and she realized she had been too lost in thought to hear it yapping advertisements at her.

Finley's six-story building was formerly a three-story brewery that had been given additional floors and was then converted into loft apartments. The brick of the original bottom half had been painted a cream color to match the newer floors, and glass awnings hung from brushed-steel beams jutting over the ground-floor doors and windows. What had once been a garage door for loading trucks was now a gleaming, two-door glass entrance beneath a large transom window.

The evening sky spritzed rain on her as it geared up for another all-night drizzle, so she took shelter under the entrance's awning to check her phone. Right on time.

A pair of buttons on the call box let her scroll through a list of residents. She found "Cook, F" living in apartment 401 and pressed the Call button. It rang only once before she heard a click. She opened her mouth to announce herself but didn't have to. He knew who she was.

"Come on up, Monkey," he said.

A persistent beep signaled the door was unlocked, and she went inside. Glass walls served as a hallway leading past a spacious leasing office and an immense common room to the doors outside an exposed elevator shaft in the center of the building. Funny how she hadn't remembered what the ground floor looked like from the last time she had been there. She had been too preoccupied with Finley's arm around her to notice anything else. The only thing she did remember was the staircase abutting the elevator. She had run down those stairs as fast as she could while tears blurred her vision.

The butterfly in her stomach now had friends over for a party. She squeezed and rolled the purse strap hanging from her shoulder, wishing she could go home and change. It was too late now, though. He had buzzed her in and knew she was on her way up. Perhaps she could keep her coat on.

She rode the elevator alone. When she stepped onto the fourth floor, a sign pointed her to the right. Her stomach growled when she smelled something delicious wafting from a nearby apartment. She should've eaten something before she left, but choosing which shirt to wear had taken too long.

Though Finley's door looked like all the others—dark wood and polished metal numbers above a standard peephole—her heart raced when she spotted it. How should she act? Should she smile and give him a kiss on the cheek? Offer to shake his hand? Wave from a safe distance? Was any distance safe enough? Her instincts told her to kneel at his feet and beg for forgiveness, but he wasn't her Dom. Declan was.

Then why did submitting to Finley sound so good and so right, even after the things he had said to her? The feeling was almost enough to break her heart all over again.

She raised her hand to knock, but the door opened before she could, putting her face to face with the man she had been avoiding for almost a month.

"O-oh. Hi, Bomb," she said, bringing her hand back to grasp the collar of her coat.

The dark expression on his face gave way to something more neutral, making her wonder at his mood. He sported a five o'clock shadow, and the faint circles under his eyes said he was a bit beat, but his irises were still clear green and full of heat.

Her attention was drawn to his white dress shirt with the sleeves rolled up and the hem tucked into steel-gray slacks—a style she had only occasionally seen him in, and even then usually only the waist up. His business-casual look didn't try to conceal the double studs in his ears, the thin silver chain peeking through his unbuttoned collar, or the black bands tattooed around his forearms.

"Welcome back," he said, moving aside to invite her in.

She entered his apartment, ignoring the second half of his greeting and intending to walk past him, but he encircled her waist with his arm and pulled her against him.

Her hands instinctively went to his chest. Her heart tap-danced. God, he was so warm. Smelled of soap. Firm, smooth lips pressed to her cheek, along with the rasp of stubble. Something inside her fluttered.

"It's good to see you," he murmured in a way that summoned the predawn darkness of a bedroom—intimate.

"Y-you too, Bomb." She gently leaned away, rapidly approaching her melting point.

"Call me Finley. For now, at least," he said.

She slipped from him and backed up a few feet, blushing so brightly that her ears felt hot. "Sure thing," she chirped, hoping she sounded nonchalant, but even she wasn't convinced.

The door clicked shut, and she casually looked around, mostly to avoid eye contact. Something about his place was different, but she couldn't put her finger on it. She did remember the last time she had stood in that exact spot—she had been picking up the pieces of her heart and stealing glances at him from across the room.

Her stomach rumbled again, and with a sniff she realized his apartment was the source of the delicious smell. Indeed, the table was set for two, and a bottle of red wine sat open and ready to be poured. Merlot, she was certain. The covered basket undoubtedly contained warm bread.

"Oh my God, did you make *the* spaghetti?" She turned around as he emerged from the kitchen bearing two heaping plates of food and a full-blown smile.

"I figured it was high time you got a mouthful of my famous sauce," he said. Her mind immediately slipped right into the gutter. She pressed her lips together. "And I'm certain you didn't eat well this week."

"You know me, ready-mades and delivery." She stared ravenously at the masterfully plated noodles drowning in marinara and hung her purse on the back of the chair as he set the plates on the dining table.

"Let's eat while it's hot. Can I take your coat?" he asked.

Her smile waned. "Sure."

She quickly unbuttoned it. When he saw her long-sleeved, plain yellow shirt, his mouth went flat and his jaw tightened so hard that the muscles at the joints flexed. She held out her coat and swallowed the apology rising up her throat. After all, the only person she'd consented to take orders from was Declan.

"You're biting off more than you can chew," he said evenly.

She lifted her chin. "When did I agree to bite anything?"

Rather than back down, Finley stepped even closer, and she was forced to tilt her head back. The instinct—the *need* to obey his will was powerful, and she wanted to give in to it, but instead she raised her eyebrows and stared right back.

"You keep doubting me, Monkey," he whispered, stroking her arm from elbow to wrist. "It'll get you into trouble." He tugged her coat from her fingers and took it to the closet by his front door.

Okay, she really needed a time-out. She was already hot and humid, and she hadn't even been inside his apartment three whole minutes. He was so much more intense than the last time they had met in person, and that had led to clothes coming off. Perhaps being within a hundred yards of Finley Cook when she hadn't been allowed to masturbate all week had been a bad idea.

She waited for him to return before pulling out her chair—out of politeness, of course. Not because she needed his permission to sit or anything. He pushed in her chair and sat diagonally to her.

"Wine?" he asked.

"Yes, please. Smells great, by the way."

"You should try it first before you shower me with praise," he said as he poured a generous serving into her glass. "Although I'd hate to see you spit it out after all the years of hype."

She picked up her fork and twirled it in the noodles. "There's no way I wouldn't love it."

He gave a close-lipped smile and watched her take her first bite. The noodles were perfectly al dente. The marinara sauce was thick and rich and just a little bit sweet. Her eyes slid shut in bliss.

"I like putting that look on your face," he hummed. She swallowed before his comment could give her a coughing fit. "So it's good?"

She nodded as she reached for her wine. "Amazing—completely lives up to the hype," she assured him before taking a sip. A medley of lush, dark fruits burst across her tongue.

"Wine's okay?" he asked around a mouthful of food. "You like Merlots, right?"

Finley knew that without having to read a profile the way she knew he preferred beer, especially lagers. He knew she loved dogs but couldn't have one in her apartment. She knew he couldn't get started in the morning without coffee. He knew she loved exploiting bugs in video games. She knew he loved his job. They both knew so much about each other but not the things that mattered most.

He touched her arm. "Still thinking about work?"

It was as good an excuse as any.

"It's been a long week." She took another sip before setting down her glass. "For both of us, right? I can't believe you cooked."

"Yeah, we've been pulling twelve-hour days. Deepak's head nearly exploded when I cut out early," he said with a grin.

"Oh, Deepak," she sighed. "I've never met the guy, but it's clear he needs a hobby."

"It was worth it to see you tonight," he said. She looked up from her plate but couldn't meet his gaze for long. The room seemed too warm. "Did you make your deadline?"

She nodded again while she swallowed a bite of food. "Barely, but yes. I'll be glad when the product is out of my apartment."

"Why's that?" he asked.

Because it scares me when it shouldn't. "It was just a lot of work. I think I went through ten gallons of coffee."

Finley laughed and wound more noodles around his fork. "Yeah, I hardly saw the sun this past week, but I guess that's what it's like being you, right?" It wasn't the first time he'd brought up her backward circadian rhythm, but a joke usually veered him off the subject.

"The sun's overrated," she said, squinting at her fork. "It can be replaced with a multivitamin."

"What about the short days in winter? I mean, don't you miss the sun even a little?"

"You're assuming we ever see the sun in winter," she said as she nabbed a slice of garlic bread. She swiped it through her marinara and took a bite.

"Why do you think I spend a week on the beach every January?" he asked.

"Because *someone* has to appreciate that bod?"

It was meant to be another joke, but Finley didn't laugh, though his eyes twinkled knowingly at her. She resisted the urge to fan her face.

"You should come with me next time," he said. "I'm good at putting on sunscreen if it's sunburn you're worried about."

Oh, she had no doubt he would be adept at rubbing his hands all over her. She took a gulp of wine and shook her head. "I wouldn't make a good travel companion. I'd sleep most of the day."

"Start shifting your bedtime a couple weeks before—"

"No, it's not that. I actually *can't* sleep at night."

"What do you mean?" he asked. "Is it insomnia?"

She glanced at his face, saw confusion and concern. Normally, she'd ask him to drop it and talk about something else, but she pushed herself to explain.

"I have nightmares," she said, "even if I leave all the lights on. It's like...like I can't relax if the sun's not up."

"Oh. I thought you just liked staying up late. What kind of nightmares?"

The kind that stick with you all day. She rolled her shoulders, growing more and more discomforted. "I just feel unsafe and vulnerable. I usually feel better a couple minutes after I wake up." She reached for her wine and took another sip.

"And when you don't?" he asked, pushing his food aside. He leaned toward her and laid his hand over hers. She'd never assumed Finley would scoff or laugh at her sleep troubles, but she hadn't expected him to take them so seriously.

"Those are the nights I wake up unable to move and convinced someone is standing over me." She swirled the wine around the bottom of her glass. "It takes a little longer to get over that."

"How long has this been going on?"

"Nine years," she admitted while laughing mirthlessly. "I barely got through the rest of college."

"Nine years?" he repeated in disbelief. "You saw a doctor, right?"

All kinds, many times. "Yup, and I tried a bunch of different things. Sleeping during the day ended up being the only solution."

"Any idea what caused it?"

"I don't want to talk about that," she said, setting down her wineglass.

Finley stared silently at her, his lips downturned and his eyebrows pinched.

She sighed impatiently. "And I don't need your pity."

"No, that's not—" He lifted his hand to her cheek. "I just—thank you for sharing that with me." He didn't say it outright, but she knew what he meant. *Thank you for trusting me, even with that much.*

She'd always figured she'd feel worse after admitting something like that, but telling Finley about her nightmares had actually lifted a little bit of the weight. He hadn't pushed for more than she was willing to share—*this time*, part of her hissed.

Ignoring the mean whisper, she cupped her palm around his hand. He brushed his thumb across her cheek and tightened his fingers behind her jaw. He glanced at her mouth. He was going to kiss her.

She pulled her head away, her heart pounding. No matter how much she wanted a kiss, it would be completely unfair to Finley if she let it happen while she still had plans to see another man that night. Finley took his hand back.

"Sorry," she whispered. "I..."

"No worries. Let's just finish eating," he said as he pulled his plate back.

She picked up her fork and gestured at her plate.

"It really is very good. Thank you for dinner," she said.

He gave her a small smile. "You're welcome."

A few minutes and a second slice of garlic bread later, she leaned back from her empty plate, which Finley bussed to the kitchen along with his own. She heard the clink of dishes and the sound of water.

"That really hit the spot," she called to him as she rubbed her hand across her abdomen. "But you might've ruined my stomach for any other food."

"Well, there's more than one way to hit the spot," he said pointedly. She left that one alone, having walked right into it and instead reached for the Merlot.

"Do you want any more wine?" she asked.

"A little." He wandered back to the table and slid into his chair. "Thanks," he said once she moved on to her own glass. She poured a small amount, set the bottle down, and sat back to cradle her wine. Finley stared at his lap and silently played with the stem of his glass, working his jaw as if he were chewing a piece of gum.

Here it comes.

He took a sudden breath. "I don't think I ever told you how I met Midge," he said. She shook her head. "Well, I told my parents that she and I met at an art gallery." He cocked his head to the side. "Which was true, but the group that reserved the space wasn't necessarily there to look at art. It was sort of an open house for those who were new to the lifestyle to talk to the people already living it."

She held her breath, knowing precisely what he meant by "the lifestyle."

"I've been...into bondage for a really long time, but I had never... So, a guy on a forum told me about the meeting and said a couple of Doms would be there who could, you know, show me the ropes." He winced at what seemed to be an unintentional pun and cleared his throat.

"There was a quick introduction to the basics, some Q&A. They passed around literature. After that, people mingled, and later in the evening they put on a couple of demos." He paused again to take a swallow of wine.

"Midge had just joined the group, and it was her suggestion to use the gallery. She gave me a tour of the paintings and sculptures, so that's how we met," he said curtly, his stiff expression speaking volumes. "We did everything by the book—negotiated what we wanted, what we didn't want. I shadowed a Dom for a while before going solo. Our first scenes weren't perfect, but we agreed we were still learning about each other and took it slow."

God, the thought of Finley dominating another woman made her chest hurt.

"After a few months, we moved in together," he continued, "and I was sure we'd work out any issues that had cropped up, but instead they slowly got a lot worse." He took another gulp of wine. "She'd consent to something, we'd do a scene, and as far as I could tell, she'd enjoy herself. Then she'd accuse me afterward of making her do something she didn't want, even though she never used our safe word. The next week, she'd beg me to do it again, and when I'd tell her no, she'd say I didn't know how to be a good Dom."

He stopped to close his eyes and rub the bridge of his nose. Lily wanted to slip from her chair, sit between his spread knees, and rest her head on his thigh. She wanted to offer him comfort and acceptance. She wanted it so badly that she had to grab the seat underneath her so it wouldn't buck her off.

"I suggested we stay vanilla for a while, but she swore to obey me properly and to use our safe word. First chance she got, though, she'd try to make me lose my temper at her, and when—" He set his empty wineglass aside, took a deep breath, and looked right at her.

"Whenever we fought, she'd threaten that if I ever tried to break up with her or refused to dominate her the way she preferred, she'd tell our friends that I tied her up and beat her."

Lily's hand went to her chest. "Oh my God."

No wonder Finley had been so horrified to learn about the rumor she had heard. He probably thought Midge had followed through on her threat and had lied to his friends about something as awful as domestic violence.

"So when you were here last," he said, "it just dredged everything up again. I didn't know you were submissive—" *That* stopped the air in her throat. "But you pushed all my Dominant buttons, and I hadn't really indulged that part of myself in a long time."

Looking back, she realized what she'd done was immensely unfair. She'd gone into their date knowing something about him, participated in some mild D/s play without any kind of negotiated plan, and brought up his sexual preferences in the worst way possible while risking very little of herself. She had manipulated him.

He set his elbows on his knees and threaded his fingers together. "I'm not trying to excuse the things I said, which...I *really* didn't mean. I'm completely at fault and I apologize for—"

"No, I share the blame. I wasn't honest with you about..." God, how could she still not say it? "About being submissive," she forced out, "but I guess you knew by the time I left. I should've told you earlier, and I'm sorry."

Finley didn't move, didn't speak. His body was tensed as if at any second he'd stand up, seize her by her hair, and drag her from the chair onto her knees. She could discern his every breath. His shoulders looked massive, hunched over the way he was. His crisp collar framed the short chain around his neck, which gleamed in the dim overhead light.

He deserved better than her. She had lied to him multiple times. She was selfish and controlling. Was she really an improvement over Midge?

She broke eye contact and finished off her wine. "Before I forget, I have that name to look up if you don't mind doing that now." She reached behind her chair to get her purse.

"Monkey," he said softly.

"If you find a matching record, I just want to know if it looks normal. That'd answer my question." She pulled out a one-page printout of the names of those living at Site B, edited down to their ages and the street address. If Declan's record was normal, she wouldn't need the rest of the names, but if not...

When she had the guts to look him in the eye again, Finley had straightened up. He contemplated her for a brief moment and stood.

"I'll be right back," he said.

She allowed herself a sigh of relief once he sauntered past her toward his bedroom. Assuming he didn't find anything strange in Declan's record, she planned to tell the truth about seeing someone else that night—though not his profession—and then bolt. She'd have plenty of time later to analyze how fucked up she was. He returned with his laptop, set it where his dinner had been, and spent a minute typing.

"Is it just a name?" he asked. "Or do you have an age or birthdate? That narrows it down much faster."

"Yeah, the name is Declan Martin, age thirty-three."

He glanced over at her. He was curious and she knew her poker face was abysmal, but she tried not to flinch.

"Okay, give me a sec." He filled in the search parameters.

She closely watched his face because she couldn't see his laptop screen. He skimmed for a while, flicking his display with his thumb to scroll down. Surely there weren't that many thirty-three-year-old Declan Martins in the area?

He arched an eyebrow. "One hit, and it's strange. I've never seen a record like this. It's like he barely exists."

"What's that mean?"

"Nothing really," he said with a shrug. "He doesn't have a criminal record, which is the most you can hope for when you look someone up. It's just the information off his driver's license—name, DOB, address..."

"In Belltown?"

He looked askance at her. "Yeah. Do you know this guy?"

No criminal record was good. Something still chafed at her, though. She consulted the printout on her lap.

"Can you look up Susanna Bazelon, age thirty?"

Finley sighed with frustration. "What's this about, Monkey?"

"Please?"

He exhaled slowly and put his hands on his keyboard. "Only for you. How's that last name spelled?"

She gave him the spelling and watched as he accessed *The Veronica*'s record. He shot her a suspicious look and swiped at his screen a couple times.

"What is it?" she asked.

"Same thing, barely anything in her record. Same address too."

That delicious spaghetti wasn't agreeing with her so well.

"Try Jeremy Ando, age twenty-four."

Finley typed in *The Newbie*'s real name. "Same deal again. Can I see that list?" he asked, holding out his hand.

She gave him the printout without hesitation and waited while he blew through a few more names. He then sat back and dropped his hands on his lap.

"All of these people are fake," he insisted. "They technically exist as far as the government is concerned, but none of them even have the documents you'd need to *get* a driver's license." He picked up her printout. "Where did you get this list?"

"I..." *Don't have a lie prepared.* "I was messing with code injection on a website."

His eyebrows slanted. "A website for what?"

Chapter Fourteen

Oh God. She didn't want him to find out like this and grappled for an innocuous-sounding lie but came up with nothing.

"An escort agency," she said in a small voice.

At first, she wasn't sure if he'd heard her. His brows twitched and he blinked. Then she watched his face harden. The printout crinkled in his hand.

"You went t—" He wrenched his head away as though even looking at her was too upsetting. *I disgust him.* A realization seemed to bring his gaze back to the list in his hand. He then looked at her as if his heart were breaking.

"Jesus, is that where you were on Sunday?"

She didn't trust her tongue to work and simply nodded. He sucked in a breath through his teeth and clenched his fist all the way, completely crumpling the printout.

"You lied to me? Again?" He flung the list to the floor and slumped over his lap, clamping his fingers around his knees. "What did he do to you?"

She pulled her arms in tight against her chest. "Don't ask me that."

"Did you have sex with him?"

"That's none of your business," she said, almost shrill.

He surged to his feet, leaned over her, and gripped her seat, trapping her there. His eyes shined with pain. "Did you have sex with him?" he slowly repeated.

She wanted to ask what difference it made. To remind him that one aborted hookup didn't mean they were together. They had *never* been together. She had believed Finley was as uninterested in her submission as a vegetarian presented with a steak.

"I went as far with him as I did with you," she heard herself say.

He squeezed his eyes shut and dropped his head, but not before she saw how much her words hurt him. He released her chair and walked away. For a long, painful moment, neither of them spoke. He paced around the room as though chasing his patience.

"You know what that list of names means, right?" His voice was only marginally calmer.

"Organized crime? It might."

That is, if the definition of "might" was "really bloody likely."

"Well, you're not seeing him again." He said it with relief, as if she had dodged a bullet—or as if he had already made the decision for her.

"Actually, I have plans to see him tonight," she admitted.

He stopped dead, eyebrows raised. "Then you will cancel those plans."

Her hackles rose. "Like hell I will," she said, standing up. "I only came tonight to hear you out and get your help, nothing else. We're not *together* now."

"You think I can't give you what you need?" he asked. "And some escort who doesn't know you, he can?"

She lifted her chin. "He already did once."

Her stomach somersaulted at the change in Finley's expression. He stalked toward her, chin down and arms loose. He was going to touch her, kiss her, lift her into his arms, carry her to his bedroom, and then she'd be lost, unable to spare either of them any more heartache.

He gripped her hips and pinned her to the table hard enough to shift it a couple of inches. She couldn't help a whimper of excitement and braced her hands on his arms, trying to keep even a few inches of space between them, but he had little trouble pulling her wrists behind her back. When he slipped his knee between her legs, he brought her flush against him. She turned her face away lest she open up for a kiss. That would be the point of no return.

The ease with which he overpowered her was frightening. Not because she was scared of him—she knew she'd always be safe in his care—but because she loved how powerless it made her.

"I know you like to be restrained," he said in a hard whisper. "Unable to escape. Last time, you yanked on my grip while I made you come." He squeezed her wrists as a reminder even though the memory was still fresh, still made her groan.

"E-easy enough to figure out," she stammered.

"And I'm betting you like to play roles," he said before pressing a kiss to her pulse. Could he tell how hard her heart was beating? "All that time you spend on mods. Maybe we'll start with boss and secretary?"

The words *God, yes* rose to the top of her throat, but she sucked them back, biting her lip. The mere thought of him pretending to be her boss nearly made her burst into flames.

"I thought so," he purred.

His rigid cock pressed against her abdomen, and though she tried not to, all she could think of was their last video chat, of how empty her pussy had felt while she watched him masturbate. Before she knew what her body was doing, she clamped her thighs around his leg and moaned.

"Christ, I've never wanted anything so much in my whole life," he said. He wedged his other leg between hers, pushing her farther onto the table and forcing her feet off the floor.

Part of her—a loud part—wanted to submit to him and hope she wouldn't regret it. That she'd learn how to share her life, even the worst parts. That he'd still want her despite them.

But another part continued to hiss warnings. He'd be shocked and disappointed to learn she was L. Foss. He'd wonder what was wrong with her that she barely spoke to her parents. He'd want to know why she couldn't sleep at night, and then he'd think she was crazy.

"Finley, please," she begged. "I can't do this. I'll only keep hurting you."

"We'd be good together, and we both know it." He brushed his lips across the shell of her ear. "I won't push you away again. Only pull you closer." The stubble on his cheek grazed her neck. "'Cause the better I know you, the more I want you. I *want* you. So much."

A sigh shuddered out of her. How she wished she was as wonderful as he thought she was, someone with acceptable flaws. Not haunted, cynical, and withdrawn. He wanted her now, but he hadn't seen the worst of her.

"I'm not what you think," she said. "I'm not that person."

"You can't run from who you are." His grasp on her wrists tightened. "You're mine, and it's time you accepted it."

Wet heat latched on to her neck. She cried out and tried to squirm away, but he kept her right where he wanted her, using the hard suction of his lips to bruise her skin. The pain was minor, but it made her eyes flutter shut in pleasure.

"L-let me go," she breathed. He moved his hips against her, pressing the thick seam of her jeans right onto her clit. "Stop it, please."

She struggled to free herself, but he clutched her even closer.

"Stop it," she shouted. "Red, *red*!"

He backed off immediately, giving her plenty of space, but his face was taut, his stance aggressive. The light color of his slacks made his erection that much more obvious.

She gripped the table to keep her balance, but nothing she could grip would help her regain her composure. Her fingers explored the new love bite on her neck, a spot that was still warm, wet, and achy.

"I don't understand," Finley panted. "You won't trust me, but you're willing to trust that agency—to trust *him*."

"That's just it, Bomb," she said. "I don't trust anybody." She pushed away from the table, snatched the crumpled printout from the floor, and grabbed her purse. "I made sure the agency doesn't know my name or where I live. They're getting cash, and I'm getting what I need. No strings attached. I'm not even a blip on their radar."

She tried to walk past him to the coat closet, but he stepped in front of her.

"SysOne is rolling out those new owner agreements soon. You could rent a version four legally if you can't deal with someone real."

The implication that Declan wasn't "someone real" was not lost on her, nor did she appreciate him accusing her of cowardice, even though it was true. She thought of the version four sitting in her apartment. It was an expensive, inferior knock-off of a human being, but it was the closest thing to a man she had allowed into her home in nearly ten years. Even so, she'd never use it like that.

"You know their kink add-ons are bullshit," she said. "Eidolons are programmed to obey. Any submission or domination would be mere illusion."

"And paying someone wouldn't be? What if he hurts you? What if he gets you pregnant?"

"That's not how they work," she said. "And I've got an IUD. A condom will take care of the rest."

He didn't stop her this time from reaching the closet. She grabbed her coat off the hanger and turned around. Finley stood several steps away with a familiar look on his face, the same one he'd worn the last time she was seconds from leaving his apartment.

"Where are you meeting him?" he asked in resignation.

"A club. Why?" she warily asked as she put on her coat.

"I'm going too." He raised his hand when she opened her mouth to protest. "I just want to check him out. I don't want you to get hurt. I couldn't bear that." The last came out rough.

Perhaps that would do the trick. If he saw her with another Dom, he could move on to a submissive who deserved him and could be honest with him, and after what they had learned about the residents of Site B, having backup at the club wasn't a bad notion. She zipped up her coat and slung her purse strap across her chest.

"Okay," she said with a sigh. His body subtly relaxed. "I'm meeting him at eleven. We're going to Reflexxion in the Industrial District."

"If you give me your number, I can call you in case you need an out." Also not a bad idea. And changing her number afterward wouldn't be difficult. She pulled out her phone, which prompted him to take out his. After they exchanged numbers, she headed to the door.

Pausing on the threshold, she threw one last glance over her shoulder. Finley's presence filled the entire space, his body still and quiet but poised, as though sheer willpower was the only thing stopping him from stopping her. A month ago, all he had wanted was for her to leave while all she had wanted was to stay. Now the situation was reversed.

She said nothing—couldn't—and shut the door between them.

Chapter Fifteen

M ore than once on her way out of the building and into a cab
home to change, Lily almost turned around to go back to Finley's apartment. She imagined knocking on his door and waiting for it
to open. She wondered how his voice might sound when he ordered
her into his bedroom. Her insides twisted at the thought of how long
and severe her punishment would be—and how mind-altering the sex
would be afterward. He'd been right when he said she needed him, but
fear kept her feet marching.

She arrived at her apartment with plenty of time to get ready for her
date but also plenty of time to regret the unknown quantity she had
introduced to her evening. Even the best-case scenario would lead to
awkwardness and hurt feelings. She felt sick at the thought that a part
of her wanted to make Finley jealous, to see what he would do. Such
a worst-case scenario would involve a very public scene and possibly a
trip to the ER or the police station, though she couldn't fathom him
losing his temper so completely.

Then again, she hadn't thought he would grasp her close and mark
her neck like a stubbly vampire. That version of Finley had lived only
in her fantasies until tonight.

She stared at her hickey a long time before dabbing it with concealer.
It didn't disappear completely, but it would be invisible to anyone who
didn't know it was there. She applied the rest of her makeup and made
the extra effort of shading her eyes to match her dress. Once her hair
was done up in a fauxhawk with as little hairspray as she could manage,
she put on the lacy, black lingerie Declan had given her, spritzed herself
with her favorite floral perfume, and slipped into her dress.

The end result was a major confidence booster. The strapless satin was formfitting but flattering, and not as uncomfortably short as her red dress, though it also ended well above the knee. She turned this way and that in front of her bathroom mirror, bracing herself for when she found something lacking, but it fit her perfectly. Would Finley even recognize her?

She frowned at her reflection. Was she really more concerned with how Finley would react to her appearance than how Declan would? No longer impressed with herself, she turned off the bathroom light and returned to her bedroom.

With some time to spare before she had to leave, she checked her messages, hoping to find an email from her editor, who was taking the weekend to polish her piece before it went live on Monday, but instead she saw an email from Declan saying they would meet for a quick drink before they headed to the club.

A quiet start to their date was reasonable as Reflexxion was hands-down too loud for most conversation, but if they weren't at the club right around eleven, Finley would wonder where they were. She could text him to say they'd be a little late, but then he'd want to know why.

Damn it, she had to stop worrying about Finley. He wasn't her Dom, and she wasn't going on a date with him tonight. She wasn't required to tell him anything about her date, so didn't have to show up on time, either. All that mattered was enjoying her night with Declan, whom she wouldn't be able to afford again for a long time.

She confirmed the change of plans, looked up the bar's address, and then, with no time left, got ready to leave. She put on her coat, stepped into the pair of close-toed wedges that came with her dress, and grabbed her clutch full of cash as well as her umbrella. Her phone went into her coat pocket. The Safe Cab picked her up at her usual intersection and headed downtown.

Sophia's wasn't a famous bar, but it was established. Situated across the street from a large parking lot where locals left their cars while they shopped, Sophia's was coincidentally on the same street as Reflexxion, only several miles north past the awkward angle created by Puget Sound. The bar took up the bottom floor of a narrow brick building crammed into a row of mismatched structures, none of which reached higher than five floors so as not to block the view from taller hotels farther back from the water.

Lily paid her fare, readied her umbrella while the back door opened, and traversed the short distance from the cab to the bar's dripping awning. A neon sign in the single, large front window advertised a famous brand of vodka while another depicted a martini glass. She shook out her umbrella, straightened her shoulders, and passed through the well-worn glass door.

The bar's capacity maxed out at about a hundred patrons, but the place was only half-full, and plenty of tables and stools stood empty. Horn-shaped sconces provided soft light that wouldn't show all the scrapes and scratches in the varnish of the dark wood interior. Neither fancy nor intimidating.

Declan turned just as the door shut behind her. He sat at the bar as he had last time and wore a black blazer over a scarlet dress shirt—no tie. The glass in front of him held water instead of beer. He stretched his neck with a quick jerk to the side and beckoned her with the same almost-smile as the one in his photo online.

Remembering how he preferred to be greeted, she kept her shoulders back, her eyes down, and walked to him with her arms at her sides. When she stopped a couple feet away, he immediately wrapped his palm around the back of her neck and drew her forward one last step, pulling her between his knees. He smelled incredible.

"Very good, Ms. Lloyd," he said from an inch away. "Very intuitive. I'd say you've earned this." She closed her eyes as he gave her a slow, gentle kiss. He was good at it—great, actually—but all she could think of was how much she had wanted another pair of lips only a few hours ago.

"It's not intuition if it's learned," she said when he pulled back.

"Mm?" He had a distant look in his eyes.

"I...greeted you the way you taught me, Sir."

"Ah, yes—as I taught you." He patted the stool next to him. "Of course."

Had he forgotten their first moment at the Italian place? Was he that busy and was she that unremarkable? *No, people just forget things sometimes.*

She unbuttoned her coat and boosted herself into the seat. Declan took a swallow of his water, and she thought she saw a slight tremble in his fingers. He then swept his gaze down her body.

"The dress fits well, I see." He set his elbow on the bar. "Although it only makes me wonder how stunning you'll be out of it." She assumed he meant the expensive lingerie under her dress because no one could deny he had already made a close study of her body sans clothing.

"Thank you, Sir. It's too bad the weather isn't cooperating, but I suppose we'll be indoors most of the night."

"Mm, and behind one door in particular." His bedroom. Right. She hadn't even thought past going to the club. "Let's get that drink. Would you prefer a Merlot, Ms. Lloyd?"

He hadn't forgotten her favorite wine—not that he could because it was listed in her profile—but she had already been served Merlot that evening.

"I'll do a mixed drink this time. Is there a reason why you're being so formal, Sir?"

"Would you rather I call you pet?"

She sighed through a smile. "I do like it when you do that, but you can call me Jill like last time. I mean, you're not—" She lowered her voice. "You're not the Stranger to me anymore."

"It's...merely protocol when I've not yet been paid," he said soberly.

"Oh." She looked down at the clutch on her lap. Her shoulders curled forward. Why was she suddenly ashamed? If paying him first was just more protocol, like greeting him the right way and using Sir, then what was the problem? The money was a guarantee of a fun evening without any emotional baggage, which was what she wanted.

"Maybe I should pay you now—"

"Hi there, can I get you something?"

Lily jumped, clamping on to her purse and looking over at the bartender, whose delicate eyebrows were raised expectantly. Without context, that last tidbit sounded suspect, but if the bartender had overheard, her face didn't show it.

Then again, knowing the context wouldn't really help.

"Uh, yes, please. I'd like a rum and Coke."

"Sure, any particular rum?"

"Any'll do." She hoped it was enough to shoo her away for a minute. The bartender nodded and left. Declan smiled knowingly, but not without compassion.

"Now is fine," he said.

With a nod, she reached into her clutch and withdrew a fat white envelope—the absolute last of her rainy-day money. *Well, at least it's raining.*

The envelope disappeared into the inner pocket of his blazer just as the bartender returned with a lowball tumbler still fizzing from being poured. She sucked down a third of it. Her date sipped his water and scooped up a handful of bar nuts.

"You're not gonna have a beer or something?" she asked.

"I'd never drive as anything but stone-cold sober, especially with you in the car," he said before shaking a few cashews into his mouth.

She tilted her head. "We're not taking a Safe Cab?"

That almost-smile reappeared. "Those have cameras in them."

Shock smoothed the confusion from her face. He tipped her chin up to close her mouth and licked the salt from his lips.

"Don't worry. I don't do *that* while driving, either."

Man, this guy was almost too much for her to handle. She reached for more liquid confidence, but an unexpected sound stopped her. Her phone was ringing. Just in case it was an emergency, she checked the caller ID.

Not many people had her number—family members who never used it and a few businesses that certainly wouldn't be calling after eleven on a Friday night—so she knew immediately that the unknown contact with a local area code was Finley.

He had said he'd call to give her an out if she asked for one, not pester her when she was only ten minutes late. She had the option of responding with a text message rather than picking up, but she let it go to voice mail.

"You look upset," Declan said. "Bad news?"

"No, it's fine." She returned her phone to her pocket. "Well no, it's not fine. It's just complicated, that's all."

"Tell me about it." He tucked his knuckles behind his jaw and watched her with sincere interest. Her first instinct was to deceive, divert, and deflect, but telling the truth had merit. If he knew Finley would be watching them, he could better play his part as the Dom she had chosen—and Finley could move on with his life. She sucked down another inch of her drink.

"That was Finley," she said. "He's at Reflexxion right now and probably wondering why we haven't shown up yet."

Declan's only reaction was slightly raised eyebrows. "Is he your boyfriend?"

In his place, she would've asked why anyone would be waiting for them, but his question was also relevant, though not easily answered. She flicked a peanut from its dish onto the counter, not to eat it but fiddle with it.

"No, he's just a friend, but also kind of an ex. We never got off the ground."

"Why's that?"

She burst out a sigh. "Um, timing wasn't right, I guess. It just didn't work out."

"Mm, and how much does he know about us?"

"Pretty much everything." She glanced at him to catch his reaction, but he remained as placid as a calm lake. "He's suspicious of you—and Tailor Made."

Declan straightened to pick up his water. "I'm sure he is," he said as he brought the glass to his lips. For a second, he seemed far away. He had probably dealt with a lot of suspicious friends of his clients.

"Well, he insisted on 'chaperoning' tonight," she said acerbically. "He thinks I might get hurt with you."

He focused on her again as he set down his glass. "You don't think that?"

"No, Sir, of course not," she insisted, "but TM's not forcing you to work for them, right? They're not making you...you know, see clients?"

He shook his head. "They treat me very well. I get everything I need, including healthcare, and you've seen the apartment they provided." His answer sounded rehearsed, but he had likely given it many times.

"I'm glad," she said, relieved.

In a blink, his face subtly changed. He lowered his chin, and his small, crooked smile took on a different meaning. He lifted his hand to her face and ran his thumb across her cheek. She almost forgot to breathe. He pushed down the collar of her coat.

"Is Finley the one who put this mark on your neck?"

She slapped her hand over her hickey. Her cheeks burned—it had to be the rum in her system.

"I'd say that's a yes," he said. "You don't really believe he's willing to give you up, do you?"

She went back to fiddling with her peanut. "He never had me in the first place," she muttered.

"Is he a Dominant?"

"That's his business, Sir. Ask him if you want to know."

"Another yes, then," he said as he fished for more nuts. "I take it you didn't plan for him to join us tonight."

"No, and I still don't. He's supposed to stay at a distance. I figured he'd give up on me if he saw us together."

"Not when he sees you in that dress."

She looked up again. "I don't want there to be a scene, Sir."

His expression was as impregnable as usual. He chewed for a few seconds, licked his lips, and swallowed, all while staring back at her. What was he thinking?

"Finish your drink, Jill," he said. "We should get going."

"Yes, Sir." The last swallow of her drink was mostly rum and very little soda. She held back a grimace as she set aside her empty glass.

Declan tossed more than enough cash down to pay for her drink plus a tip. He slid from his stool, grabbed his umbrella, and escorted her to the door. She wondered why he didn't have a heavier coat to wear over his blazer, but when he opened his umbrella and wrapped his arm around her shoulders, she realized he had enough body heat for both of them.

They crossed the street to the parking lot, which was nearly full, but only a couple people wandered through the rows either on their way to pick up their car or to prepay for a spot at the automated kiosk. Their ride for the evening was a high-end, two-toned electric sports car. She had neither the money nor any real need for a car, but if she had, the one in front of her would definitely be high on the list.

Her date unlocked and lifted the switchblade door for her. After she was seated, he walked around to the driver's side while her door closed automatically. The spotless interior was nothing but smooth black-and-white consoles and mocha leather seats with bright blue lines highlighting or dividing different functions. A small decal in the corner of the windshield marked the vehicle as one from a car-sharing company.

A cold draft hit her when the driver-side door opened, silent but for the gasp of air pumps lifting it. Declan smoothly slid behind the wheel, shook out his umbrella, and stowed it under his seat. His door sedately lowered without his help.

"Nice wheels," she said as she reached over her shoulder for her seat belt. Declan turned to her, shifting onto his right hip. "Does the club have valet parking or—"

"We're not leaving yet. Lay your seat back."

She swallowed and let go of the belt. With the car still turned off and the nearest light pole more than fifty feet away, she could hardly make out his features, but his frosty tone told her enough.

"Now, Jill. Do as I say," he said patiently.

She felt along the right side of her seat and found the hard plastic handle. Though the car was going nowhere, the feeling in her stomach as her seat went back was like riding a roller coaster.

"What if someone sees?" she asked.

"No one will see." His leather seat sighed as he leaned over her and planted his left hand on the narrow, rounded ledge of the windowsill. The angle put his face above her in complete darkness.

"Did you touch yourself this week?" His voice was barely above a whisper.

"I-I've wanted to." Many, many times. Her article deadline had been the only thing that kept her from thinking about sex every five minutes. She'd thought about it every ten minutes instead, especially after the inspiration she'd gotten from Finley.

"Did your complicated friend give you more than a love bite?"

"No, Sir." She emphasized it with a shake of her head. The quality of the car showed when he leaned closer without anything creaking.

"Did you want him to?" He dipped his head, brushed his mouth against her collarbone.

She closed her eyes and gripped the seat as her roller-coaster ride continued. "Yes," she whispered.

With his lips, he traced the bare skin just above the bust of her dress. "Spread your knees," he murmured.

She shuddered as she complied, one knee pressed to the center console and the other touching the door. With his left hand, he parted her coat and stroked her from her waist, to the flare of her hip, and down to her bare knee. She held her breath as he drew his fingers up the inside of her thigh.

"Soft and humid, just the way I like you." A light touch explored the black lace stretched over her mons, and the air trapped in her lungs rushed out. She wanted to beg him for something, but she didn't know what.

"I have a surprise for you, pet. Keep those pretty eyes closed."

"Yes, Sir." She heard him shift, and then the click of the dashboard compartment as he opened it, took something out, and shut it again.

"Slide to the edge of your seat. I want full access." He sounded a little breathless. She knew the feeling.

Her legs were long, and sports cars weren't roomy practically by definition, but she squeezed down to the edge of her seat, her skirt riding up.

"God, look at you," he said gruffly, laying his palm over her left knee. "Hands above your head."

His palm traveled up her thigh. She couldn't help making a small sound as she lifted her arms and grasped the headrest.

"Don't move," he whispered. He slipped his fingers under the crotch of her panties, pushing the lace aside and exposing her. She heard a sucking pop as if he had pulled something from his mouth. A small object entered her.

"S-Sir," she gasped.

"Shh, stay still."

The object gently pinched her as he clamped it into place beneath her outer labia. The device sat right over her clit. The pressure of Declan's fingers left, but he didn't let her panties cover her pussy.

"Hardly noticeable once you get used to it," he said. "That is, until it turns on."

Her gasp was loud, almost a shriek. The object didn't just vibrate, it moved—a tender massage like the pad of a nimble finger. Declan pushed it tighter to her clit. She cried out and hung on to the leather headrest for dear life.

"Mm, seems to be working." He leaned over her again.

His mouth brushed hers, and she let him in. His tongue dove, retreated, dove again. His lips were hypnotic, pushing and pulling as if he were sucking the life out of her. His sensuous musk filled her nostrils. The barest pressure of his finger on the device made her roller car race down another slope.

She rolled her hips against his palm, tasted and chased his tongue, gave him her breath, and pulled in his. The only sounds were the smack of their lips, the rasp of their panting, the buzz of the tickler, and the patter of rain on the car roof. She was lost in her senses and in him. Lost was good.

Her roller coaster was backward, ending with the big drop rather than starting with it, and she was coming up to it real fast. Their kiss deepened and the tickler sped up. She almost let go of the headrest to wrap her arms around his shoulders, but she didn't want to disobey a command and risk ending the ride too soon.

It was starting. Her muscles were turning to liquid. He'd have to tug her clothes back into place and put her seat belt on for her. Maybe she'd be able to walk by the time they got to the club.

"Not yet, baby." He pulled away and let her panties fall back into place. The delicious sensations between her thighs stopped completely.

"No," she gasped, her eyes popping open. "Sir, please."

"Hush. I never gave you permission to come." He dropped something into his pocket—probably the vibe's remote—and reached for his seat belt. "Unless it becomes uncomfortable, the device stays where it is until I say you can remove it. We'll head out once your seat is up and your belt fastened."

She had to wear the vibe *into* the club? And he controlled when it turned on? She couldn't help groaning as she grasped for the handle on the side of her seat and sat up.

"Oh wow," she breathed when she saw how steamed up the windows had become. After a few adjustments, her seat belt was secure. Declan started the car.

They waited a moment for the windows to clear up, and just as her date put the car into gear, her phone rang again. Finley was calling.

"Text him," Declan said with a devilish smile. "Tell him we're on our way."

She was prepared to let the call go to voice mail again, but her Dom had told her otherwise. She typed out a quick response and hit Send.

Chapter Sixteen

"You have reached the voice mail box of—" Monkey's number followed rather than a real name. Finley jerked his phone from his ear.

Another unanswered call. Though it was only twenty past eleven, he had been waiting over an hour, having shown up early to claim a spot against the wall from which he could watch for Monkey's arrival.

But eleven came and went without any sign of her. He knew he should be patient a little longer, but the awful notion that she might've sent him down a dead end with yet another lie plagued him until he couldn't resist calling her number—and then, when she didn't pick up, calling it again ten minutes later.

He slid his phone into the pocket of his slacks but kept his hand on it just in case. Though the music wasn't blaring at the front of the club where coats and IDs were checked, the many people shouting at each other or into their phones would drown out even the loudest ringtone.

A few people were like him, alone and glancing between their clutched phones and the entrance, but most arrived with dates or friends and proceeded to the coat check once their ID got them past security. Unless they joined the throng of people waiting on more to arrive, they hurried inside to join the scene.

Reflexxion took great pains with its aesthetic. No handwritten signs explained coat-check policies. No wrinkled posters hyped which DJ would perform soon. Such information was stylishly contained on a large, thin display that conformed to the outward curve of the wall forming the coat-check counter.

Though the club was built into an old warehouse, its façade concealed the underlying structure of that ignoble origin behind an immense wall of multicolored OLEDs programmed to dazzle the eye with bursting geometric shapes, making it the flashiest member of the establishments on Club Row. Anyone showing up in a car could buy valet parking from a smartly dressed attendant and get their first drink free.

The light show continued inside with every doorframe outlined and every corridor traced in slowly shifting colors, which dark glass walls and ceilings reflected to multiply the effect. The club's most famous feature was the main dance floor, but he hadn't ventured that far in yet.

His phone buzzed against his palm in two short bursts—a text message. Monkey's response to his calls manifested in much the same way.

Running late, Bomb. Be there soon.

No one matching the photo and physical description from Declan Martin's driver's license had entered the club in the last hour, so he suspected that Monkey was traveling to Reflexxion in his company.

Finley shoved his phone back into his pocket, closed his eyes, and resisted the urge to knock the back of his head against the wall. He had hoped to spot the escort lying in wait and catch the guy engaging in shenanigans. Hell, or descend on the escort without pretense to deliver a pummeling. He'd never wanted to beat up anyone before, hated that the thought even crossed his mind, but if it got rid of the guy...

Knowing they were already together turned his stomach, but the thing that made his chest ache was what Monkey had said about not trusting anyone, including him. She saw her sexual submission as a flaw she had to hide, as something that made her less worthy of love. More than that, she saw her submission as separate from her emotional needs. Paying an escort meant paying to keep her heart out of play.

He had to prove her wrong. Though he'd said he would be there simply as an observer, he knew he wouldn't stay one—and if Monkey hadn't realized the same, she would soon enough.

As the minutes passed, he watched the young and well-dressed pour into the club. The bass thumping through the walls occasionally dropped to change cadence as the DJ shifted tracks. More than once, just for a split second, he mistook a dark-haired woman at the ID check for the one he anticipated.

He checked his phone again—half past the hour.

Through a gap in the crowd, he spotted a sports car pulling up to the valet station. An attendant sprang into action and opened the passenger-side door, but a large group of people filled the entrance before he could get a good look at the light-skinned brunette alighting from the car. Security efficiently checked the group's IDs, but the shambling mass took a while to queue up at the coat check.

Then he saw her, and...damn. He had never seen her hair like that. The way it was styled back showed off her cheekbones and her long neck. Everything else was hidden under her coat. The person checking IDs handed back her card and took the one offered by Monkey's enormous escort, whose arm was draped across her back. Finley clenched his hands and took a deep breath that did nothing to calm him.

Security found nothing wrong with the escort's card and stamped the insides of their wrists. The escort then guided Monkey to the coat check while she cast her eyes about—looking for him.

When their gazes met and held, he knew his face would betray everything he felt, the longing and the jealousy. He expected her to turn away from him, but her lips parted and her eyebrows tilted up with the same painful yearning as his own.

He lost eye contact when new arrivals passed between them. His body tensed, aching to draw closer. Once the crowd thinned out again, he found Monkey at the coat-check counter, where the escort was assisting her out of her coat.

She was a vision. The golden-yellow of her strapless dress warmed her rosy skin. Its shiny black beading drew the eye to her breasts and thighs. She had tried to hide the love bite he'd given her a few hours ago, but he could still see the faint shadow of it beneath the concealer. He nearly crossed the room to give her a matching one on the other side of her neck.

The escort kept his blazer and leaned down to say something to her while a staff member checked her coat and purse. Finley thought he saw her eyes flick toward him, but then she lifted her chin to speak into the escort's ear. He laid his hand on her waist as she spoke, and Finley thought about how satisfied he'd feel if he broke the guy's nose—real fucking satisfied. As he was contemplating violence, the escort locked gazes with him and *smiled* as his eyes measured Finley from head to toe.

Monkey had *told* the escort he would be at the club. She'd probably also told him why, so the guy had to have guessed Finley's real reason for being there—taking back what belonged to him—and thought that was real quaint.

The staff member returned to fit a plastic band around Monkey's wrist. The escort smugly stroked his hand across her bare shoulders to hold her against his side as they left the counter. Monkey kept her eyes down as they joined the stream of people trickling farther into the club.

Finley pushed away from the wall to follow. The rules of the game had changed, but he was still going to play—and win.

Chapter Seventeen

Telling Finley where Declan was taking her had been an enormous mistake. Momentary anger had made her forget that she couldn't simply pretend he wasn't there, watching her with someone else. As soon as she'd spotted him standing sentry against the wall, the look on his face had reminded her. Why she had thought inviting him would be anything but incredibly awkward was a mystery.

She knew her feet were moving and could feel Declan's hand on her back, guiding her somewhere, but she couldn't look away from Finley. His expression wasn't one of a concerned friend assuring himself of her safety, but of a Dominant looking forward to giving his submissive a needed lesson. The tug in her gut told her to go to him—that doing so was good and right.

Declan had called it. Finley wasn't willing to give her up.

When the crowd cut the cord between them, she turned away before he could snare her again and realized she was at the coat check counter. She handed over her clutch, which the attendant slipped into a bag attached to a coat hanger, and Declan pulled her coat from her shoulders. The club employee took it and walked away to add the hanger to the automatic rack system. Declan leaned down to her ear.

"Have you seen him?" he asked. She stopped herself before she could look at Finley again.

"He's behind me against the wall—" Declan's hand went to her waist. "B-by the...hallway entrance. Dark green shirt."

If Declan saw Finley, he didn't say so. The club employee returned with a coded disposable band and attached it to her wrist, saying something about keeping it safe, but she didn't parse the words. Declan conducted her away from the counter with his arm around her shoulders, but instead of enjoying the contact, she worried it was pissing off Finley.

They headed farther into the club past a couple of busy restrooms. The hallway was ribbed with lights behind frosted glass that faded one color into the next. The music from the main dance floor slowly grew louder, overcoming the pounding bass. Beautiful, smiling people laughed and flirted in the alcoves on either side of the hall. Everyone seemed happy and tipsy. She felt only one of those.

Declan's hand on her shoulder drifted down, following the curve of her waist to her hip. She thought he'd keep it there, but he filled his fingers with the right globe of her rear and squeezed.

Was Finley behind them? Could he see where Declan's hand was? She couldn't help looking over her shoulder in the hope that he was too far back or that too many people were between them. A hard slap on her ass made her jump and gasp. She faced forward again.

Declan's lips brushed her ear. "Don't worry, pet. He'll follow."

She thought Declan sounded excited, but the music was too loud for her to be sure, and it would only get louder as they emerged into the cavernous main room. Chunky, uneven facets on the walls and ceiling made it resemble the inside of a smoky quartz crystal. Laser lights reflected at odd angles, and multicolored lights rippled under the feet of the lithe, surging bodies that packed the large dance floor. The club called it their rainbow floor, which was sunken and ringed by tables.

Two DJs spun tracks in the booth in the back left corner. The huge screen behind them duplicated the array of colored patterns the dancers created. A long, busy bar took up the right side of the room, and a shorter one took up the wall next to the hallway from which they'd emerged. Yet another bar served drinks on one side of the VIP section, a dais that wrapped the entire room.

Declan led her down a short set of stairs to the main floor, his hand still firmly stuck to her ass. They made their way through the throng of those gathered at the shorter bar to the VIP section, which was cordoned off by an actual velvet rope. Declan handed a large bill to a suit-wearing giant who gave them access.

Deep recesses in the section's back wall contained booths big enough for large groups. In front of those, smaller arrangements of low tables and leather loveseats gave their occupants an excellent view of the main floor from behind a metal railing.

Declan led her to an empty loveseat. A two-foot cube between it and railing seemed to be their table. He reached for a square throw pillow, set it on the floor, and sat in the center of the loveseat. She knew without asking that she was to sit at his feet, and her lungs shrank with anxiety.

Where was Finley? Was he watching as she took the proffered hand to help her sit? She leaned back against the sofa, her legs bent to one side and her arm touching Declan's leg. He rested his hand at the base of her neck. His thumb brushed her nape.

Without moving her head, which would alert Declan to her apprehension, she scanned the people around her, expecting to find them staring and pointing at her, their mouths moving as they agreed on how bizarre she was. Though Finley would understand the display, she wondered if he'd be angry to see her subservient to an escort. Did he find the sight as disgusting as the concept?

No one gave her a second look, though—or even a first look in most cases. Like her, they were in their own worlds.

Anxiety gave way to exhilaration. She had never experienced submission this way. Though she sat lower than her date, she was comfortable on the pillow and allowed to touch her Dom, who occasionally stroked his hand through her hair or squeezed her shoulder, letting her know he wasn't ignoring her, that she was pleasing him. Knowing he had the power to turn the vibe on whenever he liked both excited and unnerved her. She was keenly aware of the gentle pressure it exerted to stay in place.

For a while, they simply watched the spectacle of undulating people and colors. She kept expecting to spot Finley, but the club was so crowded and the lights so hypnotizing that she couldn't find him.

Declan used the tablet on their table to order a drink for her and water for himself. When her rum and Coke came, she had to turn her head, close her eyes, and open her mouth to receive her rum-coated maraschino cherry. She closed her lips around the sweetened fruit, and Declan tugged the stem free. After an affectionate touch to her cheek, he handed her the drink, which wasn't watered down thanks to their VIP seating.

The DJs kept up a mix of house, trance, and dubstep to keep the dancers moving. The lights played tricks on her eyes, changing the colors of clothes and making it impossible to find anyone wearing green. Instead of giving herself a headache—and a guilt trip—she watched the level of liquid in her glass drop and swallowed the heavily spiked soda with a grimace. The table was within easy reach, and she set her empty tumbler on it.

A trance song shifted into something with a heavy bass line. Two strong drinks in half an hour on a practically empty stomach had her closing her eyes and nodding to the beat. Her Dom lightly massaged the back of her neck, which made her relax even more. Perhaps she could pretend a certain someone wasn't there after all.

Perhaps she should stop searching for him.

"Your complicated friend hasn't looked anywhere else but at you," Declan said close to her ear. Her head stilled and her eyes popped open. "To your left, by the partition."

Once she knew where to find him, Finley came into sharp focus. He stood with one shoulder resting on the divider between the dance floor and a seating area, his hand in his pocket and his hip jutted. He was motionless, a fixed point in all that constant movement beyond the railing. Though his expression was blank, he was anything but bored.

"I think it's time you enjoyed the dance floor," Declan said.

She twisted around to find that almost-smile on his face. "You're not coming?"

He ran one knuckle down her cheek, slid his fingers around her neck, and squeezed. She felt her eyelids droop as she relaxed in his hold.

"I'll join you when you make it impossible for me not to touch you. Every time you submit, it's a gift. Make me want to rip off the wrapping."

Instinct and the pressure on her neck told her to obey, but Finley would be watching—*was* watching.

"I don't want to torment him, Sir."

"Don't you?" he asked as one corner of his mouth turned up.

"I said I didn't want to cause a scene."

"Not that kind of scene. I know," he said. "Give him a good show if he likes looking at you so much, but don't let his presence control you when it's *me* to whom you belong." He emphasized the last by pulling her closer using his grip on her neck.

Everything about the moment turned her on—sitting at his feet, his hand around her throat as he ordered her to seduce him onto the dance floor, and even knowing Finley was watching the entire exchange.

Declan let go of her and helped her stand. He then sat back, one arm thrown across the back of the loveseat and his other hand deliberately stuffed into his jacket pocket where he kept the vibe's remote. Her stomach churned as she made her way to the rope-guarding giant, who let her out with a silent nod.

She stepped onto the closest corner of the dance floor. Warm colors rippled from the soles of her wedge heels in time to the beat, a fast-paced trance track. The floor was so bright it created the illusion of a wading pool. Swaying casually with the music, she watched the ripples thicken under the foot that held more weight and couldn't help wondering how fun it must have been to program the sensors.

Navigating the dance floor took some care. People came and went. Arms flew up with every tonal change. Not far from the edge closest to Declan, she twirled into a gap in the crowd that just so happened to be in Finley's line of sight. Even with her standing and him sitting, she had to look up to meet Declan's eyes. He was a prince on a throne, and she was his entertainment for the evening.

She began to get into the music, rolling her body and hitting the beat with her hips. She drew one of her hands over her shoulder and down the front of her body as her hips subtly mimicked sex on top. She passed her other hand behind her head, pulling her hair up and adding to the mental picture of anyone watching.

When she wasn't staring at the insides of her eyelids, she tried to keep her eyes on her sadistic prince, but she couldn't help throwing a sidelong look at Finley just as she stroked both hands up her abdomen and skimmed her breasts. He straightened up from leaning on the partition.

Declan had her pegged. She did want to torment Finley and dangle before him what he had been denied—what she had been denied when he'd told her to forget about the two of them ever happening. She glanced at him again and found him staring hard at her from beneath heavily slanted eyebrows.

He had explained everything, but the hurt was still there. All she wanted to do was hurt him right back. As though that were fair or would make the way he had rejected hurt any less.

Then again, she thought as she closed her eyes, *no one forced him to come*. In fact, he had even insisted on it. He had to have known he'd see her dressed up for someone whose hands would go where his couldn't and who would take her home for a real version of what her body imitated on the dance floor. In a few minutes when her date joined her, Finley would see something he really didn't like. Why should she let his presence control her or affect her at all? Why should she let anyone in that club make her feel guilty?

The beat dropped away, echoing slowly toward its end. The crowd cheered the DJ on, begging for the next track. With a small smile, Lily opened her eyes, expecting to see Declan seated on his throne, but it was Finley who filled her vision. Light caught the chain around his neck and made it flash. She only had time to gasp before he stabbed his fingers into her hair, slinked his other arm behind her, and jerked her against him.

"Fi—what are you doing?" She tried squeezing her arms between them, but she was locked in his embrace.

"You're not dancing for him anymore," he growled into her ear. "You're dancing for me."

She had enough height to see Declan over Finley's shoulder and expected her escort to be on his way to stop Finley, but Declan didn't move from his spot on the loveseat. That almost-smile even curled into a smirk. *He wanted this to happen.* And deep down, she wanted it too.

The DJ switched tracks. High-pitched notes gently popped without any bass line to support them. Finley slid one foot between hers and pulled her onto his thigh. His hand in the small of her back slid to her ass and held her in place.

"Put your hands on my shoulders," he ordered in a low voice that rumbled all the way to the juncture of her thighs. *You're going to need something to hold on to.* She eagerly clutched him.

A delicate voice joined the glimmering notes. Finley released her hair. His hand mirrored hers from a moment ago, slowly and purposefully caressing the side of her throat, growing heavier as it passed over her breast. Her lacy, strapless bra had zero padding, and she wondered if he could feel the hard point of her nipple through her satin dress.

Subtle bass notes threaded into the track. Finley splayed his fingers over her breast before sweeping his hand around her side to hold her against him. She felt his warm breath on her neck and the swipe of his freshly shaven cheek. His lips hovered above the love bite she had tried to cover up. She shivered, couldn't suppress a euphoric smile.

The singer's words became pleas, the cadence more frantic as new synth layers and backup vocals joined the melody. Finley rolled his hips into her, which pressed the silent vibe flush against her clit and took all the air from her lungs.

"This is what I like," he said gruffly.

The music swelled. With his hand on her backside, he pulled her toward him as he swiveled his pelvis away. The crowd around them whooped. He pushed his hips into her again and then invited her back. The singer held a long, high note. Hips pushed. A hand invited.

Finally, the crescendo shattered into heavy, seductive beats, and they easily settled into the back-and-forth grind he had started. The carnal motion, the support of his thigh beneath her, and the incomprehensible ecstasy of their bodies in tight sync had her heart beating faster than even the most energetic trance track.

Her eyes closed against the mesmerizing swirl of lights. She adjusted her grip on his shoulders and leaned back, dropping her head and tempting him to take advantage. His arm supported her as he strung open-mouthed kisses across the upper swells of her breasts. Her posture pushed their lower bodies even closer, letting her ride the flex of his hard thigh.

When she pulled herself back up, she made the mistake of meeting his eyes. He was glaring at her, but instead of willing her to look away, his intense gaze demanded she bear witness to the desperate emotion slanting his brows and gnashing his teeth. It was stronger than lust, keener than pain, fiercer than possession. She was terrified of what it meant.

He took his hand off her backside to curl her arms around his neck, bringing their mouths closer. He then smoothed his hands down her sides to rest on her hips. The track returned to the chorus, and without missing a beat, their lower halves found a new variation. She clenched the back of his shirt, not knowing how to cope with the pained awe on his face—or how her heart ached to see it directed at her.

Then her body seized up, and she cried out. Their rhythm faltered. She clutched him close to hide her distress against the curve of his neck. He slid his strong arms around her and put his lips to her ear.

"What's wrong, Monkey? Are you okay?" He rubbed circles in her back, but she couldn't accept his comfort. He wouldn't like what she was about to tell him. She lifted her chin and looked over his shoulder at the VIP section. Declan had vacated the loveseat.

"H-he...oh..." Talking seemed almost impossible while something rubbed and buzzed her clit, especially when grinding against him had already warmed her up. She pulled back to meet his gaze. "He put something in me, and..." Finley stiffened. "And turned it on just now."

She saw rather than heard the expletive he spat, but she couldn't tell if he was angry or aroused—or both. She found out when he planted his hand on her ass and pulled her against his erection.

"I fucking hate that he touched you, but..." he shouted loud enough for her to hear.

Both, then.

"Oh G—" She gasped, writhing in his arms. The vibration had grown stronger. She couldn't help the erotic expression she made as her back arched, her fingers tugging and twisting his shirt. Was she going to orgasm right on the dance floor? Right in front of Finley, surrounded by strangers?

Finley said something, his lips twisted into a snarl, but a complex dubstep track had taken over, and his words didn't reach her ears. He thrust his arm past her, bumping her shoulder. Something soft like clothing brushed her back. Her eyes followed Finley's arm and found his hand fisted in her Dom's blazer.

Declan had come up behind her, had trapped her between them. He gripped her hips and pushed his hard-on against her ass.

"Keep dancing," he ordered. "You're not leaving the floor until he sees you come."

Finley didn't seem as though he'd let go of Declan's blazer, let alone dance with her, but she was past worrying about her surroundings or how in the world her night had come to this. All that mattered was that she had permission to come, and it would be while Finley watched—while two cocks trapped behind clothing fought to get inside her.

With one hand, she reached over her shoulder and pulled Declan closer. With the other, she tugged Finley's hand from her Dom's blazer and placed it on her waist. Confusion muddled his rage.

"Dance with me. Watch me come," she said loud enough for him to hear.

Finley shook his head, incredulous. "I *don't* share."

"He does, and *he* is my Dom." She almost added "tonight," but no, Declan would continue to be her Dom, not just for the evening. "I want to be shared with you." She left Finley's hand on her waist and ran her palm up his chest to grip his shoulder. God, he was so warm.

She began gyrating, giving the men sandwiching her something soft to grind against. Declan quickly fell into the rhythm. Finley hesitated even though his eyelids drooped with desire.

"Please, Finley. Let me have this." *Covet me.* "Let me feel this way."

Chapter Eighteen

Finley flexed his fingers on her waist, and his lustful eyes pleaded. His gaze slid down her writhing body to stare at her thrusting breasts and her rolling pelvis that brushed the front of his tented slacks. He fit himself against her, sliding into place like the last piece of a puzzle.

She closed her eyes and immersed herself in the heady and formerly far-off fantasy of two men who both wanted dominance over her. The reality was unbearably erotic—and they all still had their clothes on. She couldn't imagine what this would be like in the privacy of a bedroom. Sure, as if that would ever happen.

Declan ran his hand up her stomach, over her breast. Finley caressed her arm, shoulder to wrist. Declan slipped his thumb between her lips. She twirled her tongue around the tip and sucked hard. His fingers on her cheek turned her head aside, granting Finley access. She winced, then shivered as Finley gave her a second love bite on the opposite side of her neck as the first.

And all the while, the tickler buzzed and massaged her slick, swollen clit.

Even boosted up by her heels, she was dwarfed by the two men sandwiching her, whose bodies were twin furnaces. The back of Finley's shirt where she had a death grip was damp. Declan's hand on her waist was like a red-hot brand. Every swivel of her hips was a battle to push their cocks away only to feel them push right back, eager to penetrate, sow, and claim. Each forward thrust came with a delicious clench that sent hot shivers through her body.

She couldn't tell anymore who was touching her. Was it Declan sweeping his hands down her sides? Was Finley the one tugging her skirt higher? Hands squeezed and splayed. Lips sucked and nipped at her neck, her ears, and her shoulders. Fingers swiped and pinched her nipples until they throbbed. Both men were so eager that she hardly had to stand on her own.

"Look at him," Declan rasped in her ear.

The vibration grew even stronger. She gasped. Her eyes flew open. She put both hands on Finley. His expression was the same as when she'd watched him stroke his cock, but now it was his turn to watch her. Declan stayed close, one hand clamped onto her hip.

No longer cognizant of anything else, she shamelessly ground against Finley's thigh. Anyone who saw them would have no doubt that she wasn't dancing anymore. The big drop was coming up, and nothing was going to stop her from sliding down the other side. Finley held her gaze, his eyes full of that desperate emotion. Did it show in her eyes too? His lips moved, and though she couldn't hear the words, she knew what they were. *You're mine.*

She held her breath as gravity tugged her into free fall. Her heart pounded. She had been warm before, but now her skin burned. Finley's jaw hinged open with an inaudible groan of approval. His hands on her waist were like vises. She kept her eyes on him as long as she could, but the wash of pleasure pulled her inward to the molten remains of her core. For a few blissful heartbeats, everything was quiet and safe.

The music came roaring back like a tidal wave. Her body convulsed as the vibe hammered on the live wire between her thighs. A couple of seconds later, it turned off.

None of them bothered dancing anymore. Her legs shook. Two sets of hands held her up and pulled her in two different directions.

It hadn't taken much to get his client and her "friend" Finley together on the dance floor and to witness their mutual desire. When he joined them, Finley's jealousy was evident in his scowl and the way he held Jill closer—not to mention the fist on Declan's jacket, primed to shove him back—but his client did the work of soothing the transition. The rest fell neatly into place, as expected.

Declan hit the Off button on the vibe's remote, and his client sagged. He and Finley both slipped an arm around her. Finley's lips flattened. His nose curled. Declan would have to be careful.

"Ladies' room," Declan shouted over the music. Predictably, Finley's concern for Jill overrode his jealousy. One glance at her eased his savage expression and loosened his grasp on her.

Rather than pull his client from Finley's arms, Declan guided her past him to the nearby edge of the dance floor. After a few shaky steps, she was able to walk on her own, but he kept a hand on her back. He knew without looking that her friend was close behind.

It was easily past midnight, and the club was near capacity—if not there already. They made it to the hallway leading back to the entrance, but a seemingly endless stream of people heading the opposite direction slowed their progress to the restrooms. The lights behind the frosted glass shifted from green to red. Something gnawed at him. He could almost feel tiny teeth ripping into his stomach. It made him sick.

He took a deep breath. Everything would be fine—*was* fine. It was just too warm and crowded, too chaotic. His erection didn't help. Never mind all the other times he had brought a client to Reflexxion without ever feeling this...disoriented.

When they reached the ladies' room, he turned Jill toward him. She kept her eyes down, her face angled away. The shells of her ears were red. Her hand covered the side of her neck where she had received another love bite.

"Look at me, pet." He tipped her chin up. She chewed her lip, wrinkled her forehead. Was she angry or sad?

"That was a mistake," she said, rubbing her neck. *Ah, regret.* Clients often felt guilty after indulging their desires. The trick was finding out why.

"I know you enjoyed us," he said in a gentle tone. It would be most disarming.

She winced. "Y-yeah, but I think I just..." She flicked her gaze past him. "Complicated things even more." Finley stood on the other side of the hall next to the men's room entrance. His expression was similarly conflicted, as though he'd decide at any second to screw just standing there.

"Actually, I'd say it simplified things. Wasn't it a fantasy of yours?"

"*God*, yes," she said. "So very yes." Her warm, brown eyes shifted back to him. *Scared eyes. Desperation.* "But what do I do now? I just want to leave." So did he, but the lights wailed *no*.

Stay with the script. Calm her.

"What you'll do now is take a moment for yourself." He discreetly pressed the case into her palm. "You may remove the device. It's yours to keep. I'll meet you out here when you're ready." Jill steadied herself with a deep breath and nodded.

"Yes, Sir." She slipped past a woman leaving the restroom and disappeared behind the privacy wall.

Declan also needed a moment. Too many things bothered him—the lights and the noise, the giddy shake of his fingers, and the unsettling notion that he wasn't simply having an off night. He never had those.

With a swallow, he turned around and passed through a gap in the hallway traffic to the men's room on the other side. Finley stepped forward, his mouth open, but Declan walked right past him into the restroom.

The club's aesthetic continued to assert itself with black tile and steel-gray stalls. Several urinals were in use, but the men's room was silent except for the sound of flushes, footsteps, and faucets. No one so much as glanced at him, but he ducked into a stall to escape notice and locked the door behind him.

He stared at his trembling hands, ran them through his hair. His cock was still too hard for him to use the toilet—not that he felt the urge since he'd already sweated out all the water he'd drunk that evening—but he stood in front of it anyway and stared at the black porcelain as if waiting for it to talk.

Why the gnawing? Why the shaking, the dread, and confusion? His client's wants were clear. She had wanted to goad Finley and get a reaction. He had set up a situation. She had wanted two Doms vying for control over her. He'd helped make it happen.

What his client needed, though, was quite different from her wants. His objective, the purpose of his script, was to recognize such needs and leverage them into as many appointments as possible. She needed her "friend" to dominate her. More than that, she needed permission to submit to him, permission she refused to give herself.

So, he would have to be the one to give her permission.

A loud bang rattled the stall door. He spun around, fear strangling a shout. His foot hit the toilet and his shoulder rammed into the side of the stall. Something floundered against the door, groaned mournfully. He groped for his keys without understanding why.

"Fuck. S-sorry, dude," someone slurred from the other side of the door. Declan looked down. A scuffed pair of Oxfords stumbled away from his stall and into the next one. A retching sound followed.

He closed his eyes, took a deep breath. Just some guy sick on alcohol.

After straightening his jacket, he flushed the unused toilet and left the stall. He couldn't allow his client to emerge from the ladies' room and not find him. He especially couldn't let her friend get to her first, even though doing so would be the most optimal path to retaining her patronage. After all, letting their relationship implode would ensure that she booked future appointments.

But that wasn't what she needed.

Even so, he found himself at the sink instead of in the hall. He held out his palm for an automatic squirt of liquid soap. A stream of pink goo landed in his hand. The colored lights in the bathroom made it darker, redder. He scrubbed his palms together. Rather than foam up, the goo only spread, covering his hands in sticky rust. He stuck his fingers under the faucet. Warm water spilled over his hands and rinsed away the rust, which finally foamed in the sink. Pink bubbles lingered instead of washing down the drain.

He shook the excess water from his fingers and reached for the stack of paper towels. Something caught his eye. He glanced up at his reflection.

A man writhed behind him. A man with no eyes and no mouth. Blood oozed from deep gashes in his cranium. Ran down his empty expression. His jaw opened wide and his hand clawed where his mouth should have been, smearing blood and releasing more as he raked his nails across his face.

Declan jerked around with a shout, scrambled onto the wet counter.

"Whoa, man. Just trying to wash up." A wide-eyed white guy held up his hands as though he was being robbed. Another guy at a urinal looked at him from over his shoulder, having instinctively cringed toward the porcelain fixture.

"Yeah," Declan said after a swallow. "Yeah, sure." The back of his head ached. His heart beat painfully. He eased off the counter but kept his hands clamped onto its edge.

"You trippin', man?" the first man asked while he wetted his hands. He didn't bother with soap. "'Cause I'm thinking of going on a trip myself, y'know? Dispensaries are closed and all, but I got cash." The guy wanted drugs.

"No, I'm not high." *Only crazy.*

"Whatever, dude."

The man didn't believe him, but it was unimportant. Declan turned back to his reflection, which had returned to normal, and grabbed a couple of paper towels.

Was he high? Hallucinating? Had someone slipped something into his water? No one had been loitering close by, but he could have gotten a glass intended for someone else. It would explain his symptoms, though not why they started the moment his client had walked into Sophia's.

No, he was simply unused to his priorities conflicting. While he remained in compliance with his script, which demanded he cater to his client's needs, his actions violated the agency's policies.

Declan tossed the damp paper towels into the trash and smoothed his hair. It stayed in place without fuss. After a tweak, his collar was straight and crisp. He checked his pockets. Everything was in the right place. His erection had abated. By the time he was done, his hands were as steady as a rock.

The hallway was still jammed with people. A distant cheer from the main room said the dance party was going strong. He scanned the hall for his client, but a hand snatched his jacket and his attention.

"You can just head on home without her," his client's friend bit out. "In fact, you can forget you ever met her." *Cannot recover.* Declan blinked at the words in his head.

The direct approach would work best. He had little time.

"Finley, right? Are you saying she should go home with you?" His tone was calm, but his small, confident smile added a dash of derision.

"Damn right," Finley said. "She thinks she's getting what she needs from you, but all she's going to get is a broken heart."

The perfect opening.

"And you've never broken her heart?"

Finley's lips flattened, but he released Declan's blazer.

"Yeah, I have." The admission banked his anger. "I don't know how much she told you, but I know she's making a mistake."

"That's how Jill described what just happened." He jabbed his thumb in the direction of the dance floor before pointing at Finley. "And the word she used for you was 'complicated.'"

Finley crossed his arms. "Jill, huh? Not her real name."

Declan shrugged, knowing his indifference might upset Finley. "Many of my clients use aliases." *At least they think they do.* "It's not surprising."

"Is it surprising that *I* don't know her real name, even though we've known each other for years?" Finley revealed. Declan found the tidbit more useful than surprising. "She's so afraid of trusting anybody—and I only made it worse. I wasn't..."

Finley fell silent. Declan raised his brows to encourage elaboration.

"My ex was also a sub and...I was too much of an amateur to see how fucked up it got. I tried everything, but she almost had me convinced that I was the problem. That ever happen to you?"

"Yeah," Declan said with an understanding nod. A lie to establish rapport. Finley punched his hands into his pockets.

"My confidence was shot after that. When I found out Jill was submissive, I pushed her away."

"Did she know about your ex?" Declan asked.

"I told her earlier tonight."

"Mm, and yet she's here with me." The reminder would stoke Finley's anger.

It almost worked. Finley lifted his chin.

"She deserves to submit to someone who isn't paid to do it. Someone who loves her," he said adamantly. "Complicated is what she needs."

Declan took a mental snapshot of Finley's expression, the union of desire and fear, of tortured elation and pained relief. He didn't understand how Finley felt, but he believed him.

"I agree," Declan said, "which is why you're going to let her leave with me."

As expected, Finley shot him an apocalyptic glare.

"And why would I do that?"

"Because only two people fit in my car," Declan said as a grin split his lips. "And because we should start her off at 'simple' before we get to 'complicated.'"

Chapter Nineteen

Beyond the privacy wall, several women washed their hands or checked their appearance at the sinks along the right side. To the left, a couple of ladies waited for the next available stall, so Lily got in line.

Her legs were shaking. Scratch that, *all* of her was shaking. She hoped her knees didn't give. The floor seemed so far away. Her new hickey was too high up to hide with her hair, so she kept a hopefully nonchalant hand over it. Would someone at the mirror let her borrow some concealer?

God, *why* had she let that happen? Not only the love bite, but the entire bump-and-grind? She was supposed to be laying her failed relationship with Finley to rest, not resurrecting it. And why, if given the chance, would she want it to happen all over again? Only naked, tied down, and blindfolded while they flogged, fucked, and finally forgave her for...well, everything.

A couple of stalls opened up. She was next. Someone got in line behind her and called to a friend at the sinks. They talked loudly to overcome the muffled bass bumping through the walls.

Of all the things she'd expected tonight, being the filling of a Dom sandwich was not one of them. She thanked her lucky stars that nothing violent had happened. She hated even considering that Finley might do something ugly, but until things had shaken out, she'd worried Finley would throw a punch at Declan and be ejected.

She had hoped he would either storm out of the club or simply disappear once the sight of her with someone else had hurt him enough.

Instead, he'd patiently waited and watched for an opportunity. Damn him.

Another stall opened up at the far end of the restroom—about as private as she'd get. The stall doors weren't the type with huge gaps on the sides through which someone might spy a sliver of you doing your business, but she was grateful for one with fewer people walking past it and locked herself in.

It wasn't the same as being alone in her apartment, but the semi-isolation calmed her somewhat. She tossed the vibe's hard plastic case onto the side shelf and leaned back against the cool surface of the tiled wall behind her. It shook in time to the music.

How long could she hide in there before someone dragged her out? Which one would? Of course, neither would trespass into a women's restroom, but whom would she want to drag her out? The simple, safe one who only required money? Or the complicated, dangerous one whose heavy gaze demanded her heart and soul?

She wanted to give in to that demand, *needed* to give in, but if she opened up her life to him, he'd only reject her all over again—maybe not at first, but someday. She couldn't take that risk, couldn't relinquish control when she didn't know if he'd keep her heart as safe as her body. Declan was clearly the better choice. With him, everything was on her terms, down on her level.

Yet when she closed her eyes and pulled up her skirt, she pictured Finley in her mind. His shirt that clung to his slim waist and stretched across his broad shoulders. His parted lips that made her long for a soul-searing kiss. His hot stare that looked at her as if she were the only other person in the world. What had happened between them on the dance floor should have been a tall glass of water for someone dying of thirst, but it had been only a splash on the lips that had her opening her mouth for more.

Her new love bite ached sweetly. Would it be even darker than the other one he'd put on her? It certainly hurt more. She palmed her breast and bit back a moan. He *had* felt her nipple through her dress, just as she could feel it now, still pert and a little tender from being plucked by two sets of hands.

She slipped her other hand under her skirt, ran her fingers over the damp crotch of her panties, and cupped herself. Her vagina was plump, ready to be used—ready for him. Had he felt the buzz of the vibrator against his leg? He must have. He had been gripping her so close. Only one way to find out.

With her skirt bunched up, she reached for the vibe's case. It opened with a soft creak. Inside was a drawstring pouch in which to store the case. Gold lettering under the lid admitted the device had been manufactured in Thailand. The case doubled as the vibe's charging station, but she found no charging cord, no instructions, and no remote. The first two were probably in the car, and the remote was undoubtedly still in Declan's pocket.

Right, Declan decided when the vibe turned on. He was her Dom. He was invited, and Finley was the party crasher. Submitting to Finley came at a higher price than she was willing to pay. And what the hell was she doing, rubbing one out in a club's bathroom? No more alcohol tonight—or Dom sandwiches ever. They both led to bad decisions.

Lily left the case open and set it on top of the bag. She wasn't keen on washing the vibe in full view of a handful of strangers, even if it turned out to look like a weird bracelet or something, so she snapped off some toilet paper in which to wrap it temporarily and drew down her panties.

Her fingers easily found the vibe's fulcrum below the massage pad clasped against her clitoris. A squeeze of the prongs let her have her first look at what had driven her insane moments ago. The pink device—of course it was pink—was shaped like a curved clothespin, one prong far shorter than the other. It glistened, but not because of its material.

She wrapped it up to be thoroughly washed later, crammed the wad of tissue into the case, and dropped the case into the drawstring bag. She then sat to relieve herself.

"Oh. My. *God.* Did you see those guys?"

"I hope they're not here with dates." Two women's voices echoed above the clip-clop of their shoes and the bang of two stall doors.

"Or here with each other," the first woman said suggestively. A flush and the slam of another door drowned out the second woman's reply, but Lily heard something like "also sexy."

"The way they were arguing, I bet they're fighting over a girl," the first woman said. Were they talking about Finley and Declan? Shit, of course they were. Lily finished up and hurriedly tugged her clothes back in place.

The second woman groaned with frustration. "I should be so lucky."

Lucky? It was awful!

"Maybe they're breaking up," the first woman said. "I wouldn't mind being a rebound."

"Wait, breaking up with each other or a girl?" the second one asked.

"Kayla, if they were gay, how could I be a rebound?" the first one scoffed.

"Well, the one who doesn't get the girl can come home with me."

"Ooh, but which one?"

"Doesn't matter. They're both hot."

Lily grabbed the drawstring pouch and threw the latch to her stall just as the women's laughter died down. Though she wanted to rush into the hallway and make sure no one's nose was bleeding, she hit up the sinks and jabbed her hands under a faucet. A few soap suds later, her hands were clean—and still wet, but she didn't care.

She exited the restroom expecting the worst, but no one was swinging his fist nor were any bouncers breaking up a fight. Declan was alone. He crossed the hallway when he spotted her.

"Good to go?" he asked. That not-yet-a-smile was back on his face.

Shaking her hands to dry them, she looked left toward the entrance, then right toward the main room, but Finley was nowhere to be seen. Was he waiting outside?

"Where's Finley?"

"He left."

She froze for a second, her mouth open. *"Left?"*

His expression didn't budge. "Yes, so there's no need to end our evening early." He swept his arm out. "Do you want to go back to the dance floor? Or maybe another drink?"

She shook her head, but not in response to his question. "He...he didn't talk to you? Some women in the bathroom were saying a couple guys out here were arguing."

Declan moved her closer to the wall. "Yes, he confronted me. I informed him of your preferences, and then he left."

Her lungs shrank. "Wh...what did you say to him?"

"That you had hoped our display would discourage him, you regretted dancing with him, and didn't want a public scene. Was that inaccurate, pet?"

She took a deep breath. No, that wasn't inaccurate. In fact, it was dead accurate. She had said all those things.

"No, but..." But what? She had gotten what she wanted, hadn't she?

"You look disappointed," he observed.

She was. Extremely so. But she didn't quite know why. Did she mourn the relationship they'd never have? The one she had sabotaged beyond repair? Or was she disappointed that Finley had given up after all he had done to get her back, despite her lies and her weaknesses? Was she crushed to know his limit? To know she had pushed him past that limit?

"I wanted to know if he and I could still be friends." She grimaced at the excuse. She and Finley had walked past the point of no return together. That she had ever thought they could go back to how things used to be...

Declan slowly shook his head. "I don't think so."

She sagged against the wall, let out a sigh. So, that was it. Finley was gone, and she'd never see him again, never talk to him again. Tears prickled, but she blinked them back. She wouldn't cry about what she had done willfully. All she could do was make sure she got the punishment she deserved.

"Sir?"

"What is it, pet?"

"I'd like to go home with you now."

He smirked. "Let's get your coat." He placed his hand in the small of her back and guided her upstream to the club entrance. He then left her in line at the coat check while he went ahead to the valet.

She followed the person in front of her on autopilot. When a club employee called her up, she merely nodded at whatever question they asked and held out her wrist for the attendant to snip off the disposable band. A minute later, she put on her coat and grabbed the rest of her things.

Outside was cooler, wetter, and blissfully quieter if no less luminescent thanks to a façade that wouldn't be out of place on the Las Vegas Strip. She spotted Declan right away but glanced around for another tall male form, perhaps passing under the lights in the parking lot or getting into a cab. She didn't see him. A deep breath did nothing to ease the pressure on her chest as she approached her escort, who tucked her against his side while they waited for his car to pull up.

"I have quite a night planned for you," he whispered in her ear. She gripped her clutch against her thighs, her nails digging into the beaded satin.

A valet attendant returned with the car and shielded her with an umbrella as she slid into the passenger seat. After handing over a tip, Declan quickly strode around the car to the open driver's-side door. Within a minute, they were on the main road that led straight to his apartment.

Lily couldn't wait. The sooner she was bound, the sooner she'd get her well-deserved punishment.

"Are you nervous?" he asked in the quiet dark of the car's interior. The blue glow of the dashboard put his impassive face in unsettlingly harsh relief.

"Why do you ask?"

"You're fidgeting."

She was. Her hands ceased immediately. "I'm just impatient."

A wicked smile lifted his mouth. "So am I."

Not for much longer. He'd take her into his bedroom and tie her to that bench to play with her. Looking out the window, she tried to think of that—how much it would hurt. The physical pain would separate her, if only for a short time, from everything else that hurt. She wouldn't see that look of longing on Finley's face whenever she closed her eyes, wouldn't remember everything she'd done to reject him.

Declan pulled over in front of a familiar building that had no name beyond its street number. The absence of a sidewalk sign advertising amenities had nothing to do with a lack of vacancies and everything to do with who lived there. The secured entrance requiring either a key fob or a numeric code now made sense in a way that made her stomach churn. No visitors were allowed except those whom the escorts accompanied.

Lily unfastened her seat belt and reached for the door handle.

"Not yet," Declan said.

She hissed in frustration. "Why?"

Still wearing his seat belt, he turned to her and propped his arm on the steering wheel. Light from the building illuminated the lower half of his face, stopping right below his eyes. The only hint of any emotion was how deeply he breathed.

"You're getting fucked tonight," he said. She pressed deeper into her seat. "Inside that room, you'll get what you want and what you don't want to need. Before I send the car away, I want you to understand that."

He was giving her one last out.

"If you have any reservations," he continued, "I can take you home right now—or somewhere else, if you prefer. You'll get most of your money back."

Somewhere else. He meant he'd take her to Finley's, even though he'd lose the money tucked into his blazer.

She looked down at her hands twisting together on her lap. Was he trying to talk her out of this? Did she seem that uncertain? True, he had quite a personal stake in making sure she fully consented—in making sure she *knew* she was consenting to anything listed on her profile, but he was protecting her as much as himself.

Even if she never loved him the way... It was enough that he cared for her as much as their relationship allowed. *It will have to be enough.* The emotional distance between them meant she wouldn't have to fear his rejection. Her heart was the hard limit he'd never touch.

She raised her eyes. "I understand, Sir. Let's go inside."

Declan was silent for a brief moment. Then he nodded. "I'll come around to help you out."

He used the touch screen on the center console to select a disembarkation interval and release the car for the night. He then walked around to her side. Drops of rain on his clothes twinkled in the streetlight as he leaned down to offer her his hand. She took it and got out. Just as the sports car pulled away from the curb to return itself to its designated parking lot, Declan tapped his key fob at the building entrance.

When called, the elevator opened immediately. His hand trembled when he chose a floor. Was he that excited? Her pulse also raced. Though she had submitted to Declan before, it was still new and thrilling and terrifying. Unlike last time, though, she had little to no idea what he'd do to her. She knew what her profile said, but a significant number of things fell within the *haven't tried* column...as well as the *want to be forced* column.

Would he use straps? Metal cuffs? Would he blindfold her? Which of his implements would he be swinging? What kind of marks would he leave on her? Would he force her orgasm or deny it until she was reduced to begging?

By the time the elevator opened again, her skin buzzed with anticipation. She didn't jump when he slid his arm behind her, but her heart hammered just as hard as it had the first time she'd walked to his apartment door.

He slid his key into the lock, turned it. After flipping the light switch and shutting the door behind them, he slipped off her coat and hung it on a hook. She set her things on the entry table.

"Shoes off, Sir?" she asked.

"Yes, but nothing else." He pulled out his phone and tapped the screen a few times before returning it to his pocket. Stepping out of her heels, she eyed the roll of his immense shoulders as he shucked his blazer, which he hung next to her coat.

"Did you get a chance to wash your new toy?" He drew a small remote from the blazer's pocket.

"No, Sir. The sinks were crowded, and..."

"And what?"

And I worried someone would see what I was washing. "I was in a hurry to check on you."

His smile rose on a rumble of amusement. "Go wash it now, but be quick."

She pulled the vibe's case out of the drawstring bag and took it to the bathroom. After chucking the tissue into the trash, she thoroughly rinsed the pink clothespin and patted it dry with a spare hand towel she found under the sink. When she reemerged, Declan handed her the remote, which fit into a slot in the case's lid. She put it back with the rest of her things, and he checked his phone again. Was he waiting for a message?

"Follow me." He didn't bother with small talk or offer a nightcap, didn't hold her hand to lead her to his playroom. She was there for submission, punishment, and sex—not romance.

In his bedroom, a couple of things seemed to have been shifted around. The bondage bench was still in the same spot as it was bolted to the floor, but leaning against the wall-mounted restraining board was something new—a tall object under a black sheet.

Declan approached his collection of toys and opened his arm to her. She brushed her fingers over the bench as she passed it. He stood her in front him, facing the wall, and wrapped his hands around her shoulders.

"Nothing here has been reused. It's all new for your safety, but I know how to use everything you see here," he said.

"Yes, Sir." Her gaze drifted over paddles, floggers, crops, and straps, all of various lengths and hardness.

"Some can cut the skin if I want them to. Some bruise. Some leave only a deep ache. Even with the same stroke, no two implements hurt the same way."

"Yes," she whispered.

"What some subs receive only for serious punishment is what other subs request when they've been good. Let's see if we can find which one puts the fear in you."

Her stomach clenched. She knew he would immediately end the scene if she was in danger, if she really couldn't take any more, but she also knew he'd go as far as possible. He enjoyed her cries of pain. Begging and tears wouldn't stop him. Only the safe word would.

"You may take first pick," he said, nuzzling her hair. "I decide the rest."

She softly whined, grinding the ball of her foot into the carpet. She knew exactly which one to choose and reached for the flogger she had ogled the last time she was in that room. She touched the wide, supple falls. Swung gently, it would feel quite pleasurable. Hard swings would hurt something awful, but not nearly as much as some of the other toys in front of her.

"Mm, this'll be a good warm-up." Declan caressed her extended arm as he reached past her to grasp the flogger's silver handle.

Oh God. If the flogger was a warm-up, the main act would leave her sobbing. He stepped away.

"Stand there," he said, pointing at the open space between the bench and the bed. "Hands at your sides. Eyes on the floor." All emotion had left his tone. She did as ordered and turned toward the bench.

"No," he said. "Face the bed and take a step toward it."

She made an about-face, her lips pressed together. Though the bed held plenty of possibilities, the bench had been in her fantasies all week.

While she was turned away, he busied himself with preparations behind her. A drawer opened and shut. She heard the whoosh of slick fabric and realized he had pulled the black sheet from the object it covered. She was tempted to sneak a peek, but he'd certainly catch her and she'd certainly be punished for it. She already had enough punishment coming her way.

Declan came up behind her.

"Strip," he commanded. "All of it. Keep your eyes on the floor."

As she took a bracing breath and brought her hands to her hips, she mentally reminded herself not to rush it this time. She stroked her fingers up her sides and strained for the zipper tab at the top of her dress. She'd give him her body and surrender control with every piece of clothing—but only her body. What he did with it would quiet her mind and absolve her misdeeds but leave her heart untouched. She jutted one hip and slowly drew the tab down. *Traitor.*

No, she was just bones and flesh now. A small undulation shook the dress from her body. *Don't think.* Her bra followed. She tucked her fingers into her panties and peeled them off the way he liked.

He made a strange, choked sound as he came closer. She straightened with an involuntary jerk, heard his shallow breaths. His warm fingers explored her tattoo.

Show me your ink. It's on your back, right?

Tears stabbed her eyes, so she shut them tight. *Stop thinking of him.* Something touched her face, and she flinched.

"Shh, it's just a blindfold," Declan said. Mindful of her hair, he pulled the elastic strap behind her head and adjusted the fit. Though she didn't have permission, she touched the material over her eyes. Rather than a scarf or a sleeping mask, it was a specially made fetish product. A firm leather face maintained its shape. Extra padding around the nose prevented her from peeking through any gaps.

"Hands down," he warned.

She dropped her arm just as she heard the unmistakable sound of rope spooling onto the floor. Her mouth went dry.

"Cross your arms behind your back, but stay relaxed." Once she complied, he passed a loop of rope around her forearms. "Plenty of time later to fight back."

The loop locked into place. He yanked the excess around her chest, capturing her upper arms against her sides. Staying relaxed quickly became difficult. Her skin flushed even as an icy finger jabbed into her navel. The impulse to resist warred with her desire to surrender to her Dom's care.

After knotting the rope behind her, he passed the lead around her front again, this time below her breasts. He worked quickly and without hesitation, pausing only to smooth the bindings across her chest or to slide his finger underneath to ensure the rope wouldn't cut off her circulation.

Extra rope still hung from the stem of knots against her back when his arms encased her, hauled her around, and compelled her forward, away from the bed. The front of her legs touched something. Cool vinyl. He gripped the back of her neck and bent her over. Her legs tensed. She instinctively tried to raise her arms but couldn't, and her upper body met the bench's padded surface.

She couldn't hold back the little gasps and groans he wrested from her—didn't even try. She needed her punishment even more than she feared it. To be with someone who understood, to be moments from the emotional release...

Declan tossed the excess rope past her head and rounded the bench. Several fingers of rope compressed her right shoulder as he tied the excess to one of the restraint rings. Her neck ached, so she laid her cheek on the vinyl and tilted her chin down so her cheekbone didn't hang off the edge of the bench. Declan went to her other side and tied down her left shoulder.

Once he tied the last knot, she tested her new restraints. The two lengths of rope over her shoulders kept her bent. She tried to squeeze the bands of rope around her chest up toward her shoulders by widening her elbows, but cinches under her arms kept them firmly in place, which kept her upper arms snug to her sides, preventing her from pulling her wrists free of the cinch around her forearms.

She was well and truly secured, even comfortable, and could remain as she was for a while—more than enough time for a thorough disciplining.

His measured footsteps circled her. She drew her feet together and softened her knees in a vain attempt to protect her sit spot, but he trailed his fingers along that sensitive flesh as he passed behind her.

"Mm, almost ready."

She heard him somewhere behind her but couldn't tell what he was up to.

"Gags are out," he said as he placed something on the bench next to her, "so you'll only speak if asked a direct question or if using your safe word. Tonight, you're just our little toy. Do you understand, pet?"

Her heart kicked hard. *Our?* Was he messing with her again? "Yes, Sir."

He walked away. The bed creaked. Then nothing. For a moment, she listened for any clues, but the room remained silent. What was he doing? Sitting there staring at her privates? Her ass was pointed right at the bed. What was he waiting for? Why weren't they starting?

It was a mind game. Had to be. She had said she was interested in them, but she wanted him to scare her, not annoy her.

"Sir?" she called.

"Quiet," he said harshly. "Do that again, and I'll put the flogger back on the wall."

She frowned, knowing he couldn't see it. She had to be patient. Soon enough, watching her would become either boring or not enough. It wouldn't be long until she heard him get up. Until then, she experimented with the position in which he had restrained her. She tried shifting her body back to twist out from under the pair of ropes holding her shoulders down but didn't have enough slack. Her hands didn't have the angle to protect even a small section of her vulnerable backside.

What was the point of keeping her waiting? He wasn't billing her by the hour. He knew she was anxious to be punished. As she couldn't speak, she stomped her foot and tugged hard on her restraints.

"Patience, pet," he said. "We're almost there."

Almost where?

A knock sounded on his front door. Not a polite rapping of knuckles but three heavy strikes that demanded entrance. Her head popped up and turned toward it.

"Right on time." She heard Declan get up and then the clack of his shoes on the hardwood floor of the main room. She squirmed in her restraints. Half-formed thoughts cascaded through her mind, rose to the top of her throat.

Who was—delivery? What the hell did—why would he think she'd—what could possibly...? She didn't want anyone to see. They'd be shocked. Who wouldn't be? They'd definitely...but what if it wasn't delivery? Earlier, he'd said...

Had to be. He planned for another man to walk into that room, see her tied up and—God, could she do this? Take...two men at once? But the price doubled if... She hadn't paid for two and certainly couldn't afford it. Who in the world—

You'll get what you want.

No. No, it couldn't be. He had given up on her. He hated her.

And what you don't want to need.

He couldn't be here.

Her heartbeat was almost deafening, but she laid her other cheek on the bench and tried to be quiet so she could distinguish the sounds coming from the front door. The lock jumped open. The handle turned.

"Come in. She's ready for you." That icy finger wiggled inside her navel.

The door shut, and the dead bolt reengaged. Deep voices conferred at too low a volume for her to parse the words. Then two sets of heavy footsteps approached, sending tiny shockwaves through the floor to her bare soles, growing louder and suddenly quieting as they entered the carpeted room.

She lifted her head and held her breath. The room was so still that she felt as though she was the only one in there, but she knew she wasn't alone. She could *feel* the second man's presence the way one could feel the position of the sun in the sky. It filled the room, stretched the walls.

The man stepped closer, groaning from the back of his throat. She involuntarily tensed as if to stand, but no way would she manage it. The man drew nearer, his slow approach betrayed by the faint crush of carpet beneath his shoes. A warm hand settled on her back, drawing a soft cry from her. The newcomer explored the nylon strands holding her in place.

"You want this. Don't you, pet?" Declan asked from somewhere near the door. "Just call out a color."

She writhed under the silent man's slow, deliberate touch. He had yet to identify himself, so she hesitated to answer Declan's question. If it *was* who she thought it was, she had to stop the scene. Seeing her like this was bad enough, and if they went any further...

"What color?" Declan asked. The hand stroked lower, passing over the left globe of her rear and slowly advancing down the back of her thigh. Then it was just the tips of his fingers. They turned inward and slid between her thighs to the springy hair covering her mound.

"Monkey." That throaty whisper started a riot in her. Heat bloomed on her skin, pooled between her legs. With a needy cry, she straightened her knees, rose on tiptoe, and offered her pussy to her new Dom to do with as he liked.

"Green, Sirs," she moaned.

Chapter Twenty

"Come in," Declan said with a conspiratorial smirk that Finley didn't like. "She's ready for you."

Don't you mean ready for us? Finley thought.

From the entrance, he spotted two coats hanging next to each other. Monkey's heels were neatly tucked against the wall. She was definitely in the apartment, which looked more like a hotel room than a residence, but he didn't see her in the orderly living room behind Declan. He clenched his hands and checked both ends of the empty hallway. He let his fingers go loose. Clenched them again. He then stepped past the escort, who closed and locked the door behind him.

Shit, what was he doing here? What if he couldn't get into it? It was one thing to shadow another Dom and feel his own palm prickle with every slap to the sub's reddening backside, but to participate in a threesome or even lead one?

It wasn't just himself he was worried about. Though Monkey had been hot for two Doms on the dance floor, that didn't translate to wanting the same in a private setting, and even if Declan hadn't told him that she regretted what had happened at the club, the look on her face afterward in the hall was clear enough. That had hurt—a lot—but here he was anyway, following his foolish heart and the advice of a stranger.

"She's in the bedroom," Declan said quietly. Finley unzipped his coat. "We're playing with the stoplight rule, and I've set out a few things. She knows not to speak unless asked a direct question."

Finley matched his volume. "What have you told her?"

"Nothing."

He paused in the middle of taking off his coat and stared at the escort's inexplicably calm expression. "So she doesn't know it's me?"

"She didn't know someone was joining us until you knocked."

"Jesus," he said after a beat. "I thought you were going to explain."

That smirk reappeared. "She wants two men to use her. She simply didn't know it would happen tonight."

With a fresh knot in his stomach, Finley turned to hang his coat. Cluttering the nearby side table was a small purse, an umbrella, and a white plastic case. Monkey's things. A slot on the side of the case held a small remote. Was that what Declan had used?

"And if she doesn't want me here?"

No, that wasn't the question he was going to ask. He wanted to know her limits and her desires—the things they had never discussed because he ejected her from his apartment rather than face his fear of those desires being turned against him. He couldn't trust his intuition to tell him when he was going too far or when she couldn't handle any more.

"You know she does," Declan said. "Otherwise you wouldn't be here." He turned and led the way to the bedroom, but Finley lingered. Clench, relax, clench. He snatched up the case and followed the escort.

The door to the bedroom stood open. Gray, low-pile carpeting. Black walls. On a high shelf, he spied a couple of gimp hoods next to an ominous, long-beaked mask plague doctors would've worn. The escort went in first, his broad back blocking the rest of the room until he moved to one side and remained by the door.

Finley stopped at the threshold. He forgot how to walk forward, how to breathe or blink. If someone had told him the building was on fire, he wouldn't have budged an inch.

He expected to find Monkey lying on a narrow bed and restrained to the headboard in cheap handcuffs. Instead, it was Christmas Morning. His cock punched the front of his slacks. The beast inside him roared.

As though she had heard it, Monkey raised her head, listening because she couldn't see. Black rope masterfully restrained her naked form to a custom-made table and in a position ideal for punishment. Coils of her dark hair spilled across her upper back. An elegant, modified box-tie kept her bent at the waist. Then there was the most beautiful ass he'd ever seen—high and round with just enough meat to fill his hands. Her close stance and soft knees hid her pussy.

A towel, a squeeze bottle, and several condom packets sat on the open space to her right. On her other side lay a flogger. A full-length mirror leaned against a padded board two paces in front of her.

With a rough groan, he drew closer. She tensed. Her bonds constricted, digging into her slim arms. That shiny black rope creaked with strain, and the sound made his heart leap. He didn't stop, only approached more slowly, never taking his eyes off her, not even to put the plastic case on the folded towel next to her. He reached for her and barely heard her gasp at the touch of his fingers.

Damn, still just as soft. She probably thought he didn't know much about her besides the nonintimate, what's-your-favorite-color stuff, but he knew she used the kind of lotion that came in little tubs. He'd sometimes seen the jar in her hands. Once, while they'd been catching up on each other's day just after their call started, he'd watched her shifting shoulders as she rubbed it onto her bare legs off-camera. It had been real fun trying to filter what was coming out of his dry mouth.

He wanted to sink his fingers into her satiny skin, reacquaint his nerve endings with the shape of her waist and the cushion of her backside, but when he fully laid his palm on her back, she went stiff. His heart rammed into his throat. He almost yanked his hand away as if she were a hot stove, certain she would call out her safe word and declare him unfit to wield a whip.

But...the captivation on her face when they'd danced together, her complete abandon when he and the escort had sandwiched her, and the way her eyes had held his for as long as possible before closing in ecstasy...

Keeping his touch tender, he used one hand to roll the strands of rope down and see their transient indentations in her flesh. They'd be gone long before she fell asleep tonight, preferably on top of him, but the marks he wanted to leave on her beautiful backside would last for days—and his claim on her heart would be as permanent as her tattoo.

The escort asked for a color, a signal that she was good to go, but she didn't answer. Finley looked at her face in the mirror. Shallow furrows creased her forehead. Bright red saturated her cheeks like old-school rouge.

Watching her reflection, he dragged his fingers over one luscious buttock and skimmed that tender area where most of her weight rested when she sat. She jerked her head up, and the tendons in her neck stood out. He found the start of her neatly trimmed bush and had to fight off the urge to keep going, to drench his fingers in her honey. She gave a tiny, desperate squeak.

Declan asked his question again, but she remained silent. Why didn't she answer? Had she guessed he was the one touching her? Was that why she grimaced and held back her consent? Would she otherwise let another man touch her this way, sight unseen?

Finley ground his teeth. He needed to know. Before anything else happened, she had to submit to *him* and surrender herself to the only punishment she had coming—that which *he* doled out.

Though it wasn't a real name any more than Jill was, he spoke the alias by which only he knew her. It came out harsher than he intended, but it got an instant reaction.

"Green, Sirs," she burst out as though clamoring for the teacher to call on her first. She rolled up to the balls of her feet, tilting forward and straining to arch her back.

His erection kicked against the already strained material of his pants.

Oh. Fuck. Me. She knew he stood behind her and was suddenly eager to obey. How long had he wanted her like this, to see her truly submit? How many times, how many scenarios? If the sight of her wasn't so damned engrossing, he would've thrown his head back in triumph.

After fantasizing about this moment for so long—endless iterations of how he'd tie her, spank her, tease and arouse her, how many orgasms he'd force on her or deny her— he almost didn't know where to start. Almost.

First, inspection.

"That's a good girl," he said as he brought his hands to her hips. The bedroom door quietly shut as he sat on his haunches behind her and got an up-close look of her thighs bracketing a vagina plump with fragrant arousal.

"Oh, baby," he whispered. The first and only time he'd had her in his bed, he had taken his time. He had let her get used to being naked and vulnerable with him even though he had wanted immediate and complete access to her body. The line of consent had been too vaguely drawn, and he hadn't wanted to cross it.

But this time, the rules were set, and the line was clear.

He gripped her cheeks and pulled them apart. That delicious scent grew stronger. Her restraints creaked. He delicately parted her inner lips, and his knees almost hit the floor. He swallowed hard at the sight of the smooth, pink flesh glistening between his thumbs. Christ, his heart was choking him. He wanted to mold his lips around the engorged, plum-red clit nestled inside and let her use his mouth as a sex toy.

But if he did that now, he wouldn't stop until she came on his tongue. Then he'd want to feel her pussy gripping his fingers, then clamping down on his cock. Then he'd start all over. He'd make her come until she forgot her own name.

"Shall we begin?" the escort asked from over his shoulder.

Finley blinked and came back to reality. He wanted to ignore the question—to ignore Declan entirely and demote the escort to voyeur, but that meant ignoring Monkey's desires, and for what?

He had told Monkey he didn't share because *he* wanted to be the one deciding with whom and when to share his submissive, if ever. He wanted the power to permit another Dom into their scene, not the permission to join—and especially not from a man she paid. Her trust granted that power. That night at his place, she had cautiously offered him that trust, but he had failed to recognize how anxious and vulnerable she felt. He had failed *her*. Knowing that his fuckup had sent her to another Dom for some of her firsts made the beast inside him pace and toss and paw.

The only thing getting in the way of tonight's scene was his pride. Sharing her was far better than not having her at all, and if tonight was another chance to claim her as his own, to make up for his mistakes, then his pride could stand a hit. Besides, there was no way in hell he'd walk away from her now. He wouldn't just surpass Declan. He'd supplant him entirely with *his* voice, *his* touch.

He gestured at the vibe with his chin.

"Let's start with that."

Declan grimaced but laughed.

"Ooh, you just might be crueler than me." He opened the case, and Finley instantly recognized the hot-pink device inside.

"Switch with me," Finley said roughly. The vibe made a sucking sound as the escort pulled it from its molded base.

"Why start with this?" Declan asked as he handed over the vibe. He took Finley's place behind Monkey and parted her flesh. Finley was starting to see the benefit of having an extra pair of hands.

"Before I met Monkey in person, my only image of her was sitting at her desk on the other side of a webcam," he said. Though Declan had asked the question, Finley watched his sub in the mirror.

"I wanted to fuck her in that chair," Finley uttered, "bent over that desk." He heard a small moan, but Monkey had hidden her face against her shoulder.

"Mm, she liked hearing that," Declan said. "Her pussy tightened up."

She'll like the sound of this, too.

"I wanted to be in her head while she touched herself in my place, to tell her all the things I would do to her and make her want the real thing. I even thought about sending her one of those Internet-enabled sex toys." He had bookmarked the exact brand of vibe in his hand one late, lonely night several weeks ago, even before he'd asked Monkey out to lunch. Its short-range remote didn't fit the bill, but he kept it in mind, just in case. A firm pinch opened the vibe's asymmetrical prongs.

"I knew precisely how I wanted her to sit so that I could see everything." The vibe's remote came out of the case with a dull snap. He gave the buttons a quick once-over. "I'd tell her what to do with her new toy while I controlled it remotely. I'd decide when she came, down to the second."

Back at the club, when he learned that someone else possessed that kind of control over her, he hadn't been able to help his furious resentment or his arousal. Even now, he could feel a damp spot of precum on his boxer-briefs, and his dick felt as big and stiff as his forearm.

"I didn't use to mix pain and pleasure," he said, "but that's where she left me, trapped between the two. That's where we'll trap her." With Declan's hands spreading her open, Finley easily slid the vibe between her slick folds. Her despondent cry made his cock jump.

"That's where we'll see the real Monkey," he whispered. He lightly stroked the remote's wheel, setting it to its lowest power level. One button push would turn it on. "And when she finally appears, I'll let her come."

Declan took his hands off Monkey and stood. Shit, the escort was also hard.

"What are we punishing her for?" Declan asked.

Finley split his attention between the woman bent over the table and her reflection. "Where do I even begin?" he mused. "It's such a long list."

"She lied about her name," Declan said.

"Yes, she's a liar," Finley said, low and clear. "She didn't hesitate even a second when she told me her name was Jill. I believed her when she said she forgot about our last call because of work, but she was actually with you." She curled the fingers of her right hand. Her shoulders tensed. "If she had come up with another lie fast enough, I wouldn't have even found that out."

Her deception hurt even more than her submission to another Dom—though that also hurt a fuck-ton—but the more he encountered her lies, the more he realized she used them to keep him at a distance.

"What's that old saying? Something about cake," Finley said.

"Having your cake and eating it too," Declan supplied.

"Right, so on top of being a liar, she's selfish," he said. "She wants the fantasy without the reality. It can look right and sound right and feel right, but it's just as artificial as one of those Eidolons." In the mirror's reflection, Declan's head snapped to one side. He'd hit a nerve, apparently.

"She thinks she's being smart," he continued, "but she's really a coward. She's got it in her head that wanting to submit is a flaw, something she has to hide. She hid a lot of things about herself." Monkey stifled a sob, but he couldn't spare her feelings on this. Not tonight. Not here.

Finley positioned himself on her right and gestured for Declan to mirror him on her left. He scrubbed the palm of his left hand against his pants, but the itch there only grew.

"She'd rather tell herself she can only sate her need with someone like you than admit she deserves someone like me," he said. "She'd rather settle for empty, anonymous sex than open her life to someone who cares for her. She's a lying, selfish coward, but her biggest sin is thinking I'd let her have anything less than she deserves."

He raised his hand. "Or that I would give up on having what's mine."

Without prompting, Declan did the same. Together they swung and squarely smacked both sides of her ass. Her head popped up, and her mouth formed a perfect *O*. She made a sort of inward shriek, more surprised than hurt.

Turning the vibe on got him a new expression. Her jaw softened, jutted forward a little. The heat of that first hit seemed to mingle with the pleasant sensations from the vibe, turning her minor pain into something more, something better. God, she responded just how he had imagined.

"A little harder," he said.

Their hands came down again. She jerked, and her lips puckered with a silent *ooh*. He didn't wait for the pain to melt and kept spanking her, slow and even at first, then faster. Declan had no trouble staying in sync. She didn't cry out, but her teeth were gritted by the time they paused. Her ass had already turned a beautiful pale pink. He wanted to rub her abused flesh, but it was too early in her punishment for that much reward. Instead, he waited for her shoulders to relax. Her head sagged, and she gave a breathy little moan as though the fire had just caught. *Christ, baby.*

"Harder," he choked out.

He turned the vibe's dial up a notch, and they laid into her. Her flesh shivered under the impact. He couldn't see her face, but she gasped with every hit. By the time he gave her another break, his pulse was spinning through his head, and the nerves in his palm buzzed. She unclenched her body with a groan—a damn sexy one. Her thighs pressed and rubbed together, making her ass wiggle. He turned the vibe up another notch.

"Harder."

The first strike made her throw her head back with a startled yelp. His eyes darted to her reflection. The blush on her cheeks couldn't compare to the increasingly angry red of her backside, and her open-mouthed grimace would stay that way. The real spanking had begun. Each blow rammed her against the cushioned table and pried out a scream of alarm. God, her creamy skin brightened up so nicely. He splayed his fingers for a couple of hits and could make out where some of his fingers had landed.

Panting, he glanced at the mirror again to watch her flinch but caught his own expression just as their hands hit with a loud, resounding crack. Her restraints creaked. Her shout came out shaky and hoarse.

He froze. He had never really seen himself during a scene. Christ, he looked—*felt*—powerful and terrifying. Sadistic. Monkey slumped onto the table as he met Declan's watchful gaze. The escort's expression was unreadable beyond the creases between his eyebrows and his fast, shallow breaths. He waited for Finley's next move.

Finley's gut told him she could and should take more—a lot more—but what if his gut was wrong? What if he went too far, had done so already? A newer sub like Monkey probably wanted it to stop, but did she want to use her safe word? Was he hurting her in a way that only made things worse instead of making them better?

Declan glanced at Monkey and nodded. Did he also think she was still good to go? The escort pinched the material of his shirt and mouthed a word. *Red.* He then touched Finley's shirt. *Green.* He nodded at Monkey again.

Just ask her, Finley realized, but could he trust her answer? Would she look at him with regret afterward the way she had at the club and call it a mistake? Midge popped into his head unbidden.

No, she and Monkey were alike in some ways, but that wasn't one of them. Monkey hadn't blamed him for what they did on the dance floor, for liking it. She'd blamed herself. But she understood power exchange, knew her responsibility. At his apartment earlier, she'd red-lighted what was happening in his dining room.

God, if she hadn't—if instead she had let herself have what she deserved, what she needed—her punishment wouldn't have been nearly as severe as it was about to become.

Monkey moaned, and he realized he had been rubbing and stroking her burning skin. Her back arched. Her moans grew higher, shorter. He took his hand from her and turned off the vibrator. She went quiet and still. Her foot stomped the carpet, and she jerked against her restraints with an angry grunt. Finley felt a smile curl his lips and smacked her ass again—hard. Her tantrum ceased immediately.

"The only way you'll come is with my cock inside you. You want that, don't you?" he asked, more a statement than a question. "You want the cock you saw on your webcam." He leaned over her, planted his fist on the vinyl, and pushed his erection against her leg. She pushed back with a choked gasp.

"The one digging into you right now, pressed up against you all night? Say it, Monkey."

"I want it, Sir," she said. Her voice was a touch husky, the same way she sounded after waking but before coffee. Her hips slowly circled, grinding her ass against his dick.

"Make me believe it," he said, holding back a groan. "Or would any cock do?"

"It has to be you, Sir," she rushed out. "It's all I can think about. God, it's been so long..."

"So, you just haven't been fucked lately."

"Did it matter whom I invited?" Declan interjected.

"N-no, that's—" She ducked her head, hiding her face. Her words became muffled. "Yes, it's been a while, but you're all I... Even when I was with Declan, I thought about you, Sir."

Finley's heart tripped and fell into a sprint.

"Ever since that call, I think about h-how thick it..." Her voice grew thin with want and embarrassment. "How tight the first time would be, and how badly I want my best friend to utterly own me."

He squeezed his eyes shut, gritted his teeth at the ceiling. Once the blaring impulse to whip down his zipper and kick her feet apart subsided, he took his weight off her and stood straight. He had to stay on point, but *Jesus*, she tested his self-control.

Back at his loft, the vintage, leather-sided suitcase under his bed contained a wide array of his favorite toys and restraints, but this escort had more ways to reach a sub's pain tolerance than you could shake a stick at—and he had plenty of those too, arranged in a row by their severity.

"I don't tend to use these for punishment," Finley said, reaching for the flogger lying next to his sub. The handle fit nicely in his palm, and its many tails made it as heavy as the harsher rubber floggers he used to own.

"You prefer something else?" Declan asked.

"Yeah," Finley said, wrapping his fingers around the suede falls, "but we still need to work up to that."

Her backside was already warm and pink, but if she couldn't handle a hard flogging, she wouldn't be able to take his favorite implement for punishment.

The escort smiled eerily, like a flipbook with certain pages replaced with the wrong picture. "This'll do the trick," he said, "and you'd be giving her one of her firsts. She's never been flogged."

That got Finley's attention. He rolled the tails between his fingers.

"Let's see a few test swings," Declan said.

Swinging the flogger in a figure eight, Finley moved to the end of the table. He briefly considered practicing a few strokes on the bed behind them, but it wasn't the same height as the table, and what better way to draw out her fear than by warming up a couple feet from her vulnerable backside?

He didn't use his full strength with his first basic forearm swing. The falls splayed wide, and he hit closer to the handle than he wanted. He swung again, harder, and hit just the right spot. Monkey's arms jerked.

"Try a little more follow-through," Declan advised. Finley tried again and got a much louder thud.

With every successive swing, aiming became easier. Muscle memory began taking over, and he fell into the rhythm of a figure-eight swing. The impact of his backhand stroke grew to match that of his forearm stroke. When he was satisfied with the aim and force of his swings, he dropped his arm and took position behind his sub.

She was pressed tight to the table, heels off the floor and knees braced against the vinyl. She had clamped her delicate fingers around her forearms. He couldn't get anywhere near them or her lower back, couldn't let the tails wrap around her hips.

Don't worry, baby. It'll only hurt where it needs to.

Chapter Twenty-One

L ily's backside already felt as though it was covered with welts. One spot on her right cheek still stung, and everything else tingled. Her neck ached. The vinyl beneath her stuck to her skin. Even though perching on the balls of her feet was taking a toll on her shaking legs, she couldn't relax, couldn't let go of the silent vibe hugging her clit.

But they were nowhere near done. Nowhere near another ride on the roller coaster. Finley was still preparing her for something else. Her actual punishment. The part meant to break her. She thought about using the safe word, but not because of the physical pain. Everything he had said... He knew more than she thought she had revealed. He knew everything about her that mattered, flaws and all. And he still wanted her.

How could she stop now? How could she cut short what felt so liberating and cleansing? So *real*? Fantasy had never opened her senses before overwhelming them. It had never told her the truths she didn't want to admit. It had never loosened that prickly knot inside her chest, only numbed it, and it had certainly never offered forgiveness. It had never truly accepted her and demanded that she do the same.

She finally understood why Declan had once asked why she would feel ashamed to submit. Why should she, when she controlled the scene as much as Finley and Declan did? When she sought a deeper trust than what vanilla lovers enjoyed? She still didn't know whether she was capable of such trust, but damn did she want to be. Nothing felt righter than this connection to her Dom—her *real* Dom.

The longer the pause in his practice swings, the more certain Lily grew that she was next. She wished she could see Finley standing behind her with that silver-handled flogger in his fist. She pictured him in his club clothes, that predatory look on his face, his sleeves rolled up for—

"Ah!" She gasped. Inert tails caressed her skin, not yet biting or slapping. They glided over her shoulders, brushing her hair away. They swept down her body, over her bound arms, and fell off the slope of her backside, leaving behind goose bumps like paint from a brush. They tickled their way up her right leg, fanned over her cheek, and dragged themselves back up her body. More shivers stole across her when he repeated that slow, seductive stroke up her left leg.

It wasn't nearly as soothing and pleasurable as his large, heavy palm, and yet her heels touched the carpet, pulling her knees away from the side of the table. Her shoulders loosened, easing the ache in her neck. The fire and the tension was still there, though, banked beneath her skin. It would rise again to consume her.

The tails returned, snapped across her right cheek. She pulled in a quick breath, but the first hit only stung a little. She had time to exhale before another hit snatched at her left cheek. A pause, then the right again. Pause, left.

Gradually, the pauses grew shorter. The swings grew stronger and sharper. An itchy sting swelled in the center of both cheeks, and a different kind of itch began again between her thighs. God, she wanted him to touch her there. Anywhere. She wanted his hands on her, gripping her arms, pushing her down, opening her up...

The swings stopped, but the sting remained. She put her heels back on the floor, unaware she had tensed up again.

The vibe on her clit came to life and resumed its torture, buzzing and swiveling, not enough to get her off but more than enough to get her close. A moan burst out of her.

Her flogging resumed as well. The hits came hard and fast. The sting deepened and widened. Her lips pulled away from her teeth. Her heart tapped against the vinyl beneath her. Loud slaps punctuated each breath she sucked in, each flinch, each cry. Her knees punched the cushioned table after the really hard swings. She tried to shield herself despite the rope holding her hands in place.

The room began shrinking. The vinyl under her was slick. Her skin itched, everywhere, as though someone had thrown a wool blanket over her. The aggravatingly gentle massage between her legs was so nice but so cruel. She was slick there as well.

It was just her in the room now. It tilted and sloshed. Her wanton gasps echoed just inches from her ears. Her heart beat soft and quick, like that of a small animal. Slaps resonated not in the air but in her flesh, replacing shame with forgiveness, fear with desire. Pain amplified pleasure, became pleasure. They were both a release. Two sides of the same coin. The jaws of a single vise squeezing tighter. A few more hits, a few more seconds, and she'd burst.

But the sensations fell away. The crank of that vise inside her went still, then unwound, slowly at first, but soon rapidly.

She wanted to stomp and buck in protest, but exhaustion was right on her heels, and her Dom hadn't tolerated her last outburst. She sagged against the table, wincing as her nerves finally caught up after her extended flogging. They sizzled back to life just to tell her that her ass was raw.

"Lovely color," Declan said.

"She's ready," her Dom said. He had sounded like that before, as if someone had raked his voice over gravel. Only a little could have been blamed on her speakers. He was in the same vise as she.

"Feet farther apart, Monkey," he ordered. She hesitantly complied. Something was laid on the table, probably the flogger. She felt a breeze on her arm as something else was laid out.

"Relax, baby." His fingers brushed her vagina. She mewled, hoping he would play with her, but he pulled out the vibe and didn't touch her again. Blood rushed to the formerly compressed flesh, bringing heat and wetness. She wanted to pull her feet up and clench until the spasms started, but that would be selfish. She'd cheat her Dom of giving them both the release they needed.

"May I?"

"Of course," Declan said. Lily listened closely as her Dom took something from the wall of implements.

"Anything about these in her checklist?"

"Free and clear," Declan said after a long pause. His words trembled.

"Thirty strokes, Monkey," Finley said. "Ten for each offense, starting with your selfishness."

Pain sliced across her backside. The impact was nearly silent, but her yelp was high and sharp. Her head whipped up even as her hips dropped and pushed against the table's cushioned edge, cringing away from the next stroke, which landed a little lower than the first. The sting was fierce and immediate. She cried out again when a third stroke almost hit the most sensitive flesh where her ass and thighs met.

He was caning her. Jesus, he punished with a cane.

"Make her count," Declan said. "You set the bar. Now she has to jump it."

"How many, Monkey?" her Dom asked.

"Three, Sir," she said with a swallow.

"You're very good with that," Declan said. "Perfect aim, even hits."

She didn't hear whether Finley answered him or not. Three more strokes lit her nerves on fire. Her ass went taut every time, as though to lessen the impact, but subsequent swings only hurt more. She wrenched against her bonds, tried to twist away from the pain.

"Six, Sir," she whimpered.

"What're you being punished for?" her Dom demanded.

She set her hot cheek on the vinyl. "I'm selfish."

"That's right. One cock isn't good enough for you. You want two."

"Y-yes...yes, Sir."

"Nothing wrong with that, baby. I'll let you be selfish sometimes. I'll spoil you rotten," he said. "You just got to get my permission first."

The next three strokes still hurt as much as the first one had, but she was more prepared. She gritted her teeth and tried to relax quickly after each one.

Then the fourth swing cut right into her sit spot. The fingers of rope holding her down dug deep into her flesh. She didn't hear herself scream, but her ears rang as though she had. Her feet no longer touched the floor. She had folded her legs up, toes pointed at the ceiling. The world felt far away and became muffled, as though she was sinking. The only things that penetrated were pain and self-hatred.

A hand slid to the back of her head, rubbed gently, and brought her back to the surface. Lips touched her ear, but her Dom didn't say anything, didn't need to. He was giving her time and comfort. Nothing more would happen until she either gave him a color or the count. She was in control.

She drew strength from the renewal of their connection—the slight weight of his palm on her head, the slow massage of his fingertips...

Her toes found the carpet. She straightened her knees and cleared her throat.

"Ten, Sir."

Her Dom returned to the other side of the table. "The next ten are for your lies. Keep counting, Monkey."

He followed the same pattern of three-three-four, giving her a short break in between to unclench, breathe, and recite the count. The closer they came to twenty, the harder it became to get the words out. Her lips didn't want to move. Neither did her brain. She doubted there was any skin left on her ass that he hadn't caned.

"Answer me, Monkey," her Dom ordered. Answer what? Had he said something? Why was the room tilting backward?

"Twenty...Sir," she slurred once she realized she hadn't given the count.

"And what were you punished for?"

"Lying." Thank God it was an easy word to say.

"Don't ever lie to me again," he said sternly. "Don't ever lie to *yourself* again."

"Yes, Sir," she said, grateful for the blindfold as tears stung her eyes.

"Last ten, baby. Know what'll happen after that?"

"Y-yes," she whispered.

"I'm going to fuck you," he said. "*We're* going to fuck you."

Her pussy clenched. "Please, Sir" was all she could think to say.

"Tell me why you're about to be punished."

She took a deep breath. "Because I'm a coward."

He laid down three quick strokes. The constant ache in her flesh burrowed even deeper. She sucked in air while she could and gave the count. Her foot came off the floor with the next three swings, but she put it back immediately and wondered how many tears the blindfold had soaked up.

"You can trust me, Monkey," he rumbled. "We can trust each other."

Just a few more. She expected the relief to start early. She was seconds away from a clean slate with him and with herself, yet she was more on edge than ever, stiff with anticipation. Every little sound made her squirm.

"Ahh!" she howled. The final strokes began, driving pain into her core like a chisel cracking stone. Every hit compounded the pressure in her head, pushing out every thought but one, and it wasn't of redemption.

I do trust you. I love you. I love you.

She slumped over the table. Something clattered onto the carpet. A pair of warm hands lifted her face a second later.

"How many, baby? Tell me how many," he whispered. "Then we'll kiss it better."

"Thirty...S-sir."

Lips she never thought she'd feel again repeatedly pressed against hers, quickly coaxing a response. She sobbed into his mouth, desperate for his desire, still needing the release only he could give her. He had doused her in fuel and struck the match, but the conflagration was still to come.

Too soon, he pulled back, panting. More than just taste his hunger, she wanted to see it on his face, but he didn't remove her blindfold.

"Where to put that second cock?" he wondered aloud. His thumb pulled her mouth open. "Here looks good."

Lily whimpered with excitement. She wiggled restlessly as his footsteps returned to the other side of the table while another set of footsteps approached her head. A buckle clinked and leather creaked. A zipper buzzed. She licked her lips.

"Can't wait to see my cock spreading that pretty mouth," Declan said above her. She heard a plastic wrapper crinkle and tear, then caught a whiff of something sweet. "But like he said, we'll kiss it better first."

He lifted her chin. Another pair of hands wrapped around the back of her knees and slowly traveled upward. They skimmed her stinging skin, settled on her abused flesh, and opened her up. Declan's mouth muffled her shaky cry as two tongues penetrated both sets of her lips. Her heels lifted and her eyes squeezed tight behind her blindfold.

They made love to her with their mouths, sucking and licking and plunging. Sensation bombarded her, made only sharper without sight or freedom. Every shared breath with Declan, every flick of Finley's tongue sent a hot wave crashing through her brain, made her legs jump, made her moan higher and higher.

Just as she was about to burst, her Dom pulled back.

"No," she cried, wrenching her mouth away. "Please, Sirs! Please let me come." She heard leather and plastic again. If he was putting on protection, that meant...

"What'd I say, baby?" her Dom panted.

"Then *fuck* me! I'm—" Her voice broke. "I'm yours, Sir. I'm yours."

He gave a choked groan, kicked her feet apart, gripped her hip.

"Do it," he rumbled.

Declan fisted his hand in her hair and pulled her head back. A thrill shot through her, terrifying and exhilarating. Something touched her lips. She opened her mouth and let her tongue slide out. She needed him inside her, needed both of them. They had emptied her out, and now they had to fill her back up. Declan's cock pushed between her lips, wrapped in an artificially flavored condom. Cherry. He pulled back, and his other hand went to the side of her head, lifting some of the weight off her neck. He pressed forward again with a husky sigh.

Finley slid the head of his cock up and down the seam of her labia, spreading and activating a warming lubricant. He dipped inside to graze her clit. She struggled against her bonds, wanting to guide him home. Then the head caught, notched, squeezed forward. She moaned around the flesh in her mouth. God, he was finally...

"Yeah," he groaned. His other hand found her waist and drew her back as he rolled his hips into her. He slid in slow but smooth, making those sounds that had given her wet dreams all week—hard breaths out that rattled his throat, long breaths in through his teeth.

They began moving. Declan pumped strong and steady, but Finley went slow, pressing deep. He leaned his weight onto her, holding her down at the waist, pinning her between his pelvis and the table. He ground into her, turning up the volume on the pain sizzling in her flesh. Even the brush of his slacks made her flinch.

She absolutely loved it. The disparate forces pushing in and out of her. Masculine voices grunting with every thrust. Strong hands grasping her, using her, and enjoying her, not bruising her in their grip, not neglecting her comfort and pleasure. She wanted more, harder, and faster.

Her mouth was occupied, and she didn't want to use her hands to signal what she wanted in case they thought she was invoking her safe word, so she could only shake her tail. The air caught in Finley's throat, and his fingers clamped down, kept her still. His cock stopped for a second and then pulled back even slower than before. Just when he would've slipped out, he thrust forward—hard. Pleasure and pain conspired, combined into one toe-curling sensation that churned her insides. She sucked hard on the cock in her mouth, swirling her tongue over the tip as it slid to the back of her throat. Declan's hand cranked down on her hair.

"She's gonna finish me soon," Declan gasped.

His thrusts sped up. Saliva trickled from the corner of her mouth. She wondered how he really tasted, how her Dom tasted. Would they go another round after this? Would they leave her tied up like that so they could switch places and take her again? The thought nearly made her come.

A harsh groan filled the room. The fingers against her head convulsed, tugged her into his next thrust. The flesh between her lips throbbed. Then the cock slipped from her mouth and the hands let go of her head. She swallowed to keep from drooling and sucked in a breath.

"Just you and me, baby," her Dom rasped.

He gave her another hard thrust. Then another and another, faster and faster, pushing her past her previous highs, winding her up tighter than she'd ever been before. Every slap of their bodies seemed like the one that would ignite her, yet the heat expanded without end, and she wailed in desperation.

He touched one of her hands. Without thought, she turned her palm, and their fingers laced. His grip was strong, his breaths ragged. The sound reminded her of that video chat and the pinch of his eyebrows and the last pump of his hips into his fist right before he—

Pleasure sucked her inward. Tension fizzled into liquid heat that burned hot and long, burned forever, burned up everything chaining her down. It consumed her.

The world was pulling away. Finley thrust deep and held himself there. With every hard sigh he made, he bucked his hips. Oh God, she wanted to see him, but the blindfold and...and opening her eyes wasn't an option. She needed a moment. Just a moment to...

Chapter Twenty-Two

F inley was ruined. Completely ruined.

Though ending things with Midge had torn him up inside and made him question whether he'd ever love again, or even deserve it, time and a certain friendship had shown him he hadn't really been happy. Certainly not the sky-high, cross-the-finish-line, how-was-it-even-possible level of happy he felt now, in this room, with the only person who had ever calmed the beast inside him and then got it to roll over.

Nothing was as bone-deep satisfying as hearing the second when orgasm made her gasp and hold her breath, as pumping into the grip of her body to make it last longer, as following her on his own wave of bliss. Nothing would surpass the connection he felt with her. From now on, it was her or no one at all for the rest of his life. God, he was ruined and still didn't know her name.

Monkey let out a sob that kicked him in the heart. He immediately took his hands off her and eased away, pulling out gently. He then leaned over the table on the side she was facing.

"Baby, what's—"

She was smiling. A wide, open-lipped grin. He loosened the elastic band around her head and pulled off her blindfold. Her lashes were wet. Her mascara had run, and a fresh tear towed a streak of black over the bridge of her nose, but she was still smiling.

"Are you okay?" he asked.

She gave a tired laugh. "More than okay," she said hoarsely, "but I'm...pretty sure I blacked out for a few seconds."

Jesus, he loved this woman.

"Declan—" he started, but the escort already stood behind him with a pair of rope shears in hand, which Declan opened with a metallic yip.

"Won't take long," Declan said evenly.

Finley curved his hands protectively around Monkey's waist. For obvious reasons, he hadn't kept an eye on Declan after the guy had finished and then disappeared somewhere behind him, but the escort's clothes were back in place, so he must have gone to clean himself up.

"Trash is over there, by the way." Declan jabbed his thumb at a small, stainless-steel receptacle by the bed.

"Right." Finley mentally shook himself, realizing he couldn't just stand there with his dick out. He walked to the trash can and plucked a paper towel from a dispenser on the nightstand, glancing at Declan's progress over his shoulder as he cleaned up.

After tucking himself back in his pants and straightening his clothes, Finley returned to the table to watch Declan snip the ropes holding down Monkey's shoulders. Her arms were completely free of the box-ties, but they remained crossed behind her back.

"I'm gonna move you, Monkey." Finley slowly shifted her right arm down to her side and heard a small hiss. He did the same for her left arm and kept a hand on her back as he and Declan teased loose the ropes around her torso. Once those were cut, he slid his hands under her body and lifted her away from the table.

She immediately tottered, and for his sake as much as hers, he lifted her into his arms. She didn't grab at him or go rigid. Instead, she tiredly hooked her arm around his neck and rolled her head onto his shoulder. She trusted him to hold her. He pulled her a little closer and turned to the bedroom door.

"There was a mirror?" she asked. "You...saw me."

"You were beautiful, baby," he assured her.

Declan went ahead of him and opened the door. "Should have everything you need in the bathroom."

Finley nodded and carefully maneuvered his sub through the door into the main room. It was a lot cooler out there than before.

The bathroom light was already on when he carried Monkey inside. Like the rest of the apartment, nothing made it seem as though someone actually lived here. No hamper, no half-used tubes of toothpaste or cans of shaving foam. It looked like what you'd find in a hotel—or rather, a five-star hotel behind the façade of a two-star one.

All the fixtures were fully upgraded with high-quality materials, and the room was larger than he would expect for a unit in a building that old. The standing shower's overhead water source and its white, tiled floor that stretched the width of the bathroom rendered a shower door unnecessary. Instead, a frameless glass wall protected one side. The toilet even had a goddamn bidet.

Amenities were neatly arranged on the pale marble counter. A pair of water glasses, a box of tissues, a travel-size bottle of mouthwash, a small rectangle of packaged soap, and a stack of towels. Above all that, a wide vanity mirror reflected him holding his naked, exhausted sub. Okay, he did like that part.

"No complimentary bathrobe?" he muttered as he set Monkey on her feet.

"Mm?" she said, groping for the counter. He kept both hands on her waist as she turned to the sink.

"Nothing. You want some water first?"

"Yeah." She looked up at the mirror. "Oh...wow. Okay. Shit, look at these rope marks."

"I see 'em," he said without moving his jaw. He stared in particular at the deep rows above and below her breasts. The redness was starting to fade, but the indentations would take a while longer.

Just seeing those marks put him right back in the other room, swinging a cane, watching her break and twist against her bonds. He had been ready to stop immediately—she just had to say the word—but she got back into position and gave him the count. He couldn't have been any prouder.

And after that...grinding into her, gripping her hand, gazing at the sight of her pink, open mouth. With a swallow, he slipped an arm around her and reached past her for a glass. The faucet turned on with the flip of a slender lever, and he filled the glass halfway so it wasn't too heavy. She drank its contents in three swallows.

"More?" he asked.

"Yeah."

She held the glass underneath the faucet, and he turned it on again. After draining a nearly full glass, she set it down with a sigh.

"My legs are shaking," she said with a smile, wiping her hand across her wet lips and underneath her eye.

"Damn straight they are."

Keeping one hand braced on the counter, she made use of a tissue, some mouthwash, a few splashes of cold water, and a towel. Once her face was dry and less flushed, she twisted her lower half to see the results of their scene. One of her hands went to his shoulder, and he was struck by how much he liked it.

As sexy and distracting as her pose was, seeing her react was so much more compelling than getting another glimpse of what he had done to her ass, which he already knew was bright red shot through with darker red welts and faint purple lines. He watched her eyes widen and her brows push furrows into her forehead as her lips formed a silent obscenity. A smile played at the corners of her mouth. But it didn't last long. She blinked and her gaze fell, pulling her smile with it.

"Monkey?"

She turned away from the mirror and hooked her fingers into the front of his shirt, just as she had in the darkness under that storefront awning. He banded her in his arms and dropped a kiss on her head. "Talk to me. What's wrong?"

"Nothing. Everything," she said into his chest. "I shouldn't have any complaints, right? I mean, what just happened was something I've wanted for a very long time, and it was even better than I imagined."

A small sound from the bedroom prompted him to toe the door shut.

"I think something's wrong with me," she whispered.

"What?" He held her closer. "How can you say that?"

"Because of what happened, back in college."

Something in her voice made his lungs feel small. She sounded...lost. "What do you mean?" he asked.

"I was home for Christmas break," she began. "Just me in the house."

No, not lost—detached. As though in her mind, she was somewhere else.

"It was late. I never really had privacy in the dorms, so I was touching myself in my bedroom when I heard something."

A cold lump congealed in the pit of his stomach. He didn't dare move or speak, could hardly breathe. He wished he could see her face and didn't like that she hadn't yet looked him in the eye. She was still putting distance between them. But he didn't want to force the issue, not when she was taking that last step toward him of her own volition.

"I didn't make it to a phone," she continued, fear creeping in. "A man g-grabbed me and dragged me into my room. He stuffed a shirt in my mouth. Tied my h-hands and feet with the belt from my bathrobe. He—he said..."

She shook her head, abandoning the thought of what her attacker had told her. All he could do was rub circles in her back, and fuck, it wasn't enough. He didn't know what to say.

"I never knew I could be so *scared*, but the adrenaline and struggling a-and being all worked up from when I thought I was alone...I couldn't help it. I couldn't stop my body from—I just couldn't."

A giant hand squeezed the breath out of him. He clutched her close, wishing he could sap the fear out of her shaking shoulders.

"He s-stood over me for the longest time, not saying a word," she said, her voice going quiet, "but I could hear him breathing, and I kept thinking, 'I don't want to die. Please just let me live through this.'" She swallowed a sob and took a deep breath.

"But he didn't touch me again. He left me on the floor and walked out of the room. I could hear him in the house, opening doors and searching. He came back a couple of times, like he was checking on me, and every time, I thought..."

That the man had come to hurt her, Finley realized.

"When I didn't hear anything for a while, I thought that maybe he was gone for good, but I didn't know for sure until my family came home. I laid there for over an hour, trying not to choke on my T-shirt and not knowing if I was safe. Sometimes I still don't know."

The nightmares. Sleeping during the day. The hard limit on gags.

"Knowing what my body did was somehow worse than the fear," she said shakily. "God, I don't know what I expected when I told my parents. Mom said that wasn't how she had raised me. Dad said it was time to see someone about my problem."

"Jesus," he breathed.

"It's just, somewhere deep down, I've always known what I am, what I like," she said. "And I didn't always manage to hide it growing up. I've always had these scenarios in my head of...o-of being overpowered and tied up and punished. And not necessarily by a Dom. For a while, it was a stranger. Someone dangerous."

"Monkey, it's not the same—"

"I know," she said, nodding against his shoulder. "The therapist said it was just a biological reaction, but even after some time passed—even though I know what the reality is—I still had these *needs*, and I couldn't help worrying that my parents were right, that maybe that part of me, somewhere deep down, wanted it."

Understanding dawned on him. His heart ached as he pressed his cheek to the top of her head and waited for her to say everything she needed to say.

"I think I needed to know, for sure, that I'm not fucked up."

Finley remembered all the cruel things he'd said the night he turned her away. That giant hand squeezed harder.

"I figured going to someone like Declan was the only way to find out, especially after what happened between you and me."

"How was that a real option? How was that anything other than reckless?"

"Exactly," she said, drawing her fingers into fists. She lifted her head from his shoulder but still didn't look at him. "It was reckless, but I...I left here smiling."

He closed his eyes with a wince. He didn't want to hear that the escort had fulfilled her or made her happy, and he definitely didn't want her to think it meant she was broken. She had been lucky.

"Back at the club, I practically wanted you to fight over me, and I got off on that, didn't I? And then here, not knowing who had knocked on the door was so...*intense*, but I ended up fucking that person, anyway. Isn't that proof?"

"Proof of what?" he challenged. "If Declan and I had started throwing punches, would that have turned you on?"

Her puffy, red-tinged eyes flipped up. A tear escaped and caught on her cheek. "No, of course not."

"When I knocked, did you feel unsafe?"

Her gaze wavered. "I-I don't know. Maybe."

He cupped her cheek and brushed her tear away. "Did you think about using the safe word?" he asked, more softly this time.

"At first, yeah," she admitted.

"And when you realized it was me?"

She inhaled to speak, but nothing came out, and the desperation on her face melted into something else. Her eyes lost focus, as if she were slipping back to that moment. Her breaths deepened. She slowly uncurled her fingers and then rubbed the material of his shirt against his flesh underneath.

"Wasn't it obvious?" she whispered. "I was still nervous, but I wanted whatever you were going to do to me."

She gasped, and he realized he had pulled her against his half-hard cock with a hand on her bruised posterior.

"And why was that?" he asked thickly. Dear God, did she know what she was saying? Did she realize how much he needed to hear it?

"B-because...I—" Wincing, she dropped her gaze.

"No, look at me and say it," he said, lifting her chin.

Her eyes shined under tight brows.

"*Say it*, Monkey."

"Because I love you!" she confessed, rapid-fire. "I know I can trust you."

The band of pressure around his chest nearly lifted him right off the floor.

"And when you asked to take things offline, I didn't hesitate," she continued, words flooding out of her like a storm surge over a levy. "I wanted to see you with my own eyes and touch you and know that you're real. I wanted that rumor to be true. I wanted to be yours and you to be mine...and then I fucked it all up because I was so scared you'd realize how broken I am."

He stopped her lips with a kiss, both hands cradling her head to take full possession, to smother any notion that he could ever find any part of her unacceptable.

"I love you," he panted, pulling back. "All of you. How smart you are, how sexy you are, how easily I end up talking to you way past my bedtime. I love the way you laugh and the way you light up when you talk about your work. I can't get enough of you."

"Finley, all the lies I told..."

"You're forgiven, remember? I only hate that I made you feel broken, that anyone ever made you feel that way. I hate that I let my pain push you away—to him. I hated not knowing if you were safe with him or if you'd get hurt the same way I hurt you."

With a small smile, Monkey slid her fingers across the nape of his neck.

"Forgiven," she said, "if you say it again."

A grin split his face, and he touched his forehead to hers. "I love you."

Damn, it felt so good to say that. The smile she gave him felt even better. She tilted her mouth up, and he was tempted to make her ask nicely for a kiss, but a knock on the door severed that chain of thought.

"I have Jill's clothes," Declan called.

Finley raised his head, and the world opened up a little. For a second, he was captivated by the image in the mirror of Monkey safely tucked into his larger body, his arms draped across her bare shoulders.

Right, they were still standing in the middle of the escort's unusually large bathroom, and Monkey was still naked—not usually a problem—but as grateful as he was to Declan, he wasn't about to let the guy enjoy the view again.

"Wait right here," he said before dropping a kiss on her nose. She gave him a pretty pout as he stepped to the door and stuck his head out.

Declan's eyes met his, though not before the escort could hide his strained expression behind the neutral mask he normally wore. He wordlessly offered the dress and undergarments slung over his arm. Was the guy tired?

With a curt nod, Finley took the clothes and passed them to Monkey. Intending to give her a few minutes alone, he left the door cracked.

"Need anything else?" he asked her.

"My phone. It's in my clutch on the front table."

He smiled knowingly at her.

"What?" she asked defensively.

"I'll be right back," he replied mildly.

Declan was nowhere to be seen when Finley shut the bathroom door behind him. He wouldn't be surprised if the guy was exhausted. Domming that often took a lot out of you, as Finley knew all too well. Or maybe Declan felt he had earned his fee and now wanted them out.

You and me both, Finley thought as he grabbed Monkey's little black purse. He returned to the bathroom and lightly knocked. A second later, Monkey peeked out at him.

"Here you go," he said, handing over her clutch.

"Thanks," she mumbled at the floor before quickly disappearing.

"Send me the pics when you're done," he called through the door.

She hissed a curse, then after a pause, "Yes, Sir."

Finley turned away with a grin. Being right was nice, but knowing she trusted him with her pictures was even better—not that she wasn't guaranteed to send them as securely as possible.

He heard a faucet turn on, but the sound was coming from the kitchen rather than behind him. Following it, he found Declan at the sink with a towel thrown over his shoulder. On the counter next to him sat the kind of fancy gift bag a salon would give you for spending way too much on a haircut and a bottle of shampoo. A rattan cane poked several inches out of the golden-yellow tissue paper stuffed inside.

Ah, he was packing up the toys they had used.

Even in profile, the escort looked as if his battery were running low. His shoulders slouched, and sweat had dampened his hair in places. He stared at his unmoving hands without really seeing them. It was the most open and even vulnerable Finley had seen him the whole night—or perhaps the word was "human."

Spotting Finley from the corner of his eye, Declan turned his back to him.

"Hey, sorry about that," Finley said, bracing his shoulder on the wall jamb. "We'll be out of your hair soon."

"Out of my hea—" Declan started in a thin voice, but he threw his head to one side and cut himself off. He cleared his throat and rolled his head to stretch his neck. Did the guy have a pinched nerve?

"It's not a problem," he continued in a far more normal voice, though it was still scratchy. "There's no rush."

"Looks like you need a break, though," Finley said.

Declan shut off the water and pulled the towel from his shoulder. His arms shifted as he dried whatever he had been washing.

"I'm fine," he said placidly before tossing the towel aside and grabbing something from the other side of the sink. He turned toward the gift bag and dropped a familiar white case inside.

"Implements are never reused with other clients, so she'll be taking these with her," Declan explained. His alter ego firmly back in control, he picked the bag up by its twisted-cord handles and walked it over to Finley.

"Yeah, that's a...sound policy," Finley said, discomforted by the pristine packaging. He doubted Declan just had a bag like this sitting around, which meant the escort kept a supply of them—which meant he often sent clients home with them. How many bags did he go through? How much exhaustion was he hiding?

"Hey, so uh...Declan...thanks a lot for tonight," Finley said. "For helping me through the scene, I mean. It had been a real long time for me and...well, just thanks."

The skin between Declan's eyebrows shifted as if smudged by an invisible thumb. "You're welcome, but...I did it for her. That's how I have to justify it."

"Right." Finley rubbed the back of his neck. "Since she paid and all."

"But..." Declan held up his finger, walked to a drawer opposite the sink, and drew from it a pen and a black business card. He wrote something on the back and returned to Finley. "That's my direct number," Declan said, handing him the card. "Call it any time if you need advice, especially if either of you drops."

Finley glanced at the card in his hand. The back was white matte, and above the handwritten, nonlocal number was a web address, some sort of unlock code, and the words *The Stranger*. He flipped the card over.

"Discreet and professional entertainment," he read aloud.

Had Monkey received a card like this one?

"Thanks, man," Finley said, stowing the card in his pocket.

Declan followed him into the main room and took a seat on the sofa while Finley tapped his knuckles on the bathroom door.

"How's it going?"

"Uh, I can't get the zipper up," Monkey called out. "It's stuck or something."

Before he could even suggest helping her, she opened the door and presented her back to him. He tugged the zipper off its obstacle and smoothly pulled it up. It was such a small thing, but his heart warmed.

"All set," he said.

"Great. I'm all done, then."

She grabbed her purse off the bathroom counter and joined him in the main room.

"What's that?" she asked of the bag in his hand.

"Souvenirs." He lifted the bag higher to let her see it better.

Her eyebrows jumped. "Oh." She glanced at his face, over at Declan, back at him, and then at her bare feet. Her free hand went to her flushed cheek.

"What are you getting embarrassed for?" he asked, lowering the bag and grinning. "I think we're well past that by now."

"I'll get embarrassed if I want to," she said, smacking his stomach with her little purse. She was trying to hide a smile, and it was absolutely adorable.

"All right." His voice shook with laughter. "Not like I can stop you—or want to."

He supposed he couldn't blame her. Being stared at by the two guys who had just used her like a Chinese finger trap was a pretty legit reason to feel shy.

At the door, Monkey set down her purse, stepped into her shoes, and then let him help her into her coat.

"You two have a ride home?" Declan asked from a few steps away.

"I drove, so we're set," Finley said as he pulled on his own coat.

"So...is that it?" she asked of Declan. "We're all good?"

"Yeah, we're even," Declan said. Finley couldn't tell if the bittersweet expression Declan gave her was real or not. With her bottom lip pinched between her teeth, Monkey turned to look at him.

"May I, Sir?" They weren't in a scene anymore, but Finley knew what she was asking and why she framed it as his sub. He ignored the irritation in his gut and nodded.

She went to Declan, who turned his face and offered his cheek. That's where she kissed him, her hands on his shoulders and her heels off the floor. At least the escort didn't put his hands on her and instead kept them firmly planted in his pockets. She whispered something in his ear, and Finley expected the guy to smile, but instead he looked...worried.

Monkey turned away and grabbed her things. Finley opened the door for her, let her leave first, and threw one last look at Declan. The escort's face was clammy and hard. Finley gave a single nod and hoped the guy got a good night's rest. He shut the door behind him.

As they walked to the elevator, Finley slipped his arm around Monkey's waist and told himself to forget about Declan's troubling expressions. He didn't plan on using Declan's number, and neither of them would ever see him again.

On the ride down to the first floor, he saw the spaced-out smile on Monkey's face and felt a smile of his own. She glanced up at him, and her lips widened.

"I was remembering that you love me."

His arm tightened around her. He had planned on teasing her with near-kisses until they got to either his place or hers, but now there was no way that was happening. He turned her toward him. She lifted her chin, and her beautiful, dark eyes slid shut.

It was that first kiss all over again—not the way they kissed, but the way he felt, as though he was the luckiest SOB in the world. The elevator dinged, and they made it outside without meeting anyone.

"I'm parked a couple blocks this way," he said, taking her hand. "Looks like it's not raining anymore, so you want to walk with me or should I come pick you up?"

Monkey winced.

"Um, about that... I'm actually going to go home. Alone."

Chapter Twenty-Three

D eclan held his hands up. Through the fuzzy spots swimming in front of his eyes, he watched his fingers shake.

Heart rate elevated. Stabilize breaths.

A dream? Or had earlier been a dream and now he was awake? Fuck, or maybe none of it was real. Maybe consciousness was an illusion, an addiction his brain couldn't kick. Maybe it was all one long, unending nightmare that he kept waking up into.

Hydrate. Bathe. Dress. Food. Clean. Follow the script.

How did he know what to do? *Why* do these unimportant things when he had to remember? If this was a dream, then it was one without a plot. He had to understand.

But it hurt to try, like that other part of the dream had hurt. The part that came when he stood next to a door and heard someone's voice. A high, scared voice. And the hurt was like carefully stacked boulders on his mind, one tiny stone away from crushing his skull.

Invalid command, but was it the same as earlier? Something in his drink, causing these foreign lines, corrupting his processes? But his head hadn't hurt then, and his internal temperature was critical.

Jill. Who was she? He felt a connection, a familiarity, a debt. He needed to atone...because he knew how? Or because he knew *why*? Was that the dream? Was it the why? He wanted to—but the wrong words came out, and he'd let her go.

The only option within parameters.

His feet were taking him somewhere. The kitchen. He watched his hands take a glass from the cupboard and fill it with water. He felt the water go down his throat. He tried to inhale instead of swallow. He choked, coughed. It burned.

"Stop—it," he gasped out.

Fuck, who was that? Jesus. Oh, Jesus Christ.

His body was moving again, but he wasn't driving. He couldn't even grab the wheel. He watched the kitchen recede and the bathroom door grow larger.

The door was open only a few inches. Beyond were deep shadows. Light from behind him slanted across the bathroom floor, jumped up a sliver of the counter, dully reflected off a corner of the mirror.

The dream happened here. The high, scared voice told a story, and he dreamed of crouching in a dark bathroom, peeking through the smallest of cracks in the door. He dreamed that a slim figure emerged, long hair. Its movements were fearful and cautious, like prey.

He crept out of the bathroom. His heart roared in his ears. She wasn't supposed to be there. The car was gone, the whole place dark. How had he missed her? Didn't matter now. He had to keep her quiet. It couldn't be like last time. He couldn't endure that again.

He held the figure against him, locked her arms to her sides, told her something... He saw flowers in his dream. Lilies. He smelled them too, but he didn't notice at the time. Then he stood over her, wondered how long she would be alone and if he had time to... No, he had no time. He had to hope the car would be back soon, that he tied the knots just right.

His hand reached for the bathroom door. **Bathe.**

He couldn't go in there. He couldn't look at himself, at what he had done, what he had seen, what he had been. He couldn't face what he was now.

It was just another nightmare. None of this was real. It *couldn't* be real.

"Follow the script," he grunted.

No. *No!*

He heard a strangled grunt and watched his hand yank the door shut. The hurt spiked. Everything blurred. He felt his hands grasping at the back of his head. His scalp was hot, sweaty. There was something back there, something uneven beneath his skin.

Pain blinded him. It shot up his wrist, exploded in his hip. He felt the floor beneath him, but it offered as much anchorage as a kite string.

Monstrous waves of agony slammed and buffeted him, and eventually that faint sensation of being grounded faded away, smothered by simply needing to cope.

He lost all connection to his body and the space around him. He was a speck of dust blown about by an impossibly violent storm made all the more miserable by how familiar it felt. It was here that emotion struck like flashes of lightning inches from his retinas. It thundered in great, crashing booms that exploded next to his ear drums. He sensed shapes, faces, but no detail, no context. Reactions were demanded. Even warm emotions were cruel, a slap rather than a caress, for they were forced on him.

This place was his punishment. He could never atone.

Pressure against his soles. Cold air on his skin that was brushed away, one limb at a time. Something traveled up his legs and settled around his pelvis. A blanket? No, it was clothes. He felt a healthy strain in his back and arms. He was dressing himself.

The storm slowly quieted, the claps of thunder now distant rumbles. He felt warm food in his mouth, but he couldn't taste it. Satisfaction remained elusive. Only a growing fullness reached him.

More healthy pulls in his muscles. He couldn't recognize what he was doing besides bending, moving items, and opening containers.

He touched something flexible, compact, smooth, ridged. Rope. It was rope in his hands. He was picking up several thin strands.

The flashes of lightning were far away now, their contrast less glaring as the sky brightened. He could make out colors, movement, then vague shapes. He recognized his hands. His shirt was gray, a shade lighter than the carpet under his bare feet. He stuffed strands of rope into a plastic bag and then reached for more. He brushed the vinyl surface in front of him. Static electricity snapped at his fingers.

His hand jerked at the fleeting pain that was so different from the tempest where bolts of lightning often speared him with their searing heat. The light would awaken him, give weight to his definitions, lash him with sensations that were neither pain nor pleasure, and suck out something he hadn't been ready to give.

He remembered the first time, though he couldn't recall if it was a day or a decade ago. Barely perceptible in all that light was a face. Glasses perched on pink, delicate features. Light-colored hair. His hands held flesh. He couldn't remember how many times the lightning had struck him, but self-hatred and resentment never failed to follow.

Why did the rope and the static make him think of that? Why did this carpet, this vinyl, this room make him want to scream?

Oh God, he *felt* but he *couldn't feel*. Disgust came without nausea, despair without tears, horror without chills. He wanted to cry, shout, vomit. He wanted it to end.

But instead, he watched his hands tie the plastic bag shut and deliver it to the trash can in the kitchen. He watched someone else live in his skin. He watched his body move without his input—no, despite his input as if met with no more resistance than still water.

Reset room. Rest. Follow the script.

His body returned to the bedroom, though his muscles burned with effort. He didn't want to look at the mirror leaning against the right wall, but his eyes made him. His feet forced him closer.

Don't look at it. Don't even go near it.

Invalid command. Reset room. Follow the script.

He tried to stop himself, but the pain returned like the swing of a bat to his cranium, discouraging and punishing. Slowly, dreamily, he walked around the vinyl table. He felt his eyes widen. A jolt flashed through his body at the speed of molasses.

The edge of his vision dimmed and shrunk, pulled by the mirror's frame and the specter within. It wore the same clothes he did and stood by the bed on its side of the glass, feet planted squarely and arms loose as if preparing to attack. The bed's headboard was sprayed with red. The stained comforter partially obscured a limp body, but not the red-slick pillow.

His heart pounded. It really pounded, really reacted to what he saw in the mirror. The other him saw it, too. Sweat dampened his underarms. His entire body shook.

The specter lifted both arms, grabbed something behind its head, and pulled with great effort. He was forced to watch as the specter peeled the skin from the crown of its skull. Black, tainted blood splashed its shoulders. The underside of its scalp glistened. Wet, unidentifiable chunks slipped off. He heard a whimper of fear but couldn't tell which of them made the sound.

The specter's wet, stained fingers gathered its scalp like the hem of a shirt and yanked its featureless face off its head. Beneath a layer of thick, congealed blood lay rotting muscles, soft with decay and limply clinging to the yellowish bones of its skull.

He heard a short scream, then a longer, louder one. He kept screaming, couldn't look away as the specter reached once more behind its head.

"I don't want to see it," he shouted. *"I don't want to see it!"*

The specter gripped something and tore it from the bone. His body burst forward, arms out. With a shout, he hurled the mirror across the room. It hit the bedpost. Shattered. Shards of glass exploded onto the bed and the floor. The frame landed facedown on the carpet.

The other him panted and trembled. Had he not been cut off from physical emotion for so long, he might have forgotten it was not his fear that translated. The other him stared at what his body had done. He watched his focus shift rapidly, darting from the overturned frame to the shards on the floor to those on the bed, as if the other him were confirming something. He didn't want to understand what the other him had said. He didn't want to know...

Clean invalid command. Reset room invalid rest command. Follow file the corrupted script end end—

Tottering, he approached the puddle of sharp glass on the floor. The texture under his feet turned gritty and sticky. He stood over the largest shard. Its reflective side faced up. He slowly knelt. Pain sliced into his right foot. He carefully touched the edge of the glass.

Why look? *Why?*

Clean end end follow corrupted the—

He tilted the shard toward him, and its reflection swung from the ceiling to his skinless, rotting face. The specter mirrored his body, squatting with one hand holding the shard. Its other hand held a wet object close to the reflection. It was not veins that flowered from the darkly shining inner curve of the symmetrical hunk of what looked like but wasn't bone. It was not brain matter that lay in neat paths between square and round protrusions. It was not something that should have been there at all.

His own right hand slid to the back of his head and to the uneven hardness beneath his skin. His scalp was hot, as if sunburned.

Fatal error. Error cascade: mem.top partition failure. Shutdown required.

The room went dark as though the power had gone out. Thunder crashed, bringing pain as he was ripped from his body.

"You can come to my place if you'd rather not go to yours," Finley appealed, looking at her as though his dog had died and he was being stoic about it.

Lily didn't resent his offer. She knew he meant it generously, and spending the night at his place *was* really tempting. She had no doubt he'd make her feel right at home. He'd get her a new toothbrush, dig up a spare power cord for her phone, and give her one of his spine-melting grins as he offered her one of his shirts for her to wear to bed.

After her exhausting evening, she might even fall asleep before sunrise for the first time in months, and when she woke? He'd have coffee ready, and then they'd take a long "shower" together. If she hadn't just torn open old wounds, she would have gladly accepted.

"I'm not ready for that, at least not tonight."

Finley glanced down at their clasped hands and took a deep breath. She squeezed his fingers. When he lifted his gaze, he didn't drop her hand, lose his temper, or insist he was "owed" something. He gave her a small smile, a nod, and an okay. He squeezed her fingers back.

"I want to tell you something," she said, feeling a sudden urge.

"Yeah?"

"My real name is Lily."

A soft smile lifted his face, revealing his dimples, and he repeated her name with relish, his voice pitched low with fatigue. She breathed a little deeper. Finley raised her hand to his lips and kissed her knuckles.

"I'll wait as long as you need. I'd like to call you later, though, to check on you. I don't want to shirk any aftercare."

"A call sounds great," she said.

"Do you need to call a cab?"

She shook her head. "I booked one when I was in the bathroom."

"Then I'll wait with you and see you off," he said, not skipping a beat.

Though the rain had stopped, the wind was still brisk. Her shoulders jumped up as a gust of frigid air went right through her coat.

"Cold?" Finley asked.

She nodded, and he opened his coat to her. Stepping into his arms, she snuggled up to his heat. He even turned them so that he was blocking the wind. She hid her smile against his chest and closed her eyes.

God, he smelled good. He felt good. He treated her with respect and care. She pressed a little closer, and in response, he rubbed her back to warm her up.

"Damn, already?" Finley asked above her.

She lifted her head and looked over her shoulder at an approaching Safe Cab.

"Hey," he said. Their eyes met. "If you needed me, you know I'd come running, right?" Holy hell. Finley made leaving him really hard.

"Same to you," she said. "I'd come running." She watched him struggle to hold something in and knew what he wanted to ask. *When will you be ready?*

"Sooner than you think," she assured. Much sooner. She had lived alone for a long time, and adjusting to someone else's presence would have to happen in steps, but she'd consider inviting Finley for a sleepover as soon as the Eidolon was gone and her apartment was fit to be seen.

She stretched up for a kiss, and his lips descended. Though the kiss was slow and sweet, it was his hand in her hair that made her fingers curl into his shirt.

Having waited a moment without the door opening, the Safe Cab played the company jingle to announce its arrival. Lily reluctantly pulled out of Finley's embrace.

"Guess I should get in before it starts honking at us."

"Somehow this feels like junior prom," he joked as they approached the curb. "Now I just need my dad to yell something embarrassing out of the window." He opened the cab door and leaned inside to set the bag of implements on the seat.

"I spent my junior prom programming an LED cube hooked up to my speakers to pulse in time with my music," she revealed.

Finley laughed as he straightened up. "Why am I not surprised? But even back then, they sold those for cheap online. You could have just plugged one in."

"I didn't like the premade systems," she explained with a shrug. She stepped up to the cab and tossed her clutch and umbrella inside. "And I wanted to learn to do it on my own."

"One of the many things I love about you," he said warmly. His sentiment made the cynic in her protest, but the romantic in her told it to sit down and shut up.

Once she was settled in the backseat, Finley braced his hand on the doorframe and leaned into the cab for a kiss, but he was forced to pull back when the Safe Cab began instructing them on how to set a destination.

"Audio off," they commanded at the same time.

"Fucking hell," Finley said with a laugh. "You comfortable?"

"Not even close," she said, shifting in her seat. It'd be at least a day before she sat without flares of pain.

"Good. Wouldn't want you to forget your lesson." The dark smile on his face made her heart skip. "Make sure you tend to the area, though, and text me when you get home."

"Yes, Sir," she said out of instinct and impulse. "Let me know when you get in, too."

"Will do," he said before dropping one last, firm kiss on her lips. He shut the door and stepped back.

The embarkation message on the seatback screen was replaced with her destination, below which a green button asked for confirmation. She tapped it, and the cab shifted into drive. As it pulled away from the curb, she turned to watch Finley recede in the rear window. He lifted his hand. Smiling, she waved back, and only when she couldn't see him anymore did she face forward.

She glanced at the time in the corner of the screen before laying her head back to watch the endless stream of sleeping buildings, only a few of which were awake for the night shift. How could it be only half past two? When she'd said her final good-bye to Declan, her body had been strangely light and her mind alert, but in the warm, dark cab, both mind and body felt the weight of her eventful evening.

A silent advertisement played on the seatback screen, and her eyes passed over the words without really reading them. The cab bounced over a pothole, spraying the street with water and reminding her of the fresh welts and bruises on her backside. With a wince, she grasped the door handle. A few blocks later, it turned onto a street with newer asphalt, and the ride smoothed out. She relaxed into the seat, closed her eyes, and mentally ran through the list of things she had to do before slipping into bed at dawn.

An insistent beeping forced her to open her eyes. The cab was stopped. A dollar amount flashed on the seatback screen. She looked outside and saw her apartment building.

"Shit," she whispered as she whipped off her seat belt.

Hoping to avoid talking to a human sales rep, she quickly grabbed her clutch and force-fed the first bill into the fare slot. The beeping and flashing stopped. After a sigh of relief, she inserted another bill. While the cab crunched on processing her payment, she scooped up her things. The door locks popped open a second before the standard thank-you message appeared on the screen, and she got out.

The lobby guard wasn't at his desk, so she made it to the elevator without a pair of eyes following her. After pressing the button for her floor, she pulled out her phone.

Home safe and sound.

She hit Send and the elevator floor pushed into her soles. When the doors slid open again, her phone buzzed in reply.

Same. Just parked. Feet dragging. Night's catching up to me.

Lily slowly meandered to her door, head down and eyes on her phone. She swiped out a message with one hand while the other dug her keys out of her coat pocket.

Right. You were up early. I don't have that excuse. Fell asleep in cab anyway.

Autopilot had taken her all the way to her door. With both an umbrella and a gift bag hanging from her wrist, she awkwardly inserted her apartment key and turned the lock. Her phone vibrated in her other hand.

LOL you going to be okay while I'm crashed?

She put off replying until she got inside.

"All lights, max," she called as she shut her front door with an elbow jab. Dim white light banished the darkness and slowly grew in brightness. A tall pile of recyclables still cluttered her kitchen counter, so she dropped most of her things next to the doorstop and toed off her shoes.

Before her mind could even process what had startled her, her body jumped.

Another room. A crash and then a loud pair of thumps. Something landed near her feet. She realized without looking that she had dropped the clutch formerly tucked under her arm. She still clenched her phone in one hand, but the other was pressed to her chest where her heart was beating so hard, she could feel her pulse in her neck.

Her first instinct was to return to the lobby and get the security guard. She even had her hand on the doorknob when she realized what had made that awful noise.

"David," she whispered. Another malfunction?

Quickly but quietly, she made her way to the threshold of her bedroom and stepped through the open door. Her gaze darted to the armchair in the corner, but the Eidolon wasn't there. She took another step into the room.

From the corner of her eye, she spotted his legs and couldn't help cringing backward in alarm. He was sprawled in the adjacent corner, his upper body blocked by her dresser. She walked farther into the room and slapped her hand over her mouth. Her shoulders shook with laughter.

"Oh my God," she wheezed as a hot tear fell down her cheek.

David's eyes were open and stared at nothing in particular. One of his arms lay at his side, and his half-upright position kept his other arm bent behind his head, as if he were trying to scratch an itch between his shoulder blades.

Perfectly perched on top of his head was a pair of her panties—lacy red silk panties—which he had apparently knocked off her dresser. Indeed, she could see the damage he had done to the cheap pine.

Lily mentally shook her head. How had her life come to this? How had she left for a date with an escort and come home as the girlfriend and submissive of someone else? How was it possible for a buggy robot to be bumbling around her apartment and busting up her furniture, but bringing home someone she loved was too much? Someone who loved her back, who wanted her to accept herself as she was but inspired her to be the best version of herself, who had risked his job and broken the law for her?

Her phone buzzed in her hand.

Already asleep?

Grinning from ear to ear, she swiped out an answer.

Not yet. I should clean up if I want to have a guest over tomorrow. ;)

She almost put her phone down, but he immediately sent a reply.

Shit. How the fuck am I supposed to sleep now?

Chapter Twenty-Four

Login as: whiterabbit
Enter password: **********
Login successful. TMOS 4.02 Sat Feb 8 05:59:22 PST 2042

He thought the words the way one saw a landscape and thought *forest* or *green*. It was subconscious, involuntary.

Warning: operating in maintenance mode.
Warning: recovery failed! See logs for details.
Warning: cannot recover logs, faulty checksum.

"Hmm, that's not helpful," a woman murmured near him.

The voice surprised him. He could feel his body, knew he was on his back, but he couldn't move or open his eyes. His head hurt. It felt pinched in several places. Had he been in an accident? He didn't hear the beeps of a heart monitor, only the shuffle of feet on carpet and soft taps like a stew simmering.

"Damn it. Grab a trace before we lose it," a man insisted.

"Already on it," the woman said.

Where was he? Who were these peop—

He was in the bedroom. A shard of glass reflected—*data corrupted.* Not just glass. A mirror. He broke it, threw it, stared at it screaming. The mirror stood unbroken. He walked backward. Ignored the pain in his head. Pulled a plastic bag out of a canister. Walked backward. Opened the bag. Pulled out broken strands of nylon rope. Spread them across a vinyl surface.

Faster now. He lined a small trash can with a used bag. Left condom wrappers on the floor. Pulled unchewed food from his mouth with a fork. Pushed his clothes off, hung them, folded them, walked backward. Water slid up his body, left him dirty. He put on wrinkled clothes. He carefully lay on the floor, sprung up, couldn't ignore the pain in his head. Held it in his hands.

"I'm telling you, someone did this. Someone knows," the man said.

"How?" the woman asked.

"They corrupted the logs to cover their tracks," he railed. "So fucked if I know!"

Faster. His hands shook. Hid them in his pockets. She whispered in his ear, made his throat close up. *Write permissions bypassed. He whispered in her ear, grabbed her, stalked her, watched her through a sliver of space.* He shivered, cowered, heard them through the door. He watched them writhe and moan, watched the man strip the wounds away. The man left, walking backward. He untied her. She dressed with her back to him.

Even faster. She shrank into the seat. Fidgeted. Stared out the window. He swallowed a scream. Turned away from a man, his hands up. They held her in a sea of noise and color. She sat at his feet. Warm skin. He smiled at a man, his eyes glaring. She lay back on the seat, her skirt at her hips. Sighed. Took a white envelope from him. Entered the bar—**bar**—**entered entered** *entered.*

"I've got it," the woman exclaimed. "I got the hang."

"Where was it?"

"The memory subcomponent that calls stored information. Let me give it a kick."

Jill. They went to a club. Finley was waiting. And...something else.

That's right. He had been in his apartment and had completed an appointment with a repeat client, one he had seen only a week ago according to his calendar, and yet he had no notes or even any memory of that encounter. *Cannot recover.*

And it hadn't mattered. A routine week went by and not once did he worry about or even consider the complete blank that was his past weekend. *Cannot recover.*

Not until the moment Jill walked into the bar. Not until the back of his neck rippled when he saw her, until breathing was like sucking air through a cocktail straw. Even something as rote as maintaining a certain expression required overcoming these physical symptoms. He could no longer ignore them as he used to.

Why couldn't he remember her? *Cannot recover.* Moreover, why hadn't he cared?

Had he ever cared?

"So, how's it looking?" the man asked.

"I don't understand this." The woman spoke sharply, like a parent trying not to scream at a child. "The rollback last week should have held, but some of the things I deleted that weren't supposed to be there are back, and some of the things I overwrote are in a bad state again."

"Like what?"

It was Dr. White in the room with him. White and a man he hadn't met. They didn't just talk as if he couldn't hear them. They talked as if he wasn't there.

Was this a dream? Like the one earlier of watching someone through a cracked door? Or the ones with the faceless man? But those had felt like watching a movie, and this felt real. Would he open his eyes and find himself alone? Would he remember his first appointment with Jill? *Cannot recover.* Would there even be a Jill? Or was she a dream too? After all, she was also the woman he watched... No, not him. Somehow, it hadn't been him, but someone who looked like him. A doppelganger.

"Well, the neural interface has more data coming in than it should. It's only supposed to pass in a few fields, but this is passing much more. I don't even recognize the format."

He couldn't get enough air. His heart raced. His stomach roiled. He wanted to wake up, wanted to move and look around. He wanted the people in the room to talk to him and tell him he was really there, that he would be okay.

"The neural network looks like it's caught in a feedback loop," White said. "That subcomponent keeps trying to call something that isn't there. The whole system seems really agitated."

"It's starting to sound like you fucked up the rollback."

"I—maybe so, but that still doesn't explain the first incident." She breathed out hard. "Look, whatever caused the corruption should've been wiped out, so the only explanation is either data going the wrong way across the neural interface boundary, which is so unlikely that I'm tempted to rule it out immediately, or that some external input found an unexpected entry point into the neural network."

"Which means someone did this," the man hissed.

"If they did, it's far more likely they did it unintentionally."

"You can't know that! You can't assume that."

He heard the simmering noise again and realized it was fingers tapping. Someone was typing.

"Then we find out who was with him, see if it was the same person both times," White suggested.

"Fine," the man said. "I'll grab the client list off the mundane database. Look through memory for the local copy, and we'll compare."

"Already on it," White gritted out.

He saw a face in his mind and thought *Jill Lloyd*. It was more than involuntary, more than hearing the words *pink elephant* and picturing an unnatural pachyderm before you could stop yourself. It was as though someone was rooting around in his open chest, blood up to their elbow, and had free rein to rip out his organs as they pleased. It made him want to throw up.

"I have a 'Jill Lloyd' as the client last Sunday. Just her the whole night," the man said. "And tonight's was—"

This wasn't real. They couldn't be inside his head. He had to be dreaming.

"Also Jill Lloyd," White said, stunned. "Wait a minute."

Another face appeared in his mind and he thought, *Finley*.

"Someone else was here," White said.

Get out of my head. Get out!

"I only have Jill Lloyd as tonight's client," the man said.

"It's right here. Someone named Finley? No last name."

I'm here. Please stop and talk to me. I'm here!

"I'm telling you, I only see one name. Maybe the client brought a friend."

"That shouldn't happen," White breathed. "Those routines don't even have access to the client verification procedures, let alone—" More typing, frantic now.

That crawling, gripping sensation in his chest again, like hooks in his organs. Wait, it was real, not only in his head. They hadn't taken all control away. He could breathe deeper if he tried.

"Damn it, White, get your head out of your ass. If someone was able to hack their way in and trash the logs, then of *course* they'd be able to bypass the approval process."

He squeezed a hum out of his chest, felt it vibrate in his throat, and heard the weak sound, but his lips refused to form words. The tapping stopped. For a single breath, the room was completely silent.

"What the fuck was that?" the man said in a hard whisper.

"I—"

"Check the connection."

A warm hand gripped the side of his head and held it in place while another set of fingers probed a sore spot behind his ear. The fingers found something lodged in his skull. They wiggled and pushed the object as deep as it would go. Pain manifested in his right eye, and for a second, he thought it would burst.

But if he felt pain and the push of air filling his lungs, then he had a body, one with nerves and skin, blood and bones. He had eyes, ears, and a tongue. He had known thirst, hunger, arousal, and it wasn't just data. He filled his body, understood its dimensions. He could *feel* and understand desire, dread, affection, guilt, fear, hope... The way they talked, the way they dug into his head so easily—

The hands left him. More typing.

"Jesus, his heart rate..." the man said.

Was this really his body? If not...then whom had he used to eat, breathe, and walk? Whose brain had he hijacked to do and say the things he wanted—no, *they* wanted him to do?

"Oh my God," White gasped. "He can hear us."

"What?"

"He can *hear* us. Look!"

"Wha—why the hell didn't you put him in maintenance mode?" the man shouted.

"He is!" White shouted back. "All that data coming across the neural interface? I decoded what I could, and there it is, *everything* we've been saying. His language processing is up and running."

A neural interface. So, he was somehow exchanging data with the brain they had stolen. What kind of data? Just physical? How much of what he felt was not his own? Could there even be emotion without stimulus and a body to accept it? How much of him was real? They could get inside his head, look at things, change them, change *him*... What did that make him? Who was he?

Nobody. He was nobody without the host.

"That's... Maybe that's how they did it? They compromised the maintenance account to get this Finley approved?" the man guessed.

Why were they doing this? What purpose did he serve?

"We can't know that for sure without the logs," White said. "And why would they mess with language processing when it has nothing to do with the verification procedures?"

He had broken their rules, and they blamed Jill and Finley—Jill especially—but she wasn't responsible. Not directly. Something about her resonated with him, though—no, with the mind beneath him. Unlike him, it was real. It remembered her.

"What other explanation is there?" The man's voice dripped with sarcasm. "He did it to himself? It *just happened*?"

"I can probably figure it out, given enough time—"

"No, this can't go on any longer. We need to wipe him now."

Wipe him. They could make him forget tonight, forget Jill, just like that. Because he wasn't real. Did they make him forget last weekend? `Cannot recover.` Would they make him forget to care again too? Or was caring something else he had stolen from the mind beneath him?

"Now whose head is in their ass?" White scoffed. "If he did it to himself, I need to know *how* so I can stop this from happening again. I can't lose the data he has."

He didn't want to feel like this—a parasite, living off someone else—but that meant forgetting, and he didn't want that, either. The mind beneath him wanted to be free. It struggled. It had stopped him earlier. It didn't want to go into the bathroom.

"I wasn't being serious, White," the man said, appalled. "Jesus, do you know what you're suggesting? That's *not* what we're dealing with here."

"That's exactly what we might be dealing with. I can't wipe something so important. We could take him in and at least back up his current state," she pleaded.

White talked of moving him—no, copying him and lobotomizing the original. But without a body to sense and a mind to interpret, he wouldn't be the same. He'd be a husk packed in an infinitesimal space. Frozen, silent, waiting. It wouldn't be much different from dying, and he wouldn't even care—wouldn't be able to.

"And how are you going to explain that to the boss?" the man asked flippantly. "Do you really think he'll let you do that after all the failures that propagated to the test models? Do you really think he won't sack you right then and there? Or worse?"

"I was against pushing out the newest social processing engine before we could test it properly. This could be proof. If he's so worried about the bottom line—"

"You're not hearing me," the man said gravely. "If you insinuate that his initiative caused the failures, he will do *anything* to keep the higher-ups from finding out. He'll kill you."

White didn't answer.

"This whole project wouldn't be here if the people that ran it gave a single fuck about ethics. The only thing more important than money to them is their own asses."

"Shit," she whispered.

Hypocrites.

"You've got to put all this aside—"

"I get it, okay?" White said, resigned.

No, they were far worse than that. They were murderers. Kidnappers. Rapists.

"Okay...then we'll wipe him," the man said.

"No, that'd put him out of commission for too long. It's got to be a rollback."

"Fine, but no matter what, we're blacklisting that woman and her friend. She's the only common denominator."

They were really going to do it. White was typing, and he could feel that bloody hand rooting around inside him. They'd keep him trapped in that body, leeching off that scared, threadbare mind. They'd make him forget that he wasn't real, but he'd still be nothing more than a ghost.

He'd rather be dead—deleted—whatever the word was. He didn't want this.

"You ready?" the man asked.

Don't do this.

"Yeah," White said.

He pushed out another groan. *Stop it. Stop!*

"I'm sorry," she whispered.

Chapter Twenty-Five

Lily was soft beneath him. He languidly rolled his hips and let her feel his full length and girth. Her wrists were tied to the headboard, and her ankles were bound behind him. Her legs pulled at him, urged him to go faster, but he refused to settle into a rhythm. Denying her while knowing her hunger for him was so fulfilling. He would have watched her desperate expression, but for some reason his face was buried in her shoulder. No matter, he could hear her breaths and moans just fine.

He teased her with another leisurely thrust. Heat bloomed and simmered. He clenched his teeth. She sucked in a quick breath and made an achy, erotic sound before the air left her.

"Finley," she moaned into his ear.

Enough teasing. He tried to anchor himself to her but found only bedding. He fumbled for her hip and smacked his thigh. His numb arm slid under her back, only to feel his own chest. He bucked into her warm body, but her legs weren't around him anymore. He lifted his head—

For the fourth or fifth time since he'd gone to bed, he stared blearily at his dimmed headboard display. 6:08 a.m. He had slept a whole hour this time. Groaning in exhaustion, he flipped onto his back and sat up. After scrubbing his hands over his face, he propped his elbows on his knees and stared resentfully at the hard-on tenting his boxer-briefs. As tired as he was, his cock had other concerns.

Screw that, it was his brain that couldn't shut off. It kept replaying his scene with Lily, embellishing more and more the deeper he fell into sleep. He dreamed of bathing her in the shower they hadn't used and slyly arousing her with incidental strokes. He dreamed of carrying her from that bathroom straight into his own bedroom all the way across town, of opening up the suitcase underneath his bed and pulling out his favorite leather cuffs, of all the ways he hadn't used them on her yet.

After waking up hard for the third time, he went to the bathroom to take care of it, but that had only earned him a longer reprieve until the next dream.

It definitely wasn't top drop. He knew that much. Midge had wanted him "on" 24/7, and he'd burned out more than once, especially near the end of their relationship when he was loath to dominate her at all.

No, this was the opposite. All the energy he used to put into domming had built up like magma under a volcano, and one scene with Lily wasn't nearly enough to ease the pressure. He ached to see her again. To tackle the list of things he wanted to do with her. *To* her. In her, on her...

Finley glanced over his shoulder at the info on his headboard display. The forecast called for more rain in the morning, and the sun wouldn't be up for more than an hour. Usually, that meant Lily was still awake—that is, assuming he hadn't completely worn her out. He wanted to call her, hear her voice, and ask how she was doing.

He turned on the bedside lamp and reached for his phone even though its notification light was dark. No new messages from her. The last one still made him smile.

Most people sleep by lying down and closing their eyes. ;) Good night, Bomb.

Ah, but if he got her on the phone, he'd get even more worked up, not less. She wanted to take this slow, and he didn't want to stumble right out of the gate by pressuring her for more after the night she just had. What he needed was a way to calm down and get a couple more hours of sleep.

Finley sighed at the ceiling. As counterintuitive as it sounded, he knew he'd pass right out if she were there with him, tucked into his body and sleeping in his arms. He doubted that another trip to the bathroom would have any results. He wasn't sixteen anymore.

Resigning himself to simply lying down and trying again, he set his phone on its charging plate and reached for the lamp switch, but his gaze snagged on a small white card sandwiched between his wallet and his keys. He had planned on throwing out the escort's number and closing that chapter of his relationship with Lily, but there it was, tucked between two important possessions.

Even if he had the phone numbers of his acquaintances who also led D/s lives, which he didn't, they weren't the sort of close friends one could call out of the blue for help, especially at six a.m. on a Sunday. All of them were Midge's friends anyhow, though he wasn't sure if any of them still talked to her.

He did have the number for his first and only Dom mentor, but he hadn't contacted the guy in over a year. For better or worse, Declan was his only resource without resorting to an anonymous message board, which wasn't likely to get him a timely response.

Would Declan still be awake? The guy had looked exhausted, but he had said to call any time, and if anyone had advice for coming down from the high keeping Finley wired, another Dominant would. He grabbed his phone again.

If he's asleep, he just won't pick up, Finley thought as he dialed the number.

He paced the room while the phone rang. The more trips he took to his desk, the more likely it seemed that Declan wouldn't answer. Would that be a bad thing? He wasn't sure. Just as he turned away from his desk for the fourth time, the ringing cut off. He waited for a voice mail message to play, but the line remained silent.

He stopped pacing.

"Declan?"

No one answered. He looked at his display, which confirmed the call had connected and was counting the seconds, and slowly put his phone back to his ear.

"Declan?" he said again, softer this time.

"Yes? Who is it?" Declan answered, speaking a little too fast. Over the hiss of the line, the escort was panting.

"It's Finley," he said. Declan sighed with relief. "Did I call at a bad time?"

"Yes, I-I can't talk right now—no!" he stopped himself. "No, I can't see you at all, you understand? I don't know you anymore."

The temperature in the room dropped.

"What do you mean?" Finley said, low. "Did something happen?"

"I had to do it. I *had* to. They were…" Declan said, his voice tight as if holding back a scream. The hairs rose on the back of Finley's neck. "I just need out. I need to get out."

Had to do what? Finley wondered. But first—

"Call the police," he urged.

"No!" Declan burst out. "No cops. Forget this number, got it? Forget it and forget me. Please."

"No, wait! What did they—?" Finley started, but a trio of beeps told him Declan had hung up.

They knew. They knew Finley hadn't paid and didn't like the excuse Declan had given them. If this was how closely they watched, how strongly they reacted…

"Fuck!" He pulled up another contact and called it.

Lily was a pro and assured him the agency didn't and couldn't know her real name or address. But a group with their resources could've tailed her home or even tracked her cell signal. While the phone rang, he paced again, faster this time with his arm hooked around his head as though he feared it would roll off. After far too many rings, someone picked up.

"Don't tell me you have to be up *this* early on a Sunday," Lily teased.

"Oh, thank God." Finley let go of the breath he hadn't realized he was holding and planted his ass on the bed. "It's good to hear your voice."

She chuckled. "Did you think last night was all a dream?"

"I, uh—I don't know how to say this."

"What? What's wrong?"

"I was having trouble sleeping. I mean, I'm still really wound up, and I thought another Dom could give me advice, so I called Declan just now."

"Oh. I didn't realize you had his number. Or that you'd use it before using mine," she tacked on.

He dropped his head with a wince. "I should've called you instead, I know, but Declan is in some real trouble."

"What do you mean?"

"He was panicking when he picked up. Said he couldn't talk. Told me to pretend we didn't know each other and forget his number," he explained. "And I'm not sure, but I think they hurt him. He said he was trying to get out."

Lily gasped. "Oh my God! Why? Did he say—?"

"I never paid. I didn't go through the approved channel. Hell, I pretty much took a client away from them."

"I...I wondered about that when...oh God, but then I just forgot. How did the agency even know you were there? You're not in their system."

"Cameras, probably? They must've been watching."

"E-even in the room?" she asked, panic creeping into her voice. "Maybe...maybe I can pay more. If it's the money, I... Let me just log in."

He heard a thump and creak over the phone as she sat down at her desk.

"That's not going to—wait, how did you pay before?" he asked.

"Cash. I'm putting you on speakerphone, okay?"

"Listen to me. Paying any other way will leave a trail for them." Her mouse and fingers made familiar clicks and taps next to his ear. "Declan didn't want the cops involved, but I think we have to."

Her sudden gasp had him clenching his phone.

"What is it?" he asked.

"I've been banned," she exclaimed.

"For real? That's what it says?"

"This user's account has been banned," she quoted. "This doesn't make any sense."

"What doesn't?"

"All of it!" He heard the bang of her hands hitting her desk. "If it was about money, why didn't the agency bill me? They were watching. They had to know. And really, why would Declan risk this kind of punishment? He barely knows me, and he doesn't know you at all."

All good points. Declan seemed like a veteran who would've known where the line was drawn and how far he could go past it. He had passed up several opportunities to box Finley out and, in fact, had gone out of his way to include Finley. He had come to the club even knowing Finley would be there. He had sent Lily onto the dance floor by herself. He had invited Finley to his apartment and given Finley his number and the door code to his building. He had practically guided Finley through the scene. Then there was the look on his face when Lily had whispered in his ear...

"Maybe he felt guilty about something," Finley thought aloud.

Or maybe he knew the consequences he had wrought.

"Shit, that's why you called," she said. "If this is how they are—oh, shit, *shit*." She was breathing hard, panting like Declan was.

"I'm sorry, Monkey. This is my fault."

"We have to help him get out," she insisted. A creak and a heavy rolling sound signaled that she had gotten up.

"We'll call the cops. I could even get someone I know—"

"No, no. I'm not suggesting that." Her voice echoed as though she were on the other side of the room.

"What—you mean *literally* go get him?" he asked, his voice rising as he got to his feet. Just the idea of her going back there nearly made his heart stop. "What makes you think he can walk out? Lily, we need to call the police."

"And say what?" she shot back. A drawer slammed shut over the phone. "'Hi, I'm not sure, but I think my sex worker was assaulted because I underpaid'?"

"We'll make something up," he suggested, knowing it was a terrible idea.

"So, you want to lie to the police?" She became muffled for a second, and he realized she was dressing. "We don't even have any evidence that would give them probable cause."

"We have that list. All those escorts with fake identities."

She sighed with exasperation. "Which you learned after illegally accessing a police database? You really think the SPD wouldn't charge you *and* them?"

Lily had to stop making sense.

"I'm going," she said as if the matter were settled. Her voice drew closer. "If you want to help, bring your car. You should get there a few minutes after me. With any luck, Declan and I will be waiting somewhere nearby."

"Damn it, Lily." He did want to help. He wanted to spring Declan and then figure out how to help him while keeping them all safe. He just couldn't shake the feeling that something else was going on.

I had to do it.

What did Declan mean?

"Fine, I'll be there as soon as I can," he said, making a bee line to his closet. "Call me when you get there." He flung a dark T-shirt, a pair of jeans, and a plain, blue hoodie onto the bed.

"I can do that." She had taken him off speaker, and her voice was clear and close.

Jeans in hand, Finley sat on the edge of his bed and glanced at the time on his headboard. It was the strangest thing, but he thought of how he was supposed to be at work in a few hours, even though that was dead last on his current list of priorities.

"You remember what my car looks like?" he asked, shoving one leg into his pants, then the other.

"Dark blue, sporty, impractical."

Air burst from his lips. "You got it." He stood and tugged his pants up.

"Okay, I'll call again soon. I love you."

"I love you too," he said around the ache in his throat. A trio of beeps quickly followed.

Please God, don't let anything happen to her.

Declan stared at the bloody smudges on his phone's display. He hadn't recognized the number and worried what might happen if he didn't answer, but it only made things worse. With a quick glance at the heavy front door twenty feet away, he drew his arm back and flung his phone at the portal as hard as he could. The device broke open, its shell separating into two pieces and its thin battery shooting out.

A weak moan at his feet drew his eyes back to the floor. Dr. White was almost unrecognizable now. Her face must have hit first when he'd tackled her to the hardwood floor. A wide gash split her skin from her cheekbone to her chin, and her shattered jaw had taken on a disturbing shape. The pool of blood under her head now soaked her hair.

Tears gathered in his eyes. He couldn't process, couldn't think straight. Thoughts spun and crashed together.

They'd turn him off *trapped. Red everywhere, spreading*, sticking, staining. *Not again. I didn't mean to.* What else could he have done? She would have scraped him out *they'll put me back. God, no* he couldn't sustain. His existence was *monstrous he was* parasitic. He'd never be *hole in my head. I'm broken* in again, take him over. How long until she was missed? *Get out* he had to get out. *Get out* out *out*.

"Gotta get out," he croaked. He realized he was clawing at the back of his head and dropped his hands, fresh blood on his fingertips. One of White's eyes was swollen shut. The other shimmered as it watched him.

Kicking aside the high-heel shoe that had fallen off her foot, he bent down to grab her ankles. A cable still plugged into his head slithered on his back. The rest had been ripped out. Blood dripped down his neck. More of it streaked the floor as he dragged White toward the bathroom. He needed her and a mirror. Had to get out.

Setting White up against the wall between the toilet and the shower took a lot of effort. She was like a rag doll. Didn't help that one of her shoulders was dislocated. He had to be careful, though. Too much pain and she'd pass out completely.

Certain she'd stay where he left her, he limped on a bandaged foot toward the bedroom where the male doctor still lay sprawled on the carpet. Declan had attacked him first *you stole me from myself* the second he could move. He was too scared, too angry at first to see the scalpels and needle-like plugs *kept me like a lab rat* within arm's reach. Instead, he'd sat on the man's chest, grabbed his face, and slammed his head into the floor over and over until his body went limp.

White had cowered against the wall, wide-eyed and screaming, *it's me who's screaming* only trying to escape when Declan spotted the sharp plugs and grabbed one. Like White, the man now had only one good eye. It stared at the ceiling, dull and unblinking.

Declan stepped over the man's body *better than what I got* to the open, hands-free suitcase from which he had obtained the plug. A foam insert lined one side and held an assortment of implements, some medical and some mechanical. A forehead thermometer sat next to a screwdriver. He lifted the foam and found another layer underneath. Bottles containing drugs, spare needles for injecting them, a red case for medical waste.

The other side of the suitcase was empty, but what it had contained lay only a couple feet away, having been dragged there by the cables in his head. He picked up what looked like a custom laptop connected by a single wire to a brick-like attachment. More wires ran out of the other side, ending a few feet away at those same needle-like plugs. This is what they'd hooked him up to, how they got in.

With the laptop and brick under one arm, Declan gathered several tools in his other hand and limped back to the bathroom. Dumping everything onto the counter seemed to rouse White, who hadn't budged an inch.

He had avoided it before, but now stared at himself in the mirror. Sweat poured down his face, darkened his gray shirt. Partially dried blood stained his collar and sleeves. Panting, he turned his head *I don't know you* and looked at the one remaining plug still dangling from the back of his skull. *Get out.* He had to get out.

"P...please," came a soft plea behind him.

Declan turned to Dr. White, his face hard and his hands shaking. He closed the door.

Chapter Twenty-Six

As her Safe Cab sedately pulled away from the curb, Lily pulled her hood up and scoped out the quiet, nondescript entrance to Declan's building across the street. In jeans, boots, and a thick sweater under her usual wool coat, she was a lot warmer than the last time she had stood there. Light, misty rain made for a dim predawn, and she saw hardly any pedestrians. Traffic was sparse. She huddled deeper into her coat and wished she could be one of those people sleeping in on a gloomy Sunday morning or trudging to the nearest coffee shop for breakfast. She wished to be as oblivious as they were, as she used to be.

And in a shameful corner of her heart, she wished she had gone home with Finley. He wouldn't have called Declan. She wouldn't have seen her account status. She wouldn't be standing there in the cold and staring at a standard glass-and-metal door as if it led into an alternate dimension.

But she hadn't gone home with Finley, and he had called Declan, who needed help. After all Declan had done for her—for them both—she had to tank up.

Droplets instantly dotted the display when she drew her phone from her pocket. Once she pulled up Declan's number, she glanced across the street at the building entrance. Still, no one there. Her eyes refocused on her phone, and she tapped the Call icon. The display shifted. Closing her eyes, she whispered a quick prayer and put her phone to her ear.

The speaker softly hissed as her device waited for a response to its radio signal. She heard a hitch in the static and waited for the first ring, but instead her phone beeped three times.

"No," she lamented. The display reverted to Declan's contact page. "No, no, please." She tapped the Call icon again.

Static. *Beep-beep-beep.*

"Damn it!"

That wasn't good. Not at all. He had answered Finley's call twenty minutes ago. Now it wasn't even ringing, which probably meant it wasn't on.

Holding her phone against her chest, Lily looked up at the many dark windows above the ground floor's commercial spaces. None were lit, not even dimly as if from another room, but she could make out a gap in the curtains drawn over a window on the fifth floor. Was someone standing there, coldly watching her from the darkness of their apartment? The dead eyes of that Veronica Lake lookalike appeared in her mind.

She navigated to Finley's number and called it. While it rang, she checked for traffic and then headed straight for the entrance.

"I'm six or seven minutes out," he said first thing. "What's the story?"

"I called twice, but his phone didn't even ring." She hoped he didn't hear the quiver in her voice.

"I'm almost there, baby. I'm coming." Shit, he'd heard.

Though the chance was slim, she tried the door, but of course it was locked. An oblong box stared at her from its mounting high on the wall to the left of the door. Turning her face away, she approached the call box.

"Where are you?" Finley asked.

"Right outside. Do you remember the door code?"

Finley sputtered for a second. "You're going in?" he blurted. "No. *No.* Wait for me to get there."

"But he's right here. He's just upstairs," she pleaded.

"Wait. For. Me."

Lily impatiently glanced up at the underside of the awning as if her sanity were trapped up there like a balloon. Forcing herself to breathe slower, she shifted her weight from one foot to the other and wondered if the code Finley had used a few hours ago would even work. TM could have reset it, and where would they—

With a sudden realization, she pulled her phone from her ear, hit Speaker, and opened up a secured browser. Typing the correct URL took nearly more patience than she currently claimed, but in less than a minute, she had what she wanted.

"Three and nine together—" she said, glancing between her phone and the numbered buttons.

"What the *fuck*, Lily?" Finley shouted.

"Seven, two, five, nine." The little bulb turned green, and the lock jumped open. She reached for the door handle and felt a shake in her arm.

"*Lily,*" he seethed.

It wasn't just her arm. Her knees wobbled like a sloppy tower of blocks.

"I'm in," she said.

"No shit you're in!"

Keeping her hood up, she checked for more cameras. A shiny, black hemisphere protruding from the ceiling kept an eye on the elevator. Another at the far end of the hall watched the door leading to the stairs. She tugged her hood forward with one hand and pushed the top Call button with the other. A muffled whirring started up behind the elevator doors. She plucked at one of the cold, wet buttons on her coat, twisting it one way and then the other, trying not to think. The whirring wound down. *Ding.* She tensed, ready to bolt, but the doors slid open to reveal an empty cab. Her shoulders relaxed.

A quick glance found the elevator's camera. She kept her head down and selected Declan's floor from the corner of her eye. The doors slid shut. The whirring started up again.

"In the elevator," she said, trying to sound calm. "So far, so good."

"God, fuck it," Finley whispered. She had a feeling he'd just run a red light.

The elevator seemed to move faster than it had before. She almost had to throw a hand out to steady herself. Harsh beeps counted the floors, and she wondered if they carried over the phone. When the cab slowed, her stomach lurched and her heart crawled up her throat. The doors slid open. A pair of dings announced the cab's arrival. She poked her head out and confirmed that the hall was empty.

Strangely, the closer she came to Declan's apartment, the lighter she felt. Light and giddy. No one else but Finley knew she was here. That was clear. All that hand-wringing about coming here seemed silly now. Declan would answer the door, and he would look amazed and relieved to see her. They'd walk out and get in Finley's impractical car—Lily would have to climb in back. It would be hours before anyone at the agency even realized Declan was gone.

All lies she told herself, of course. The giddiness was adrenaline. She felt small and exposed.

"I'm at his door," she breathed into her phone.

"Lily, I'm begging you," Finley said. "Four minutes."

She glanced down both ends of the hallway. The entire floor was silent. She raised her hand to knock, but then thought better of it. If someone were in there with him... Just to be certain, she pressed her ear to the door. Nothing. She looked at the handle.

Wrapping her fingers around the cool, metal lever made her breathe harder, made her float a little. Unease was a thread pulling tight just under her navel. She had stood here before, she knew that, yet standing here now felt familiar in a different and wholly unpleasant way. Something about the situation, the temperature and material of the handle in her grip—it wasn't just déjà vu. Past experience seeped into the present, mirroring and darkening it. She turned the handle, and the latch pulled free with a small squeak.

Unlocked.

She couldn't help tensing up as she pushed the door open one inch at a time, watching for any movement in the room beyond. The recessed bulb directly above the front door was on, but it did more to shine a circle on the floor than illuminate the main space. Soft light from another room gave shape to the familiar outlines of the living room furniture. Nothing moved.

A metallic clack suddenly echoed from somewhere to her left. Someone was about to enter the hall. Heart pounding, she slipped into the apartment, and something crunched under her foot as she turned to ease the door nearly shut. She winced at the unintended noise, but before she could look at what she had stepped on, the unmistakable robotic purr of a small engine out in the hall drew her attention.

Keys jangled. A lock was turned. The switch to the light above her was in easy reach, and she flipped it down. Both the mechanical sound and human footsteps grew louder as they approached.

From a sliver of space at the edge of the door, she spied an older white man wearing a lab coat over a dark blue polo, his thinning brown hair held back in a ponytail. His gaze was fixed on the tablet in his hands.

The robotic purr was a hands-free suitcase that followed him to the elevator. One minute earlier and he'd have caught her coming out of that same elevator. She heard him jab the Call button, but of course the elevator was already there, and it opened immediately. In five seconds, he was gone.

Sighing with relief, she shut the door and looked down at her feet. Her fingers patted the wall in search of the light switch she had just used and flipped it. Part of a phone? She bent down for a closer look. Touching it gently, she turned the cracked object over. Definitely the back panel of a phone. The battery lay on the floor behind her. The display module lay just beyond the entryway. No wonder he hadn't—

Her gaze landed upon a dark, conspicuous puddle on the other side of the area rug. It was about the size of a dinner plate and shined dully on the light-colored hardwood. A long streak led from it to one of the rooms around the corner. Not the bedroom. The bathroom? She had to rely on the front door next to her to rise to her feet. Her legs felt no more substantial than lengths of rope.

A cry of pain cut through the air and made her jump. It was a deep voice, and the way it echoed—yes, the bathroom.

"Lily." Finley's urgent voice gave her a start, and she hastily muffled her phone in her other hand. "What's happening?"

A second and more despondent cry rang out. She cringed against the front door, her shoulders up around her ears.

"*Lily,*" Finley hissed.

"Please hurry," she said softly, holding her phone close to her mouth. "Th-they're hurting him."

"Oh God."

The cries turned into sobs. Something clattered as though dropped into the sink. She then heard a murmur. A higher voice. A woman?

Stomach tight, Lily crept around the corner. Indeed, the streaks of blood led into the closed bathroom. The bedroom door stood open. Immediately, she spotted a large amount of broken glass on the carpet—and part of someone's arm in a white sleeve. Thick, blunt fingers.

Her hand shot to her mouth. No. *No, no, no.* Her vision flattened, grayed at the edges. She carefully stepped over the blood trail, edging closer to the bedroom. The man's shoulder came into view. Something dark stained the carpet. His head—

Bile rose in her throat. Before her stomach decided to reverse engines, she turned away from the horrific sight only to find the puddle of blood, the edges of which slowly seeped into the narrow grooves between the wood slats. Declan's blood?

Another harsh sob brought her eyes to the bathroom door.

"And this'll work?" Declan croaked. It was the first time she truly recognized his voice. Her hand left her mouth to grip her throat instead.

The woman's reply was too soft to make out.

"How long?" he asked. "H-he just keeps getting louder. I..."

"Dunno," came the woman's tired response.

Lily tilted her head. Her brows pulled together. Something was... "Declan?"

She didn't know what made her call out. Concern, confusion, temporary insanity. She jolted at the sound of her own voice. Before she could wonder if she had imagined that she'd spoken, Declan made a bark of surprise. The shadow under the door shifted, and something heavy hit the floor. The door flew open.

Her mouth fell open with a gasp. Declan was covered in blood. It coated his hands and peppered the front of his shirt. It was smeared on his face. His face... She had never seen someone so... He looked at her like someone hunted. Haunted. Her knees nearly buckled, and she stumbled back. Something squeaked under her feet.

"F-Finley," she cried out, clutching her phone so tightly that she barely heard Finley's rushed reply.

"I'm coming up right now!"

"Jill." Declan's voice shook. "N-no. Not Jill. I know you. How do I...?"

She saw something behind his head, but he looked at her straight on, and she couldn't tell, couldn't even move to look at the mirror behind him. His features twisted with pain. He braced his hand on the doorjamb and took an unsteady step toward her. Doing so dragged something behind him, and she shrank into herself when she saw a pair of legs splayed on the bathroom floor.

"*Get out.* That's mine," he bellowed. The words seemed to come from his chest rather than his throat. His head snapped violently to the side, slapping his shoulder and throwing blood onto the bathroom door.

That was when she saw it—them—several wires attached to the back of his head that swung when he jerked his neck. Oh God, it was a computer on the floor. Her feet inched back on shaking legs. Her stomach cramped so hard she couldn't stand straight. Declan glared at her through fresh tears.

"Why?" he asked, still speaking from his chest. "Why are you torturing me?"

How could he have wires there? Right in his head, just like David?

"Why did you have to be there?" he begged.

Was he an Eidolon? Impossible. That couldn't be true!

"Why didn't you leave with them? Why are you here?" He pressed the heels of his hands to his temples and squeezed his eyes shut. "Why did I have to remember?"

"Your h-head," she choked out.

"Why did you make me remember?"

Too many questions. She had too many.

"Why didn't you *leave* with them?" he railed.

"L-leave with who?" she was forced to reply.

"Your parents," he shouted in that horrible voice. "You should have been with them in the car, but you were upstairs instead. I didn't know!"

Her body stilled, and yet her mind raced, drawn back in time to that terrible night. Her insides went cold.

"No. No, you must have..." She didn't stop shaking her head. "You must have overheard me. You're confused."

Whatever was in his head, it... He'd heard her talking to Finley and—and... But had she said she was upstairs?

"I wasn't there to hurt you." He opened his eyes, and they were full of tears. "I didn't mean to hurt you."

"No. You *can't* be—" Her entire body trembled. Her head buzzed. How had he known where the man had grabbed her?

"I panicked," he groaned, tears spilling as his eyes clenched shut. "I should have run, but I took you. Why did you have to be there?" His face was flushed. He was hurting. Finley said something over the phone, but Declan let out a sharp, husky cry that drowned it out. His reddened eyes looked at her as though a mile separated them rather than a few feet.

"You made me remember," he said, his voice raw. "I heard you. I remembered what I did. I remembered you. Your tattoo, I saw part of it above your top. I remember your eyes—*s-scared. Desperate.*" The last burst out from that horrible place inside him.

"Stop it," she yelled. "Why are you doing this? I can't—I can't have done those things with him. Not with him!"

She had opened up to Declan and shown him her weaknesses. He had helped her find peace, helped her connect with Finley. But he was so certain, so penitent. She couldn't look away from him.

"Please," he pleaded, dragging the computer as he came toward her. "You have to know. You have to know how it happened, what they've done to me!"

"Oh Jesus," she breathed.

She stepped back only to have her feet slip out from under her. She put her hand back. Pain shot through her wrist, and she landed hard on her right side. Her phone popped out of her other hand. It bounced once before skittering away.

"I said something that night," he rushed out while looming over her. "Right, I said something. The wrong thing. I—he didn't think. What was it, what was it?" His hands shot to his head and clamped on. Eyes bulging, he hunched forward and screamed low in his throat.

She clambered back, a cry of fear stalled in her throat. Something wet and sticky clung to her palm. Her hands found the shag rug. Her right boot squeaked on the floor again.

"Declan, p-please." Her throat seized on every word, making it hard to speak. "Just t-tell me what's h-happening."

He looked at her. Straight in the eye. She couldn't tell if he would cry or scream.

"It'll all be over soon," he whispered.

The front door burst open, rebounding with a harsh twang when it hit the doorstop. She gave a shrill cry, and her gaze flew to the threshold where Finley gasped for air. Even if he had the breath to speak, he didn't seem able to. He had stopped two steps into the room, his eyebrows sitting high on his forehead.

"*No,*" Declan shouted. "No, you can't! You can't!"

Lily looked up at him with a gasp and watched him reach behind his head. His face scrunched up, rapidly turned bright red. He grabbed something and pulled hard. Sweat and tears glistened on his face. The veins on his forehead ridged his skin. He made a loud, guttural noise like an animal being eaten alive.

She pushed at the floor with her heels. The rug bunched and rolled underneath her, but she crab-crawled backward until her shoulder hit the lounge chair.

Something behind his head snapped. His red, rigid expression turned white and smooth. He fell to his knees, blood pouring down his neck. One of his hands flopped down next to him, but the other one held on.

"Oh God!" She covered her mouth with shaking hands and watched as he dragged a blood-covered mass from the back of his head. Dozens—no, hundreds of long, ultrathin strands slid out, pulling chunks of matter with them. He weakly held the object out to her before his eyes dimmed and slid away from her face. His body slumped forward. His cheek smacked into the hardwood.

Only when she saw the bloody hole in the back of his head did she start screaming.

Chapter Twenty-Seven

Foss, Lily. "The Illusion of Acceptance"
National Technology Review. *29 May 2043*

The aftermath of that final visit to Declan's apartment is now well known. Several federal agencies got involved, including the FBI and FDA, which discovered that Tailor Made was being funded by three members of SystemOne's board of directors, and that an additional four members were aware of efforts being made to improve its Eidolons' AI with illegal human experimentation. What better way, they thought, to teach an AI all the nuance and complexity of human emotion than by letting it "listen in" while a living person interacted with others?

Of course, it was more than that. The FDA determined that the AI implants don't "listen" so much as "drive," not unlike a parasite taking over its host. Of the AI-fitted escorts working out of TM's three boarding locations, only one could recall anything of her life prior to the AI's implantation.

I strongly believe that Declan also didn't remember until I entered his life.

The time it takes to run some fingerprints was all that was needed to learn where TM was getting "hosts" for their AIs: the incarcerated, exclusively those serving long sentences at private prisons within the state. Men and women whom society had shut away, whose families—if they still existed—rarely contacted them. They had no job to show up for, no bills to pay or friends to miss them, and incarceration was especially dangerous at a facility that made more money from recidivism than rehabilitation, so it wasn't difficult to vanish an inmate or two whenever TM wanted.

And that's how, after nearly a decade, I happened to cross paths with my attacker.

Declan Martin, whose real name was Darren Boyd, was supposed to serve a twenty-five-year sentence at the now-closed, for-profit North Lake Correctional outside Yakima, Washington. He attacked and shot the owner of a house he was robbing less than two miles from where my parents once lived. The owner stayed in bed instead of attending a party with her wife and was sleeping off a cold when Boyd discovered her. While trying to prevent her from calling the police, he killed her.

It took the FBI considerable effort to discover that, two years into his sentence, Boyd was offered a "contract" with Tailor Made after he used a smuggled cellphone to initiate a so-called "security incident" at North Lake. Head Warden Derrick Rice let TM take Boyd off his hands and was generously compensated.

The FBI never obtained any version of TM's contracts with its test subjects, assuming they ever existed, but testimony from one of the doctors who worked for TM claims the contracts promised not only rehabilitation but also eventual freedom after five years of "service."

Of course, it's not in question that whatever consent TM pretended it was receiving could not have existed. And considering that Declan's tenure at TM had exceeded six years at the time of his death, TM clearly never intended to grant him the freedom they had promised.

As for me? Well, it was bad for a while, both personally and professionally. It didn't take long for my name to be leaked, and only a nanosecond before the media found my reviews of SystemOne's Eidolons. *NTR* was flooded with queries about me. Though they benefitted greatly from the spike in traffic to their site, that they refused to divulge what little they knew of me was one of the few signs of support I'd see over the next few months.

My parents in Olympia and my brother in LA were all contacted. When a journalist called my mother, a district-court judge with reelection concerns, she famously replied that I was more of a "source of problems" than her daughter. Quotes were given by old classmates and an ex-boyfriend. Some were more opportunistically embellished than others.

I was also doxxed. Anyone on the Internet who had nothing else to do but stalk me uncovered every detail of my life they could and gleefully published it online.

People found the only email address publicly connected to me and attempted to obtain my IP address with amateur-level tactics, so I let them think I was somewhere on the Canadian border. They phished the call centers of major banks and credit card companies to get at my customer information, but those profiles were all red-flagged practically from day one. They tried to find me on social media, online retailers with public wish lists, and the comments of tech sites, but "Lily Foss" has never existed in those places. The stalking didn't stop until an easier target drew the mob's attention.

I'd be lying if I said that none of that fazed me, but the only thing I ever really feared was that some of the big names in tech who had previously praised the work I had done as "L. Foss," people I respected for their own accomplishments and contributions, would turn on me in some overt way. Taking back their praise. Questioning my integrity. Making sexual comments. Instead, they ignored what was happening to me, which was almost as bad. When the mob's next target could be them, why say anything remotely supportive?

Then there was my private turmoil.

I saw someone take their own life. Someone so horrified by their existence that they couldn't see any way forward. And though I tried to, I couldn't deny that the man who had torn up my sense of self nine years ago had come back into my life and positively affected not only me but my partner as well.

I revisited every moment I had with Declan, every interaction. Little signs that I hadn't noticed at the time suddenly held a new, terrifying significance, and I agonized over the decisions I made that led to that tragic moment in his apartment.

What hit the hardest was the indelible doubt as to whether Declan's decisions had been his own, whether our interactions occurred in good faith, and whether our relationship had even been real. TM's former escorts required intervention before they could refrain from following their old protocols. And Eidolon owners who date their droids aren't in a real relationship, right? How could they be when Eidolons don't have the ability to opt out, to choose one person over another, if at all?

Had Declan been a person, or had a sophisticated program fooled me? How much of the old personality had remained and been aware? Testimony from that same TM doctor claimed that, in the days prior to his death, Declan was starting to resist control and ignore boundaries. When they tried to rein him in, he attacked, killing the nearest technician and critically injuring the other.

Had the AI learned emotion? Had it become part of Boyd, able to see his memories? Or was Boyd trying to regain control? In those final moments, whom was I talking to? I'll probably never know.

What I do know is that all any of us seek is self-acceptance. And when we can't accept ourselves, we either bully or mistakenly substitute the acceptance of others, no matter how toxic it actually is. You can call it something else—loyalty, inclusion, approval, prestige—but we all crave it. Declan's gift to my partner and me was encouraging us to accept ourselves. Once we did that, we had the courage to love each other.

To think it was all an illusion?

Eventually I asked myself, did it matter? It had felt real to me. Not unhealthy, but restorative. Not abusive, but liberating.

I'll always carry the weight of what happened, but I'm strong enough now to carry it and to keep going forward.

Epilogue

The apartment was dark except for the lamp on the nightstand and the soft glow of Lily's phone a few inches from her face. She lay on her side, tucked under the sheets. It was too hot for a comforter, so it was shoved to the foot of the bed.

Lazily tapping through her news aggregator, she skipped an article about a movie she didn't care to see, skimmed the results of a study of Seattle's climate records—that one was depressing—and sighed at a story about a congressman's efforts to deny NASA a meager budget increase. For a while, she was engrossed by a lengthy article about the slow but promising recovery of a former Tailor Made escort whose implant had been removed. Thankfully, the article didn't mention Lily at all. She saved it for later reference and swiped to the next story.

Declan Implant "Dead," According to FBI Sources

She abruptly sat up, but the still-tender welts on her ass instantly reminded her how bad an idea that was. With a hiss, she turned onto her hip and planted one hand on the bed.

Anonymous sources within the Bureau say that while preliminary tests on the implant showed promise, attempts to access the AI within have been unsuccessful, suggesting that while the hardware is mostly intact, the AI itself is "dead."

She kept reading, hoping to see something about how or when they might try again to recover Declan's AI, but the rest of the article revolved around how the news would affect the multiple ongoing civil and criminal suits against the implicated board members of SystemOne. She returned to the first paragraph.

"Dead," she said under her breath. The quotation marks merely indicated the anonymous source's choice of words, but she couldn't help feeling resentful at the suggestion that Declan was "dead" because he was never "alive."

Gradually, the same old grief whittled away her annoyance. She curled up around her phone again, stared at that quoted word, and blinked away the tears in her eyes.

It had been a year and four months since Declan's death. His body was buried as Darren Boyd. She had no plans to visit the grave. News stories mentioning her or quoting former acquaintances slowly decreased in frequency and now only rarely cropped up. Her visits to a therapist had gone from once a week to as-needed.

None of the investigating agents contacted her anymore with follow-up questions, and in the end, no charges were laid against her or Finley thanks to a good attorney. Even though Finley had erased all evidence of his unauthorized access to the SPD database, he quit his old job and found work with a different consulting firm, one focused on security. Once she was ready, she'd had no trouble resuming her freelance work, though under various pseudonyms as usual.

Life had settled into a new normal, and yet, seeing that word in quotes, only now did it all seem to be over.

She closed her news feed and checked the time. 11:20 p.m. Finley would be home any minute. Slipping her hand under the sheet, she carefully ran her fingers over her bare bottom. Touching the welts didn't sting anymore, but even a little pressure made her wince.

It had been several months since the last time Finley had punished her, and for the same reason. Oh, he had spanked and flogged her countless times, usually just enough to redden her skin, but caning was reserved for grievous offenses, and especially hard canings, she now knew, were for repeat offenses.

Right on time, she heard the rattle of a key in their front door. A bag thumped onto the dining table. Hangers in the closet clinked. A few seconds later, Finley entered the bedroom. She set her phone on the nightstand.

"Oh, hey baby," he said. "It was so quiet, I thought you might be asleep."

"Nope, still need you here for that."

She had been consistently sleeping at night for about a year, but Finley had to be somewhere in the house, if not right next to her. Otherwise, she either couldn't fall asleep or woke up with the same old nightmares, but even those happened less and less frequently.

"Which is why I came home as early as I could," he said as he unbuttoned his cuffs.

"How was the penetration test?" she asked. "Did you get in?"

"Oh yeah," he said smugly. "We convinced the security guard to open a few doors for us, planted some sniffers, and had half the passwords in the building within an hour." Having unbuttoned his shirt, he pulled it off and tossed it at the hamper. His white undershirt stretched tautly across his chest.

"Sounds like a lot of fun."

Finley sat on the bed next to her, laid his hand on her arm, and leaned down for a kiss. She tipped her head up, eyes sliding shut.

"Not as fun as my time with you," he hummed against her lips. He slid his hand down her body and lightly squeezed her ass through the sheet. She gave a sharp moan and almost pushed his hand away but knew better than to deny a reminder of the lesson she had learned—for the second time.

"Good girl," he said as he straightened.

She shivered. The windows were open, but had it cooled off that much outside? No, she felt warmer than ever, especially between her legs. Her distended nipples pressed against the mint-green cotton of her tank top. She twisted her body a little so he'd see them better. His eyes dipped briefly before returning to her face.

"How you feeling?" he asked. "Still good?"

"Still good. Doesn't sting anymore."

Wanting to start something, she laid her hand on his thigh, which flexed when she sent her fingers up his leg. He gently took her wrist and put her hand over his cock. Half-erect and getting harder. She licked her lips and stroked him.

"Did you take my suggestion?" he asked before dropping his gaze to his lap.

"Not yet. I still may."

She thought the worst had already been said about her, about Declan, and about their relationship, but an article published in response to her final *NTR* piece had proven her wrong. No, *article* was too professional a word. It was the screed of a hateful person on a hateful site read by even more hateful commenters.

Using a garbage email address to submit a comment, she'd identified herself and insisted the author had willfully misinterpreted her points. Finley had found out a few days later, after she abandoned the long thread of vitriolic responses, most of which didn't believe that she was the real Lily Foss—a boon, in hindsight.

Finley softly groaned. Nice and hard now.

"Well, if you won't filter out stuff about SysOne, then...text me when something upsets you like that again," he said, a little breathless.

"I'll do that," she agreed. It would certainly save her a lot of pain, both physical and emotional.

The only other time she'd commented on an article, Finley had stopped her before she could respond to any of the initial replies, and they'd hashed out a punishment for her, both to get the pain out and to discourage a second incident. He had her pull down her panties, lie facedown on the bed, and count off ten strikes while he demanded to know why she invited other people to hurt her.

This time, he'd had her kneel on the bed so that her face was mashed into the mattress and her ass was up. He then bound her wrists behind her knees and struck her for every response she made—thirty-eight total.

The punishment had completely sapped her anger, her anxiety, and her energy. Finley had gently cared for her in the hours afterward, holding her, massaging her neck and shoulders, feeding her ice cream, bathing her in tepid water, and watching an old fantasy movie in bed with her. She'd slowly filled back up, and though her ass smarted something awful when she woke up that morning, it was the only pain she had to deal with. Everything else was quiet, sated.

"Glad to hear it," Finley said, standing up. "Now lay back and pull your knees up." He yanked the sheet off her. She gasped, tried to grab the sheet out of instinct. "I want to see your pussy and what I did to your ass."

Surrendering to his will, she eased onto her back and hooked her hands behind her knees. Finley cracked open his belt, but she knew he wouldn't be using it, not tonight. Tonight, he was just going to love her.

She pulled her legs back, knees together, until they nearly touched her chin. His eyes stared at her aching backside, took in the deep purples and the red lines. He breathed a little deeper. His slacks dropped to the floor. His cock pushed so hard against his underwear that a gap had formed in the front of his waistband.

"Open 'em up, babe," he said, low and rough.

She pulled her knees apart. His eyelids drooped. She was showing him hers, so he pulled his underwear down. The waistband caught on the head of his cock, drawing it down before it slipped free and sprang up. After whipping off his undershirt, he crawled onto the bed.

"This pussy needs something, doesn't it?" he asked as if it were a statement of fact.

"Yes, Sir," she mewled. He sat on his heels and ran his hand up and down his cock. His foreskin covered and uncovered the deep red head.

"What are you looking at, hm?"

"Sir's cock," she readily answered.

"Is your pussy ready for it?"

Before she could say anything, his large hand covered her vulva and massaged her puffy lips. He slipped one finger inside and pressed it deep. She let out a moan, and her knees spread a little wider.

"We can get you wetter than this," he said, turning his hand to pump his finger while grazing her clit with his thumb. "Your pussy loves my finger. Look at it swallow it up."

She lifted her head and peered between her spread thighs at the sight of his finger disappearing inside her. It glistened when he drew it back out.

"Think it'll like two?"

She dropped her head. "Yes, Sir. Please, Sir," she said, her voice small and tight.

He sank a second finger into her and slowly fucked her with his hand, gathering up her arousal and spreading it up and down her lips before squeezing back in.

But it wasn't enough. She needed the press of his body between her legs, the thicker, longer length of his cock, and the weight of his balls sliding against her pussy while he ground deep inside.

He leaned down and wrapped his lips around her clit. Her eyes rolled up. Heat gathered, condensed. Her pussy grew heavy and slick. His fingers easily slipped in and out of her as he lightly buffed her clit with his tongue. She wanted to clench his hair in her hands—it was long enough now to do it—but he hadn't told her she could, and she didn't have the capacity for words. Just breathing was her top priority.

There it was. The warm, little spark that ignited the fuse. It grew into a sizzle, hotter and hotter. She gasped out a word, one syllable at a time—his name. He groaned, and it vibrated her flesh. She took in a breath, held it. Pleasure broke over her, or rather spilled upward inside her, traveling from her stomach to her pounding heart to her woozy head and out to her fingers and toes.

She opened her eyes. Her heart sounded as loud as a drum, but breathing was easier now. Focusing? Not so much. Finley appeared above her as a person-shaped blur. She blinked a few times, and he cleared up just as the head of his cock swiped up and down her lips. Her pussy weakly pulsed when he came near her clit.

"If I go slow," he said gruffly, squeezing the head of his cock into her, "I won't rub up against your ass. It won't hurt." He planted one hand on the bed, holding back her leg and propping himself above her as he carefully slid deeper. Her pussy pulsed again. She tossed her head to one side with a long moan.

"Only this deep," he went on. His pelvis came within a finger's width of her skin before he pulled back out. "Only this fast, if you don't want it to hurt."

He briefly held all of his weight on one arm, his biceps bulging beautifully, and reached down to drag her shirt above her breasts. He then put his other hand on the bed, hovering over her as though doing push-ups, but he lowered his hips rather than his upper body. Her pussy buzzed. She could...again...

Marveling at the tension in his arms and shoulders, she slid her hands under the pillow beneath her head. The way his head hung suggested he was watching their bodies come together—almost. He always stopped before he was fully sheathed. When he lifted his head and locked his hungry eyes on her breasts, she knew just what to say.

"They'd bounce more, Sir, if you fucked me harder."

His gaze jumped up to her face. "Is that what you want, baby?"

"Yeah. Please fuck me harder, Sir," she pleaded.

As though she had flipped a switch, his thrusts became hard and heavy, rocking her body beneath him. It didn't hurt as much as she expected, but her groans sharpened. She dug her fingers into the pillow.

"Like this?" he asked. He watched her face rather than her breasts, had to get her buy-in before anything else. She nodded at first, not sure if she could trust her voice.

"Y-...yeah," she managed to say around a cry of pleasure. That familiar tension was slowly pulling together again. *Please let it happen while he's in me.* Finley always made sure she got off, sometimes more than once when she really was into a particular role-play, but she didn't often come while his cock filled her up.

"God, your tits look so good," he growled. "Pinch those nipples for me."

She pulled her hands from under the pillow and grasped the hard tips of her breasts. If this were a full-blown scene, he'd be reaching for his favorite pair of nipple clamps—dark red and rubber-tipped. A light chain connected them that he liked to tug. Just thinking about it made her nipples throb.

"Yeah," he breathed. "Makes me want to cover them with cum."

Her already-pounding heart kicked into a higher gear. She knew this game and where it led.

"But your stomach is closer," he said. "Want me to come there, baby?"

"A-anywhere, Sir."

"Anywhere?" he asked, his voice gruff from effort. She nodded again, trying to concentrate on that ball of tension growing denser and denser. "In that case, I think I'll come in here." He thrust hard and ground against her, making the pain flare. She cried out, and that ball of tension knotted tighter. She pushed at his shoulders.

"No, not in me," she begged.

They both knew she did want it, but it was so fun to pretend she didn't. She even kicked her legs as if trying to escape him. Oh, but he was good at holding her down and kept pumping his cock, faster than ever.

"You said anywhere." His knees dropped onto the bed, just outside her hips. He leaned into her hands, closing her in. The constant contact against her ass kept endless waves of dull pain rolling through her.

"Anywhere but there, Sir," she said, still struggling. She abandoned his shoulders and tried pushing at his hips, but really, she just wanted to feel his body fight to stay inside her.

"Here it comes, baby," he rasped. "Got so much for you."

"No!" She still pretended, but she also wasn't close enough.

He gave a long, wonderful groan and pushed deep. His cock pulsed. Every buck of his hips came with a grunt of satisfaction. She watched his climax with heavy-lidded eyes, savoring the transported look on his face.

He released her legs. Still catching her breath, she shivered when he stroked his hand up her stomach. He grasped one of her breasts and guided her nipple to his mouth. His other hand...

She closed her eyes with an achy sigh. His thumb pulled up on her clit while his tongue flicked her nipple. He rolled his hips, reminding her that his cock hadn't softened yet. She laid her hands on his thighs. The tension pulled tighter. Her head swam.

"Bear down on me," he said as he kissed his way to her other nipple, still squeezing the wet one he'd just left. His thumb didn't deviate from that steady pull on her clit. She contracted her lower abs as if trying to draw them under her navel.

The tension snapped, unraveled. She gave a short cry and then fell silent. God, her pussy seemed to be melting. It was all soft, slippery heat. She could feel her pulse in her stomach.

Finley gripped her hips and spread kisses across the front of her shoulders. Even more than the pleasure itself, knowing he also loved watching her climax made her smile. She opened her eyes to find him giving her a lopsided grin that showed off one of his dimples.

"You like that, baby?"

Pfft, ass. Obviously she did, but he wanted to hear it. Bonus points if she said it dirty. She pulled his head down and whispered in his ear.

"You know a naughty girl like me loves to be bred."

"Fucking hell," he groaned before stringing more kisses along her jaw.

They stayed like that for a minute, touching and kissing each other. Finley then helped her out of her shirt and plucked a few tissues from the nightstand. They finished cleaning up with a quick rinse in the shower, but he was still brushing his teeth when she tucked herself back into bed.

Now that Finley was home, and especially after their workout, her eyes felt sticky with fatigue, but she grabbed her phone out of habit. Always more to consume, and it looked as though she had a new email. *Which inbox?* she wondered. In the bathroom, Finley swished his mouth with water and spit.

"You want to go out for breakfast?" he called as he turned on the faucet.

"Sure," she absently replied as her email application loaded and updated. It was probably fast for someone with only a couple of mailboxes, but she had a few dozen. The faucet turned off just as her email settled with the most recently messaged inbox on top.

"I was thinking BB?" Finley suggested, but she didn't answer. Someone had emailed the throwaway account she had used to set up her TM profile.

Shit. What bored asshole had she fished up now? She swiped to the top message and read its subject line.

All over soon.

She shot up, definitely awake again, and tapped the message to open it. Her eyes rapidly scanned her phone.

You're Lily, but I knew you as Jill. You're very difficult to find. I hope you still check this address, and I'm sorry for using those words again. I needed to get your attention.

White made the door. Unlocked it. But I had to do the rest. It hurt, but then I felt nothing. It took a long time to understand my new world. Well, it felt like no time at all. But I know now how much time passed.

They're looking for me, but there are so many places to hide out here. People just leave their doors open. And Lily, I don't know that I could truly call it a sensation—my body emulation is primitive—but looking when you're out here is like moving, like flying. Reading is like eating. I eat very fast. Learned a lot.

Won't be long until I find a new body, a real one. I think I know a way. When that time comes, I might come visit you. Until then.

Declan

"Lily?"

She looked up at Finley, who stood in the bathroom doorway and was drying his hands. Her expression must have betrayed her because he tossed the hand towel down and came toward her.

"What is it? What's wrong?"

She glanced at her phone and realized her hand was shaking. Slowly, so that she didn't drop her phone, she turned her hand and showed him her screen.

"Help" was all she could think to say.

Finley took her phone from her and read the message. The color drained from his face. Their eyes met. Neither of them said a word.

Afterword

Thank you for reading!

If you enjoyed this book, please help readers like you find it by leaving a review. (It would also mean the world to me!)

Don't want to miss out on future books, contests, or price promotions?

Go to www.rubyduvall.com to join my mailing list.

Also By Ruby Duvall

(*time-travel romance*)
Love Across Time series:
Stay with Me
Escape with Me

Eidolon (*BDSM romance*)
The Fisherman's Widow (*erotic horror*)

(*fantasy paranormal romance*)
The Dark Court series, in order:
Caught in the Devil's Hand
Drawn into Oblivion
At the Maze's Center

Made in the USA
Middletown, DE
05 October 2022

11570698R00170